Coltswood

Jules Revel

2026

Bywater Books

Print ISBN: 978-1-61294-333-6

Bywater Books First Edition: January 2026

Printed in the United States of America on acid-free paper.

Cover designer: TreeHouse Studio

Bywater Books
PO Box 3671
Ann Arbor MI 48106-3671

www.bywaterbooks.com

To the artists and activists who have given so much.
Beloveds, comrades, friends—together we persevere until all are free.

And in honor of those we lost.
What is remembered lives.

The Replacement
October 2002

DEB WOLF KNEW SHE would have to be the one to break.

It had already been three full minutes since she'd entered Professor Belinda Coltswood's office and the woman had yet to meet her gaze. As she waited Deb looked around. Afternoon light illuminated a massive abstract painting on one wall; shelves lined the other. Not industrial metal shelves like any other office, but carved blond wood with books arranged by color, like a palette.

Wolf took in the details, but her eyes returned again to Coltswood herself, whose attention remained fixed on the papers strewn across her desk.

"Deb, is it?" Coltswood did not look up. Her indifference appeared too practiced, too complete to be coincidence.

"That's right." Deb rested her ankle on her knee, a slim black notebook poised on her thigh.

"Do people call you Debbie?"

"Not more than once." She wasn't often the one answering questions, but this situation required finesse. She clicked her mechanical drafting pencil either from nerves or from irritation. Even she wasn't sure, but the slick metal feel of it comforted her.

"How about Deborah?" Coltswood asked, stealing a glance. Her eyes widened for just a moment.

Deb caught that look and tilted her head slightly to the left. It was a tell, a sign she was amused, softening up, but she let it happen anyway. A few dark errant curls fell over her brow, and she pushed them back.

She kept her voice level. "Sure, some people call me Deborah. Doctors, lawyers, police officers."

Deb watched for any indication, however slight, any open acknowledgment of what they both knew was true. Coltswood made none, but her lack of eye contact said plenty.

"All right, Deb, I assume you'll want to start from the beginning?" Coltswood's hands still riffled through essays, sorting them into stacks.

"Oh, come on now, there's no need to stand on ceremony. You can still call me Wolf." She grinned and supposed it was the same teasing grin she'd always had, flashing the crooked eyetooth that Belinda had once called the only flaw in her perfect face.

Belinda Coltswood looked up, her expression unreadable, her gaze not quite meeting Wolf's. "Hmm. Why didn't you just stick with that?"

"Well, it's my last name and Wolf Wolf didn't sound very employable, though it would make one hell of a byline."

Coltswood didn't answer.

"I suppose I could have changed my last name. Maybe borrowed someone else's, but it didn't occur to me at the time." She raised one dark brow. The right side of her mouth lifted in a bittersweet twist. "At any rate, no, we don't need to start from the beginning. Gemma sent me the notes and the tapes, so I think I'm up to speed."

Her tone remained calm, almost detached. Nothing in it to suggest the strange thrill she had felt listening to the recordings her colleague had sent. The whole flight, from Logan to Cedar Rapids, she'd gazed out at the sun above the clouds and let Coltswood speak directly in her ear—recounting in as little detail as possible her upbringing in New York, her move to Iowa, her painting process. Through the turbulence outside of Chicago, and the crying infant who sat two seats away, Wolf had been absorbed by Bel's unmistakable voice. She swore she could hear all of the unsavory chunks being carefully edited out, the snags sanded down until they were as smooth as Bel's smoke and honey timbre. Wolf would rough it up, gouge the surface. It's my job, she told herself, though that wasn't entirely true. This was hardly an investigative assignment. Her job here amounted to a glorified puff piece. Two articles and enough material to cobble together a mini memoir, which would molder away in an archive somewhere under the city. It was good money though, and she was glad Gemma had talked her into it, especially now as she sat in Belinda's office seeming calm and collected while the professor did her best to mask her apparent anxieties.

"I'm surprised you do this sort of thing," Belinda said coolly, picking up a stack of papers and neatening them like a person desperate for something to do with their hands. A few slender silver bangles clattered on one wrist.

"Journalism?" she asked, though this wasn't quite journalism, was it? More like public relations.

"No, journalism makes sense, but isn't this a bit beneath you? No teeth. Or are you planning to eviscerate me?" Bel stared, their eyes fully meeting for the first time.

"The awards committee would hardly appreciate that," Wolf replied.

"True. So I suppose we all sell out in the end."

The comment, likely intended to wound, perked Wolf up. She lifted her pencil. "Do you think you've sold out?"

The leather chair creaked as Belinda leaned back, looking a shade deflated by Wolf's eagerness to turn the tide. "No. Selling out would imply I was something before, which I no longer am. I'm what I've always been, a painter who sells her work for money. Tawdry, I know, but no different than it ever was."

"You haven't always been a professor though. Was teaching a concession?"

"Hardly. It was a practical consideration. I thought you listened to the tapes?"

Another jab? Wolf nodded, features placid. "I did. You took a job here in 1993 shortly after leaving New York. You were hired on the recommendation of Herb Watson, former director of the Fine Arts program and longtime friend of your uncle Anderson Meredith. But that's all a matter of public record, isn't it?"

"You would have made a fine lawyer, Deb."

Wolf raised her brow but said nothing.

"Yes, you have the facts. So what are you driving at? Do you think I'm defiling my craft somehow by teaching?"

"I want to know what you think." She gripped her notebook, the veins in her hands pushing up against her skin.

"Hmm. No, I don't think that. I think it's a good job, and obviously my craft hasn't suffered. At least the committee awarding the Hirsch Prize doesn't think so."

"Obviously," Wolf concurred.

The Hirsch Prize was based on artistic merit; a committee of seven people had made the decision. Wolf hadn't seen the paintings in question firsthand, but she knew they must be worthwhile. She didn't want to insult Coltswood on her artistic talent, especially when there was no basis for it. She tried another approach. "It must have been a big change, moving here."

"Of course, but I needed a change about then."

"Why?"

Belinda shot her a look of pure disgust. Wolf knew Gemma wouldn't have gotten that look, but Wolf figured she deserved it. It was such a strikingly familiar expression that Wolf almost laughed with surprise. A memory of one of their more epic public arguments swirled at the periphery of her consciousness. "It's not fiction. I can't just write whatever comes to mind, you know?"

"It's not relevant," Bel replied with obvious agitation.

"We can come back to it. What is relevant?"

"I think Gemma had everything relevant for you to know. I told her my background, my philosophy on painting, and some of my teaching philosophy as well. I don't know what more you need."

She's trying to dismiss me. Wolf had fended off this kind of behavior countless times. Haughty politicos caught with their hands in the campaign funds, local judges accused of mishandling cases—a stream of people much more powerful than Belinda Coltswood had tried to turn her away. Still, she found this galling.

"Do you teach today?"

"Tomorrow at two."

Wolf made a note. "Can I observe?"

Belinda fussed with the papers again, though the stacks had already been neatened and re-neatened. "It's a graduate studio course. I don't know what you'd get out of it."

Wolf shrugged. "It's always nice to see people in their element. I'd rather watch you paint, but I don't suppose you'd be up for that yet."

"Or ever."

Wolf forced herself to sound more casual and assured than she felt. "So, tomorrow afternoon, two o'clock. Which building?"

"This building," Coltswood replied reluctantly.

"Great. I'll meet you here." Wolf closed her notebook.

She let herself out of the office with no further comment and walked slowly outside. The late afternoon light glazed everything rose gold. Voices lilting with youthful vivacity mingled in the courtyard to her left. A sudden pang of despair struck Wolf in the chest. It was a feeling so familiar she didn't even wonder at it anymore. Years ago she might have asked herself, *what's happening? Is it the lighting? The sound of young voices raised in amusement? Have I been somewhere like this before?* She would have dug around in her brain for some logical memory to explain the abyss that had abruptly opened in the depths of her being. Now, she just let it happen. She walked to her rental car and sat behind the wheel. The door had scarcely closed before tears coursed down her face.

No one noticed.

People rarely did.

The Messenger
May 1987

THE HALLWAY SMELLED WORSE than usual. A stench of mold and cleaning chemicals assaulted Deb's senses. She had work in an hour. She needed a snack, a shower, a change of clothes—and precious minutes were slipping away. Again, Deb put her key in the apartment door and again it didn't work.

"It's broken." She turned to face the building supervisor who stood in front of her, holding his hands up like she'd pointed a gun at him. One of his hairy nipples poked out at the edge of his too small tank top.

She cleared her throat and aimed for a less faltering, more authoritative tone. "Open it, will ya? I've gotta get to work."

He raised one shoulder sheepishly. "Look, I'm just the messenger."

"What the fuck is going on? What message?"

"It's uh. I need your key."

"My key?"

He nodded, his unshaven jowls a fleshy ripple.

Deb clutched her Bauman's Bagels key fob fiercely and worked the useless key from the ring. With a mounting sense of dread, she pressed it into his hand. Had they been robbed? Was that why the knob had been replaced and the locks changed? For a horrifying moment she feared the worst. "My Dad? Where is he? Is he okay?"

With a confused look he pocketed the key.

"Come on. What's happening?" She whined and hated herself for it.

"Look, I don't know what to tell you, kid." He wiped a sheen of sweat from his face. His eyes darted back to the stairs. "It's, uh, it's a family matter. I just need the key."

"Where's my Dad?"

"Well uh—" He lifted his hands as if to convey his own helplessness in the situation. Red blotches spread across his cheeks. He was on the cusp of stammering some more when the door across the hall opened and a thickset woman of about forty scowled at them both.

"Get out of here, Phil. I'll do it," she said, her voice filled with disgust.

He sagged with relief then hurried downstairs.

Deb crossed her arms over her chest and glared at the woman. "You gonna tell me what's going on or what?"

"Come on, don't stand in the hall." The woman turned and walked inside.

Deb followed, for what choice did she have? The living room was lit only by a stream of weak sunlight penetrating the crooked curtains on a street-facing window. A matched but shabby set of furniture filled the space.

"You want a smoke?" The woman gestured toward a pack of Winstons on the coffee table as she walked into her kitchen.

"Um, no thanks," Deb mumbled. She bit her lower lip to stop it from jittering. Something was definitely wrong.

The woman opened a beer and held it out to Deb. "I won't sugarcoat it. He's gone."

He's gone.

At first, Deb couldn't grasp what the woman meant, but she was looking at Deb with a certain blend of contempt and warm sympathy that explained more than words. Her father had left. Not died. Not been killed. He had left the apartment. Left her. Maybe left New York altogether. Deb picked up the beer and drank.

"I saw him take two big boxes down the stairs. He didn't say anything, but then Phil was over there cleaning the place out and changing the locks. It doesn't take a genius."

Deb didn't reply.

The woman reached into her cupboard and pulled down a box of raspberry coffee cake with one slice missing. Deb almost laughed. Under ordinary circumstances she would have treasured such an indulgence.

"Name's Angie, by the way." Gooey flecks of icing clung to her knife as she maneuvered a slab of cake onto a plastic plate.

"Deb."

The woman slid a plate in Deb's direction. "That's my kid sister's name."

Deb couldn't think of an appropriate reply, so she took a bite of cake. The sugar jolted through her, a reminder that she hadn't eaten since the night before. "I like the raspberry best."

"Yeah? Me too."

"You think my stuff is still in there? In the apartment?"

Angie shook her head. "Naw. Phil's been hauling things out all day. You want me to help you check the dumpsters? I got some bags we can use. Salvage what we can."

Deb's room had been sparse to begin with. The move to the city had been on short notice. A whim. Her father lived by last-minute decisions. They'd tossed what they could in the back of his LeBaron, and left Rhode Island behind in the blink of an eye. She'd held on to a box of photos and notebooks. Besides that she had some clothes, a work uniform, and a cookie tin full of pennies. What did it matter? Even if she had it all, she had no house.

Angie swallowed her last bite and tossed her plate in the sink. "Come on, Deb, let's go see what we can find."

Grabbing two trash bags from the cupboard, she cast an apologetic look toward Deb before leading her again through the front door of apartment 3C. The bins sat in a narrow alley between their building and the derelict shell of a factory next door. As soon as they turned the corner Deb saw the wreckage of her life. The few pots and pans they'd collected from Goodwill were lying in the greasy mud. The sleeve of her coat peeked out from the top of the bin.

"Shit." She felt suddenly cold despite the mid-May sunshine.

"Come on. Let's get what we can." Angie pushed open the lid.

Fucking Berelli couldn't even be bothered to remove the hangers. Everything was trash, something to be cleared away. But who could blame him? It was his job. Her Dad was the real prick. Deb remembered how quickly they'd stuffed things into salvaged banana boxes on their way out of Pawtucket. It was almost as quickly as they'd left Staten Island when she was ten. That time it had been the law chasing him, but this time who knew? And this time she hadn't been invited.

"Keep? Sure, you want to keep this. It's still nice." Angie gestured toward a jean jacket.

Deb nodded. Angie stuffed it into a bag with the brusque efficiency of a checkout clerk. She held up a few flannel shirts, but didn't wait for a reply.

"It'll be fall before you know it," she cautioned.

"I got nowhere to keep all this," Deb murmured. She held a handful of photographs salvaged from the murky bottom of a neighboring bin. The rest were gone, who knew where.

"One step at a time."

It seemed like good advice. They went on sorting as the sun got hotter and the reek of garbage intensified.

"You got anyone you can call? You can use my phone," Angie offered.

Deb shook her head. "No, I'll manage."

At the mouth of the alley the 3:15 bus groaned to a halt. Deb looked down at the bulging plastic bag by her feet. Her overriding impulse was to chuck it back in the bin, but she didn't want to seem ungrateful, and Angie was probably right: she'd need some of it eventually. Her work uniform was trashed. Bauman wouldn't be forgiving. He'd once docked her pay for wearing the wrong color pants. Still, it was the only job she had. "Thanks for helping me. I gotta get to work."

"Wait, where are you gonna go tonight?"

Deb stared at her and then down at the bag.

Angie scooped up Deb's belongings. "Gimme this. My man is in Columbia, military thing. He'll be back in nine days. You can have the couch. Just knock when you get in, not like a cop, soft and friendly-like, okay?"

"Yeah?"

"Yeah. Go to work."

Deb nodded, unable to find any words for the gratitude she felt. She jogged toward the bagel shop and what she knew would be an unpleasant last day on the job.

When he saw her, old man Bauman scowled. It was probably unfair to call him old as he couldn't have been much over fifty, but some ancient injury had left him with a crooked spine, and it made him stooped like a man much older. The stoop, his cantankerous personality, and his accent placed him squarely in the "old man" category of Deb's mind.

"I'm sorry," Deb spluttered. How could she possibly explain what had happened? Maybe it was better to not bother. Bauman wouldn't care. She had fucked up, and that's what he would notice.

"Sorry? I don't understand. You are here to quit?" His eyes narrowed.

"Quit? No. It's just I don't have a uniform."

He raised one bent finger. "Impossible. I gave you one when you started. Size large for the shirt. I remember. It's too big for you, but I gave—"

Deb shook her head. "No. Yes. You did. That's true, but it's gone."

"Stolen?"

"No. Not quite. My father left."

Bauman looked at her, his face a knot of annoyance and confusion.

Deb felt sick. "He left the apartment and tossed out my stuff. The uniform is ruined. I'm sorry. I came anyway because it's my shift."

"Your father did this? He left you?" Bauman spoke slowly as if worried he'd lost something in translation, but he had been in New York for most of his life. His English was excellent.

Deb nodded.

"Because you are gay he did this to you?"

Her whole body stiffened. A feeling like something cold dripping down her spine caused her to clench her fists. Run. Run. The message roared from Deb's gut. But she stood still. She'd never said she was gay. Not to Bauman and certainly not to her father, but maybe it was obvious. Maybe nothing needed to be said. Maybe that was why he'd left. She felt suddenly hoarse. "I don't think so."

Bauman stood up as straight as he could, his eyes searching Deb's face. "He should not have done that. But you are an adult; you will survive."

Her throat went tight. She wasn't an adult, not legally.

Bauman opened a cupboard under the till and pulled out a blue Bauman's Bagels T-shirt and a fresh apron. He nodded toward a rack of bagels. "Go get dressed and then you can put the seeds on those."

Deb forced herself to swallow.

With his characteristic scowl Bauman pushed the clothes into her hands. "I see you're thinking of crying. Don't. We have work to do."

The Little Gorge
July 1987

BELINDA LOOKED AT WHIT stretched out on the couch. A thin sliver of mid-summer light permeated the dark curtains, illuminating him. His body was burnished gold from hours spent lounging by the sea. With some amusement she noticed he was wearing a pair of her favorite underwear, the black ones she'd gotten in Paris when they'd gone on sabbatical to visit Michel. Wordlessly, she turned her attention back to her painting and fretted her lower lip between her teeth, her shoulders tight with some unacknowledged disquiet.

"Beli. Beli, come here," he pleaded, but there was laughter in his voice, a soft teasing undercurrent.

She wouldn't be lured so easily. She kept her eyes fixed on the massive canvas in front of her. She'd only just had it framed, but now they would have to crate it up. A gallery in Chelsea wanted it, and some part of her mourned its imminent loss. *Sold out from under me, a silly thought.* She wanted it to sell. Of course she did. Not that she needed the money. No, she wanted it to sell in order to twist the knife in the collective ribs of her family, who had treated her ambitions as a joke and assured her that studying art had been simply a means of securing a husband. They had a great distaste for the notion of Belinda being known for her work. Whit was their consolation. A June wedding after her second year in college to a husband with connections, property, and class. Good breeding. It could almost make up for her living in Boston, almost make up for her insistence on painting.

They should see him now, she thought. The notion held no rancor toward him, but rather a long-simmering, feeble outrage against her own flesh and blood. She loved Whit and his many peculiarities. Not for anything would she have wanted him exposed to her parents' petty judgments. Whit, sweet as he was, would have felt hurt, even as he laughed off their gibes or later made the whole experience into some exquisite piece of performance art to amuse their friends. No, she wouldn't want Whit to have to manage such an encounter. Still, it would have thrilled her to throw this in their faces. So much of her life would appall them, and she cherished like a gem all of the multifaceted ways she might one day horrify them with the truth.

Belinda's eyes roved over the sinuous waves of paint rippling the canvas. She called it The Little Gorge. A six-foot square, painted over the course of two weeks spent holed up in a too-rustic-for-her-taste Vermont cabin with Laura Worthing, who ostensibly was there to work on her novel.

The trip had begun inauspiciously.

"I'm going to kill Peter," Laura had said when they were forced to stop their car at the end of a long dirt track. The road, if you could call it that, seemed likely to wash down the mountain at any moment.

Belinda held her tongue. Killing Peter had often crossed her mind, but it was unseemly to say so.

"I told him I wanted somewhere away from it all, not a death trap in the middle of nowhere." Laura's fierce scowl was the kind she often used to bend the will of anyone unfortunate enough to serve her.

It had no effect on Belinda except giving her the pleasure of observing the way rage lent a cooler color to her lover's eyes.

"Don't think of Peter right now," Belinda's voice had commanded as she reached her hand through the sleeve of Laura's slippery silk shirt and cupped her breast. Laura leaned into the embrace.

"You're right. Do you think you'll be able to work here?" Laura had whispered, her attitude apparently softened by the heat of Bel's hand.

As if he were aware of her thoughts, Whit groaned like a sullen child. "Beli! Don't ignore me."

He was acting positively desperate for attention now. If she neglected him any longer, he'd get petulant.

She turned toward him. "Don't call me Beli. You know I don't like it when you call me that. It's a silly name."

He sighed with mock exasperation. "Oh, Beli, please. You are a silly girl. Look at us here. Both silly as can be. Come, darling, sit beside me."

His radiant smile beckoned as he smoothed his hand over the deep green velvet of the antique couch.

She sat and he giggled, smug with his accomplishment. *He's stoned out of his mind. Listen to that laugh.* Though she didn't remember seeing him smoke or snort anything. *You've been distracted.* She focused on him then. The little lines at the corners of his eyes were deepening from too much time in the sun. He was already not a young man anymore, and his way of roasting himself would only make matters worse.

"Are you assessing me, little Beli? You know I'm far too vain not to notice. But really, if you must take my measure, get the full picture," he said, quite seriously now, his luminous hazel eyes looking into hers as he gestured at his smooth hairless torso.

Belinda obliged him. Gazing at Whit was easy. He had done all he could to make himself handsome and smooth. A living statue. Not a Greek god. No, he wasn't burly enough, unless maybe Dionysus, but she did not think of Dionysus just then. She looked at him lounging in her expensive lingerie, cocking his head down to enjoy a view of himself, and she thought of Donatello's David with his dark feminine curves. She had slept with Whit for a time when their marriage was new, but it had been years now, and they both knew neither of them had an appetite for it. Still, Whitney loved to be looked at by her, to be viewed as a beautiful object by a woman who knew beauty, adored beauty, had made it her life. Yes, Whit was beautiful still. She told him so, and he was happy with her and with himself. He giggled again and rested a hand sleepily over his eyes, palm facing the ceiling.

"Beli, let's take a nap on the deck," he suggested.

"No. It's too hot."

Whit scoffed but seemed too tired to argue. Soon he said nothing at all. His dark pink lips parted slightly but a whisper of his smile remained even in slumber. She wondered if he'd been drinking, though she didn't smell drink on him. Whit's father had died young from too much alcohol, though they called it something else for the sake of decency. That lie, along with Whit's massive inheritance, had gone a long way in securing her parents' support for their union.

Why do they still loom over me? She hated thinking about her parents so much. *Maybe I should have gone outside.* She considered the possibility that the dim gloominess of the north parlor was what made her think of things she would rather not attend to. She looked at her painting again. *The Little Gorge.* Five thousand one hundred and eighty-four square inches of homage to the labia of a woman she would have at that moment paid any price to be in the company of again. But that was another thing it was better not to think about. Besides, they would see Laura and Peter soon enough.

When she did see Laura again, it was hardly how she would have wanted it.

Whit's parties were the stuff of legend, and this one—"just a casual get-together"—more than lived up to expectations. The boat could easily fit a hundred people, but Whit had restrained himself by inviting only forty of their closest friends and rivals. Everyone was enjoying the night, but Belinda retreated outside to an empty stretch of the deck. Waves lapped, black and endless, against the yacht. They were moored not far off Cape Cod, and the soft rhythm could have lulled her to sleep were it not for the raucous shouts of the revelers. Seeing Peter and Laura together had knitted a cold knot of jealous longing in her throat. The feeling, not unfamiliar, somehow hurt more tonight. She hated herself for it. *You should know better. This is how it is. How it's always been.* She let her hand slide along the cool edge of the vessel and listened to the waves. She couldn't bring herself, even in her thoughts, to say this was how it always would be. Belinda stared across the water. There, stars filled the sky as they never did in Boston. Everything was black punctured with light. Somewhere far beyond was the edge of Europe.

Maybe Cádiz.

She closed her eyes trying to picture the scatter of bright fishing boats along the golden sand, the line of dark palms reaching to heaven. But all she could see when she closed her eyes was Laura in Peter's arms. Sunrise washing the cathedral in a spreading pool of glorious pinks was nowhere to be found. *Forget about it.* But her mind conjured with terrible clarity the way Peter traced his blunt index finger down the line of Laura's spine while they danced. Whit had seen it too and had pulled her close to him, whispering "Don't be jealous, Beli." She'd laughed. How could Whit stand it? He had so many lovers who weren't solely his own, yet it never seemed to bother him.

You're being a child. But no amount of self-admonishment eased the bite of anger that gnawed her insides. She wanted to be dramatic, to lean over the edge of the boat and moan Laura's name into the night, but that was too ridiculous even for her.

She was startled for a moment by a hand on her hip—soft, warm, and unmistakably familiar.

"It's only me. I know, I know, how disappointing," Whit teased, kissing her cheek.

"It really is." She smiled and leaned against him.

He rested his arm around her shoulders for a moment, then squeezed her closer. "You shouldn't get so emotional about these things, Beli. It's not worth it. There are countless women who'd be more than happy to do whatever your wicked heart desires, trust me."

"Bar dykes?" She tried and failed to conceal her distaste.

He laughed and cocked one brow roguishly. "Well, of course them. You'd be perfectly ravished. But plenty of elegant ladies are out there as well. The world's absolutely bursting with queers like us, Bel, so don't get morose and heartbroken over one."

"What if I love her?"

"Of course you do!"

"What if she's the one?"

"The one? Oh, Beli, do you want a divorce? Do you want to run off and set up a house in Vermont or Maine or some other bucolic setting? Maybe get a few cats?" he asked, voice dripping with mock seriousness.

"Don't tease me, Whit." She was tired and upset and in no mood for his nonsense even if she did find it comforting.

"It's my job to tease you. As your older, wiser husband, I positively must." He kissed her cheek. He smelled of vodka and the French cologne he favored. The scent made her think of a church she'd visited as a girl.

"I hope I'm not interrupting." Laura's voice was almost a whisper. Belinda heard the low murmur of apology in it, the longing too—and something in her wanted to make Laura beg for forgiveness, but she knew she couldn't manage it.

"Not at all." Whit smiled indulgently at them. He kissed Belinda's cheek once more before taking his leave.

Laura filled the place he'd vacated, fitting her side against Bel's so no space remained between them. "Finally alone."

Any thought of holding a grudge melted out of Belinda with the rustle of her lover's breath against her skin. She leaned into Laura. *So what if Whit's right? So what if I do want to run away with you?* She knew better than to say anything like that to Laura.

"I missed you," Laura whispered and she turned ever so slightly toward Bel, begging *touch me.*

Belinda complied, letting one hand discreetly rove the contours of Laura's satin-covered hip and slide across the slight swell of her stomach. "I wish we were alone."

"Hmm, me too." Laura turned ever so slightly in Belinda's arms, granting her more access.

They had been at this game for over a year, and it never ceased to amaze Belinda how restrained and yet deliberately erotic Laura could be. Bel felt the heat radiating from Laura, the subtle movements of her body drawing Bel closer, daring her to reach up the slit of her dress which beckoned welcomingly along the taut line of Laura's thigh. Belinda would have been happy to take her right on the deck, party be damned, or to hunt down an empty room somewhere below, but she knew Laura would resist any such overture. With a twist of mortification, Belinda wondered if part of Laura's delight in their relationship was the torment she inflicted by insisting on being caressed and then refusing Belinda when she yielded and yearned for more.

The Son
(January 1988)

DANIEL BAUMAN CAME HOME after the New Year, or rather he'd shown up in his father's bagel shop looking like one of those harried travelers who sometimes stumbled in searching for a late lunch. Deb had been alone, wiping down the counters in the quiet lull between the lunch rush and the evening commute when the door opened and a man in his mid-twenties hurried inside, brushing snow from the shoulders of his dark wool overcoat.

"Onion bialys two for one," she said, barely raising her gaze to his. It was about the best welcome one could hope for at Bauman's.

He put one hand on the counter and scanned the sign, though his eyes seemed to be taking in more than just the list of wares. "A sesame, toasted, with plain schmear."

His voice, a light baritone, had only the faintest hint of a New York accent.

Easy enough. She turned and reached into one of the wire baskets behind her, pulling out a sesame bagel.

"The owner around?" he asked, not sounding too concerned one way or the other.

The hairs stood up on the back of her neck, and a weird cold tingle pulsed in Deb's gut. She thought about his fine wool coat, the heavy silver band of his watch, which flashed from under the cuff when he put his palm on her countertop. *Who is this guy? A real estate agent? A banker?* "No. Sorry."

She worked the knife through the bagel and slid it into the toaster wondering if she'd said the right thing. Should she have mentioned that old man Bauman would be there in the morning? Odds were good this guy wouldn't be up at the crack of dawn anyway, and by the time he rolled around Bauman would be gone again. She caught the bagel as it fell hot from the toaster conveyor belt and slathered on the topping. It defied logic, but she wanted this guy gone.

"Sesame, toasted, with plain." She pushed the bag toward him and took his money.

He smiled at her. It was a winning smile; even she could see that. His face was handsome and his hair perfectly feathered. She noticed a few fine creases in the skin around his eyes, like the look of someone who spent their days under the sun. *Construction worker. No, too smooth.*

"Thanks," he said, still smiling.

Deb nodded and turned her back on him. Without looking, she could sense him lingering by the doorway. Maybe debating saying something else, or hesitating before going back into the cold. From the corner of her eye she watched him examine the framed photos on the wall. She knew each of them by heart, without knowing who the people were. The man lingered a moment longer, then pushed out into the snow. Deb ran a bleach-water rag over the counter and sighed.

Ever since her father had vanished without a word, Bauman's had become her world. She worked split shifts. Bauman let her sleep in the loft over the bakery storage room for ten dollars a week. She had initially insisted it wouldn't be for long, but the old man ignored her. She didn't want to sleep in the loft forever, but for now it was the best place for her and she wanted to defend it. A banker or a real estate agent, or whatever this guy was, it could only mean bad news. She shook off the uneasy recollection of his smile and told herself again he wouldn't be back.

An hour later Rebecca showed up to relieve her. By then, all Deb could think about was sleep. Her legs ached from standing, and her eyes burned from the relentless overhead fluorescence. She pushed her way into the narrow employees-only restroom and began her nightly ablutions. The tap poured pale rust-red, and she let it run until the water was clear. As always she paused and scowled at the white metal Boraxo dispenser. The powdery soap repulsed her, but she knocked her hand against the metal valve until it spit out a mound of grit. She rubbed it between her palms feeling it dissolve and slicken. Finally, she dug her toothbrush out of her backpack and brushed. Wiping her mouth with the back of her hand she had the misfortune to glance up and catch her own reflection. The mirror, a flyspecked square foot of material that had probably once been reflective, now seemed to exist only to insult whoever looked in it.

Even so, Deb got the sense she really did look like shit. She needed a haircut badly, but the cold made her hesitant to chop it all off again. Dark, nearly black, waves grew from her scalp at odd angles. Her lips were cracked from the cold. Nothing could be done about any of it now, so she dressed for bed and scurried into the loft. A curtain made of old flour bags tacked to the ceiling blocked out just enough light to make it cozy. Deb put her head down and closed her eyes.

"Bagel troll! Time to feed the drunks."

His voice punched a hole in her sleep as sure as sunshine. She rolled over in the dark and pressed her face into the pillow trying to blot him out. It was no use. As if on cue, a group of guys came through the door jostling each other and ranting loudly about some unresolved gambling issue involving a guy named Larry from the Bronx.

"He owes me. That fat bastard!"

She sighed and slid out of bed.

I'm lucky. I'm lucky. Lucky, lucky me.

A quick trip to the bathroom-turned-dressing room and she was out at the counter helping Ben slice bagels.

"He's never gonna pay you. Not in a million years. I don't care what he says. You can't trust those assholes from the Bronx. Ain't that right, kiddo?" the shortest guy of the group hollered at Deb.

She shrugged, turned her back to him, and kept working.

"Aw, don't get the kid involved."

"Probably from the Bronx anyway," the third guy barked with laughter.

"Here you go, guys. Four bucks even." Ben pushed the sandwiches in their direction and took cash from the little guy.

They lined up at the counter facing the window and shut up for a few hungry moments.

Ben emptied the tip jar and pocketed the coins as he walked back into the kitchen. Deb watched him go, grateful as always that he was massive, intimidating, and most importantly right behind her during the early hours. She didn't scare easily, but the "drunk rush" as they called it could get tricky. It helped to know there was backup. The guys at the counter seemed to lose steam as their sandwiches settled in whatever pool of alcohol filled their guts. They left together more or less sedately, though without packing up any of their trash. She tended to it. Outside a gentle snow flittered down. If she looked up into the lights, over the garbage and the drunks, it was almost beautiful. *Maybe that's how the tourists see it.*

"Coffee and a plain with lox," the next customer grumbled. He was sober and smelled like a curious mixture of diesel fumes and cold air. The transit authority patch on his jacket was worn with age.

"One twenty-five."

He left a tip. The morning went on. Unremarkable. A mix of the woefully inebriated and the painfully sober who might have benefited from a little softening of life's edges. Old Bauman showed up at four ready to work. He said nothing to Deb as he passed her, pausing to hang his coat and wash his hands. If he greeted Ben, Deb never heard it, though she imagined they might share a silent nod of acknowledgment. Their work together was often wordless, each man knowing his role in the process, each carrying out their tasks with a precise efficiency she found fascinating to watch when there was a lull between customers.

After a while, the steam of the boil made it impossible to get a clear view outside. Everything was smeared and speckled. Abstract. The convenience store across the way became a bright blur of neon through which dark forms and figures passed. Inside, everything was bagels. Bagels dumped into the vat, bagels lifted into the ovens, bagels cooling on the racks. It was the few hours of the day when everything made sense. She knew she was doing what she ought to be doing. She knew her place. But she also knew it was coming to an end. Soon her shift would be over. She'd walk out into the snow and wander. A few people had tossed coins in the coffee can by the register, and she would use those to buy a drink somewhere in the Village. That's where she ended up most days, occupying a table in a coffee shop reading the free newspapers. Sometimes she scoured every page pretending she might find a better job, or an apartment, or a lover, but mostly she just sat alone watching the world go by.

The door opened and there he was like a bad memory, the man in the dark wool coat. He looked just as well put together and handsome at five in the morning as he had in the mid-afternoon. He smiled at her, recognition lighting his eyes.

"Are you the only staff?"

"No."

His smile deepened. A dimple revealed itself. "Is the owner here?"

"Mr. Bauman, a guy here looking for you," she yelled over the hum of the fans. She imagined she could actually hear Bauman's scowl of disapproval. Part of her wanted to see how this meeting might go. She'd never seen Bauman unleash the annoyance that so clearly simmered just under his skin.

"Daniel!" the old man bellowed, not in his usual chastising way but with a note of pure joy. He shuffled quickly toward the younger man with his arms outstretched. "You surprise me!"

The two embraced, and Daniel lowered his pale forehead to old Bauman's flour-specked shoulder and held him.

"This is my boy, Daniel," Bauman announced to the room when they finally broke their embrace.

Only Deb seemed to be listening and she held out her hand in shock.

"Deb." Her voice sounded small. *Louder, clearer,* she chastised herself.

For a fraction of a second the young man seemed to hesitate then took her hand and smiled. "Danny."

Bauman nodded toward Deb. "She's a Wolf. Do you see it? Deb Wolf. No relation to the Wolfs on Orchard Street, she says, but she looks like Abe's girl, doesn't she?"

She let them look at her. Bauman had never mentioned this supposed resemblance, only asked if she was from Orchard Street when he first hired her. She wasn't.

Daniel smirked. "A little, I guess. Forgive my father, he looks for relatives everywhere."

"Psh. Did they come from Hanover, your Wolfs?" Bauman asked as if he were about to prove a point.

"I don't know. My dad grew up in Brooklyn."

"Hmm." His full lips tightened in annoyance at the mention of Deb's father and he said no more.

As if sensing some disturbance in the mood, Daniel said, "Either way, it's good to meet you, Deb Wolf."

The Send-off
September 1988

"BEL, REALLY, A BLACK dress? No, it's too funerary. Try the red," Whit insisted.

Whitney, already attired in one of his favorite tuxedos, watched from the foot of her bed while Belinda sorted through her clothes. He liked advising her, and she didn't mind the help. She had often thought if she had her own way she wouldn't have to play dress-up nearly as often as she did, but now the thought felt obscene.

"This one?" She held up a strapless red dress Michel had sent over at the beginning of the season.

He arched his eyebrows in mock seduction. She'd worn the dress only once before at a gallery opening in Manhattan. All night, men had flocked to her, some women too. Whit had watched with amusement as he fended off his own equally diverse string of suitors. "It's very becoming, you know."

She sighed and slid out of her black dress. Motionless in front of a full-length mirror Bel looked at herself without seeing. She wondered what they were doing. *A party? Really, is this the best use of our time?* Dubious, she felt none of the usual electric pulse emanating from Whit though he had gone out of his way to look the part and was doing everything in his power to ensure she did the same.

"Those are lovely," he said in a voice that neither mocked nor flattered, merely observed.

"What?"

"What you're wearing. Were you thinking of changing? Only, you looked like you were."

Bel looked down at the dark line of her underwear across her hips and sighed. "No, I was just thinking."

"Don't do that. Not tonight. Let's enjoy ourselves and our friends. Tomorrow we'll be in France."

He said nothing more, but the weight of his words hung in the air around them, expanding and filling the space. Belinda wanted to cry but found she couldn't, even when she tried. There was nothing, only a numb, cold sensation. She pulled on the red dress and hoped it might somehow transform her into the happy heiress ready to depart for an overseas jaunt just when everyone least expected it.

"Gorgeous."

"Is this the one?" She faced him for a moment before giving a turn.

He walked closer and lifted a necklace from her dressing table. "Absolutely. Come on, let's finish you off and get down to the car."

The final few meters of the drive felt like a last chance to escape, but Bel sat still and watched the Gilded Age edifice of Sea Edge mansion come slowly into view. Even in the dark, it was gorgeous. For tonight, Sea Edge was lit with thousands of tiny lights making both indoors and outdoors seem magical. *Perhaps it is a dream.* Whit had spared no expense for their send-off. The car slowed to a stop, and a man dressed in livery echoing the time of the building came forward and opened the door. Whit gave her a little squeeze. It had never escaped his notice how much she dreaded every formal affair. Despite her feelings, she always behaved flawlessly. She had been born to it. Belinda patted his hand and they walked in together.

The weather was cooperating marvelously, and nearly everyone had assembled in the gardens between the house and the ocean. A light breeze blew in off the water, cooling what had been an unusually warm evening. The scent of cut flowers mingled with the salty air. Everywhere people gathered in little groups drinking and chatting. They turned their heads as Whit and Belinda walked down a central aisle toward a low stage. She tried to read their expressions. Most were painfully neutral, unaware, even reveling.

Where are you, Laura?

Her eyes scanned the crowd. Face after face and none of them who she looked for.

"Whitney, so good to see you." A young man with perfectly coifed white-blond hair stepped toward them and took Whit's hand.

His watery blue eyes told Bel he knew this might be the last time he'd ever see Whit.

"Marek. What a nice surprise. I thought you were in London," Whit replied with genuine delight. His hand clutched Marek's in a tangle of gold and porcelain white.

"I was, but I couldn't miss this. Besides, I need to be back in New York soon. The Gladstone deal—"

Whit cut him off with a laugh. "Let's have no business tonight, not even good news."

Marek acquiesced. "Too right. Let me introduce you to my friend Patrick Reilly."

A man stepped forward and shook Whit's hand. He had the build of a boxer, but an unspoiled face. "It's a pleasure to meet you."

"What a charming accent," Whit replied, still holding the man's hand between his own. She knew Whit wasn't drunk, but had simply and obviously ceased caring what others thought.

"Is it now?"

"Indeed it is," Bel interjected, thrusting her hand in the man's direction.

Patrick took her hand and kissed it. "You must be the artist. It's an honor. Marek's told me so much about both of you."

"Has he? Well, I hope we live up to it. Enjoy your night, lads, I'm sure we'll run into each other again."

They were only a few steps away when Whit leaned close and whispered, "Christ, where does Marek get them?"

Bel laughed silently. Already the masses swarmed, and there was no time to talk about Marek's latest acquisition. Having chatted openly with one guest they were now obliged to stop every few feet and exchange pleasantries. *Tedious. But better than a formal receiving line.* She made her face look warm, welcoming. Her eyes, however, never ceased searching.

The clock in the hall chimed three and Bel kicked off her shoes, adding a dull thud to the tones.

"Where were they?" Her voice was louder than she intended, but she'd held it in the long ride home, and now was on the cusp of ranting with outrage.

Pale and exhausted, Whit slumped on the couch and waved one hand as if to shoo away her bad temper. "Word spreads like wildfire and sickness repels. What can one do? I repel myself most days. Don't be too hard on them, Beli."

"I can't." She felt like she might vomit.

"Hush, let's forget about those little details and focus on the best parts. For example, how handsome Marek's new friend is. He never would have dared bring him by me last summer. I would've snatched him right up. That adorable Dublin accent. My god. Delicious."

Belinda tried to smile, but couldn't.

"And how beautiful the Dior dress was on Carolyn. Perfect for her, absolutely perfect," he mused as he undid the studs from his cuffs.

"They should have come, Whit."

He ignored her. "And you. You stole the show as always. I told you this haircut would bring out your eyes. Simply stunning. It's like a second Evangelista has graced us." He always played up his campiness when he was trying to make her smile.

Belinda laughed, exasperation mixed with pleasure. "What does it matter, Whit?"

"A second Evangelista? It would be a sensation. I would call up my friends in Milan, and they would put you to work right away. Pity you aren't a teensy bit taller." He poked her lightly in the ribs.

She laughed and for a moment she forgot about everything—being snubbed, flying to France, Whit dying.

The Bar
October 1988

THERE WAS AN AD Deb had seen on an overpass billboard, or maybe she'd seen it on the subway: AIDS TAKES EVERYTHING. She hadn't thought too much about it. It was just one of those public service posters that peppered the city, warning against everything from house fires, to crime, to drug addiction. But she was finding out the truth of it if only at a small remove. The subway map was barely legible behind the heavy scrawl of graffiti, but Deb didn't care where this next train was headed. A break from the rain was all that mattered. Her clothes already dripped. Soaked to the skin, she couldn't take it anymore—the feeling that she was decomposing into the sidewalk like a wad of tissue.

The high-pitched squeal of the approaching train felt ominous and comforting all at once. She thought about stepping over the edge and letting it take her. She closed her eyes and leaned forward just enough to feel the blast of wind as the train passed. It would be over so quickly, not this lingering decay looming inevitably around every corner. She thought of Danny, then opened her eyes and stepped aboard the fetid subway car. She claimed a seat under a defaced advertisement boasting the renewal of the metropolitan transit authority system. Without even enjoying the irony she sprawled across a row of baby blue seats and curled her arms protectively over her chest.

There weren't too many people riding this line at night anymore. The subways were dangerous, at least that's what the papers said. Deb thought it was a little unfair. Everywhere was dangerous. Still, she kept one eye on the young man at the back of the car who clutched a wooden baseball bat and occasionally smacked it on the seat across from him as he muttered unintelligibly. *Maybe it's a ruse.* She'd pretended to be unhinged a time or two herself simply to avoid having to deal with people. After a few stops the man with the bat left and Deb closed her eyes.

She didn't know how far she'd gone when a voice roused her.

"Hey, are you okay?"

"Mmm? What?"

"Are you okay?"

Definitely a girl's voice. Deb didn't open her eyes.

"Sleeping," she mumbled.

"All right, well, here let me give you one of these."

Deb vaguely sensed something being placed by her hand and she clutched it sleepily. *Religious tract?* Sometimes the Jesus people liked to slip her a little piece of paper about how God had a plan for her. As if it mattered. But this was heavier and plastic.

"Stay safe." Footsteps departed, swallowed up in the screech of the train as it pulled into the next stop.

Deb rode to the end of the line and then back again, the plastic bag she'd been given still clutched against her chest. Finally, somewhere near Fulton she noticed the rain had stopped and she decided to head back to Manhattan. At least in the Village she might have some luck getting fed. Groggy and alone she sat up and looked at the packet of goods she'd been handed. The bag was a regular sandwich-sized Ziploc. Inside were two lubricated condoms, a clean syringe, a folded-up pamphlet and two Hershey's kisses.

"Fucking weird," she muttered but wasted no time pulling out the chocolates and eating them. At first she felt a tingle of annoyance. *That girl thinks I'm a junkie.* But then again, she was on the train in the middle of the night, soaking wet, malnourished, and passed out. *Fair enough, I guess.* She withdrew the pamphlet. It had all of the usual advice. Safer sex. Don't share needles. It wasn't moralizing or religious. She opened the page. Inside was a list of meetings. AA. NA. SA. PWAC. ACTUP. She'd gone to some of those meetings before when Danny was around, but now? She couldn't imagine going back.

She squeezed her eyelids tightly. She did not want to think about Danny Bauman. But fighting it only fed it. There he was in a perfect memory like a movie playing in the dark cinema of her skull.

She had been leaning over the small metal table at a cafe in the Village, eyes scanning the columns of advertisements. Help wanted, apartments for rent, personals. The tiny black type was smudged in places where the early morning dew had been absorbed by the newsprint. Her coffee was still steaming although she had forgotten it there beside her after a few sips. The ritual was the same day after day. Only winter had diverted her from this practice, but now since the streets were more or less free of snow she was back at it.

"Anything good?" he'd asked casually.

Deb shook her head.

"You'll never get a better deal than my father's."

"I'm not looking for a better deal."

"No? Oh, the personals then," he said dryly.

"Shut up, Danny."

"Aw it's nothing to be ashamed of," he went on with a grin.

She ignored him.

"So what's your type? Can I guess? I think older—"

"Any younger, it's a crime, Dan."

He had laughed. "True enough. But even so, I feel like you need someone who can show you the ropes."

Her glare hit him so forcefully that for a moment he held in his laughter. *These damn Baumans.* First it was the old man essentially outing her. Then Danny had done the same thing only a few months after showing up in the shop. The second he was sure she was gay he'd started inviting himself along on her trips to the Village. She was never sure why. He must have had friends his own age, but as he cracked jokes at her expense she supposed he liked having someone to pick on.

"Show me the ropes," she'd muttered incredulously.

"Don't be sensitive. We all start somewhere. You're a kid, and you're hardly even out. I don't think I'm being outrageous here."

"Look, I've had two girlfriends, so shove it," she had replied, though the admission did nothing to make her feel less awkward. Those relationships had been sexual, sure, but they'd been messy and childish. It wasn't what she wanted, though the personals didn't give her much hope.

"Okay, okay. So you're a trained professional. Still, you are skimming the personals every day. It looks desperate."

The train screamed as it turned a corner and Deb sighed, glad to stop remembering Danny if only for a moment. She rolled the smooth cylinder of the syringe between her fingers. In one more stop she'd be at West Fourth. She'd hop out there and walk to Christopher Street. Somebody would want these condoms and needles. She pocketed the pamphlet, not quite sure why, and stood by the door.

At street level, Washington Square was thronged with a lively mixture of tourists, junkies, artists, and assorted others. Someone played saxophone badly while another guy smacked two five-gallon buckets like a virtuoso. Deb breathed in the damp cool evening air, sensitive to the undertones of diesel fume and reefer. Winter was approaching, which worried her. She already missed summer. The warm weather, people in a good mood and freer with their money. She passed a few working girls and thought about offering them the baggie, but she didn't recognize these two, and got nervous at the last minute. She walked on. She'd know more people in a few blocks.

Sure enough, among a group of women congregating at the mouth of the alley by Metti's Café, Deb recognized Candy. Her height and dedication to neon green rendered her unmistakable. Deb fiddled with the plastic bag in her pocket and walked over.

"Hey Candy. You want this by any chance?"

Candy looked at her with a sympathetic smile and traced a long silver fingernail along the plastic. "Oh Wolf, I didn't know you cared."

"Well—"

"Are you street team now, baby?"

"Huh?"

"Hey, where's my chocolate? No candy for Candy, now that's just not right." She made an exaggerated sad face.

"Sorry. It was the only thing in there I could use."

"It's okay, baby, you can make it up to me." She tapped her cheek and leaned toward Deb.

With a sigh, as if she were resigned to it, Deb made to kiss her cheek but Candy turned so their lips touched just for a moment. She tasted like blue raspberry chewing gum.

"Ha! Now that was better than some little foil-wrapped chocolates."

Wolf's body reacted against her will, and she felt a flush of embarrassment.

Candy laughed. "You're not a virgin, are ya?"

"No. But hey, forget all that. What did you mean about street team?"

Candy arched an eyebrow and looked at Deb like she must be slow. "Where'd you get this?"

"I dunno. Someone on the train."

"Wearing a purple shirt?"

"I didn't look."

"Didn't look? Jesus, what were you doing?"

"Sleeping. She tried to wake me up."

"Thought you were nodding," Candy chuckled.

Deb twisted her mouth in reluctant acknowledgment.

"They're from the Violet Mission. They have the little drop-in center by the donut shop."

She had heard of it but never gone there. Things with the word mission usually meant Jesus, and she wasn't interested in hearing yet again about how Jesus was a Jew. As if that might somehow change her own stance on religion.

"They come around us ladies most nights and give us a baggie and a chat. That's how I knew my chocolates were stolen." Candy grinned and batted her fake lashes at Wolf.

Wolf leaned against the bricks, fidgeting with the buckle on her jacket. "You go to their meetings?"

"Me? No. I gotta take care of my kids in the morning, and I gotta earn at night. No time for all that."

A man walked by them looking like he was trying to not seem interested.

Wolf raised a brow and Candy smiled.

"I'll see you around," she said to Wolf's retreating back.

Wolf pulled the pamphlet from her pocket. Violet Mission, meetings on Tuesday night. Maybe they'd have snacks. That didn't help her now, though. Metti's was open, but she was broke. For the second time in a week she considered pawning her leather. It was the only thing of value she had left. She couldn't bring herself to do it; it had been a gift. Besides, she was certain the leather had more than once gotten her a free drink, and right now a drink might do.

Deb walked to the bar and did her usual "forgotten wallet" routine. The bouncer shook her head and motioned Deb inside.

"Go ahead. Behave yourself."

She knew damn well Deb wasn't twenty-one but had decided not to press the issue. What difference did it make really? Deb was a butch looking to be with her own kind, and the bouncer seemed to sympathize.

Deb nodded.

The place was less than full, but the music pulsed and people danced. She sat at the bar and shoved a handful of peanuts into her mouth. The saltiness mingled with the smoky air made her thirsty. She took a few more and chewed with a serious hunger, then pulled the rumpled pamphlet from her pocket and smoothed the paper on the bar. Sleeping on the train and begging to get by was hardly how she wanted to live her life. *I look like a junkie.* She felt sick with herself. She hated that judgmental streak inside of her, but she hated even worse the idea that she looked like she'd thrown her life away. She flipped the paper over and read the tagline: *For Justice. For Our Community. For Our Lives.*

At the end of the counter a woman with thick red curls chatted with a regular. They looked friendly, more than friendly. Like maybe they'd had a fling once and parted on good terms. The redhead resembled a 1950s pinup. All curves despite the baggy square cut of her clothes. There was something inviting about her, but Deb supposed charm was a key ingredient of the job. Deb scooped the last few peanuts from the bowl and dropped them in her mouth. She was on the cusp of swabbing the salt with her fingertip when the bartender headed her way.

"Out of nuts." Deb turned the bowl and smiled in a sort of sad desperate way that came almost as a reflex now.

"I see. What can I get you?" the woman asked with a playful smirk.

"Um, water with a lime."

It came out sounding more like a question than a request, but the woman fixed the drink, even putting a little mint leaf on it as garnish.

"You trying to stay sober?"

"No. Funds are a little low."

"Yeah? Here, have some more nuts." She refilled the bowl.

"Thanks."

"No problem, sweetie."

The music transitioned abruptly. There were some groans, and someone with an unnaturally grating voice groused about playing men's music at the lesbian bar. Deb took a handful of nuts and chomped them before finishing off her water and walking toward the dance floor. She loved this song. Danny had loved this song. They'd danced to it in one of the bars on Avenue A.

Wolf didn't look for anyone to dance with. Wolf didn't look for anything. She just danced. She didn't want to spend the whole night feeling down. Maybe if she moved enough, the memories wouldn't pull her under, but even as the music blared she could see Old Bauman looking as pale and twisted as ever. He clutched a hat in his hand, swollen knuckles mangling the wool.

"I would take you with me if I could." He sounded weak. He put one hand on her shoulder and looked up at her with a watery gaze that seemed to want to tell her more than he could say.

"Dad, the car is packed," his daughter announced.

His grip tightened. "You're a survivor. Keep doing that. Survive, Deb Wolf."

"Dad!"

Bauman said no more. He let go of her and let his daughter take his arm and lead him to the overstuffed Buick.

Danny was in the hospital. No one told Deb exactly what was happening, but it didn't look good. They were transferring him upstate. Bauman's daughter lived in Albany. She was taking care of everything. The old man had given Deb a phone number on a little slip of paper, but it had long ago vanished. Part of her was glad. She didn't want to know the all too obvious ending. AIDS takes everything.

She had stood outside the boarded-up shop and watched the car drive away.

She was alone.

After that, there was no more bagel shop, no more Bauman, no more Danny. But she could still dance. Even if it didn't work to drive her memories away, she could dance and she could survive.

When the song ended, she caught a woman watching her, and Wolf knew she'd have a bed at least for the night.

The Phone Call
October 2002

DEB RAN HER HAND OVER her face. The rental car smelled new—faintly toxic. Pointless observations like this tended to calm her. She traced the shape of the steering wheel with her gaze and tried to name the exact shade of gray. Charcoal? Slate? Concrete in the rain? She shook her head. A hollow bruised sensation lingered in her chest, but at least she had stopped crying.

Belinda Coltswood.

She turned the unfamiliar name over in her mind. She couldn't have known, would not even have allowed herself to imagine it. Professor B. R. Coltswood, Iowa, Award for painting. The label on the file hadn't meant a thing to her, but the tapes, the voice, and now—

Her phone buzzed insistently and she dug through her bag as if racing the clock. Stupidly, she thought it would be Bel.

"Hey, hello."

"Is that Deb Wolf, my favorite intrepid journalista?"

She smiled and shifted the phone to her other ear. "Danny! I didn't expect to hear from you so soon. Are things okay?"

"Yeah, yeah they're great. We made good time on the drive to Montreal, and I got your message."

Oh. Right. She had called him from a layover needing to share her suspicions with someone who would give her an honest opinion.

"I thought I ought to check in and see how you're doing with the whole, you know, interview thing?"

There was some low musical humming and chatter in the background.

"Are you at a coffee shop?"

"Oui. Now don't be evasive."

Fucking Bauman. "It's fine. We had the first interview today."

"And was it her?"

"It's her."

"Oh, drama," he gasped playfully. He didn't know the whole story, but she had gotten unusually drunk with him one night and let some of it slip.

"Come on, Bauman. I'm a professional." Her voice did not give away the fact that she'd been crying. She could be thankful for that at least.

"Of course you are. So is she hot still?"

"Danny!"

"Is she?"

"I'm not answering that."

"Okay, okay. I'll take that as a yes. Wow. So what happens now?"

"I don't know. I'll email her tonight and ask if she wants me to find a replacement." Deb let her finger glide over an old scar.

"Could you do that?"

She scoffed. "It would suck. I'm already replacing Gemma, but I could find someone I'm sure."

"Do you think she'll want that? I mean, wasn't she happy to see you?"

Deb made a garbled grunting laugh.

"So a no on that."

"I wouldn't say happy, no. Not really."

"But she must have felt some kind of way. Right?"

Deb shifted. It had been so long since she and Bel had been face to face. "I couldn't tell."

"No? Aren't you known for your exceptional powers of perception?"

"Sometimes. But I couldn't tell. She's always been good at playing poker."

The Sails
September 1989

"I DON'T WANT TO be a burden."

That was the first lie. And perhaps the biggest.

Bel wanted the weight of her loss to smother them, to make their every moment in her presence a misery. She wanted them to feel all of what the last year had cost her, but she knew better. They were incapable of those feelings, and she was fooling herself to even imagine she might be able to inflict them.

Her mother made a pretense of caring. She hurried her only daughter inside and sent Elena off to the kitchen to fix them some tea. Belinda had grown up in these rooms, and little had changed since she'd moved away, but still the place unnerved her. It had never felt like hers, never been comfortable. She had fled as soon as she could, first to boarding school, then to art school, then to Whit. But now, Whit was gone. Their house in Boston sickened her. Their friends were mostly either dead or disgusted, and she sat in her mother's conservatory more than ready to lie again about what had happened.

"Lung cancer. It is just so awful to imagine," her mother said, and Belinda realized she'd been lost in thought. Who knew what she had missed, but it was an acknowledged fact that Deidre Sheraton did not need another person to talk with, just someone to talk at.

Belinda nodded. *Yes, lung cancer.* That was the genteel euphemism everyone had settled on. She supposed it was true enough. He had been gasping for air, utterly devoured by illness, a moving skeleton when he decided not to carry on any further. She wasn't crying yet, but she could feel the urge welling up inside of her. Had she been anywhere else she might have given in to it, or made an effort to, but not here.

"I do wish he would have come back for treatment, but I can understand wanting to stay in France. If one must die, dying somewhere beautiful must be a comfort," Deidre mused.

Belinda was on the cusp of telling her mother a piece of the truth. Telling her how the water had been the color of the Isabella emerald the day Whit sailed off with Michel for the last time. He was stronger somehow, knowing it was over. He climbed aboard without her or Michel to aid him. The three of them left from Camaret-sur-Mer with a perfect wind pushing them to sea. Deidre stiffened with the sound of a servant's arrival.

She inclined her head in the vaguest acknowledgment of the tea tray that had been set between them.

"Thank you, Elena," Belinda said to the woman's retreating back. It irked her mother to have the help directly acknowledged.

Deidre's expression soured for a millisecond before the mask of propriety returned. She sipped her tea. "So, will you be staying long? Your old room is available of course."

It was the same question she'd asked in the foyer. The offer of a room held no warmth and no charm. If Belinda could make them suffer, it might be worth the indignity, but no. "No, no, I won't be in the city long. I need to check in with Marek, but I go back to Boston tomorrow."

"Marek? What for? Surely, he can go to you."

Marek could have gone to Boston, but he had asked her to visit him here in the city. Not only here, but at his office. An unusual request, but she intended to honor it. He was still Whit's money man, her money man now, she supposed, and more than that, he had never abandoned them. He had flown from London to Paris their first Christmas away, when Whit had started one of the experimental drugs. It's nothing, he'd said again and again, but only Marek and Michel had seemed to care when it all came down to it. He'd come again in July when Whit was declining, and spent a harrowing week with them in a rented chateau near Nantes. Belinda had been sure it was the end, and to make matters worse their servants kept leaving them, scared off by the disease though never bold enough to say so. Even the nurse they'd hired in Paris seemed ready to bail out. Marek helped bathe Whit when he could hardly stand, and made jokes with him about all the boys they'd known in school whom they had hoped to get alone and naked. Those jokes made Whit laugh, truly laugh for the first time in months. She would meet Marek wherever he asked her to, and she supposed he knew it.

"He can, but it's nice to get out for a time."

Deidre mustered an appropriately somber face. "Yes, I can only imagine."

Belinda sighed. She imagined that in the event of Nathaniel Boyd Sheridan III's death, Deidre would be nowhere other than where she was just then. His death would hardly affect her daily life, as the Sheridans rarely occupied the same house at the same time. Even with the news of Whit's death and Belinda's impending visit, Sheridan III had decided to stay on in Virginia where ostensibly he and Sheridan IV were enjoying a break from the all of the ass-kissing IV did around Congress.

The visit dragged on longer than Belinda would have liked, and at the first real opportunity she excused herself. The women said their tepid goodbyes. Belinda endured a dry emotionless kiss on her cheek and headed off toward the SoHo apartment Whit had bought for her as an engagement gift.

I've gotten you a little painter's shack. I want you to always have a place of your own. A place to just paint whenever you like, he had told her when he proposed. He gave her a diamond too, of course. One that had first belonged to some famous lady before America even existed, but he knew jewels would hardly impress her. The shack, and all it meant in terms of his concern for her as an artist, did.

Occupying the fifth floor of a white-fronted Civil War-era building on Wooster Street, the shack had been a place for her to paint while Whitney did whatever it was he did during their trips to the city. He never visited her there, never interrupted. As she turned the key, she was glad of it, as if his lack of presence might make the place more bearable. She opened the door and breathed in the dusty wood and paint smell of a studio so rarely used. She had kept her return secret and hadn't sent for a cleaner to freshen the place. She just wanted to hide and be left alone. On the train ride into the city, she had decided she would stay here for a while, delaying as long as possible her inevitable return to Boston and the life they had abandoned. Not for the first time, she was thankful that her parents cared so little about her work, her interests, and her life. Their circles would be unlikely to overlap.

Marek looked like any other financial district denizen. Tall, well-dressed, sure of himself. Only his white-blond hair set him apart. Bel saw him immediately among a throng of suits chatting outside the Stock Exchange. He was smoking again. It didn't surprise her, but she noticed how he tossed the cigarette away guiltily when he saw her.

"Bel!" He rushed toward her without seeming to rush at all and offered a warm handshake followed by a hug.

She held him and touched her lips to his cool, freshly shaven cheeks.

"You've been in France too long." His joking tone was incongruous with his downcast mouth.

"It's good to see you, Marek."

He reflexively smoothed a slender hand over his tie. His expression brightened. "Likewise."

A group of tourists passed, pausing for photographs and marveling noisily at the architecture with such genuine awe that Belinda almost appreciated them.

"Come upstairs with me for a moment. I want to show you something. Then we can take a stroll, get coffee?"

"I'd like that."

He nodded and led the way. Bel wasn't sure she'd ever been in one of Marek's offices, and the longer they wandered through the building the more uncertain she became that she was going to one now. Still, their journey aroused more curiosity than suspicion. Marek was on her side. Of this she felt sure. Finally, he opened a door and let her into a room. It had been an office at one time, though its current use was unclear. There were boxes stacked along one wall, an unplugged lamp, and a desk with a missing drawer.

"It's a friend's. He's leaving the firm, but I thought we had better watch from here."

"Watch what, exactly?" She looked out the window and saw only the usual flow of humanity amid the stone facades.

"I'm afraid you're probably losing some money today."

"What do you mean?"

"It's nothing that will harm you. A drop in the bucket, but I thought you should know from me directly."

"Marek, you're supposed to make us richer, not lose money," she said lightly. She had never cared about such things, not really, but then again, Marek had never bothered to speak to her directly about financial matters. No one had.

"I know and believe me—"

Mid-sentence a sound blared from the ground below. Bel turned and looked. What had seemed like the everyday bustle of the corporate crowd was utterly disrupted. People were lying in the street. Others were chanting. Men rushed from their offices in agitation. Bel heard them shouting through the walls.

"Let's clear these fucking faggots out. Keep trading!"

"Don't let the queers distract you. Do your damned jobs."

Marek stood silently beside her. He watched the world below with a kind of inward intensity she had never seen. The men and women strewn across the ground held cardboard tombstones above their heads. In many of their faces she recognized the same pinched agony she had seen so many times before. These signs were a prelude to the real thing and they knew it. Again, someone sounded the horns. Without wanting to, she thought of sails vanishing in the fog. It was the sound of moving in a mist. Belinda watched as a tall bald-headed girl in a leather coat lifted an emaciated man up onto a bench so he could stand over the crowd. With one arm she propped him up and with the other she held a bullhorn to his mouth. He yelled something Bel couldn't quite hear from behind the glass.

"They're half dead," she said in a cool observational tone that might have seemed cruel to anyone who didn't know what she had endured.

Marek chewed his lip, still watching them. "Hmm. But the half that's alive is very alive."

The Horn
September 1989

IT DIDN'T TAKE LONG for all hell to break loose. People flooded the streets and alleys. Bodies went down; signs went up. Wolf lay beside two guys who had taken the train from Providence. She raised her cardboard tombstone over her head, the pavement cool against her denim-clad backside. Sirens sounded, muffled by the buildings. She wondered if the blockade had held.

"The cops are inside. The guys are locked onto the rail. The banners got dropped and everything."

Wolf sat up. Cait crouched by her feet with a gray-and-white bullhorn clutched on her lap. Reports weren't always reliable, but Wolf had absolute faith in anything Cait said. They'd known each for less than a year, but so far she had proven herself to be absolutely trustable. Cait ran the Violet Mission with single-minded, no-nonsense purpose. She helped people, she wanted people to live; that was all that mattered. She didn't grandstand, and she didn't get caught up in the sideshow debates that sometimes sucked Wolf in.

"Here, take this. I've gotta go help Tori." She thrust the bullhorn into Wolf's hands and moved through the crowd toward Broad Street like a skid loader, clearing away every obstruction.

Deb was alarmed for a moment by how complicated the megaphone seemed. Quickly, she read the dials and buttons so she'd at least have some sense of what to do. In the not-so-distant distance someone sounded an airhorn. Others joined in. This was her first big action, and it consumed her more than she'd imagined possible. The intensity seemed to guide her. The force of their collective outrage told her what to do. She scanned the crowd, and there were familiar faces. Faces from the meetings, the park, the bar, the Mission. She felt for a moment like she was waking up. She knew these people and they knew her. Even the strangers weren't complete strangers. She had a whole world now, and this was it.

Someone nudged her arm.

"Wolf, you wanna give me a hand?"

Antony looked rough these days. Truthfully, she was surprised he'd come out at all given how thin he'd gotten, yet his fierce gaze was anything but frail.

"Hey, whatchya need, Ant?"

"Lift me up on that bench there and hold me. Don't fucking drop me now." He laughed as she did what he asked.

He was so light she felt like she could have tossed him up on her shoulders. She cinched one arm around his waist and gave him a gentle squeeze. "Don't worry, man, I've got you."

She pressed the button and the bullhorn crackled. Aware that the mic was live, Ant chanted one of the familiar call-and-response lines the group had been using all day, and people joined in chanting with him for a few rounds.

"That's right! That's right! Listen, I just want to remind you of something. My name is Antony Bouras and I am a person living with AIDS. I used to work in this place, right in there on the trading floor, so I know a thing or two about what we're doing here today. And I know a thing or two about the opposition. Some of you might think these people at the drug company hate us because we're gay or because we're junkies or whatever, and that might make you feel bad, but that's not right. That's not the problem at all. They don't give a shit about any of that. They only care about one thing, and that one thing is money. Every last thing they do is to make money. So that's where we hit them. In the wallet, because that's all that matters. We want to cost them. We want them to know that they can't just profit off of us. They took government money to make this drug. They took OUR money to make this drug. Now they want to bleed us for every last penny so that a few rich people with AIDS can survive while the rest of us drop like flies. We're here to say NO!"

People in the crowd echoed back that sentiment with tremendous resolve. A few sounded the horns again. A new chant picked up. Antony swayed.

"You okay?"

He nodded and looked toward the pavement. Wolf lowered him gently to the ground.

The Church
December 1989

"REALLY, MAREK?" THE CUTTING edge of incredulity in her own voice surprised her, but it was honest at least. She kept her volume low and respectable even if she couldn't master her tone. In the cozy dim-lit confines of the club no one noticed anything amiss. Just a well-dressed woman and a man in a flattering gray suit huddled together in one of the private alcoves.

"I just think they're onto something. I'm not suggesting you lie down in the street." Marek shifted in his chair, the leather creaking under him in a groan of mild complaint. He swirled his whisky till the ice made lazy revolutions against the glass. The corners of his mouth turned down.

"Oh Marek. Of course they're onto something, but it's nothing new. The church has always been against us for one reason or another." *Us.* It still surprised her sometimes to find herself speaking openly with him about their shared condition. He and Whit had always been honest with each other. Even in front of her they had enjoyed flirtatious banter, commenting on the looks and likely preferences of the men they encountered over business. But Bel, for some reason or another, had always held herself apart. She had been discreet, all while knowing Marek surely understood her tendencies.

For weeks he had been trying to convince her she ought to get more involved. She was happy enough to write checks, to donate things for auction, but she had thus far resisted any overture to attend a meeting or a rally. Marek, for his part, kept trying without ever getting on her nerves. On the contrary, she found it fascinating to watch this dignified son of wealth and privilege talk with great animation about his late-night meetings and clandestine plots. But, when she imagined him among the rabble who had led the little Stock Exchange revolt, she found it difficult to take him seriously.

"It's all very organized," he said after a few moments of explaining the meeting process.

"You sat on the floor?" She looked at his face searchingly. Was he having her on?

He nodded. "I did. I'm no snob, you know."

"Of course not." She held in her laughter but just barely. The majority of contexts in which she'd seen Marek operate, indeed the context they were currently in, spoke most assuredly of snobbery.

"Besides, I didn't wear a suit. You've got to try to blend in. But there are all sorts of people at those meetings."

"I'm sure there are," she huffed. What an assortment she had seen already.

"Don't be that way, Bel."

"What way?" She made a pretense of feeling indignant, but Marek gazed at her with an unguarded sincerity that nearly made her squirm.

"You know what way. Look, I'm not even saying you're wrong. There are some very hotheaded people, and some people who I think might be quite literally insane with fear and grief, of course there are. It's New York. But there are so many bright and committed people. People who were probably members of a club like this one—"

"Not this one. The whispers would be unmanageable."

"Maybe not this exact one, but you get my meaning. There are people like Whit at those meetings. People who just want to live, Bel. Is that too much to ask?"

"Of course not. No, it's not." The question sobered her.

He shrugged, perhaps a little embarrassed with himself for getting emotional and mentioning Whit whom he had carefully avoided bringing into these discussions. "Anyway, I'll be there. I'm going to go inside with them and be a legal observer."

"Marek, is that wise?"

"I don't know if anything I do outside of work is wise anymore. But I have the training and with the way I look I might be better able to avoid arrest."

"What a scandal to have my adviser and friend arrested." She laughed lightly and swallowed the rest of her wine.

"I could resign if that's what you want, Bel. I'd never want to cause a problem for you or the family name."

Her hand shot across the table, and she closed her fingers over his wrist. "Never. You've always handled Whit's affairs beautifully and as far as I can tell you still are, even with all this. Maybe especially with all of this. I would never want you to resign. And even if you did, we're friends, Marek."

"We are."

There was no question. "We are."

He pressed his lips together, the crease between his eyes deepening. "Perhaps you'd like to meet someone."

"One of your activist friends?"

"She runs a program providing food, safer sex education, and some medical services. She's doing a tremendous amount of work with not much economic support. When you told me you'd like to stick to financial contributions, Cait Hanson sprang to mind. I could arrange a meeting, and you could see what kind of person you'd be backing."

"Is that what Whit would have done? Had a meeting?"

"Yes, typically. I'd handle the money side of things of course, but he always wanted to know who he was working with."

Someone in an adjacent alcove had lit a cigar, and the pungent smoke wafted through the room. She suddenly felt aware of how much she disliked this place. "Do you come here often, Marek? To this club?"

The turn of conversation seemed to disorient him. "Um, well, no. Not often. I don't even know why I come here at all really. It was my father's club, my grandfather's, Whit's too. Both of our families have been in for ages. It's private, and, I don't know, familiar in a way."

"I think I was impressed the first time Whit took me."

"And now?"

"I resent not being able to swim in the pool."

Marek scoffed. "It's not very nice anyway. Lots of fleshy old men soaking in the buff."

Belinda made a face.

"Exactly. So should I—"

"Yes, fine. Arrange a meeting, but not at the rally. And not here, for god's sake." Her voice was merry but did little to mask the contempt she felt.

Marek's expression warmed. "He always said you were no great fan of this place. I wasn't sure I believed him. I'll arrange for drinks. Upper West Side?"

"Is she coming from the Village?"

"Most likely."

"I can meet her there; it's closer to my place anyway."

"Do you have a driver?"

She bristled a little, not at Marek so much but at the suggestion that she kept a team of people to meet her needs. It was the kind of thing her mother might believe in, but she resisted. "No. No driver. I can sort myself out. I grew up in the city, remember?"

"Of course." He made a note in his slender leather book and slipped it back into the inner pocket of his jacket. Bel wondered if he had a different book for his activist dealings or if, rather perversely, his professional and personal lives were melding into one. Names of lovers, and comrades, and bankers, and brokers all pressed together in the pages, rubbing lead onto lead.

"Will you be there? At the meeting?"

"No, I'll let you two sort things out. I'll pull together some financial statements beforehand just to guide our thoughts on how we might be most useful."

"Hanson, you said?"

"Mmm."

"No relation to the developer Hansons up the river?"

"She never mentioned it, but she tends to stay very much on topic."

"Unlike some people." Belinda smiled. "Let's get out of here, Marek. I've got a few paintings being shown at Winter's. We could walk through and see how they look."

Marek arranged for them to meet at a place neither of the women would have chosen for themselves, but which suited their needs. The tavern was well stocked and quiet. Bel took her time getting there. She hated sitting at a table waiting for a stranger. The feeling of being observed alone and expectant always made her uneasy. When she opened the door, she was alarmed by how dark the interior seemed after walking in the glare of winter sunlight. She blinked as her eyes adjusted. It took only a moment to pick Cait out among the clientele. She was seated at one of the green leather banquets reading a copy of the *Times*. She raised her eyes over the paper and seemed to nod her head in a vague motion of recognition toward Belinda.

"Cait Hanson?" Bel paused at the edge of the table.

Cait stood and extended her hand. "And you're Belinda?"

"I am. Lovely to meet you." Bel took her hand. Cait's attire had all of the femininity of a bottle of scotch, yet her face was remarkably pretty even without a trace of makeup.

"I appreciate your willingness to meet with me. I was surprised when Marek suggested it. Please, let me get you a drink. Wine? Something stronger?" Cait inclined her head toward the bar, and a shock of ash blonde hair fell across her dark gray eyes for a moment before she brushed it away.

"Wine. Something dry."

As Cait walked away Bel felt a pang of regret at not having been more specific about her drink, but she'd survive a glass of bad wine if needed. She watched Cait lean against the bar and hail the young man who was lazily drying glasses. He had the look of someone who would rather be absolutely anywhere else. After a brief exchange she returned with two glasses of red.

"He said this is their best." Cait gave her own drink a practiced swirl.

"Let us pray," Belinda joked and watched with pleasure as Cait's mouth curved in amusement.

The wine had been acceptable, and Cait pleasant company, but it scarcely explained why a few days later she found herself at the church protest. Bel pulled her thick wool coat tighter around herself as she stood on Fifth Avenue looking across the intersection as winter light washed St. Patrick's in cool shades of lilac and periwinkle. Her eyes watered with bitter cold. She had agreed to take a look, that was all. To take a look at the rally where Cait and her people intended to pass out condoms and clean needles despite the fact that a few of them had already been arrested for doing just that a week before.

It was early, but the crowd was getting thick. There was an element of the carnivalesque, which Belinda had expected. Rows and rows of people in paper pope hats, an assembly of clowns, and then, perhaps even worse, the extremely earnest women in their sensible shoes raving about abortion access and human rights. Cait was around somewhere, but Belinda had lost track of her. Police wagons waited at the edge of it all, doors open and ready to swallow. She didn't know where Marek figured into things. The last time she'd spoken with him they were preparing to arrange a regular flow of money into the Violet Mission's coffers. Neither of them had mentioned the rally.

A round of chants rolled through the crowd.

"Teach safe sex! Just say no is not enough!"

A woman clutching a little blue bag from Tiffany's paused beside Belinda for a moment and watched. Wearily adjusting her scarf, she drawled. "Well, the gays have always had a flair for the dramatic."

It struck Bel as funny, though she didn't laugh and the woman walked off with the same disappointed air with which she had arrived.

The studio did not heat well, no matter how much warm air coursed through the vents. Belinda closed the door behind her without flicking on the lights. The chants of *Fight AIDS* still echoed in her head. Alone in the cool darkness, mind wracked with voices, she looked up through the skylight into the orange-tinged night. Her body ached from too long spent standing in the cold. She had promised Cait she'd look in, but looking soon became consuming, and she found that she could not leave. She had seen Marek only briefly, but his smile at the sight of her just beyond the police barricade had glowed with astonished gratitude. She hadn't known she might be the source of such a smile. He seemed like a different person in his blue jeans and neon ski jacket, his hair peeking out from under a cap. Cheeks pink with cold, he looked like a boy. She had never seen him look youthful, free.

The ring of her phone startled her. No one was supposed to know she was in New York, except of course for Marek and now Cait, to whom she'd given her personal number on a whim after too many glasses of Burgundy. She hurried toward the sound, vaguely aware of a sudden frisson rippling through her.

"Hello?"

"Salut, Bel!"

"Michel, is that you? The connection is fuzzy."

"It's me, yes. I had to harass Marek for this number. Sorry to disturb you. I'm sure you want some peace, but you've been in my mind lately."

"You never disturb me, Michel. How are you? God, it must be late there. Are you all right?"

"Yes, yes, I'm fine. Just thinking of you. I ate one of those madeleines au miel de sapin today."

Belinda sighed. Whit's love of those particular treats was a subject of some renown. Part of her could not imagine ever eating one again, yet she knew that if she were in Paris she might feel compelled. She wondered what shop Michel had gone to. Had he made a special trip just for the peculiar sweet suffering, or had the moment happened automatically? A treat with a friend, not thinking at all of those no longer here until the taste of honey saturated him with the bittersweetness of recalling Whit's singular passion for fresh madeleines.

"Are you painting?"

There was no reproach in it. Michel always supported her. His connections in the art world had helped her immensely. She looked over at the part of the room where she usually worked. Things were empty. However much she liked to claim that she was here in New York to paint, the truth was she hadn't done anything interesting in a long time. "Eh."

"Very well then. I won't feel bad for asking a favor."

"You should never feel bad asking me for anything, Michel. You know that."

"Well, I need a hand. To be frank, a companion is what I need. I'm going on an excursion for work, and I hate the thought of going alone. It'll be a few months. I think perhaps we might be of use to each other. You could show me around the States, and then accompany me south."

"South?"

"Yes, is your Spanish any good?"

"Probably better than my French."

Michel laughed. "Bueno. Come with me, Belinda; help me trade treasures. We'll have a marvelous time of it."

Belinda flopped down on the overstuffed chaise and tucked the phone against her shoulder. "Tell me more."

"Well, we are loaning out some art to various museums in the western states and picking up some work from the US and Mexico. I've been asked to play the dignitary. But, I would rather do it with someone a bit more dignified by my side," he jested.

"Someone female, perhaps?"

"Ah certainly, and why not?"

"Hmm."

"Come with me. I've got meetings to attend. You know the sort of thing, but there will be talks, dinners, museum tours. I expect there will be many interesting people to meet along the way, and a beautiful woman who knows art can enhance any encounter." His pitch was intentionally too solicitous. If they'd been face to face, Bel would have been laughing at his delivery.

"What are you loaning out?

"Ah, Bel. It's all very hush hush. If you come, you'll get a deliciously private viewing."

Again she made a noncommittal sound.

"Am I enticing you?"

"It will take more than that," she said, though she was enticed. Michel had shown her so many wonders over the years, even allowed her to handle some. By not telling her what or who they might be traveling with he allowed her imagination to fill in the blanks with obscenely delightful possibilities.

"You are the perfect woman for me."

"Pfft. Why is that?"

"Because I can hear you salivating over the prospect of running your fingers over the Winged Victory of Samothrace, or is it touching the head of Akhenaten?"

"Ah, so we're trafficking in antiquities, are we?"

Michel's laugh cut through the cottony quality of the international call. "Don't rush to judgment. I know how you enjoyed the workshops. Ah, Bel, share this adventure with me."

"So I'm the perfect woman for salivating over a statue, is that it?"

"Yes. And because you know me, and despite it all you love me still."

His voice, so familiar and yet distorted by distance, made her chest tight with memories she'd been managing to suppress. "I don't know."

"Darling, if it's too much, I understand. Truly. But it could be good for both of us. It's been too long and I think we'd have a wonderful time."

"I'm sure we would. Let me think about it. When would you need an answer?"

"Of course, think about it. Next Monday?"

"I'll call you either way."

"All right, my Bel. We'll speak soon."

He did not wait for her goodbye. Belinda listened to the dead air for a moment before clicking off the call. She walked through the room still clutching the receiver, wondering if perhaps a trip was what she needed. A pile of aborted paintings lounged against the wall, each more boring than the last. She probably needed to get laid. She pushed that thought aside. Somewhere, like a tickle in her brain, the chants from the church protest started up again. God, she hated all that public emoting. She could only imagine how Sheridan IV would mock it, and then she cursed herself for being like her brother in this small spiteful way. Even if she found the rally awkward and futile, she could see the beauty of it. She thought of Marek's rosy face, the rows of shining police helmets, the way the breath of the protestors lifted in cool blue clouds through the frosty air. She was remembering the woman with the Tiffany bag when the phone blared in her hand. She jumped, fumbling the receiver.

"Yes? Hello?"

"Hi. Belinda?" a pleasant yet tentative voice inquired.

"It is."

"Oh, I, I'm sorry for calling you at home. It's just, you gave me the number and I was wondering if you made it home all right."

"Miss Hanson?"

"Cait, yes. I'm sorry." Her voice was sweet. No one would have imagined the protest pickets and flat cap that came along with it.

"Don't be."

"I shouldn't have troubled you. It's just I saw you at the rally, and then you weren't at the debriefing. It got me a little worried, I suppose."

"I appreciate your concern, but I made it home without any trouble. No officer in his right mind would harass a well-dressed woman on Fifth Avenue."

"I suppose not." Cait laughed, a light easy chuckle, and Belinda felt a sting of pleasure in her amusement.

"And you made it home in one piece, I assume."

"I did, yes. None of our crew got arrested, and we handed out over two hundred kits. All in all, a successful day."

And yet the Catholic Church remains. Her own sarcasm ran a background commentary that she tried to ignore as if it were coming from an inappropriately loud neighbor. "So, Cait, are you meeting Marek tomorrow?"

"Yes, I need to get him some documents. I think we said before noon."

"Excellent. Well, maybe I'll see you then."

"I'd like that very much. Okay, well, sorry again if I disturbed you."

"Not at all. Good night, Cait."

"Good night."

Outside a siren blended with the sounds of the city, moving closer and then passing. It had been five months since burying Whit, eight months since she'd so much as heard from Laura. A letter. Stilted and cool. *I hope all is well.* Though the sight of Laura's tiny precise handwriting had brought her instantly to tears, Belinda had tossed it in the trash and made no reply. She could not overlook Laura and Peter's failure to see them off. Whatever she had felt, whatever she had wanted, it was over. Of course it was. So why was she hiding in New York? And if she was hiding, why alone?

The Courtney-Hall Foundation, named for Whit's maternal grandparents, was primarily managed by a man named Lewis whom Belinda had never met. Marek's involvement there had always been modest, and, except for a good view of the park, his office reflected as much. The desk was oak and mostly empty; the walls featured a few small works of art, but nothing ostentatious. Belinda slowly glanced around.

"Somewhat less than you imagined?" Marek asked with a smile.

"I suppose. Is that—" she walked across the room to look at one of the paintings. The curve of an ancient lane, all warm pink stone in the evening sun. "How did you get that?"

"Whit gave it to me when he told me he planned to marry you. I suppose it was after your trip to London."

"It's not very good." She wrinkled her nose. She had stopped painting with watercolor years ago.

"I like it. That was one of his favorite places. I think it charmed him that you painted it."

"Pfft. I painted everything back then. I don't know what I was thinking. It was as if there weren't cameras. Sad little thing with my travel easel. Anyway, I brought something to celebrate with." She pulled a bottle of wine from her bag.

"Ah, a very nice bottle. I take it you and Cait hit it off?"

"She's not my type if that's what you're suggesting."

He opened his eyes wide, the picture of innocence.

"But, she is interesting. Dedicated like you said, and I'm happy to lend our support."

Marek flipped open a folder. "I'm heading to London tonight, could be a long stay. I don't know if you want the details."

"No. I trust you, Marek. Whit always trusted you."

"Yes, but you are technically in charge now."

"I know, but it's really not my thing. Business."

"It was hardly Whit's either."

It was true. Whit had never cared much for the empire he oversaw. The only part of it that appealed to him was traveling and meeting people. Whit loved people with a kind of open-hearted energy Bel could neither muster nor comprehend. She fidgeted with the wine bottle and looked at the clock.

"What time is your flight?"

"We leave at three. I can make room for you if you like."

"Mmm. Tempting, but I don't think so."

Marek looked ready to try a bit of coaxing when a knock on the door interrupted them. Bel felt a stutter in her pulse and wondered for half a second if she was excited by the prospect of seeing Cait again. She hardly had time to consider it. Marek opened the door and revealed not Cait but a lanky youth dressed inappropriately in a motorcycle jacket and torn black jeans. She hoped this wasn't an intern. *I'll speak to Marek about it.*

"Mr. Hall?"

The voice was low but definitely female, Bel noted and she took a longer look. The visitor was nearly Marek's height. Although her face portrayed a cool certainty, she fidgeted with the buckle of her jacket as she waited for a reply. Her hands were long and fine like a musician's.

"I am."

"Cait told me to drop this with you. She got caught up in a meeting and didn't want to make you wait." The girl dug around in her messenger bag and pulled out a thick manilla envelope, extending it toward Marek.

Bel had the distinct sense she'd seen the girl before, but couldn't place her. She didn't want to stare, but at the same time she found she was cataloging everything about her: the determined set of her jaw, the dark straight line of her brows, the jagged locks of hair poking out from under a woolen watchman's cap, the nerve-bitten nails of her fingers. There was something striking and sad about those hands.

"Ah well. That's too bad, but we understand." Marek took the envelope and set it down on his desk.

Bel had been hoping to see Cait. She had thought they might make a night of it.

"Here, take this." Bel thrust the wine at the messenger who took the bottle with a crooked grin.

"Tip or message?"

"Huh?"

"Do you want me to deliver this?"

"Yes, please, if you can."

"Sure, I can."

The messenger smiled and again Bel felt the sensation of familiarity. But something in that smile troubled her, as if she were being mocked.

"Here, I imagine this is enough." Bel pulled a fifty-dollar bill from her purse and held it haughtily in the girl's direction.

"Seriously?"

More than that? Really? What do messengers make?

The girl put the bottle in her bag and looked back at Belinda. "That's too much. I can't take that."

Belinda expected the girl to look away, to turn toward Marek since she herself was clearly not up to the task, but the girl continued addressing her. "Who should I say it's from?"

"Belinda."

"Belinda." She took a pen from her pocket and jotted it on her hand. "Got it. Is that all?"

Bel nodded and turned her back on the girl, feeling certain that she would tell Michel yes.

The Van
December 1990

THERE WAS A GROOVE IN the shoulder of Wolf's black leather jacket—a dent paler than the rest and as wide as a finger. She touched it absentmindedly. It was the right shoulder. She always used her right shoulder, and occasionally she thought she must have a matching divot in her bones from all of the times she had helped carry a body over the past few years. Their coffins were light, lighter than they should have been, but heavy enough to last forever in her leather.

Wolf pulled the coat closed around her and crossed her arms over her chest, stuffing her numb fingers into her armpits, desperate for warmth. She wished she could turn the van on and run the heat for a while, just to get a break from the frost, just long enough to feel her nose again. But there wasn't much gas left, and who knew when someone might need her to run them to the hospital. She leaned her head back against the window and sighed. It was dark in the van. She had pulled the makeshift curtains closed, and only a little of the sulphur-yellow streetlight leaked in around the edges. It was quieter than usual outside. She had parked in a crumbling neighborhood that flanked the East River. Cops in the Village had been harassing her lately, but so far no one bothered her here. Down by the water, only the most desperate people were still milling around. The bitter cold wind had driven everyone else inside or underground. Before the van, she used to ride the subway all night sleeping in fifteen-minute intervals, waking with a start to make sure no one had tried to rob her. It was the only way to stay warm. The memory of that made her feel a few degrees cozier; at least the van had locks.

"Thanks, Dave," she mumbled in the darkness.

The ghosts of the letters spelling *Dave Cohen Electric* were still visible across the side of the dark blue Econoline. Dave had been dead since April. She wasn't sure where he was buried, or if he'd been buried at all. Sometimes she wished she did know so she could drive by and thank him in person, but no one bothered to tell her.

She thought about Dave every day.

Dave had been the last guy on her Thursday night rounds. The soft black bag that kept the meals hot was mercifully light by the time she trudged up the narrow staircase to his fourth-floor apartment. His place wasn't much, about twice the size of the van with a tiny two-burner stove and a mini-fridge.

That April evening there was a slip of yellow paper taped to the door. Final Notice. She didn't read it, just knocked again. There was no reply. She hadn't expected one. Dave hadn't been doing very well. The week prior, Wolf had called Cait and asked for a nurse to be sent. She wasn't sure what came of it, but no one had told her Dave was dead, so there she was with one hot meal knocking on his door as the final notice slip hung crooked and ignored.

After a third knock she tried the handle. Unlocked. She supposed Dave wasn't worried about being robbed. The apartment stank. She sniffed the air trying to mentally sort out the odors. It was rank, but it wasn't rot. She hadn't walked in on a body yet, but she knew it was a real possibility and she held her breath as she moved toward the bedroom. Dave looked awful, but he was alive.

"Hey," he muttered.

"Hey, Dave." She reached into the thermal bag. "I brought you some—"

He cut her off with a groan and shook his head.

"Yeah, right, never mind that. What can I get for you?"

He closed his eyes and she moved closer to him.

Shit, you don't look good, Dave. "Hey, you want me to see if I can get a nurse over here? Is there somebody I can call?"

"No. There's no one."

"Look, Dave, maybe a nurse could help, get you some better pain-killers at least."

He barked a short laugh that devolved into coughing. The table by his bed was covered in pill bottles. Wolf scanned them for anything helpful. She didn't know much, but every day she was learning something new. When he finally caught his breath, he wheezed, "No phone."

"There's a pay phone outside the bodega where I can make a call. Seriously, Dave, you just tell me who and I'll get them on the line," Wolf assured him. She wanted there to be someone, anyone who could help make this situation less miserable. It didn't usually bother her being alone with sick people, but this was another level and she felt unprepared for it, which was perhaps the most unnerving thing of all.

"There's no one. Am I your last one?" He nodded toward the bag.

"For tonight, yeah."

"Want to just hang out for a while?"

"Yeah, sure, man."

She sat down on the edge of his bed, and he laughed again.

"What? What's so funny?"

"Long time since there's been a girl in my bed," he spluttered though a cough. "You're gay, right?"

"Yeah." She figured she'd made that obvious enough with her shaved head and *Dykes Do It Better* T-shirt.

"Are the girls holding up okay? The gay girls? Or are you guys getting it now, too?"

Wolf shrugged. "Some, but not many. We're okay mostly."

"So you're just doing this for fun? You a religious person or something?"

Wolf spat out a bitter laugh. "No. Not by a long shot. Why, are you religious?"

"Atheist."

"Yeah, me too. I don't think God would do something like this." She looked around the room.

Dave nodded.

"I just do it cos no one else is gonna look out for us."

"I'm not gay," Dave protested, but it was a moot point. He had told her months ago that he was pretty sure he'd caught the virus cruising the Village. He probably didn't remember saying it now.

"I don't care."

"No?"

"Nope." She didn't care, not really, but it pained her to think he was in the closet on his deathbed.

Dave closed his eyes and sighed.

"You really don't have anyone I can call for you? A friend or some family or something? Even long distance, I don't mind." The bodega phone was one of those where you could call anywhere for fifty cents. She used it sometimes in moments of weakness.

"There's no one. Really. Pathetic, huh?"

Wolf shook her head. His skin was a sickly shade of gray in the undertones.

"I don't have people either, just the Mission," she told him.

A long moment passed, and Wolf thought maybe he had dozed off, but then he looked at her, his dark eyes lucid. "Where do you live?"

"Here and there. Nowhere really. Maybe I'll get a place out in the Village someday, but I don't have any place steady yet."

"Can you drive?"

"Sure. You want to take a road trip?" she asked with a smile.

He laughed and coughed. "No, but look, go to my front room. Is there a van down there still? Parked in the dirt lot?"

She did what he asked, and sure enough there was a van in one of the tenants-only slots. "Yeah, there's a van there. That yours?"

"Yours if you want it."

"Dave?! I can't take your van. If you want to get rid of it, I can help you sell it. You can use the money to pay off some of these bills, keep the lights on." Wolf furtively looked around the place. It seemed like Dave was holding on by a thread financially. She couldn't imagine why he'd want to give something valuable away when he so obviously needed the cash. Then again, she didn't know what it felt like to be irrefutably dying.

"Take it. Seriously. I got no one. I'd probably have died months ago, and no one would have been the wiser. You and the Mission are the only ones checking on me. You got no place? Well, now you do. Keys are on the fridge. Go get them." He nodded toward the kitchen.

Shivering in the van, Wolf remembered how he took the bunch of keys from her hand and held them almost lovingly for a moment as he told her about the van and the locked toolboxes inside of it.

"You can sell those. Give the money to the Mission. I won't need it," he said. She wanted to comfort him, to disagree, but she could tell he was probably right, so she just said thank you.

By the next day he was dead. Cait told her a nurse had gone by to check after reading Wolf's report and found him. That was all the information anyone had. No obituary ran in the paper. No one mentioned the van, but even if they did, Wolf wasn't worried. It was all legal. Dave signed the title that night, and the registration was good until February.

Outside it started to snow. She watched for a moment; the flakes swirled in the dark so beautifully until they reminded her of ashes. She closed the curtain and lay down.

The Observation
October 2002

WOLF ARRIVED LATE. If anyone had asked, she would have said it was an accident, a failed alarm, or some difficulty with parking, but it was intentional, though she wasn't sure why. Maybe she wanted to see Belinda look up at her like an errant student. Maybe she wanted, somewhere subconsciously, to see her disappointed glare. Or maybe she just wanted to make her wait, to let her wonder for a moment if Wolf would show up at all.

There was no way of knowing if Belinda had wondered anything, but the expression she cast toward the creaking door at 2:16 p.m. was a distinctive mix, first withering and then indifferent. Wolf tried not to smile. A warmth spread through her that seemed to say, *there, you got what you wanted.* She went to the back of the room and took a seat on one of the tall metal chairs. The girl in front of her looked over her shoulder just long enough to make sure she wasn't blocking someone's view and went back to mixing her colors between clinical glances at the nude woman on the stage. Wolf took in the scene, jotting notes about things she wasn't sure she'd ever care about again.

Seven students arranged in a semicircle. A low stage painted matte black. A smell of turpentine, and some sort of perfume. Floral, not Bel's. A naked woman, long-limbed, blonde.

The model reclined on an Edwardian couch of unevenly worn, coral-pink velvet. She had an open book sprawled across her chest, though it scarcely did anything in terms of modesty. Her eyes were closed as if sleeping, one arm lazily tucked under her head. She was older than most of the painting students, but probably not yet thirty. Her mouth and nipples matched the velvet rather prettily, and Wolf wondered if she had been selected on that basis. With a flicker of amusement, Wolf noticed that the student in front of her seemed to be exclusively focused on the model's left hand, which was limp over the spine of the book. Hardly a painting that required a nude model, but well executed nonetheless.

Professor Coltswood stood on the other side of the room, looking over the shoulder of a student who was working on a large canvas, though nothing quite as sizable as the pieces that had garnered the Hirsch prize. Wolf double-checked the dimensions in the notes Gemma had given her. One had been six feet by six feet. Another ten feet long and seven high. She wished she could see more than slides, but slides were all that could fit in the dossier. Wolf watched with interest as Coltswood leaned forward and said something to the young man who nodded and wiped his brush clean. She moved on to the next student and repeated the process, always speaking in confidential tones so no one save for her intended audience might hear her words of advice. Wolf knew she was staring, but, as no one was looking at her, she let her gaze linger for a moment on the delicate curve of Coltswood's ear and the slender silver ring that pierced her helix. *That's new.*

"Professor?" a student called and Coltswood turned, her eyes meeting Wolf's for a fraction of a second.

Caught in the act.

She was thankful she didn't tend to blush. But her heart hammered hard all the same.

"Will we have the same model tomorrow in the studio?"

"No. Do what you can now. You won't have this pose again, so make the most of it." Coltswood turned back to the painter at her side.

Make the most of it.

The art model intercepted Wolf as soon as class broke up.

"Hey, I'm Vic." She put her hand on Wolf's bicep and squeezed like they were old friends. Wolf turned toward her only to find the woman's other hand extended, a smile on her coral pink lips.

"Deb."

"Deb, are you an artist? I noticed you weren't painting."

"Ah, no. I'm not an artist. I'm a journalist."

"Oh really? Not for the campus rag, surely." The playful indignation in her voice was pure flirtation. Wolf knew this, but still she laughed.

"No, no. I was with a paper out east until last month, freelance now."

"Freelance by choice? Interesting."

"It creates different opportunities."

"Like coming to Iowa and sitting in on an art class?"

"Just like that."

"So, what's the scoop?"

Wolf looked over her shoulder on instinct. Belinda was the point, but she was nowhere to be seen. Wolf tried to keep her face neutral, but she was pissed at herself. *So much for making the most of it.* Being on a new kind of assignment was making her soft already. Or maybe it was seeing Bel again that was throwing her off.

Something showed in her expression. Vic picked up on it. Her eyes rounded and brows raised. "The prof? Oh, is that all big news again?"

Wolf scoffed. "Sounds like you know something I don't."

"No, no."

"What was the big news?" If she was going to lose out on a chance to talk to Coltswood, this might be the next best thing.

"How long have you got?" Vic was all direct eye contact and close proximity. Wolf stood her ground.

"Oh, I've got time." She could feel the little current between them. Like a barely there filament that flashed in a shift of light. She was sensitive to that sort of thing, having survived off it for a while. But that was a long time ago. Even so, a pulse like this had its place in her professional world. It was a starting point for a conversation, a seed to cultivate, a source of information eager to spill.

"Take me for a drink and I'll tell you all about it." Vic's hand passed over Wolf's wrist. The touch was soft, fleeting, but definite. It was easy to lean into her game. She was gorgeous and she knew it. And she didn't bother hiding her attraction. It was the kind of thing Wolf always appreciated.

"Where do you recommend we go?" Wolf replied with the same easy confidence.

"Follow me." She took her bag from a hook and led Wolf outside. It had been a long class, but Wolf was surprised to see how low the sun had gotten. Autumn often took her by surprise.

"Have you been modeling for a while?"

Vic smiled. "I'm in grad school. It's how I make beer money."

"Nice. What program?"

"Neuroscience.

"Really? That sounds interesting."

"It is. Here we are." She turned toward a dingy little place festooned with university pennants, opened the door, and held it for Wolf.

The interior was about as original as the exterior. Beer posters, more football paraphernalia. The floors were tacky. On a big screen over the bar a college basketball game played silently. No one seemed to be watching. The only patrons, a group of boys, circled around the pool table. The bartender glanced up from his book and smiled at Vic in that particular way men smile at women who are out of their league.

"Hey, Vic, what can I do for you?" The book was forgotten. All of his focus was on her.

She welcomed it and leaned over the bar ever so slightly. "Jaime. Hey, how's things in the bio lab?"

"Oh it's going okay. I think we've sorted it all out." He tugged at a lock of his hair as he spoke.

"Glad to hear it. Give me a pint of whatever's in the local tap." Vic paused to let Wolf get an order in.

"I'll take the same."

"You got it. Two Millstreams coming up." He washed the glasses with a flourish and filled them until a thin rivulet of froth spilled over the sides.

"Keep a tab for us, Jaime."

"Sure thing."

Wolf let Vic pick a seat and wasn't at all shocked when she chose a cozy booth in the back of the bar out of Jaime's line of sight.

"So, you're a journalist from out east."

"That's right."

"And you're writing about Coltswood?"

"About art." *Why not tell her?*

"For what paper?" Vic asked.

"Ah, it's not like that. It's a different kind of project."

"Oh. Is it?"

"It is. So neuroscience. Are you training to be a surgeon?"

Vic, mid-swallow, shook her head. "No, I study pain."

"Physical pain?"

"All pain interests me, but right now, yes, mostly physical."

There was that glimmer again, the filament in the breeze. Wolf let Vic look right into her eyes. *You have to give to get.* "So, what was it you thought I was writing about?"

Vic's mouth curved so slightly, so slowly. "Well, like I said. It's old news really, I don't know why I thought you were here about it, but it did cross my mind. What kind of journalist are you?"

"Freelance."

"Right, but before that. I mean, do you cover arts and leisure, is that it?" She raked her eyes over Wolf trying to see something but apparently not coming up with whatever she looked for.

"I've covered a lot of things over the years. Writing is funny like that."

"Never sports, though."

"No, never sports."

"Hmm. Anyway, there was a thing that happened with Coltswood a few years back. If you've been digging around about her, I'm sure you've come across it somewhere."

"The professor's not really the focus of what I'm doing," Wolf lied, her mouth partly obscured by a hastily raised glass and a guilty swallow that she knew looked normal. She'd found she was a good liar when she needed to be, even if deception bothered her.

"Ah well, maybe it doesn't even matter then."

"Maybe not, but why not tell me anyway. We're here after all."

Vic delayed, talked about other things, tried to get Wolf to do the same, but Wolf knew she'd spill eventually.

"It's all secondhand of course. I was finishing my bachelor's. Psych and bio if you're wondering." They were well into beer number two. Vic had stripped off her flannel during a round of darts, and Wolf was watching her absentmindedly stroke her own collarbone as she spoke.

"What year was that?"

"Ninety-six."

"So, spring of '96, you're in your senior year, getting ready to graduate with a double degree, neither in art, so how did you know the professor?" Wolf asked. She picked at the damp napkin under her glass, itching to pull out her notebook.

"I didn't, not really. But I lived in a house with some students of hers. They all loved her. You saw how they are, all vying for her attention. Desperate for some praise."

Wolf wasn't sure she'd noticed that, at least not any more than what she'd always noticed in college classrooms. A handful of talent, a healthy dose of anxiety, a few people eager for approval. Coltswood hadn't seemed to play favorites, despite the obvious disparities in skill among her students. Still, it was only one observation. Who knew?

"Anyway, they were so torn up about what happened I couldn't really avoid hearing about it. One day they went to class and the studio was locked. There was a sign on the door, very official looking, saying that all of Professor Coltswood's classes were suspended for the foreseeable future. This was like an absolute slap in the face. Johnny especially was destroyed; he was doing a senior project. It was his whole life as far as he was concerned."

Wolf nodded. Vic was on a roll and didn't need any coaxing.

"Anyway, Johnny and our other roomie, Kayla, got it in their heads that they were going to get to the bottom of it. At first they were worried something tragic had happened. A car accident, a sudden heart attack, the kind of thing that the admin wouldn't want to traumatize the kids with, but would require them to stop the classes. They were in the library searching everything they could. When they would have been in the studio, they were combing all the local and regional papers, calling hospitals. Nothing. Then they figured maybe she got a better job so they called some art schools to see if she'd been hired. Still nothing. At some point, about a week in they were getting pissed off because wherever the prof was, they wanted to finish their work. The grad students have their own studio space, and Johnny figured they might have a clue, and even if they didn't, maybe they'd let the undergrads into the main studio. Anyway, according to those guys, Coltswood had gone to a meeting with the dean and never come back. There was a buzz of suspicion, but nobody knew what was up. Kayla thought maybe they should round up all of the art majors and plot some kind of petition or protest or something to get the studio reopened and to get an immediate replacement so that they could finish out their semester."

"Makes sense."

"Right, they were always like that. Dedicated but kind of crazy too, you know? Activist types."

"Sure."

"Well, they contacted everyone, but there was this one girl they couldn't track down. Finally, they found out what dorm she was in and got hold of her roommate. The roommate says Missy—that was the art girl's name, Missy. The roommate says Missy had to go back home to Estherville, or Algona, or one of those places outside of Storm Lake. Anyway, her parents pulled her out of school because, and here's the juicy bit, because 'Professor Coltswood defiled her and was leading her into an unnatural life.' That's an exact quote. I'll never forget it. I was just barely poking my toe out of the closet and the thought of all that kind of blew my mind."

"I can imagine it would."

"Right? A professor and a student in a lesbian tryst. What a scandal! But I was also really drawn in. I don't think I'd even seen Coltswood before, but it definitely got me thinking, what was that like? Having an affair with a professor. I mean I don't blame either of them; they were both adults, but the parents made a big thing of it of course."

"What happened with the professor?"

"I never got all of the details, but she was gone for a year. I saw her around again in fall of '97. Forced sabbatical is my best guess."

"Is that when you started modeling? When she came back?"

"No, I started in my first year of the Ph.D. One of my friends over in Michigan started modeling for extra cash. I figured if she could, so could I. It's easy money."

"Who was the professor then?"

"Some stand-in they hired for a year and then dumped. Professor Morris? Or Morrison maybe was the name. I don't really remember. I mostly worked with the studio attendants. There've been a few of them over the years, Harry, Shawn. The new one is Kelly."

"And so she was gone for a year, then back just like that?"

"Just like that. Weird, right? I suppose there was nothing they could do. She hadn't broken the law. I mean they probably broke the law trying to force her out."

"Probably. And she's never said anything about it?"

"To me? No, she avoids me. She doesn't say more than a passing greeting, and most of the time not even that."

"Is she close with anyone?"

"Someone who might know the story, you mean?"

Wolf nodded. Vic poured her another beer. They'd moved on to a pitcher. It was going to be a long night.

"Not that I can think of. She has a few students, of course, who she's closer with just because they're hers. The painting MFAs for example, but she's not friendly with them. You know what I mean? Some profs will go out drinking or turn up at a party. She's not like that."

"A partner? A girlfriend?"

Vic laughed. "Not that I've ever seen. Why, are you hot for teacher? I wouldn't blame you. I've thought of it myself, but I prefer someone a bit taller, and who isn't my boss."

It was late when Wolf got back from the bar. Alone and cold, she fumbled with a set of unfamiliar keys. The first too small; the next fit but didn't turn. Whooping madly, university boys on mopeds raced each other down the dark lane, their shadowy forms briefly illuminated by pools of milky street light. It started to rain. Fat cold drops in a slow patter. She didn't know whether to laugh or cry.

Fuck.

Wolf shoved her messenger bag under her jacket and worked a third key into the doorknob. *Finally.* The lock unbolted. She hurried in and shucked off her shoes, leaving them askew on the rubber mat beside the door. Relief was instant, but incomplete. The stink of beer and cigarettes wafting off her clothes made her feel filthy. What she needed was food and a shower. That wouldn't solve everything, but it would be a good start. Offloading her bag and her jacket, Wolf wearily padded toward the bathroom where a pale purple nightlight glowed.

She stripped and stood in the cool room, not bothering with the overhead light. She wanted to ignore the world, to stay in the dim glow where she didn't have to think.

Turn your back on her and she slips away.

Wolf stepped into the shower and let the tepid water beat down on her head. She hadn't gone home with Vic. That was one thing she could be proud of in all this. The hum of attraction hadn't won out, nor had her desire to forget about life for a while. It would have been so easy. The woman offered directly, but Wolf said no. She finished her fourth beer of the evening and left alone.

She'd drunk too much, eaten too little, and smoked half a cigarette, but she hadn't slept with a source and that was something. Still, when she closed her eyes, Wolf could see the model as she had been in the studio, a silent assemblage of angles and soft curves. It was better remembering her that way. It kept Wolf from dwelling on the things she'd said.

Wolf rinsed her hair, hoping the smoke wouldn't cling to it. There was something perverse in the pleasure Vic took telling that story. Maybe it had become something like a fantasy for her, the thought of Coltswood and an innocent farm girl from Algona or wherever she was from. Wolf tried to imagine herself in Vic's place, but it was hard. She'd never been closeted, and she'd spent her youth in the streets. College for her had been later, and by then the interpersonal bits of the ordeal had been distractions to avoid. But maybe, if she'd been a kid living a sheltered life, the story would have seemed enticing. Either way, it sounded like bullshit to Wolf. Though not like a lie.

Vic wasn't making it up. Still, Wolf didn't believe it. Couldn't believe it. *Are you defending her?* The question passed over her like a cold draft across her throat, drawing her awareness suddenly away from everything else. *Am I?* What did she really know about Coltswood after all? It had been years since they'd last seen each other, and even then, what had she ever really known?

The Blockade
January 1991

WOLF WASN'T IMMEDIATELY SURE what she'd walked in on, but Brenda held her shoulders hunched up the way she did when delivering bad news. She struck that pose entirely too often. Cait sat behind her desk, staring blankly at the stacks of paperwork in front of her. Claim after claim, every slip of paper a desperate person hoping for some kind of relief.

"So they declared war?" Cait asked.

"Yeah, that's the word. I mean, I don't know if it's all official yet, but it's imminent, I guess. They've called a meeting tonight."

Cait took a deep breath. "All right, I'll spread the word."

"I can help," Wolf offered.

Brenda looked over her shoulder at Wolf who still leaned in the doorway. The look she shot Wolf wasn't openly hostile, but the antagonism shone clear. Since its inception, Violet Mission had officially employed only a small number of people, and Wolf had been added to the part-time payroll not long after she and Cait met. In return, Wolf gave every free moment of her life to the Mission, but she knew what people thought of her. She knew Brenda in particular called her Cait's lapdog. Wolf couldn't understand that sort of jealousy. There was just too much work to be done to turn help away.

Brenda fumbled in the pocket of her shabby mint-green puffer jacket as if her fingers were still numb from the cold. She passed Wolf a mildly crumpled quarter sheet listing all the details under boldfaced type decrying *Money for AIDS Not War*. A thick stack of them was stuffed into each of her pockets. "Here."

"I'll be there. Should I bring anything? Or anyone?" Wolf tucked the flier in her pocket.

"I don't think so. Well, I had better get back out there." Brenda zipped up her coat. A collection of mangled ski lift tags dangled at the end of her zipper.

Wolf couldn't help but wonder if Brenda ever got out of the city at all, never mind as far as the slopes. Maybe she liked to keep the tags as a talisman, a reminder that she'd had fun once, maybe even been fun, and she might be again someday when all of this was over. Wolf knew people loved to play that game with themselves. *What will it be like when this is over?* But Wolf had started to strongly suspect it never would be.

"Hey, you know I can hit one of the streets if you want and hand 'em out. Cover more ground." Wolf nodded toward the fliers.

"Yeah? Okay, sure. I was gonna head down Hudson and pin them up or drop them off at all the usual hotspots. I haven't gone past Washington Square yet. I appreciate it; it's cold out there." She passed a stack to Wolf.

See how useful I am, Bren?

"Sure, no problem, I can probably get some more of these run off if you want. Not here, not here, I know we're conserving toner. I have a buddy who works at Kinko's," Wolf explained when she saw Cait give her a stern look.

Cait said nothing, but raised an eyebrow.

"No, not strictly legal, but he doesn't mind the risk."

Cait shook her head.

Wolf loved watching Russ give a speech. He wasted no time whipping the crowd into a frenzy. Soon people were brimming with ideas on how to fight back. It didn't take much to set them off these days. Wolf herself felt like she was always on the verge of screaming, and when the people assembled in that close dim room started planning how to respond to the declaration of war, no suggestion seemed too wild to her. Cait had kept Wolf out of the cathedral.

You don't want to get arrested, she'd cautioned, and it was true. Wolf knew an arrest now could severely mess up her life, but in light of all this, what did it matter?

She leaned against the wall looking around at who was there and who wasn't. Lately it seemed like more and more people were showing up. Even as their friends died or got too sick to come to a meeting, there were more and more bodies filling in the spots they'd left behind. More and more people with HIV, but more people like her, too. People who were at the edge of it. Lesbians, or family members of infected people, those who were going to be left crying and carrying corpses.

"What did I miss?"

Wolf looked down at Nick who was pushing his glasses up his nose in a frantic, puzzled way.

"Not too much; we're kicking around ideas. Russ seems to like the idea of shutting down the trains, and those guys over there want to crash the evening news, but nothing's decided. Cait said something clever about how they want to take our eyes off of the death toll here by making more bodies somewhere else."

"Did she?" Nick pulled out his notebook and pencil.

"It's not an exact quote, Nicky."

He nodded until his glasses slid down his nose again. "Gotcha."

But he still made a note of every word. Wolf wouldn't be surprised to read it tomorrow if Nick's editor decided to run with it. Nicky said lately some of the papers were actually bothering to print things about AIDS activists that weren't merely hit pieces. He was an optimist. He always tried to get something about AIDS or at least healthcare into his stories. She admired that.

When the meeting was over, they had come to an agreement about what to do. One group would disrupt the news, another would try to take over Grand Central, and a third would rally at the UN. Nick looked like he was going to burst.

"Christ, I gotta keep this under wraps? I'll do it, I'll do it, but Christ, you guys. This is good stuff."

"I'll give you a front row seat if you want, Nick."

"Really, Russ?" Nick looked even more excited by the prospect of time with Russ.

"Sure, let's go get a drink and plan it out. You're on the team."

"It'll blow my chances of broadcast work," Nick joked. He looked back at Wolf. "You coming?"

"No, I'm going with Cait and the others who are taking the train station."

"Right. Hey, you should take notes there, write something up. I can't be in two places at once, you know?"

"Sure, I can try."

"Here, let's meet up after, okay?" Nick took a business card from his pocket. It was a little grimy and bent on one edge, but Wolf held it like something precious.

"Okay, yeah, let's meet up. I'll call you," Wolf hollered to Nick as Russ and his crew led the journalist off in a bubble of excited chatter.

Nick looked back over his shoulder and nodded, his tortoiseshell glasses slipping down his nose.

Cait was serious. As serious as Wolf had ever seen her. "Don't do anything crazy. I can't afford to bail you out."

Wolf made a face. "I wouldn't expect you to, Cait."

The lines between her eyes deepened. Not a scowl, but a face of pained concentration. "Please, Wolf, don't get into anything you can't get out of. You do more for the community out of jail than you'll ever do in it."

"There's a bail fund, don't worry, look—" Wolf pushed up the sleeve of her thermal and showed Cait the phone numbers written in thick Sharpie down her left arm. "I've got all the numbers, free legal team, and bail fund."

"Wolf, I know I can't stop you. But think about what I'm saying, please." She put a hand on Wolf's shoulder, not grasping, just a touch. "Jail's no place for you and once you get in the system as an adult it might be really, really hard to get out."

"It's no place for anyone," Wolf replied, but her retort lacked some of the force she was known for.

"No, it's not, but some of these guys who are out here gunning for arrest, they know they're dying and some of them know they've got money and connections, so for them the stakes aren't the same as they are for you. You're what, twenty years old?"

"Ish."

"Yeah, so you have your whole life ahead of you. You could do anything. I know this isn't the radical speech you want."

Wolf shook her head. It wasn't the speech she wanted, but she expected this from Cait, and a small part of her knew it was true. She also knew Cait, more than anyone else in her life, had her best interests in mind.

"I hear ya, Cait. I'll try to behave."

"That's all I can ask. Besides, I'd be in a real lurch without you. You're my best worker."

Wolf smirked. "The pay is shit, though."

"That it is, Wolf, that it is," Cait cackled and with that all of the stress between them evaporated.

Inside Grand Central Station the chanting rose, drowning out every other sound. The second the banner dropped over the arrivals board, Wolf felt the sudden and peculiar calm that washed over her just when things were most raucous. Her eyes scanned the scene. A row of men in shirts reading *Fight Back, Fight AIDS* were chaining themselves to each other making it harder for security to evict the group. A youth contingent had their own signs demanding funding for sex education. Someone was throwing condoms, and Wolf flinched as one grazed the side of her head. The evening rush commuters reacted, each in their own way. Most seemed to regard the events with bemused resignation. Some tried to push on as though getting through the crowd would be a simple matter. They hadn't accounted for just how many protestors clogged every hall and passageway. Some were lying down as if dead, taking up even more room. The whistles that accompanied so many protests echoed maddeningly off of the walls as pink and white balloons floated up and dotted the ceiling.

"Get out of my way, you queer piece of shit!"

Wolf turned and saw a thickset guy in a brown suit absolutely losing it as he tried to navigate through a knot of protestors who were splashing fake blood on the floor. *Oh shit. This won't end well.* She moved in the direction of the chaos as if pulled by some internal magnet for trouble. The fake blood flew, the guy in the suit had definitely been splashed, and his red-flecked face contorted in an apoplectic snarl. Sure enough, he threw a punch. The hallway erupted.

"Cops!" somebody screamed.

Wolf turned to look, but she could hardly see anything through the forest of bodies and signs. Behind, the melee moved closer and seemed to be growing.

Fuck.

"I'm gonna fuck you up, you fucking faggot!"

"Sit down, bitch, before you hurt yourself!"

The chants continued. The whistles blew.

"Grab this guy."

"Don't you fucking touch me!"

Then she saw it, a row of officers coming one way, a fist fight hemming her in on the other side, and there walking into it all was Cait's friend, the one with the fancy bottle of wine. *Belinda,* she remembered suddenly as the crowd seemed to swallow her. Twisting and flailing her arms, Wolf slipped out of the tussle and pushed forward, determined to intervene before things got ugly.

"Get your hands off of me!" Belinda hissed. Her fingers scrabbled against the well-muscled arms that had grabbed her from behind. The grip tightened and Belinda felt herself being lifted ever so slightly and dragged through a doorway. Panic. A sharp prickle of heat scalded her from within. Her throat constricted. It felt hard to breathe, and then like she was breathing too much. She kicked and her heel connected with her assailant's shin.

"Calm down, calm down."

The voice close, a warm breath in her ear.

Belinda clawed at the hand gripping her, nails sinking into flesh.

"Ow! Come on."

The sound of the commotion died down behind them. They were alone now in a desolate gray service hall.

Bel cursed her vivid imagination and the scream she felt threatening to burst from her lips. With some effort she took a deep breath and growled, "Let me go!"

"I'm sorry." The grip loosened.

Belinda spun and faced her attacker, unsure why she'd chosen such an absurd course of action even as she did it.

"I'm sorry. I just didn't want you to get hit."

The tall lean person behind her seemed familiar somehow. Familiar and injured, her face smeared with blood, a welt blooming under one of her dark eyes.

"The bike messenger?"

"Yeah, sure, sometimes. I'm Wolf."

"Wolf?" *Naturally.*

"Yeah, Wolf. I work with Cait."

Belinda examined her own clothes and brushed at the impeccable soft surface of her knee-length coat. She felt rumpled and stupid for having gotten grabbed, even if she was relieved to find her abductor was a bike messenger who now seemed contrite and totally harmless.

Wolf adjusted her black woolen watch cap and thrust her hands in her pockets. "Sorry again for what happened back there. I just didn't want you to walk into something. You looked distracted."

She *had* been distracted. The flight from Paris to Boston had gone smoothly enough, but travel was always exhausting. And the instant she'd opened the door to the house she had felt thoroughly overwhelmed. She hadn't been back in years, but the staff Whit retained had kept everything just as it had always been. Even the smell was unchanged, some occult blend of cleaning solvent, waxes, and scented candles. The green couch sat empty in a pool of mid-morning light, but she swore she saw Whit lounging there. Then there were the cards and letters that had been piling up for ages: a flood of holiday missives and long overdue condolences from far-flung friends and relatives, most of whom had never bothered with Whit from the moment he was diagnosed. She felt sick and angry and unbearably sad. Her only thought, *I'm not home at all, but utterly homeless.* Packing nothing, she walked to the station and took the first train to Manhattan.

"Are you okay?" The girl's face was serious and inquiring, apparently concerned for Bel's well-being.

"Fine."

"Okay. If you go that way, you'll come out by Forty-Second." Wolf nodded down the hall.

"Right." Belinda hesitated, overtaken by the unreasonably daunting thought of walking alone down that hallway.

"I'll take you." Wolf moved decisively, like she was going to take Belinda by the wrist, but stopped herself in favor of forging ahead.

Belinda followed.

"Is Cait here?"

Wolf looked back at her and raised an eyebrow. "Somewhere, I'm sure. Are you here to rally with us?"

There was something in the question that irked her. A challenge, a kind of cool dismissal from a bike messenger of all people. She rose to it. "What if I am?"

A grin, a crooked eyetooth, and an amused glow seemed to radiate from somewhere within, transforming the girl's face.

"So, what next?" Bel asked.

"Come with me." Wolf smacked her palms against the door, shoving it open. Together they spilled out into the darkness.

Cait would be there; Wolf was sure of it. The crew who distributed clean needles and condoms always made their way through the streets around any big event, and Cait would be there with her minivan full of supplies so they could re-up. It was just a matter of spotting her amid the chaos. Wolf wove through the crowd, sensing Belinda following behind. She could hardly believe she'd snatched a woman out of a train station. It felt a little like maybe they were in a revolution after all like some of the guys said. Well, action had been needed and she'd taken it. Whoever this woman was, she was important; anyone could see that.

"Oh, there she is. Hey, Cait! Look who I found." Wolf picked up her pace, hardly noticing Belinda's struggle to keep up.

Cait turned slowly as if expecting it to be nothing of interest, but her eyes grew wide when she saw.

"Belinda! I, um, what are you doing here?"

"Your messenger gra—gathered me from the train station."

Wolf smiled, pleased that Belinda seemed to recognize the method of their escape from Grand Central might not be the kind of thing Cait needed to know about.

"How did you two—"

"I saw her. It looked like she was looking for someone, so I helped her find you."

"Really? But, how did you recognize each other?"

"Are you kidding? She gave me a five-hundred-dollar bottle of wine. You don't forget that kind of thing."

"I didn't give you—" Belinda started to protest.

Wolf's laughter cut her short. "Joking, joking. But it did make an impression. Anyway, that's my delivery for the night. I'm headed to the UN. You coming?"

Cait looked at Belinda as if considering it. "Are you here to march?"

"I'm here to be helpful if I can."

Cait nodded. The two of them seemed to have an understanding. Wolf didn't need to hear what came next. It was obvious enough. "You go ahead, Wolf; be careful. I'll see you tomorrow?"

"No debrief?"

"Not for me tonight. I have rounds in the morning."

"Okay. See you tomorrow then." *Mission accomplished.* She spun on her heel and ran toward the rendezvous point, her secondhand combat boots carrying her in the direction of the drums and whistles that guided the way even over the sounds of the city.

The Skirmishes
April 1992

BELINDA SENSED A DULL ache starting just behind her eyes. She didn't know why she'd let Cait talk her into this ridiculous meeting. The apartment was small and dingy at the best of times, but packed full of activists it was hard to imagine a more unwelcoming space. The women's meetings in particular always seemed to bring out the worst in her. She had vowed to hold her peace no matter what. It took less than a moment to notice Wolf was in attendance. No surprise there; that irksome girl was at everything, it seemed. A group of young women circled around her listening to her talk about who knew what. Bel watched from the doorway, torn between wanting to be seen and wanting to walk away.

Cait passed her a plastic cup of wine. "Here, have a drink. Don't worry, it's from your bottle," she whispered conspiratorially.

There was the answer to why she'd come, or at least part of the answer. Cait was a good sort who seemed so genuinely interested in Belinda's involvement it was hard to say no. Bel liked to think she was immune to flattery, but the earnest interest of others tended to incline her toward them though she would never admit as much.

One of the activist groupies fawning over Wolf hopped onto the worn-out couch and rubbed the girl's shaved head with affection. Foolishly, Bel remembered with a sudden strange sensation almost like longing what it had felt like to be lifted off the ground and carried away. She took a drink. It was one thing to think stupid things, but another to feel them.

"Are you planning to get into the debate tonight?" Cait asked with nothing more than open curiosity. She'd clearly noticed Bel looking in Wolf's direction.

Bel took another sip of wine, hoping to blot out the unwanted memory of Grand Central. "No. I've sworn off debates. Besides, I have somewhere to be at nine so I might not even be here when things heat up."

"Ah, sounds like a good escape plan. Where are you headed if I may ask?"

"A meeting with some gallery people."

"Lovely. Are you having a show?"

"Maybe. I'm not sure I'm up to it."

Cait gave her a sympathetic look, though Bel felt sure she didn't quite deserve it.

The meeting began with the usual round of updates. A few guests from Chicago talked about a recent action they'd led in an attempt to advocate for women with AIDS. Another team announced a plan to collaborate with a group in Brooklyn to do outreach with Spanish-speaking women. These reports were the best part of the meetings. Bel took pleasure in hearing what people were doing. Although she'd been initially suspicious of some of the methods they used, she had become less judgmental. She could see the virtue of trying even if the goals were unlikely to be achieved. People who were doing something felt useful and connected. It was clearly all that kept some people alive.

She was just starting to relax and think that for once they might get through an evening without some absurd fight when she noticed one of the women from the Mission starting to rehash an ongoing argument about self-presentation. Bel suppressed a theatrical yawn. The conversation was tiresome, and she wished it were nearer to nine so she could slip away.

"We really need to start thinking about what we wear, you know? It's these little everyday decisions that are shaping our lives. When we dress the way the patriarchy tells us to, we're undermining our own authority. We're giving in to a system that's inherently designed to control our bodies," the woman explained.

There were murmurs of agreement in the crowd, and more than a few people grunted as if they'd heard it all before and weren't up for the discussion. *Well, amen.*

"I mean we need you ready for the fight, not for fashion week," the woman gestured toward Belinda who merely smiled in amusement at the accusation.

Fashion week. My goodness, it's just a little black dress.

"Whoa, wait a sec. Are you seriously trying to tell this woman what to wear?" Wolf's voice cut through the crowd. Heads turned in her direction. She was on the floor cross-legged, her knee poking through her faded blue jeans. She was, as far as Belinda could tell, the very picture of what was being advocated for.

The woman looked stunned, fair play to her. Belinda could hardly believe what she was seeing. Wolf was not her biggest fan. More often than not they were on opposing sides of these little skirmishes.

After a breath, the woman resumed arguing. "I just think she's doing herself and our movement a disservice."

"Shit! All you talk about is women's rights, and women's bodies, and autonomy for women, and you're seriously here trying to tell this woman what to wear? What a bunch of bullshit."

"I don't think we should be dressing the way they tell us to!" Brenda fired back with conviction.

Wolf hopped up from the floor and stared at the woman where she perched on the back of Cait's couch. "No. So she should dress how you tell her to because a female dictator makes it okay? Fuck that. You are so full of shit. You got no right telling anyone how to live their life."

The woman leaned forward, but Wolf left no room for commentary.

"Fight AIDS, Fight AIDS. All we fucking do is fight with each other," she yelled then stormed out of the apartment. As she passed by, Bel felt their arms brush together, and Wolf muttered an apology meant only for her.

"Well, okay. Anyone else want to tell anyone how to dress?" Cait slumped wearily back into her seat. She adjusted her lapful of paperwork and scanned the room waiting for more discussion to erupt.

The initiator of the entire fight deflated against the wall in a sulk.

"On that note, I'm off to fashion week," Bel chimed in and followed the way Wolf had gone.

The stairwell was empty and so was the street outside. Bel bit back her disappointment and reminded herself it hardly mattered. She needed to focus on the gallery, not these irritating activists.

The Ashes
October 1992

ON THE DRIVE OUT OF DC, Belinda kept remembering the way Wolf had rushed the line of police. The girl acted like she was looking for trouble, and she found it every time. As things intensified, Cait and Brenda had guided Bel out of the chaos, but Wolf had charged into the fray and vanished.

"Don't worry, she'll meet us at the rendezvous point," Cait said, pulling into the Jersey Turnpike truck stop they'd chosen as a meeting site.

Bel kept looking out the window. She wasn't worried.

A half-hour later they were all in the restroom, Wolf casually picking dried blood from the edges of a minor head wound while Belinda retouched her makeup two sinks away.

"I gave them the slip," Wolf recounted with a smile.

"You really take your chances," Cait said from inside one of the stalls.

Bel thought she sounded bored with it all. The protests, the fights—but more than anything, Bel suspected the deaths were taking a toll on her state of mind. Every day she seemed exhausted, but would never say so.

"I know, but they were hitting that guy, and he looked fragile enough without them going at him. I can take a shot better than these guys." Wolf shrugged.

It sounded like bragging, but there was an element of truth in it too. Although Belinda had tried to steer clear of the more heated zones of protest, she had seen officers using their linked clubs more than once to shove people over who looked like a strong wind would knock them down.

Belinda sensed Wolf was about to launch into one of her well-worn tirades on police brutality, but stopped when an attentively groomed blonde with the air of a woman on her way to an upscale job interview emerged from a stall. The woman scowled at them. When she caught a better view of Wolf, her bland, but not unpleasant, features shifted with a blend of horror and disgust.

"What?" Wolf stared the woman in the face. She had stopped mid-scrub, and a trickle of blood-tinged water ran from her brow to her cheek.

"This is the women's room!" the blonde announced, as if the fact were news.

A wicked grin lifted the corner of Wolf's lips, and she looked for a moment like her namesake, canine exposed, eyes intense.

"Is it?" she inquired coolly. Her voice low yet unmistakably female, her posture consummately butch. She passed as a boy with ease when it suited her. Still, useful as that was, Bel noticed confrontations like this were common, and they grated on Wolf's nerves. A subtle tic in the muscle of her jaw gave the lie to her grin.

"Yes, it is," the woman responded, turning to Belinda as if she would be equally horrified.

Bel supposed she looked the part. She still dressed like an American heiress on a casual brunch most days. Her time with the activists hadn't changed that, but her patience for stupidity and her capacity for diplomacy had suffered since Whit's death. Belinda regarded the woman, briefly sizing her up. She was tall and handsome, but her shoes were imitations of a brand she aspired to but couldn't afford.

"Wolf, show her your tits."

Wolf's eyes brightened, and behind the stall door Cait stifled a laugh.

Belinda turned toward the woman with a warm smile, like a hostess welcoming a dear guest. "Amazing, they look just like Nonnenbruch's *Huntress*, occasionally called *Artemis* by some. Have you ever seen that painting?"

The woman was silent, too stunned to say anything.

Belinda pressed on in her haughtiest register. "Ah, not likely. It is in a private collection now, as I recall, but I had the chance to see it once in person and it was magnificent. Maybe Wolf would do us the honor of posing and I could describe it to you."

Wolf's hand clutched the hem of her T-shirt, her veins standing out under the cool gold skin of her forearm. She seemed ready to enact the huntress to the best of her abilities.

"You're all sick," the woman finally spat out as she clutched her purse and hurried out of the restroom.

"Ha! Did you hear that, Cait? Princess here said tits. Ah, we're gonna bring you over to our side," Wolf boasted as if it were a personal accomplishment.

"Which side is that?" Bel inquired.

"Well, if you've been looking at Wolf's chest, I'd say you're more than halfway there already," Cait replied, washing her hands.

Wolf laughed. "No, no, not that. She's already on *that* side, I think."

Belinda felt Wolf scanning her face for some sign of confirmation, but she didn't flinch.

"I mean the radical side. She'll be throwing ashes and bricks in no time," Wolf claimed.

"Okay, okay, Wolf, you're getting carried away now." Cait slung her arm around her young friend's shoulders, an especially comical move as Wolf towered over Cait by a good six inches. "Let's get out of here before that lady rounds up a posse."

"All right. Hey, you want to ride with me?" Wolf craned her head back to look at Belinda.

"Keep dreaming," Cait said with a little squeeze to soften the blow.

But Wolf wasn't dissuaded. "Lots of leg room in the van."

"Kid," Cait cautioned.

"I can get her on our side," Wolf stage whispered into Cait's shaggy blonde hair before kissing the top of her head.

"She's already on our side," Cait replied, her tired tone conveying how well she knew there was no use trying to talk Wolf down from a plan.

Over the past year Belinda had found herself spending more and more time in their company, and she'd seen for herself Wolf was unstoppable. The threat of violence, even the very real damage people inflicted on Wolf, did nothing to dampen her commitment. The girl was at every public protest, and when things went badly, she shielded those around her or else helped them get out of danger. It was reckless and admirable in equal measure.

"No thanks, pup. I think I'll stick with the grown-ups for now."

Cait shrugged as if saying "I told you so."

"Some other time maybe," Wolf offered undeterred.

"Perhaps." Belinda pulled open the door to Cait's car.

Wolf hung back, smirking. "There's a dance at Audrey's. She's famous for a good time; you ought to come."

"See you in the city, Wolf," Cait dismissed her and got into the driver's seat. She didn't wait for a reply before starting the engine.

Bel found the music outside of the bar only a little less obnoxious than it was inside. A heavy miasma of cigarette smoke and beer mixed in the night breeze. In every direction people wandered through the streets looking for a good time. She instinctively thought of Whit and his long nights out. He'd loved to go dancing at places like this. On her walk over she had passed another venue catering to men. It had been very much his style, all pecs and sweat and throbbing bass. As she wove between the revelers and throngs of tourists, she felt such an unusual brew of feelings twisting in her gut. Remembering Whit as beautiful and free, hungry for every sensation, and then remembering with a burst of cold clarity that he was gone. The space in between, the wicked void of illness she'd blessedly blocked out for the moment, but she knew it might surface at any time. Still, for now, there was a pit of loss that opened and pulled at her like the feeling of falling that came with too much wine.

I need a drink.

"Princess—" Wolf's clear voice cut through the din.

"Don't call me—"

"You came!" Wolf bounded closer and stopped short in front of Belinda. She wore a skin-tight tank top and a pair of faded blue jeans that clearly had belonged to someone else. The fit was all wrong, but somehow it worked for her. She looked capable of anything. Like anyone she asked might follow her home.

"Here I am," Bel deadpanned, but she could feel a hint of a smile in the sound of her voice.

Wolf bounced on her heels, and Belinda wondered how she still had so much energy after the last few days they'd had. This was the girl who scaled a fence; this was the girl who screamed every chant at the top of her lungs. This was the same girl who'd pulled a bag of ashes from her pocket and torn it open over the White House lawn. Later she'd stood in the drizzle of a DC park sprinkler system washing microscopic bits of a woman named Eloise from her skin. Belinda had felt sick at the sight of it. This very morning, Wolf had run headlong into a line of police officers, shoving herself between their batons and the heads of frailer protesters while Belinda was carted off to safety.

"Let's get a drink." Wolf nodded toward the door.

"Are you even old enough, pup?"

Wolf's mouth registered a kind of annoyed amusement. She said nothing and pushed her way inside, holding the door just long enough to make it obvious she wanted Belinda's company but would go alone if need be. Belinda followed. The swell and pulse of humanity beyond the threshold seemed to swallow her entirely, but Wolf grabbed her wrist and led her through the crowd. At the bar she leaned over the rail and waved down a thickset butch with wire-rimmed glasses who seemed more-or-less happy to see her.

"Maggie, how are ya?"

"Better than you by the look of it." She gestured toward the purple welt that had darkened along Wolf's temple.

She skimmed her thumb over it. "Oh, it's nothing. Just a little souvenir from DC."

"Oh yeah. How was it?"

Wolf shrugged. "The usual."

Maggie seemed to comprehend.

Wolf plucked a cherry from behind the bar and dropped it in her mouth, drawing a smile from Maggie. Bel noticed how the skin around the woman's eyes crinkled with genuine pleasure. She tried to imagine a straight version of the bartender, a frumpy housewife perhaps careening toward an empty nest with a doting but incompetent husband. No. Maybe a schoolteacher. She had a kind of cool authority in the set of her mouth even when she smiled.

"What do you drink?"

Belinda stopped her imagination somewhere between high school math and the gym locker room and looked at Wolf clutching a green bottle of beer and staring back at her.

"Gin and tonic."

"Top shelf, Maggie. She's royalty, you know." Wolf motioned toward Bel.

Bel scoffed, but made no move to stop Maggie from getting her best bottle. It was something she would never have found in her own liquor cabinet, but it was better than she expected.

"You payin', Wolf?" Maggie asked with a dry laugh, but to her obvious surprise, Wolf pulled a slender fold of cash from her pocket and slid a ten across the bar. "Holy shit. What's this? You gone corporate on us or something?"

"Naw, sold some stuff. And Nicky bought a story off me."

"Hey, good for you, buddy."

Maggie made change, and Wolf left the coins on the counter before turning toward Bel and proposing a toast.

"To not getting arrested today," she said with her drink aloft.

"And to absent friends," Bel replied coolly.

Wolf's face sobered, and she clinked her bottle to Bel's glass. "To absent friends." She took a long drink.

Bel realized she'd never heard any mention of how Wolf had gotten involved in what she was doing. *Who has she lost?* Bel didn't want to ask. She didn't want to do anything that might worsen the dull pain she'd been staving off all night.

Wolf was here to help her forget, like the gin in her glass.

It felt good having money of her own. Maggie was clearly surprised to see Wolf buying a drink for herself, let alone someone else, and why shouldn't she be? She'd seen Wolf in the worst of it. No home, no plans, drifting aimlessly from place to place, willing for a one-night stand if it meant a bed or a meal. That sensation, as much as she hated to remember it, never went away. Even in a good moment like this, savoring a cold beer bought on her own dime and watching a gorgeous woman drink on her tab, even now the memory was close, leaning over her shoulder and keeping an eye on her. *Don't forget about me,* it seemed to say.

"Are you a regular around here?"

"Huh?"

"The bartender seemed to know you."

"Oh, Maggie, sure she knows me. She knows everyone, all the dykes."

Belinda blinked like flinching in slow motion.

"What? You don't like that word?"

Bel swirled her drink, and a faint luminescence drifted around the glass under the blacklight. "It's not one I'd apply to myself, no."

"What would you apply?" Wolf had been wondering for a while, but especially since the comment about her chest in the women's restroom.

"I wouldn't." Bel drank slowly.

Wolf watched Bel's pale throat move as she swallowed. She didn't like the "no labels" thing. In her world it seemed like a failure to commit, an act of cowardice. It made people *untrustable*, and no one could afford to go into battle with a person they didn't trust beside them. "But you like women?"

Belinda raised her brow just enough to suggest the answer was obvious.

"Are you bi, is that it?" She knew some women were cautious to admit it, especially to dykes, but Wolf didn't care; she just wanted to know.

"Hmm. I wouldn't say that either."

Wolf chewed the inside of her mouth, summoning some restraint. She wanted to press on—*well, what the fuck would you say*—but she felt in her bones that the direct question would get her nowhere. Whatever she wanted to know about Bel, she'd have to figure out subtly.

Bel made eye contact, like she was expecting something more. "No witty remark?"

"Nah."

"Hmm. Are you getting soft then?"

"Me? Oh, I don't think so." Wolf swallowed her beer, stifling a flash of annoyance.

"Hard as ever then?"

She almost choked. "Pfft. Wow. Okay. Are you flirting with me, Belinda?"

"Flirting? Hardly."

"Good, you're not my type." Wolf smirked. She ignored the unremitting throb she'd felt since realizing Bel had actually come out for a drink.

"I would say the same."

"Figures," Wolf replied.

"Indeed. Well, now that we've gotten that squared away."

"Is Cait your type?" Wolf pressed on. It was probably too direct of a question, but she risked it.

"Cait? No, but she's at least the right age."

"Ahh, you're ageist."

"What does that even mean?" Bel asked frostily.

It was like most of their spats. Wolf pushing too hard, Bel throwing up a wall. But this time Wolf knew better than to take the bait. Bel was coming around whether she wanted to admit it or not. She had gone to DC with them, and though she hadn't gotten into the thick of the march, she'd been there on the fringes being useful, chipping in. She'd been coming to their meetings too, even though she mostly seemed to be there to talk with Cait. If she had a crush, it made sense.

"How old is Cait? I don't even know. It's not relevant to me because I'm not ageist, you see."

Bel's expression warmed infinitesimally. "I thought you two were friendly."

Wolf ignored the comment. She knew too well what people thought about her and Cait.

"She's thirty-five, by the way."

"I see, and that's the right age to be?"

Bel laughed in her haughty way. Wolf found it irritating but delightful all at the same time, which was confusing. Her opinions were usually definite and unlikely to change.

"I ask because you seem close. I could see it, you and Cait."

"She's a smart woman, and I respect her very much. She's gotten so much accomplished in a relatively short amount of time," Bel replied.

It was hard to hear Bel over the music, and Wolf found she wanted to hear her. "Hey, do you want to go outside and talk?"

"Sure."

The front of Audrey's was thick with people. As they walked toward one of the few tables scattered on the sidewalk, a young woman in black leather pants broke away from her friends and made a beeline for Wolf.

Leaning up in Wolf's ear, she whispered, "Want to go out back?"

"Hey, Soph, good to see you," Wolf said in what was not at all a whisper.

Sophie took the hint and stepped back ever so slightly, one hand still resting possessively on Wolf's hip. "Were you in DC?"

"Yeah, Bel and I were there," Wolf nodded toward Belinda, trying to give the girl a clue.

Sophie's attention never wavered from Wolf. "Was it okay?"

Wolf felt Soph's eyes fixed on the battered part of her face. "Yeah, it was okay. We'll give our recap at the next meeting. Or, if you want, you can look in the *Voice*. Nick bought a story off me, and it'll run tomorrow."

"Wow, Wolf. You sure you don't want to come in and dance? We should celebrate."

"Sorry, Soph, not tonight. We've got a thing to get to. Raincheck?"

Sophie's eyes narrowed in reflexive annoyance, but she smiled anyway. "Sure."

"Shall we?" Belinda asked, her voice imperious. For once, Wolf was thankful for it.

"Yeah, yeah, let's head out." She raised her hand in a halfhearted wave and followed Bel down the street.

"Ex of yours?" Bel asked when they'd gotten well out of earshot.

"Nah. We messed around a few times, but nothing serious."

"She must have had fun."

"Of course. We both did, but—"Wolf shrugged. "Thanks for playing along. Where are we going anyway?"

"There's a cafe over on Barrow that's open."

She knew the one. It was a place she'd been to a thousand times, but she hadn't gone there with anyone since Daniel. She walked beside Bel, willing her mind not to wander too far afield. She'd spent a long time walking around the AIDS quilt in DC looking for Danny's name. *Nothing.* She couldn't be the one to memorialize him, but she wished someone had. He deserved to be remembered.

Occasionally a hint of warm amber and something green and fresh would scent the air between them. A perfume Wolf couldn't name or afford. An unasked-for pang seized her and she laughed silently at herself. *Bel's beautiful and rich. Who wouldn't want to be walking beside her?* Wolf assured herself. It wasn't anything particular or strange; she was just a type that was desirable. Anyone would have felt this twinge of wanting to be closer.

"Regretting your choice?"

"Huh?"

"Would you rather be dancing?" Bel asked.

"With you?"

Bel laughed, her head tilting back, eyes bright. "No, with your friend."

"Absolutely not."

Bel looked at her as if surprised.

"She wouldn't know *The Huntress* from a hole in the wall."

"Ah, very well then." Bel's smile changed, Wolf couldn't say how, but it was lovely.

They walked another block in silence.

"This place has an excellent fruit tart. Have you had it?"

"No." She'd never been able to afford anything from the case, but she'd seen the tarts. Rows and rows of perfect golden crusts topped with concentric circles of berries like little works of art.

"I recommend it. My treat this round."

"All right," Wolf agreed.

The cafe was busier at night than it was in the mornings when Wolf had come to sip coffee and pretend she was looking for love. Another difference was the lean freckled man in a long white apron who greeted them and asked if they planned to sit on the terrace or inside. Wolf noticed the usual scatter of small round tables was the same, only covered with white cloths and apparently off limits unless the man in the apron sat them at one.

"Wolf?"

"Um, outside."

"Very well. Please, follow me." His voice sounded like someone trying to scrub the southern drawl from their accent, but mostly failing. He led them to a table and set down two small paper menus. This was also something new. In the mornings, Wolf wandered in and stood at the counter like everyone else.

"I'll take a coffee, black," Belinda said without waiting for the man to ask.

"Yeah, same for me, thanks," Wolf added when it seemed he was waiting for her. She distractedly ran a finger over the scabs inside her hairline. Her head felt tender. It was probably for the best that they'd left the bar and the loud music behind.

"There it is, the fruit tart. But of course everything is delicious. It's up to you." Bel examined the menu.

Wolf read the price and felt her face react to the absurdity. *Six dollars and seventy-five cents. Fuck. Are they made of gold?* Still, Bel had offered, and she was the woman with the fancy wine so she could afford it. The waiter set down two cups of coffee, each on a little white saucer with a thin blue stripe.

"Will you be having something to eat as well?" He bent forward solicitously and inclined his head toward Bel.

Wolf noticed without any sense of surprise how he seemed eager to please her.

"Yes, we will. I'll have one of the three berry tarts."

Bel's glance turned toward her, and for a moment Wolf looked back rather than at the waiter who was clearly standing at the ready. It was a fraction of a second. Anticipation and offering. Belinda blinked and looked elsewhere.

"I'll have the same."

"Excellent choice." The waiter turned away.

"So, what do you know of *The Huntress*?" Bel lifted her coffee and blew softly across the surface.

"The painting? Nothing. But I've read stories about Artemis."

"Have you?"

"Stories and poems. I like old things."

A smile again, even more unusual than the last.

"Is that painting a real thing?"

"Nonnenbruch's? Yes, oh yes. It's very real. I probably have a slide somewhere. I should show it to you."

"Because I have the tits of a goddess?" Wolf asked.

At that moment the waiter stopped beside them. His face registered and then concealed amusement. "Here we are. Let me know if there's anything else."

Bel placidly unwrapped her fork and set the napkin across her lap.

"I'm sure he's heard bawdier working in this neighborhood. At any rate, I would show you primarily because it is a lovely painting. So, where did you read these stories of Artemis?"

"In the bagel shop."

Bel took a small bite and contemplated. "That's a rather unusual place for the classics."

"I am unusual."

"Very true."

"I think I liked Homer's version best."

"Did you indeed?"

"Mmm, this is awesome," Wolf mumbled around a mouthful of tart.

"I knew you wouldn't be disappointed. Wolf, why aren't you in school?"

"Like for paramedics or something?" She took another bite, smaller this time because she wanted badly for it to last.

"No. Well, perhaps. Is that what interests you?"

Wolf shrugged. "Everything interests me."

"So you could do anything."

"That's what Cait says."

"She's right."

"Maybe. But I think I'm doing all right. I'm doing something useful." Wolf didn't like feeling as though she had to defend herself, especially when she was talking to someone who had seen her in action. Wasn't it obvious she was giving it her all?

"Yes," Bel replied definitively as if she'd read Wolf's mind.

Wolf searched Bel's face for any sign that she was being patronizing, but there was nothing like that in Bel's expression.

For a moment their conversation stopped. They sat together simply enjoying their food and coffee as the city hummed around them.

"It must be difficult," Bel said, breaking the silence, which hadn't been awkward, but had been dragging on longer than Wolf was accustomed to.

"What?"

"What you do. Your work. Cait mentioned you spend a lot of time with people who are sick."

"Oh, yeah. It's not so bad, not usually. I bring them food, and I make sure they have their medicine. Mostly, I sit with them. Someone needs to do it. We can't just leave people to die alone."

"Hmm. Can't we? It happens all the time."

"Well, it's wrong." She didn't want to fight with Bel, but this was something she wouldn't budge on.

Bel nodded in agreement. "Are they all strangers?"

"Not always. Besides, at this point who's really a stranger anymore? I see people at the rallies and the meetings and the coffee shop and the corner store, and then pretty soon I'm at their house or their funeral." She shook her head.

They sipped the last of their coffee.

"You could be a doctor," Bel mused.

Wolf thought maybe she should go to school, become a medic or something, but then who would do her shift? And what was the point of planning when everything was in a downward spiral? "I don't know. It's hard to plan ahead. My only plan is the circle, I just—" she shrugged again.

"And what is the circle?"

Conversation stopped as a different member of the waitstaff weaved through the tables refilling drinks. She freshened their coffees and walked away.

"So, what is it? Your one plan for the future?"

"Oh, nothing. It's like an afterlife affinity group. Just a bunch of us who've agreed to carry each other when we kick off."

"Carry?"

"Caskets, you know. I've done a bunch of them, and the circle keeps refilling."

Belinda turned her face up to the night sky and rubbed her temple. Wolf watched her index finger run the ridge of her brow, down into the sleek dark hair over her ear. Bel took a breath and looked at Wolf again. "Are you sick?"

It was the softest voice Wolf had ever heard come from Bel's lips.

"No, no. I'm not sick. Not yet."

"Yet?"

"I mean, doesn't it feel like a matter of time, really?" The question didn't make her sad. She had accepted it a while ago, around the time Dave died, she supposed. She still got tested every month and tried to be careful, but she was swimming in a sea of infection, and T-cell counts, and viral loads. Sure, the dykes weren't dropping the way the guys were, but she'd known a few who had, and it shook her confidence. Any sense of longevity had vanished a while ago.

"No. It's not just a matter of time, Wolf." Bel looked bruised by the very thought.

Wolf hated thinking she'd brought down the mood, but the look in Bel's eyes was so real she couldn't actually regret the turn things had taken. It was a look so full of genuine concern. Wolf's muscles felt itchy on the inside. She shifted her toes in her boots but tried to stay still. Had anyone looked at her like that before? She couldn't recall. Certainly not a woman. Not one like this. Atypically, she couldn't think of anything to say.

Bel blinked and turned her attention to her coffee. "Don't be a nihilist, Wolf. It wouldn't suit you."

A distinct ache was building behind her breastbone and radiating through her ribs. Not awful, but familiar and threatening. Bel took her last bite of tart and let the sweetness distract her for a moment. *Don't be a nihilist.* She had watched Whit decline, but she had never been the one to clean him, to change him, to pump him full of potions trying to keep him alive. There had been nurses and attendants and doctors. The best money could buy. And he had Michel to sit with him when Bel couldn't bear it, and Marek too. In the end it did no good. *Who am I to lecture you on nihilism?* Still, Wolf was so young, it felt obscene to think she was only waiting for the end. For a horrifying instant she felt the prick of tears. *Not now. God, what irony.*

"I do think it's only a matter of time until we have a cure. Or at least a vaccine." Bel tried to sound convincing.

Wolf's smile suggested she had touched a nerve of hope. "I've heard that before, but you probably know more than me on that score."

"You don't go to the medical meetings. Why is that? It seems like with all you do it would be right in your line of things."

"Time conflict."

"Oh, with what?"

"My main affinity group."

Bel tried not to make a face. As far as she could tell, the yelling in most of the meetings and in the streets wasn't amounting to much, but the medical side of things made sense. It was a viable path forward. There were angles of attack that could bring them a step closer to actually saving lives. When arguments broke out in those meetings, she felt like she could understand the terms, the stakes. The other spaces by comparison were chaotic. The experience rankled her nerves. One meeting Marek had lured her to had easily four hundred people jammed into a room. When a debate over needle exchanges started, she could hardly believe the way the volume rose and the voices seemed to come from all sides. She'd pitched in some mild sentiment about the risk of arrest, but Wolf had blown up at her, accusing her of sacrificing people out of fear of the police. It had been a long time ago, but the memory lingered. Most surprisingly, she had felt nothing but respect for the girl for holding her ground, even if she was annoyed and a little embarrassed by the tone it took. Being friendly with Cait meant being around Wolf, and over the intervening months the two of them had mostly called a truce. Lately, it was perhaps something more than a truce. Bel found she enjoyed Wolf's enthusiasm, and when she went too long without seeing her, she wondered where Wolf was and worried about her safety.

"I know you don't get into all that," Wolf smirked.

"I don't like the yelling. It's not my style."

"Funny, you seem like you'd enjoy a good fight. You had no problem kicking me in the shins," Wolf joked.

"Ah, well. I thought you were going to cart me off and hold me captive in some dim little room until you could pressure someone into paying for my release."

"Did ya?"

"Certainly. I mean why else does someone snatch a person off of the ground in Grand Central Station and drag them into a hallway?"

They both laughed.

"You can fight; that's all I'm saying."

"Yes, but there are different ways of fighting."

Wolf nodded.

Bel couldn't tell if she was convinced or not, so she let it drop. "We could get another of these if you'd like."

Wolf stopped running her finger through the smudge of blackberry on her plate and grinned. "Well, I am still a little hungry."

"There's a chocolate one. If you want to try something different," Bel suggested. She saw Wolf hesitate. "I'm going to get one. Will you share it with me?"

She smiled, and Bel beckoned the waiter who took her order and cleared the plates.

"What about journalism?" Bel asked.

"What about it?"

"You're writing, aren't you?"

Wolf nodded and took another sip of coffee.

"And it sounds like you're getting published?"

"Five stories so far."

"So why not go to school for that?" Bel inquired.

"Why? I'm already doing it."

"True, but you'd learn to do it more effectively, and you'd make connections. Connections are the most important thing, truly. Your story on the needle exchange was good."

"You read that?"

"I did. Cait showed it to me. She's very impressed with you."

"Is that right?"

"Of course."

"It's weird that you two talk about me. Isn't it?"

"Oh I don't know. I ask how things are going, what projects she's working on, and you just come up." Bel carefully ignored the fact that she often asked after Wolf. *How is Wolf getting on? Is Wolf on this project? Do you think Wolf would be able to take the lead?*

"Yeah, I guess that makes sense. Just, I don't know. Makes me feel weird."

"It's all good things."

"Well, that's even weirder." She laughed, and her eyes brightened at the sight of the waiter walking toward them with another plate and two clean forks.

Bel slid the plate across the table, offering the first bite.

"God, it's as good as the other one. Mmm. Awesome."

"I never overstate my claims about pastries and desserts. I'm a very reliable critic where those are concerned."

"Is that right? And what are you not a reliable critic of?"

Women. "Well, I don't know. I wouldn't say unreliable, but my taste in art does seem a bit off center. I know what moves me and I can defend my choices quite well, but there's not always a lot of agreement among my friends. Then again, they're all medievalists or classicists. It's a different world."

Wolf looked pensive. "And what are you? Not a medievalist, so what?"

I don't know anymore. "I like things from the last sixty years or so."

"Like Nonnenbruch?"

Belinda leaned forward ostensibly so she could reach the tart. "Yes, and no. Yes, that painting is newer, but actually my friends and I agreed on the Nonnenbruch. Maybe when you see it, you'll understand why. I am going to show you the slide. I'll look for it tonight when I get home."

"Where do you live?"

"Right now? In my studio."

"Sounds nice."

"It's all right." She felt herself on the cusp of offering an invitation, but to do so seemed entirely too familiar. Besides, she had done a good job keeping people out of her space. Only Whit and Marek had ever even seen it. She supposed she should keep it that way. A bit of mystery, a bit of privacy. Those things went a long way. She was desperately thankful she'd never taken Laura there, and the relief served as a reminder of how easily a place could be soiled with memories.

The waiter arrived with a bill in a black leather folder. "No rush at all," he assured, setting it down on the table.

Bel put her hand over it before Wolf got any chivalrous and stupid ideas.

"Thanks for the desserts. They were really good."

"I'm glad you enjoyed them. Thank you for letting me lure you away from your more exciting night at Audrey's."

"I was only excited because you showed up."

"Really? And here I thought I wasn't your type."

Wolf took it lightly. Her eyes closed for a moment as she laughed. Bel admired the line of her jaw and did her best not to think about it.

When Wolf stopped laughing, it was right back to business. "Are you going to the meeting Monday?"

"Maybe. Will you go to one of the medical sessions? Just to check it out?" Bel asked.

"I don't know. I told the lesbians with AIDS team I'd come to their thing, which is at the same time."

"Maybe next week?" Bel urged, usure why it mattered.

"Sure."

"What do your parents think of all this?" Belinda asked. She felt old as soon as the words came out of her mouth, but Wolf took the question in stride as if she was used to people harping on about her age.

"My parents? I couldn't tell ya. They gave up any right to an opinion years ago." Wolf swirled the dregs of her coffee.

Bel wanted to pry, to understand what she meant, but maybe she already understood. She felt the same way about her own clan of relations.

"How about your parents? What do they think of you cavorting with the queers? I can't imagine they approve."

"No?"

Wolf exhaled in a sharp breath. Almost a laugh but without any of the mirth.

"Would you like to find out?"

"Huh?"

"What my parents think. Would you like to see for yourself?" Bel could feel herself making an error, but the question was already out.

"How's that?"

"Give me a lift and I'll show you."

"You want me to drive you somewhere? Like a chauffeur?" Wolf's voice all taunting indignation.

"If you're up for it. Can you drive stick?" Belinda asked, aware of the come-hither tone in her voice and regretting none of it when Wolf's face responded with her wicked little smile.

"Sure. I can drive anything you like."

"All right then."

"It's a date?" Wolf asked cheekily.

"Something like that. Do you have anything formal to wear?"

"What? Was that chocolate tart laced with something? Did you just ask me if I have a gown?"

"Oh, I didn't say anything about a gown, pup."

Wolf looked ready to say something cutting, but she held back for some reason and grinned. "You'll have to get me one of those little driver's getups then."

"You'd like one, would you?"

"Oh, I don't know. I think it might look good on me."

I'm sure it would.

"I'll figure something out." Bel slipped money into the black folder and handed it to the first waiter who passed.

It was late and she was tired, and she wished she had wine or gin to blame for the way she was talking and thinking, but there was nothing to explain it away. She wanted Wolf to go with her to the party Sheridan IV was throwing. She hadn't wanted to go at all, but now the thought of going with Wolf was on the table, and the idea seemed irresistible.

"What are you thinking? It looks devious." Wolf observed her with intention.

"Maybe it is. Are you still interested?"

"More than ever."

The Party
November 1992

"WHAT IF I TELL you it's for the revolution?" Bel's voice was soft and low. She smoothed down the jacket collar, careful not to let her hands linger too long on Wolf's chest.

"Ha," the girl deadpanned.

She pulled her hand away, feeling Wolf's sarcastic exhalation reverberate in the pads of her fingers.

"Is that right? Well, I suppose for the revolution."

Bel admired her choice of cut and color. The tailor had stepped out, allowing them to confer privately, but Bel sensed the man lurking at the edge of the doorway. They had gone through four other options, which now hung on a rack off to the side. Belinda had averted her eyes as Wolf changed, but she stepped close to inspect each suit, tugging at the sleeves and adjusting the lapels as if she had some deep and unshakable interest in the cloth itself. Wolf had allowed it, simply stood there almost in silence not saying anything funny or flirtatious, not even complaining, which made Bel wonder just what was going through her mind. Wolf hated the suits, that was clear enough, but the process seemed to interest her.

Belinda took a small step back and cocked her head to one side as she ran her gaze over the line of Wolf's silhouette. When she spoke, it was loud enough to draw the tailor's attention. "I think this is the one. We're ready when you are, Fielding."

James Fielding cleared his throat as he entered and adjusted his glasses without ever looking up, as if walking required great concentration on his own feet. A pale blue measuring tape hung around his neck; in his hand he clutched a piece of chalk. He had been Whit's favorite tailor, which spoke well of his talents since his looks had long ago withered if indeed they'd ever been much at all. Standing in front of Wolf he took a long look at her, then walked around her still examining. He then lifted the back of the suit coat and tugged up the waistband with a firm hand.

"For the revolution," Wolf mumbled under her breath. Bel winked at her from across the room.

"If you'd like, I could add a few touches to make the cut more feminine."

"No," they said in unison, Wolf somewhat more emphatically.

Bel suppressed her amusement. "No. Thank you."

He inclined his head slightly in a gesture of acquiescence and pulled a piece of pale pink card stock from his shirt pocket. There, he made a note before resuming his measurements.

Wolf looked good in a suit, even if she also looked uncomfortable with the way Fielding ran his hands inquiringly over the seams at her shoulders and lifted her arms.

"Will these be the shoes?" Fielding looked down at the badly battered toes of Wolf's combat boots, his face troubled. The effort he clearly made to sound neutral about the possibility almost drew a laugh from Belinda.

"No, but those are about the right heel height."

Again, he made a note. "Very good, ma'am."

Wolf stood as still as she could. She looked up at the old tin ceiling that somehow looked new. Perhaps it wasn't tin at all. Everything around her said money. If the tiles above had been actual silver, it wouldn't have surprised her. It was an alien place. Or maybe she was the alien. The room felt too tall and too full. Belinda had finally stopped looking at her, and Wolf breathed into the space the shift in attention created. In spite of herself she wondered when Bel's gaze might turn back in her direction. Wolf looked down and saw the top of the tailor's head as he hovered around the level of her ankles. The man, Fielding, had started to sweat. A distinct sheen bloomed between the sparse mouse-colored strands of hair still clinging to his rosy scalp. A smell like Christmas trees and fresh tobacco emanated from him, and it grew stronger as he moved, plucking pins from a contraption affixed to his wrist. His motions at least gave her something to look at other than Belinda and her own stupid reflection.

"Do you like this job?" Wolf asked the top of his head.

Fielding looked up at her, his right hand still clasping the leg of her trousers. There was a bewildered expression in his wide gray-blue eyes, a pin poised in his left hand. "Sir? Uh ma'am?"

"Is it a good job? Do you like it?" Wolf tried again. Determined to be acknowledged and spoken to.

The tailor glanced over his shoulder at Belinda as if seeking instruction about how to proceed. Bel didn't reply. She was appraising a stack of folded dress shirts, which all looked exactly the same as far as Wolf could tell.

The mannequin speaks! Wolf grumbled internally.

"I was trained in Florence as a young man. I could sew you a suit even finer than this one entirely by hand."

Bel looked over at them and placidly added, "It's true, I've seen him do it. Maybe if I like your driving, I'll have him make you one."

Wolf rolled her eyes, but Belinda had already turned away. "Do you enjoy it, though? Making suits."

He raised his eyes again and spoke to her directly this time. "I do, sir. I like making suits. I like being one of the best."

Fielding went back to the business of adjusting her cuff. It occurred to Wolf, not for the first time, that she was wearing at least three months' wages and now she knew with absolute certainty that as far as this man was concerned it was second-rate compared to what he could produce from scratch.

Maybe I'll have him make you one. As if she wanted a handmade suit. Like she wanted any suit at all!

She had asked Bel why in God's name she needed a suit to drive a car, but all Bel would say was *it's required.* Wolf didn't ask who required it. She didn't ask much at all about this thing she had agreed to, and as she stood there being prodded she wondered why she hadn't. Was she genuinely not curious about what they were up to? No. She was curious. She was always curious about everything, but her gut told her not to ask Bel too much. The offer felt tenuous—like a ledge Bel might back off of at a moment's notice. And Wolf didn't want her to back away. She wanted to see this through.

"How many suits do you make in a year?" She returned to questioning Fielding, as if one kind of answer might substitute for another.

Again, Fielding looked up, very much surprised.

Bel turned away from the piles of shirts and regarded Wolf quizzically. She was still fussing with a short dark lock of hair at the nape of her neck the way she did when she was deciding between suit coats. Wolf wondered if she was deciding something about her. "Are you interviewing my tailor?"

"What? I'm just curious. I've never worn a suit," Wolf replied as Fielding started to pin up along her inseam.

"Don't distract him. Do you want to get blood on the fabric?"

"For the revolution?" Wolf teased.

For an instant, Bel looked mischievous like she might take the bait, but she merely exhaled through her nose and turned away, leaving the question to hang in the air between them.

It was cold outside, but the morning clouds had burned away. Wolf waited in front of Audrey's. The street was blissfully empty this early in the day, and Wolf rolled her shoulders. The lightweight wool of the suit coat moved with her. She wriggled her arms, trying to convince herself that the problem was the tailoring, not her own nerves. Finally, a car pulled up and a door at the back opened.

"Hop in." Bel tapped the seat beside her.

Wolf looked at the man driving and back at Belinda. "I thought you needed a driver?"

"I do," she said as Wolf slid into the car beside her. "This is a cab. I'm not taking a cab to the Hamptons."

Two questions fought for supremacy in Wolf's mind. First: on what planet was this a cab? And second: the Hamptons? The second question won. "The Hamptons? When did—"

"You never asked," she replied calmly.

"I guess not."

"Are you backing out on me?"

Wolf could sense a current of nervous energy, not unlike her own, pulsing beneath Bel's well-polished exterior.

"No."

Bel sat back and let out a slow tremulous breath. "You're sure you can drive a stick shift?"

"Hell of a time to ask." Wolf gestured at the suit. She smiled to soften the blow of her comment.

Bel nodded primly and swiped at an invisible thread on her lap. "Just confirming."

Wolf caught her gaze and held it. "Yes, I can drive a stick. Can't you?"

"No."

The car rolled through the financial district. The buildings rose up ominously around them. For a moment Wolf remembered her first big rally, the banner drop inside the stock exchange. She wanted to tell Bel about it, but it didn't seem like the kind of thing that would impress her. *Do I want to impress her?*

"We're near Wall Street," she observed instead.

"Hmm. Thinking of becoming a broker now that you're all dressed up?"

Wolf scoffed. "Can you imagine it?"

"I can. I have friends who could show you the ropes."

"You're crazy."

"Ah, perhaps. You may really think so by the time today is over." Although her tone of voice tried for comedic, Bel's expression remained serious.

The Hamptons? What are we doing out there? Why do you seem nervous? Are you afraid? Wolf knew better than to ask. She would do whatever it was because Bel told her it was for the revolution, and the more she noticed how unnerved her companion was, the more Wolf believed they were in fact on a mission of some radical nature, even if it did require a suit. After all, so had breaking into Wall Street.

"Ah, yes, right here," Belinda told the driver who pulled to a halt in front of what looked like a high-class hotel. An attendant dressed in a deep green coat rushed to open the door for them.

"Right this way." He ushered them into the building.

A burst of warm air and perfume surrounded them. Wolf did her best to not look like a yokel. After all, she'd been partially raised in the city, but the ostentatious displays of wealth in the lobby and the solicitousness of the staff alarmed her. Seeing rich people was one thing; being treated like a rich person was quite another. Bel hooked her arm in Wolf's, and together they followed a gray-haired gentleman through the lobby and into another room where the sound of their footfalls was completely absorbed by a plush carpet. A few women looked up from their drinks to watch them go by, but no one saw Wolf as amiss. *It's an invisibility cloak*, she mused, smoothing down her tie as she hurried along.

The gray-haired man spoke to Bel, but Wolf missed most of the conversation. When she finally tuned in, it was to hear him apologizing.

"The usual lift is being repaired. I hope this won't be too inconvenient." He pressed the button, and a moment later the doors opened.

"Not a problem at all. I appreciate you getting the car ready for us."

"Of course, ma'am, we're always happy to meet any need. You'll find the car has been fully detailed and all necessary maintenance performed as you requested."

"Thank you, Jonas."

"Yes, thank you, Jonas," Wolf chimed in.

The man actually bowed his head deferentially and smiled. Not the tight stingy smile of someone forced to serve Wolf, but a well-practiced, almost natural smile. Apparently, the right kind of money made anything possible. The elevator stopped and opened.

"Right this way." Jonas stepped into the hall.

Bel gave Wolf a little shove out of the elevator but quickly caught her arm again and let herself be led into the parking garage. Wolf almost laughed, but the heat of Bel's hand on her arm stopped her.

"Here you are, ma'am, as you requested. The '59." He placed the key in Belinda's hand.

"Thank you, Jonas. It looks just as I remembered."

He smiled again, gave a partial bow, and left them alone with the car.

Wolf felt a tiny flutter of anxiety, or was it pleasure? She didn't know much about cars, but she knew this one must be worth a fortune.

"You can drive it, right?"

"I don't see why not." Wolf peered in the driver's side window. As of late she'd mostly driven her van, but she had operated a wide variety of vehicles over the years. In her early teens her father had run with a group of guys who traded in junked-out cars. The ones that were drivable were always needing to be shuttled from one place to another, and he had taught her how to do the task. Soon enough he let her go on the road. Although it was certainly illegal, Wolf figured it was safer than having him drive in one of his drunken stupors. Bel's voice shook her free of the memory.

"If it were warmer, we could take down the roof."

Wolf noticed Belinda was still standing beside her on the driver's side of the car. Something about her seemed sad, and the anxiety Wolf had sensed earlier had not abated.

"Don't worry, I can drive this car. Come on, you be the navigator," Wolf said.

"All right. Give me a hand, will you?"

They walked to the front of the car. The hood—which turned out to be the trunk—had been left slightly open.

"Lift it for me."

Wolf did. Inside was a spare tire and a literal trunk of brown leather bearing the initials WCH on a brass plate.

"Let's stash this in there. I hate to get too warm."

Wolf turned to see Bel sliding her long wool coat off her shoulders. Beneath the garment she wore a blue-nearly-black dress, which, despite its length, revealed more of her skin than Wolf had expected. "Fuck. Where am I driving you?"

Bel handed Wolf the coat and grinned. "The Hamptons, remember? Come, put the coat in there and let's get a move on."

Why Sheridan had decided to have his party at the old farmhouse was anyone's guess. Of course, the place could scarcely be considered either old or a farmhouse after all of the money that successive generations had poured into it, but even so, Bel couldn't help but wonder what he was trying to achieve by having them drive out so far. A birthday dinner in the city was the standard affair, sometimes coupled with a fundraising event in order to mask the extremity of Sheridan's self-indulgence. Perhaps a drive to the Hamptons was a show of fealty, akin to kneeling and swearing an oath. The old man was still young enough, being just a few years into his sixties, but Sheridan IV was gearing up for a takeover.

He was the only option. No one consulted her about business matters. She had a share of the company, of course, but unless something truly dire was afoot, they left Bel out of financial matters. She'd been happy enough with the arrangement, but now she was curious and her curiosity must be satisfied.

They still had another half hour of driving ahead of them. There was plenty of time to let Wolf in on the plan, but she hated to break the comfortable silence they'd been enjoying. Wolf's driving was better than Bel had expected. She was focused and quiet, her eyes on the road except when she stole a look at her passenger. It was a furtive glance, not intended to elicit a response, and Bel offered none, merely providing directions as needed, sometimes closing her eyes to think about how this evening could go. With anyone else a long drive in silence might have felt awkward, but with Wolf it felt soothing among the hum of the engine and the autumn glow of foliage around them.

"It can go one of two ways," she said at last.

"Hmm?"

"When we get there. It's up to you. It can go two ways," Bel explained. She found her voice somewhat muted by the hours spent not speaking.

"Tell me the options."

"First option, and probably the easier one, is you're my driver. Hired. I will pay you of course, either way, for your time. But, as my driver, you would go around to the old carriage house. One of the girls will show you the way. There'll be others there. Other drivers. I don't know what they'll do exactly, have food, play cards perhaps. I think there might be a football game on the television. It's not my space, so I couldn't say, but it would be a relaxed atmosphere and you'd be free to do what you like until the end of the party; then we'd drive home."

"I needed a suit for that?"

"Yes, even for that, I'm afraid. But more so for the other option."

"Which is?"

"This event we're driving to is a birthday party for my older brother, Nathaniel." She felt like she was giving away some kind of secret. It wasn't as if she even cared about Sheridan or his stupid party, but somehow telling Wolf about him felt dangerous. Taking her into this world seemed like revealing entirely too much.

"Okay, a birthday party, got it."

"We all call him Nat, or Sheridan, or IV, so any of those, it's all the same person. At any rate, over the past few years he has been incrementally taking over the family business. It's nothing hostile, you understand. He's been groomed his whole life to take over."

"Are you in the mob, Bel?"

"No, no, nothing of the sort." Though there were stories of some Sheridan bootleggers in the 1920s. As amusing as Wolf would probably find those tales, she didn't feel like sharing them right now.

"Okay, so Sheridan is having a birthday party in the Hamptons, and he's taking over the business, which is definitely not mob business."

"Right. I'm sure this all sounds crazy."

"That you're going to your brother's birthday party? No, that sounds pretty normal. I don't know why I'm here or why I needed a suit, but the party sounds normal enough."

"Oh, you? Well, I needed a driver, remember?"

"Right. And the revolution part?"

Bel shook her head, the diamond earrings she wore swaying with the motion. "Ah, well. It could be nothing. But I think Sheridan has some new scheme, something with Harrington and Cardwell."

"The drug guys?" Wolf's eyes narrowed.

Clever girl.

"Yes. The pharmaceutical company Harrington and Cardwell. I know we've invested in them, but I suspect it might be more than an ordinary investment. I've got the impression Sheridan wanted me to come so he could convince me to get on board with whatever he's planning. He doesn't involve me in day-to-day dealings, but my stake in the family business isn't insignificant. He would need to have my approval for any major changes."

"Are they making AIDS drugs? Is that why I'm here? Are we infiltrating? Stealing trade secrets?" Wolf's voice was mocking, but there was genuine excitement in her expression. It almost made Belinda wish there were secrets to steal.

"Don't get ahead of yourself, pup. So far H&C hasn't put out anything HIV-related as far as I know, but how can they avoid it? The funding is too tempting. I'm sure they've got something planned, or will have something soon. The truth is, I don't know enough about anything at this point. It's all speculation."

"So this is a fact-finding mission?"

"Exactly. I want to see what Sheridan is up to."

"Can't you just ask him? It's your company too."

"I could, but he would lie, even if there was no reason to. Maybe especially if there was no reason to. He's funny that way, always has been. If I show interest, he feels the need to hide his cards. I have to be my ordinary disinterested self and let him come to me. But I could also use an extra set of eyes on things."

"You want me to be your guest? To blend in?"

"Well, that might be asking a lot, but yes. I could introduce you as—"

"Your lover?" Wolf smirked.

"Pfft. Christ, no. But that would certainly be amusing. If things get too boring, maybe we should sprinkle the notion into conversation. No, no. I was going to say a friend from one of the galleries. My family doesn't know a thing about art, so it doesn't matter if you don't either. Besides, they won't care. Unless it's something they can use to advance their agenda, they simply won't ask about it."

"They sound lovely."

"Hmm, indeed. We aren't close, but I do understand them."

"Could we say I'm a photographer?"

"We could say anything."

"Except the truth?"

"And what is that exactly?"

Wolf shook her head.

"Are you? A photographer?"

"Not much of one. Nick's lent me his camera a time or two for free-lancing. Even so, I know more about cameras than I do about galleries. I don't want to sound like a complete idiot if someone decides to ask me something."

"So you want to come with me?"

"For the revolution? Of course I do."

Bel nodded and slipped a finger under one of the straps of her dress. She was fidgeting, and she knew she ought to stop as her mother would make an issue of it, start talking about nerves and loss and the need for a good doctor or a good stiff drink. A slew of unsolicited advice, which would goad Bel into an argument. She adjusted the strap one last time and noticed with a fleeting touch of amusement the way Wolf watched her. It was the kind of attention her family would notice, too, although she wondered if they would see Wolf as a woman or a boy. Either way, it was sure to scandalize them.

"Last chance," Bel whispered through lips that didn't move.

"I'm in," Wolf replied. Their shoes sounded on the massive flagstone steps. The house was less imposing than Wolf had imagined, but older too. A plaque beside the door read *White-Meredith Farmstead 1734*.

Any feeling of ease she might have had evaporated when the door opened, and she caught a glimpse of the gleaming interior. A servant of some kind ushered them in with cool formality.

"Belinda, you've graced us." A man, perhaps in his late thirties, emerged from a doorway and moved toward them with purposeful strides. He wore a navy blue suit coat and butter yellow tie that was pinned with a tiny American flag. He looked like a political hopeful, though Wolf couldn't decide for which party.

"Happy birthday, Nat." Bel kissed his cheek.

"What are you drinking? We've started without you, I'm afraid. Anders is celebrating a bit of a coup." Nat held up a tumbler of deep amber fluid with a self-deprecating smile.

"Is that right?"

"Hmm. It seems Frank Collins is no longer working at Goldman Sachs. I didn't get the whole story; you know Anders." Nat shot Bel a conspiratorial wink, then took another sip of whisky.

Bel looked bored. "Is Mother having wine or have we advanced to the next part of the program?"

"Ah. Indeed, it's still wine until after dinner, so she says. A new regimen."

They both let out a mirthless chuckle of the exact same tone.

"You brought a guest, good, I wasn't sure if you would." He turned toward Wolf and extended his hand. "Nathaniel Sheridan, but everyone calls me Nat."

"Wolf." She shook his hand firmly.

"Wolf, excellent. Is it a family name?"

"It is."

"I'm the fourth Nathaniel in a line myself, but so far I've only had girls so there's no fifth yet." He took a tiny sip of liquor.

"Are the girls here?" Bel wondered.

"They're out at the stables with Patrick."

"You have horses?" Wolf asked.

"We do. A few retired polo ponies here, but I keep racehorses in Maryland," Nat explained.

"I can show them to you if you like. You should have brought your camera," Bel interjected.

Nat smiled, "Ah you take photos, then?"

There was a note of actual interest, and Wolf wondered if this course of action had been a mistake. "I do, but the shutter needs mending. It might be a while before I get her back."

"Aw bad luck, but you know, I'm sure we have something around the house if you wanted to grab a few shots."

"Really?"

"Certainly. I'm sure Jordy knows." Nat cast a glance around, and a moment later the middle-aged man who had let them in the house reappeared.

"Sir, did you need me?"

"Nothing urgent, Jordy, but do you remember when we had those cameras sent over for cousin Alice's wedding?"

Jordy inclined his head.

"Cousin Alice is such a funny sort. She had us all taking pictures of the big day, and if I'm right we still have the ones Pamela and I used in the attic somewhere. Nothing special, mind you, but I'd be happy to hand one off to someone who knows what they're doing. Honestly, you'd be doing me a favor. I was a menace. Nothing but decapitations all night long."

Belinda caught Wolf's eye. Her expression was difficult to read, and Wolf wanted to say, *Well, thank god I didn't say galleries since this guy wants to talk shop.* The subtle indignation must have shown. Ever so slightly Bel smiled.

"Come on, Wolf, let's see about a drink. Find us, Jordy, if you manage to track those things down." Nat turned back toward the room he'd come from. Bel and Wolf followed.

Part of her should have known IV would glom onto Wolf. He had always been fascinated by Whit. At the time, Belinda had suspected his interest was driven by the novelty of meeting someone who outclassed even the Sheridans, but now she began to see IV was simply given to ingratiating himself. He did it in such an easy and almost natural way. She wondered if he felt like he was doing anything at all.

Typical.

She was the moody and difficult one, IV the golden child. People always liked him, and this was why. From the moment he met a stranger, he gathered ways to make himself well remembered. She lacked the skill. She even lacked the desire to have it most times, but now, watching him lead Wolf toward the library as if they were old mates, she was pricked with envy. She had forgotten those cameras even existed, but with the merest mention of photography, IV recalled, and now he would probably give her one, maybe both, because that's how he was.

Generous?

Bel wondered if she'd been too busy seeing IV only through the narrow frame of his ambitions, which often made him sneaky and callous. Perhaps it was unfair.

The library was an inner sanctum, rarely shared with visitors, but it was also Nat's favorite room, and as it was his birthday chairs had been rearranged to allow more seating for a select group of companions. Bel noticed her parents were not among them. More likely than not, they were in the conservatory entertaining a few guests of their own generation. The occupants of this room were younger and vastly male. Two unfamiliar men in ready-to-wear suits were filling their glasses with vodka.

Those are the ones. She knew it even without a formal introduction. These were the people he would try to get her in a room with later to discuss whatever he was planning.

Only IV would use his own birthday party as a way to broker a deal. And in an instant her original estimation of her brother was restored. He was friendly and generous, but only because it served him. He couldn't know Wolf wouldn't be useful, that she was here to spy on him, and that in her belly she probably hated everything they both stood for.

There were no candles, no songs, not even any gifts as far as Wolf could see. Nothing marked the evening as a birthday party except for a small toast given by Bel's father and another speech of gratitude given by the guest of honor himself. They had cake for dessert, three layers decorated with some of the most ornate gold frosting Wolf had ever seen, but nothing about the cake said birthday. Still, the youngest of Bel's nieces exclaimed it was her favorite and had to be held back by her nanny while a woman in a crisp white apron served dessert.

Sweat pricked Wolf's skin, a mix of nerves and too much clothing, but overall the meal had gone without a hitch. She'd been seated between Pamela, Bel's sister-in-law, and a strawberry blonde of about nineteen who seemed to be the current girlfriend of a much older man. His exact relationship to Bel remained a mystery, but he made a habit of turning to Bel every so often and saying something in confidential tones. When he did, Bel seemed forced to pretend she enjoyed his commentary. She was a terrible liar, but the man either didn't notice or didn't care. Wolf survived the evening by watching Bel discreetly and following her lead. Bel took the fork on the right; Wolf did the same. Bel paused to drink more wine; Wolf had water.

"It's so rich," the strawberry blonde exclaimed after taking the tiniest bite of cake. She leaned toward Wolf when she spoke.

"Don't worry, dear girl, you can afford it," the older man replied across the table. His cheeks were rosy with drink.

Bel shook her head subtly and took a bite of food. Wolf did the same. The cake, like everything else, was delicious. For some reason, the whole scene made her think of her father dozing off in a secondhand recliner while his friends helped themselves to their fridge and ordered Wolf around like a gopher. She took another bite of cake and thought, *Fuck you, old man. You and your friends can eat shit.* It was oddly satisfying.

She looked up and saw Bel gazing back at her. Then Bel blinked at Wolf like a cat who wants you to know they tolerate you before she resumed pretending to be amused by her tablemate.

"You had better take some pictures," Bel whispered in her ear as they walked down toward the stables. The path was wide and lined with crushed white stone. They were trailing behind Pamela and the girls, who were more than eager to get out of the house and back to the horses.

Wolf held the camera up and looked at the stable beyond. The sound of the shutter was clean and fast. She advanced the film, thankful she'd remembered enough to look competent under Nat's watchful eye. After dinner Jordy had brought a box of equipment into the hall. Nat laughed at the sight of it. *You'd think we had any talent for it with the way we've accumulated things. Here, would this one make a good replacement while yours is in the shop?* It was a Nikon F3. But for Nat, it may as well have been a disposable. He'd put it in Wolf's hands. *Go ahead, take this. Keep it. I don't ever bother with these things. Pass it on when your repairs are done. I'm sure you and Bel know more people who could use it than I do.* Jordy fished out a shoebox brimming with film and accessories. *Can you use those? Take them, take the lot. Really, you're doing us a favor. Isn't that right, Jordy?* The man agreed.

Wolf adjusted the aperture and took another photo.

"So, you do know what you're doing then?"

"Enough. I can't believe he gave me this."

"I can. He's very free with things he doesn't care about."

"It's a really nice camera." Nicky would be so jealous.

"Of course it is. Go on, take a few more shots. He'll want to see the output I'm sure, if only as a reminder of how you owe him."

Wolf was going to disagree, to defend Nat, but she thought better of it. *That's what the camera is for. To buy my allegiance.* "I'll take some photos, but only because I want to. For the revolution," she added in a whisper.

Sometime later, Bel let her brother gently steer her into the library. She'd left Wolf in the company of the girls, showing them how to take photographs while Pamela and the nanny did their best to keep the youngest from breaking something. The library buzzed with chatter. The ready-to-wear boys and Uncle Anders were huddled around the liquor cabinet filling their glasses. Sheridan III sat in a forest green leather chair talking with their cousin Carlyle, who Bel would have been happy to avoid after spending an entire meal next to him.

"Don't worry, Bel, I promise not to turn this into a board meeting. I know how boring you find these things. I appreciate you indulging me," Nat said confidentially.

"Well, it is your birthday."

Nat smiled. She knew him, knew he would be satisfied by her acknowledgment of the occasion and likely feel it bolstered his chances of winning her over. He put a hand on her arm. "I hope you don't mind about the camera."

"No, why would I?"

He shrugged. "I know you can be protective of your friends."

"Don't be silly. I'll have that whisky now if you're still offering."

"Of course I am. Here, Irish, Scottish, Canadian?" His hand hovered over the cut crystal liquor bottles.

She made a face. Nat grabbed the decanter of Irish single malt and sloshed a heavy pour into a tumbler.

He wants me drunk, she mused.

She'd had only the one glass of wine at dinner, and the other he'd fetched her when they first arrived. She was thankfully a long way from intoxicated. Bel took a slow and savoring swallow.

"Well, I think this is all of us," Nat started. Conversations fell away. All eyes turned toward him. "I wanted to have a brief conversation tonight about an opportunity that's come up this past month. As you know, our Ridgeway Unit has been exceeding expectations both in terms of the quality of contracts we've won and the capacity of the facility to meet our production goals. It's an exciting time for us, financially and in terms of what we might achieve in the area of advancing human health."

Bel swallowed a yawn. Did they need this sort of buildup? She hardly knew what Ridgeway was, but did it honestly matter? Apparently it was exceeding expectations. She took another drink. Around her, people looked appropriately delighted. She tried to muster at least a look of approval.

"A few weeks ago, one of my friends in the legislature mentioned there might be a program opening up for which Ridgeway would be a perfect fit. After some discussion with the team, it seems our lab would be suitable and our engineers are excited by the prospect. It's challenging of course, but our guys thrive on a challenge."

"This all sounds interesting, Natty, but why the conference?" Uncle Anders set down his drink and gave IV a penetrating stare. Unlike Bel's mother, Anders, the eldest of the Merediths, had long ago given up on trying to be subtle.

Taking Anders's lead, Bel's father huffed in agreement. "Yes, Anders, good question. What's the punchline, son? We should be enjoying our evening, not getting sucked into business."

Bel had never agreed more with the old man.

Nat smoothed his tie and smiled. "Of course, gentlemen. The point of concern here is our relationship with Harrington and Cardwell."

"Harrington and Cardwell? Do we have a relationship?" Carlyle blurted out, oblivious as ever. Even Bel knew they had.

Old Sheridan looked at the man like he was an idiot. Anders gritted his teeth and shook his head. If an apple had ever fallen far from the tree, it was his boy. Although Anders was the family fixer who had always managed to smooth over any proverbial bumps in the road, he had never quite been able to smooth out his son.

"Of course we do. We all have shares and they've consistently per-formed well for us," Anders bellowed in frustration. Bel wondered if Anders only suffered keeping Carlyle around because he took some perverse pleasure in bullying him. It wouldn't surprise her in the least. Anders had a mean streak, which would have been the stuff of legend in a family more prone to boasting of such things. Instead, they quietly acknowledged it was best not to cross him.

"Right, well, this project involves them." Nat started to explain.

"Are we talking a merger?" Carlyle exclaimed with more excitement than appropriate for a man who had no idea what was going on.

The ready-to-wear boys looked at each other and then into their drinks.

"No, no. Nothing like that," Nat went on. Bel was losing interest, but she managed to catch the main points. Pending their agreement on the matter, the Ridgeway Unit would provide technical support for a new Harrington and Cardwell project. The family would need to make financial disclosures to keep everything above board.

Nat was more than ready to keep talking, but Sheridan III stood abruptly and clapped him on the back. "Good to see you're not wasting time down there in DC."

"Never," he replied, veritably glowing from his father's praise.

Bel thought her brother ought to be used to the old man's approval by now, but apparently it still had an effect. She finished her drink and put down the glass with a scarcely concealed sigh. A heavy feeling settled in her limbs. The meeting had been garden-variety business. She had dragged Wolf out for nothing.

Across the room the men refilled their glasses. She watched as Carlyle, a man ten years her senior, sniffed around for a Cuban cigar like a boy begging for sweets. Bel needed to leave. The thought of even another hour lingering here made her skin crawl.

She put her hand on Nat's shoulder and said, "I had better get going."

"So soon?"

"Hmm, early meeting with someone at the gallery. You understand." She made a plausible excuse. It seemed she still felt some obligation to Nat, given that it was his party.

"Of course. Are you sure Wolf wouldn't like a smoke?"

"That's generous, but no. We really do need to get going."

He kissed her cheek and thanked her for coming. "I'll be in touch soon about the disclosures."

"You can send them to Marek."

Nat's eyes brightened, but he made an appropriately somber face. "Of course."

Bel made the rounds, saying goodbye to anyone who might otherwise take offense. Finally, she found her mother in the parlor. She looked drowsy behind her sixth glass of port, but roused herself enough to pretend to kiss

Bel's cheek and awkwardly say a word of farewell. She didn't even glance at Wolf, and Bel was forced to remember how her mother had cornered her in the conservatory and hissed, *Christ, I hope that's no replacement for Whitney!* Part of Bel wished she'd said something, anything, rather than laughing dismissively.

Jordy walked them to the car. He held Bel's door open as Wolf let herself into the driver's side and started the engine.

The Beach
November 1992

BEL RAN HER FINGER around the seam of the seat trying to find something to say. Her fingernail ticked along the stitching. The air smelled of salt and faint hints of woodsmoke. It was dark. Darker than it ever was in the city.

"Shall we go to the beach?" she asked finally.

Wolf glanced at her and smiled. "I'm your driver for the evening, ma'am. Just tell me the way."

"Please don't." She sounded as exhausted as she felt.

"What?"

Bel shook her head. "I'm sorry, nothing. It's just. I'm sorry for this evening, for dragging you out."

"What are you talking about? I had a good time. The food was top-notch. There were horses. Your brother gave me a fucking titanium F3."

"Is that what it is?" Her voice was flat. She was conflicted by the excitement Wolf clearly felt. She wanted to be happy for her, but it was difficult to stomach Natty's effect on people.

"It is."

"And that's good?"

"Oh, it's very good. I mean, I couldn't think of a better camera to take out into a protest."

Bel said nothing, but twisted her ring around her finger and stared into the night.

"Don't worry. Even a fancy gift can't buy me." Wolf looked at her again like she was trying to peel back a curtain between them.

It was an unnerving look and a more disconcerting sentiment. Bel shivered and wrapped her shawl around herself. "Go left up ahead."

Wolf turned onto the unlit road. The headlights of the Porsche cut across the scrubland that lined the street side. "I'm surprised you seem bummed out. I thought you'd be triumphant. You know? Reveling in being right."

"Right? About what?"

"About the dinner tonight. It was all about business and those research plans, wasn't it?"

"It was about stocks. Nothing about research."

"Not according to Pamela."

"Pamela?"

"I guess it's a good thing you brought me because Pamela is a talker and she seems to know quite a bit."

Indeed, Pamela was a talker, and for some reason it had not occurred to Bel that Nat might share inside information with his wife. Bel perked up and turned toward Wolf. "What did she say?"

"Those guys, the two boring-looking guys who were sort of keeping to themselves?"

Ready-to-wear. "Friends of Nat's, I suppose."

"Nope. Government."

"Government?"

"That's what Pamela thinks anyway. She actually said she wasn't sure who they were, but they've been coming around a lot."

"Interesting."

"She said, they seem to follow Nat ever since he told H&C his company might agree to work on the SEAFOAM trials. She didn't know what that meant. I asked, but it's got something to do with AIDS; she was sure of that. She seems proud of it actually. I mean she kept going on about Lady Di and all."

"You're kidding?"

"No."

"Did she say what it was to do with AIDS? Treatment? Vaccine?" Now it was Bel's turn to stare as if she might see some hidden truth in the contours of her companion's face. What she saw instead was a flicker of hope flaring in a field of anguish.

"God, wouldn't that be something? A vaccine."

The activists Bel met with seemed to think a vaccine was possible, but a very long way off. She kept that to herself.

"No, she didn't say. I'm not sure she really knows. In fact, it seemed like she didn't know much of anything about the specifics, but she was clear the company was going to be funded from the NIH and that they were teaming up with Harrington and Cardwell to work on something to do with AIDS. Apparently, they've been visited by a few senators who are pushing for even more funding for the project."

Bel let the information sink in.

"Is it above board? I mean, is it real?" Wolf asked tentatively.

"I don't know. I mean it certainly could be. Our Ridgeway Unit dealt with laboratory equipment and some specialized medical devices. All Nat talked to us about was SEC disclosures and making sure we were doing things by the book financially. It sounded like any other business venture."

"Ohh, sounds like a story there."

Bel laughed. "Don't try cultivating me like a source. You're my spy, remember."

"Yes, ma'am."

Wolf did her best to ignore the way Bel's words moved through her, warm and welcome, coiling around her insides. *My spy.* Two syllables like hot coals. Not burning but illuminating, chasing away the dark. Bel was obviously pleased with her, and Wolf fought off a surge of pride.

"You'll need to stop," Bel warned.

Wolf couldn't agree more. Then she saw the gate.

Private Members Only.

Wolf slowed the car and put it in park. From the driver's seat she watched Bel walk confidently toward a narrow stone building at the edge of the lane. Her form was bright in the beam of the headlight. Wolf raised her camera and clicked off a shot. It would be blurry, she knew, but she couldn't resist.

Bel's wrap fluttered around her as she spoke to the man inside the gatehouse. Through a clear rectangular pane, which looked shockingly like ordinary glass rather than bulletproof plexi, Wolf could see he was trim and well dressed, nothing like the kind of security guard she was used to. After a moment, he stepped out and stood with Bel, smiling indulgently as she spoke. He leaned forward and let his eyes drift from her face to her collarbones when the shawl slipped, and then to the car, which idled in the dark. Finally, he nodded, and she walked back.

"We'll drive down to the end there, and you'll see a place to park." She closed the door behind herself and readjusted her shawl. It was still well above freezing outside, but this close to the water the air was damp and chilling.

The guard opened the gate with the push of a button and nodded at them approvingly as they passed. They moved slowly between rows of sculpted evergreens whose twisted bodies were stunted by the wind until they came to a boathouse. Wolf stopped the car. To their left was a row of piers beside the nearest of which a large wooden sailboat bobbed in the black water, hull gleaming in the moonlight. Beyond lay a smooth expanse of darkness pierced only by the high white moon and a spray of pale stars.

"We can get to the sand this way." Bel nodded over her shoulder.

"All right. Should I get your coat?"

"Such a gentleman. I suppose it is cold enough. Do you want the shawl?"

Wolf thought about saying no, but when the wind turned off of the ocean, it cut through the wool of her jacket with ease and raised the hair on her arms. "Maybe."

She popped the hood and pushed a finger under the strap that held the leather case closed. The wool coat folded inside was cool to the touch. Wolf took it and tried not to think about how the silk lining that slid across her fingers would soon be sliding over Bel's naked shoulders. In a graceful motion, Bel pulled the shawl from around herself and passed it to Wolf with one hand, the other reaching for her coat.

Wolf shivered.

"Put the wrap on," Bel chided.

"Maybe when we get down by the water." Wolf folded the wool over one arm.

"Are you going to wear that?" Bel gestured at the camera around Wolf's neck.

"I guess so."

"It'll be perfectly safe in the car. Besides, there's not enough light for photography."

Wolf raised the camera and pointed it at Bel. "Oh I don't know, if we turned the headlights on there could be."

"Don't be ridiculous. You don't want to get sand in it, do you?"

Wolf put the camera on the driver's seat and decided it was best not to think about all of the ways she might get sandy.

The trail—a strip of white, soft and shifting between thick tufts of grass and occasional beach roses that scented the air—crested at a place where the horizon became one broad sweep of land, sea, and sky scarcely indistinguishable from each other in the darkness.

Waves rushed at them and retreated. Wolf looked and looked for any sign of the familiar, but there was nothing save for the red glint of a plane passing far overhead. She was sure she had never been anywhere so simultaneously empty and threatening.

"You really should wrap up," Bel warned as she walked toward the water.

Wolf gave in and put the wool around her shoulders, feeling instantly warmer and a little foolish. A memory of a book she'd read in elementary school surfaced. The creased cover bore the image of a girl in a shawl walking over a dune, her hair caught and lifted in the sea breeze. Of course, Wolf had no hair to stir in the wind. Instead, the damp ocean air sank its fingers through the scant quarter inch of fuzz the clippers left behind, and slid down her neck through a fine gap at the collar of her suit coat.

She followed Bel, trying to find the place inside of herself where she was still warm with praise. She wanted Bel closer, wanted to be arm-in-arm again.

"I've never been to a place like this."

"The beach?"

"No, I've been to the beach, but never one like this."

"A private beach, you mean?"

"Yeah, I suppose that's the difference. It's so quiet and open here."

The night seemed to rush in and steal her voice. Bel stood still looking at the water. The bottom of her coat whipped against her bare legs, and Wolf wondered how she could stand it.

"Is this the beach you grew up with?"

Bel closed her eyes and listened to the sand being sucked out to sea, the slap of the waves. She tried to lose herself in them. "I grew up in a few different places, but this is the beach I go to when I leave the farmhouse. It's a good palate cleanser."

"A chaser?"

"Exactly." She could sense the tide inching toward them.

"They seemed nice enough."

"They really do, don't they?" Bel would have liked to have sounded indifferent, but the bitter edge rang plain.

Wolf didn't ask any clarifying questions, and Bel felt sure the girl understood how deceptive looks could be.

"There's nothing wrong with them. We just aren't close."

"Yeah. Well, I liked the horses."

Bel turned to partially face her. "I like them too. Do you ride?"

"Me? No."

Bel made a face, not that Wolf could see it. "Don't sound so stunned. It's a normal question. You'll have a hard time spying with those kinds of reactions."

"Oh, am I still playing spy?"

"Not at the moment, no. I suppose not."

"Ask me again."

"Do you ride?"

"Unfortunately, no, I've never had the opportunity to try my hand at it."

Bel barked out a laugh. The sound swallowed by a crashing wave. "Very well done. All right then, you may continue to play spy."

"Not now, though." Wolf sounded tired, and Bel could only imagine how exhausting her family must be for an outsider.

"No, not now," Belinda agreed. She looked back at the ocean. "Have you gone sailing?"

"Should I be myself or the version of me that's fit for espionage?"

"Yourself."

"No. Never. Why, do you go sailing?"

"I have. I've gone as far as France to Cape Cod."

"No!"

"I have." The sound of Wolf's surprise was delightful. Bel often amused herself with the ways she might surprise her family, but this was a different thing, and she found she liked being a pleasant surprise as well as a shocking disappointment.

"Alone?"

"No. I was with people. I don't think I could manage something so far on my own, although it has been done solo. An Australian woman soloed around the world just a few years ago."

"Seriously?"

Bel nodded.

"How long does that take?"

"I think it was just under 200 days."

"God. That sounds horrible."

"Not a fan of boats, I take it?"

"As an idea, I suppose I like them okay, but 200 days alone at sea? No way."

Bel watched Wolf pull the woolen shawl tighter around herself. She had to admit it was cold. Usually after any family occasion Bel would let the wind blow over her until she was no longer thinking about her mother's snide comments or her father's aloofness, but perhaps tonight those memories wouldn't abate so easily. It was unfair to freeze poor Wolf just because she had issues.

"Do you want a drink?"

"A drink?"

"Come on." Bel led the way toward the docks.

"Are you taking me to a boat? Do you own one of these?"

"Don't sound so incredulous. It's my father's." Bel climbed aboard and held out her hand. "Come on, it's fine."

"If you say so," Wolf huffed, though she sounded more anxious than put out. Wolf who fought with the cops. Wolf, who had kidnapped her in Grand Central Station, was nervous about a boat. Bel could have laughed, but then there was the feeling of Wolf's hand in her own, trusting her.

"See, it's not so bad," Bel said once Wolf had stepped on deck.

"It's beautiful. I just—. I don't know. It's weird."

"Sure. Come on, come below deck and have a drink. You'll forget you're even on a boat." She let her fingers brush over the wood of the helm as she stepped down into the cockpit.

"I feel like a pirate," Wolf whispered beside her.

"Do you? Well, first a spy and now a pirate. You're having quite a night I'd say." It struck her again how young the girl was. How little of the world she'd seen. Bel felt old suddenly. A widow.

She pulled a key from her coat pocket and opened the sleek wooden doors that led below deck. The place smelled of polish and disuse. More than likely no one had been aboard in ages except for the staff who kept everything in a perpetual and pointless state of readiness. The cabin was just as she remembered. Lustrous wood from ceiling to floor, a low bench of seating absurdly upholstered with midnight blue leather. The galley cabinets were stocked with liquor and wine, but no food. She supposed this would have suited her mother just fine, but Belinda was certain her mother had never set foot on this particular vessel. It had been some time since she'd been here herself. She pushed away the image of sailing off Montauk with Whit and her father when the engagement had first been announced. It had been a good trip, all things considered, but remembering it now she found it was too deeply entangled with memories of Whit's last voyage off the coast of France.

"Can I help with something?"

"No. Just tell me what you'd like to drink. I've got most things. No beer, though."

"What are you having?"

Bel ran her fingers over a selection of wine bottles. "Maybe some wine. Would you join me?"

"I'd have a glass, sure. Can I sit here?"

"Of course. Have a seat." Belinda waved at the benches without taking her eyes off of the row of bottles in front of her. She chose an Italian red, determined to avoid the French vintages whose flavor might steer her mind back toward Whit and the way he'd been momentarily restored by the prospect of a final sail. She filled their glasses, fuller than she might have back in the city, and pressed one into Wolf's hand.

"A toast?" The girl held up her glass.

She remembered their toast to absent friends the night this whole plan had been spawned. She'd never actually expected Wolf to say yes, never expected she would go along with the suit and the pretense, and certainly never imagined Wolf would chat with Pamela and the kids, extracting the juiciest bits of information, the kind of information Nat would have withheld for as long as humanly possible. "To Pamela and her way with words."

"Yes, to Pamela, and to the vaccine. It can't come too soon."

They raised their glasses, and Bel took a long drink, wishing it would soothe her.

Wolf watched with unease as Bel opened a second bottle of wine. They'd finished the first too quickly, and though she wasn't drunk yet, she was well past the point of driving. They had been talking about nothing. Bel gave her a lengthy history of wine growing in the north of Italy, a good story about a volcano, some more sailing trivia, but absolutely nothing personal. It felt like Bel was struggling to stay afloat in a body of water only she could see. Wolf was happy enough to play along if it helped. The sound of Bel's voice always pleased her. But she wished more than anything that she could throw Bel a lifeline and haul her back to shore.

The corkscrew creaked, the muscle of Bel's forearm tensing with the effort. "We could take the boat out."

"Out?" Wolf directed her eyes elsewhere.

"Yes, out for a sail. It's not hard once you get the hang of it." She filled her glass and tipped the bottle invitingly toward Wolf.

"No thanks, I'm still working on this one." She held up her wine as if compelled to show proof she was still drinking.

Bel paced the length of the room, which was entirely too small for pacing, and swallowed half of her drink in one go. "Have you warmed up?"

"I'm okay."

"Do you want to go topside with me? Let's go look at the stars." Bel finished her glass and refilled it.

Wolf hated to admit how the top of the boat made her nervous. She was a terrible swimmer and the shiny deck seemed perilous. Still, the thought of Bel up there alone and drunk wasn't one she could bear. "Okay, sure."

Bel grabbed the bottle and led the way. The air outside was colder than it had been when they'd retreated, but the wind was less intense. Bel dropped onto one of the cushioned seats in the cockpit and gazed up at the sky. A bank of clouds had rolled in and obscured part of the moon, but she didn't seem to mind.

"Ah, there we go," she whispered to herself, tucking one hand under her head as the other balanced the wine glass on her chest. She wore only her dress, and her skin shone as bright as the sandy trail they had followed to the water's edge.

Wolf sat across from her and tried not to stare. She couldn't help but wonder how Belinda wasn't shivering.

"So, were you horrified by the opulence?" Belinda asked with a weak laugh, more bitter than amused. She closed her eyes, her head tilting faintly in Wolf's direction, wine-stained lips parted.

For a moment Wolf thought she had passed out, but her eyes fluttered open and she waited wordlessly for a reply.

"I've never seen anything like it."

"No."

"But that's been true from start to finish."

"Really?"

"Yes," Wolf took a mouthful of wine to mask the sound of longing in her voice.

"You haven't answered the question, though. What part offended you most? The car? The suit? Not the camera, certainly."

"Why do you think I was offended?"

Bel pulled herself upright just enough to drink. "Because I've heard you speak."

"I don't follow."

"In the meetings."

"Ah."

"Or are you a hypocrite?"

Wolf felt a twist inside. Maybe she was a hypocrite. Or maybe she was just horny. She reminded herself not for the first time that sex with Belinda would be a recipe for disaster. Not that they were fucking, but only the thought of it and here she was letting Bel off of the hook. She was one of them, the uber-elite. So why didn't Wolf hate her? Because she was pretty? And because Wolf liked listening to her tell stories, and because she liked being a spy? Her spy.

"It's all right. Maybe you're just too polite to say. Perhaps you don't want to hurt my feelings. You couldn't, you know."

The sting of those words was awful. Of all the things Wolf might like to do, hurting Bel's feelings had never crossed her mind. "Oh Princess, I'm sure I couldn't."

Bel smirked, and Wolf couldn't shake the suspicion she'd given Bel exactly what she wanted. The silence between them felt sharp and threatening. Waves lapped the boat. Clouds crossed the moon. Wolf wanted to say something, but everything she thought felt like the wrong thing to say.

What the fuck? She hated drinking, at least this kind of drinking where everything got tense and stupid.

Finally, Bel stood and walked to the wheel. She rested a hand on it and looked at the water.

"I think we could shoot over to Block Island easily enough. Do you want to be a pirate?"

"Sure, but I think we should wait until morning."

"Oh, little Wolf, are you afraid to sail at night?"

"No, but I would rather wait."

"Come on, come stand here with me," she beckoned.

Wolf noticed Bel had abandoned her glass and was holding the half-empty bottle. She walked closer, and Bel stepped back just enough to give Wolf the captain's place.

"I'll let you steer. It'll be fun, I promise."

"I'm sure it will, but like you said, I'm afraid of the dark."

Belinda laughed. "Of course. Children always are."

Wolf could feel Bel behind her, the space between them warm. She thought she might turn and bring her face close and ask, *How old do you think I am?* But she didn't. She ran her hand over the wheel and listened to the sound of Bel swallowing more wine.

"I'm not a child." Wolf walked toward the hatch, feeling terribly petulant for someone who'd just made that particular announcement. Bel caught up with her and slipped ahead, pushing open the door and descending below deck.

"No? Then come with me."

She moved with the grace of a person who was quite sober, but Wolf knew the truth. She followed but kept her distance. Bel set the bottle on the galley counter and turned toward the back of the boat. For a second, Wolf saw something sad in her face, and she wanted to go to her, but in an instant that look was gone.

Bel eyed her appraisingly. "Nineteen?"

"Nineteen? No."

"Twenty then?"

"Twenty-two."

"Christ," Bel scoffed and walked into a room Wolf hadn't known existed. She paused for a moment, then shut the door behind herself.

Wolf stayed at the counter, pondering the dregs of wine. She had decided on finishing the bottle when the door creaked open again.

"It's a good thing I'm not your type." Bel laughed and threw her dress in Wolf's direction before slamming the door shut again.

Wolf picked up the discarded garment. It was still warm, and it smelled like Bel. Rich, foreign, wonderful. She hung it on the hatch, placed her suit jacket carefully on one of the chairs, and lay down across the bench, her face pressed to the leather.

What a fucking night.

Bel woke naked in the berth. Face down, with a cool white linen sheet twisted around one leg, her other dangling off the edge of the bed as if she'd been dropped from the sky. The heater hummed. Her mouth felt dry, and the sound of gulls and waves outside seemed a special kind of torture. Bel squeezed her eyes shut for a moment, trying to remember the details of the night before. Above her a skylight allowed in the hazy morning sun. Slowly, she looked to her left and then to her right, almost afraid of what she might find. There was no sign of Wolf anywhere, though no sign of her dress either, which was a bit alarming.

Flashes of the evening came back to her. A bottle of wine, then another. Sitting on the deck in the cold. She thought perhaps she had told Wolf they should sail to Block Island. The girl being afraid of boats, or maybe just more sober, had resisted. She didn't remember undressing.

She sat up, thankful she was in one piece, and not too badly hungover. It had been a long time since she'd been so drunk. It was unseemly. She thought of her mother and felt ashamed of her own behavior. At least Wolf wasn't in the room with her. Whatever she'd done, she hadn't given in to that childish whim. Her father's boat was equipped with a compact but well-appointed head. The staff had stocked fresh towels and an array of soaps all tending toward the masculine line of fragrances. Just as well, she didn't appreciate having to choose between smelling like a bouquet or a bakery. The water heated quickly.

Bel wanted to rinse off the grimy feeling of indiscretion. She pulled the showerhead from its holder and flicked it to the most scouring setting. As beautiful as the boat was, bathing on board never ceased to feel like washing with a garden hose. She made quick work of it, reminding herself all the while that she was too old for these sorts of escapades. It was the kind of thing she had done as a teenager, though of course it hadn't bothered her then. Whatever the repercussions, she'd never chastised herself. But now, she could only think again and again of all the ways she'd been, or at least probably been, a fool. Turning off the tap she paused in the mirror and gave her hair a quick brush so it lay flat against her scalp and swept left across her brow. There were no lingering effects. No bags under her eyes, but she examined herself closely. *Christ, you're almost thirty. You can't get wasted on daddy's boat. At least do it at home.*

"I don't suppose you've seen my dress."

"Huh?" Wolf sat up with a start and blinked hard, trying to orient herself. The woolen wrap she'd used as a blanket tumbled off her shoulders and slumped to the floor. She snatched it up and put it on the bench.

"My dress? Have you seen it?" Bel wore only a towel so perfectly white it made even her pale skin seem almost tan. Behind her, the room she'd disappeared into glowed with the gold of sunrise. Wolf averted her eyes as if it were the polite thing to do, but the sight of Bel's bare feet on the gleaming woodwork seemed somehow more alarming and intimate. Her pulse leapt, and she fought to ignore it.

"I, uh, yeah, here it is." Wolf stood and went to the hatch where she'd hung the dress.

"You slept in your suit?" Bel took the dress.

"I hung the jacket up."

"Hmm. Did you think my father might show up? Or are you just modest?"

"I figured at least one of us ought to be clothed."

"Touché." Bel dropped the towel and slipped the dress over her head, leaving Wolf no time to look away.

"How did you sleep?" Wolf asked, proud of herself for maintaining at least a shred of composure.

"Well enough. There's a cafe on the beach not far from here. We should eat before the drive back."

Wolf got the distinct sensation of a door closing between them. "I'm ready when you are."

Bel gathered her shoes and her coat. She led the way above deck and locked the hatch behind them. She moved across the boat and onto the pier with a cool determination. It was the same stride she'd had in Grand Central, Wolf mused, and she thought if only she could grab Bel now and pull her away—from what she didn't know.

The First Ask
October 2002

WOLF WATCHED SILENTLY AS Coltswood read the final draft of her Hirsch Prize biography. A soft rhythmic tick emanated from somewhere in the room, and seeing no clock Wolf supposed it must be coming from the watch Bel wore. Wolf caught herself looking too intently, not at the blued steel hands or the bold stylized numbers, which were familiar enough, but at the curve of Bel's wrist, and the faint blue branch beneath her skin. This familiarity caught in Wolf's chest, and she swallowed back the sensation before averting her eyes.

The massive painting on the wall looked different in mid-morning light, and Wolf took solace there. A great lichen-green slash of paint at the bottom left caught her attention and held it. The signature in the same color. *Coltswood.* She repeated the name silently as if it might shield her from memories. *Coltswood.* After a few moments Wolf let her gaze slide back. The professor's oversized black shirt was partially unbuttoned, the soft silk folded open, revealing her collarbones, and the shadowy curve of cleavage. *Fuck.* Yes, she was still hot, and damn Danny Bauman for asking.

At last Coltswood closed the laptop, allowing one hand to linger on the slick white case, the ring on her finger gently clicking along the surface. For a long moment she didn't say anything, apparently absorbed in thought. Wolf tamped down her anxiety.

"I'm happy to make note of any changes you want me to make," Wolf offered. She opened her notebook in a show of seriousness. She was never nervous about her writing, but she wanted Coltswood to be impressed, a feeling she hoped didn't show.

Coltswood almost imperceptibly shook her head. "It's very thorough, and more complimentary than I expected."

"Well, it is my job to make a Hirsch winner as captivating as I can. You and Gemma made it easy."

For a second Bel smiled, but suppressed it quickly. Flattery did nothing for Bel, and Wolf wondered if hearing it from Wolf amused Bel only because it was unexpected. Of course, she'd carefully included her co-worker to avoid any embarrassing hint of appealing to Coltswood alone. "If you're satisfied, I'll send it on to the editor. She'll send the final copy back to you, of course, for approval."

"I am satisfied. Pleased even. I didn't expect it would be so nicely done. These things are usually so dry and formulaic."

Wolf ran her thumb over the knuckle of her gently closed fist, not sure what to say next, but knowing she needed to get to the point before her chance slipped away. "Well, I'm glad. It's my first foray into a longer form, and it's nice to hear your assessment."

"Are you having a career change then?"

"I'm still writing and conducting interviews, but yes, I have a book I'm working on." She felt her voice threaten to crack on the word "book." *Book?* It was an idea, not even a complete manuscript, and she'd taken an extended leave from her job to pursue it.

Coltswood leaned back in her chair as if she were trying to put a little more space between them.

"I wanted to talk to you about it actually. The book."

"Me?"

"It's about New York, in the '80s and '90s. About the work we were doing back then."

"An AIDS book?"

"No, not only that. It's about the women who were involved in the city at the time. Activists, artists, people who were doing things socially and politically."

"Right, but when you say what we were doing, you don't mean art."

"Not for me, no, but for you."

Bel made a low sound of derision.

"I know you probably don't want to talk about it," Wolf started.

"No, I don't," Bel replied in a clipped way Wolf knew usually shut down any further conversation. But it had never worked on Wolf.

She wasn't easily swayed, not even by powerful people who were used to getting what they wanted. She looked at Belinda, caught her gaze, and held it for a moment. "Look, I know it was awful. I was there, too."

I was there for years before you came and I stayed involved for years after you left seemed to hang in the air between them, but those words would only drive the wedge deeper. It was the last thing she wanted when it seemed like there might be some glimmer of trust here if only she managed to not fuck it up. She'd listened and re-listened to those tapes. Belinda wanted to talk; she remembered more than she let on. She wanted to let it out, and Wolf knew she should be the one to hear it, the one to write it down.

Coltswood said nothing, but she'd put a hand behind her neck and started to squeeze the muscle there as if she could quiet the turmoil Wolf threatened to unleash. Wolf had seen that look before.

"This book I'm writing is going to mean something."

"I'm sure it will, but it doesn't need me for that."

Bel's unmitigated vote of confidence unsettled her more than all the subtle jabs the professor had been slipping her direction since she'd arrived two weeks ago. Wolf tapped her pencil against her knee and took what she hoped was a discreet but steadying breath. "It would add so much. You must see that. You're a Hirsch Prize winner now, but even without that you're an expert in your field, a person who is well connected and well respected."

"Rich," Bel added, flicking up her brow as if she'd made the final and most compelling argument for her inclusion.

"Sure, but that's not the point. I don't want your money." Wolf hoped her clarity on this issue was unassailable. Was that what Bel thought this was about? Money? Financial requests for creative projects were probably something she had to fend off quite regularly, but Wolf had never once considered asking for her money.

"No? I could back you. Silently finance your project. I'm sure it would help. I could smooth the way." Bel was doing her best to seduce. Wolf knew from her tone of voice it was a lure designed to draw in a fool. Take my money and forget what you came for. A distraction.

"No. Thank you, but no. I just want to interview you. People will want to hear your story." *I want to hear it.*

"Perhaps, but isn't that what you've already written? What you'll send to your editor? My story? The Hirsch Prize winner bio and interview?"

"Sure. The bio is done, but it doesn't even scratch the surface. Let me include your story in this book."

"It won't be flattering."

Wolf couldn't quite read the meaning of her intonation. She leaned back, trying to assess whether Coltswood was aiming to insult her. She couldn't be sure, but the little glint of triumph that usually accompanied their verbal sparring was absent from Belinda's eyes. "I would write the truth and I'd write it as beautifully and faithfully as I can."

For a moment there was a look of warmth on Bel's face. A kindness in her eyes. "I'm sure you would."

"Please, just a few hours. Let me interview you and see how it goes. If you decide you don't want to do it, I'll turn off the recorder and you can have the tape or erase it or whatever."

"And your notes?"

"Huh?"

"If I decide I don't want to do this. If I change my mind, will you give me your notes too?"

Wolf looked down at the black notebook on her lap. It was packed with information from her last three months of research and interviews. It felt to her like a living being, her one last companion. Precious, and constant.

I'm gonna have to buy a new notebook.

"Okay, yes, my notes too."

The Cover
December 1, 1992

"CAREFUL," BEL SAID UNDER her breath, although she knew the men were trained professionals. If anyone could be trusted, it was them. Despite this knowledge, she had woken up before sunrise and gone to the museum to make sure everything was happening according to plan. The doors wouldn't open for another three hours. She intended to be gone long before the public arrived. Still, she imagined what it might be like. She tried to envision the looks on their faces as they passed through room after room with artworks veiled in black. Of course, she knew some would be outraged. The tourists who felt deprived of their full experience would shake their heads in a show of disapproval. But some would be sympathetic to the message—some would feel in their bones the incalculable loss of a generation and counting.

"This is the last one." He looked back at her and the other donors and curators assembled. It was a more or less likely group of people who had put their support behind the vision of how they would commemorate World Aids Day. Someone nodded, encouraging the men to go on. They lifted the final shroud and set it in place, plunging one more brilliant painting into obscurity.

One of the young conservationists who had come to help with the work excused herself, clearly overcome with emotion. Bel wondered again why she didn't cry at the sight of so much loss. She wasn't impervious; there was a feeling the sight stirred in her, but it was a void. A hole. A sensation of falling and not being able to grab anything solid. Whatever you touched was bound to fall away with you. So she stood there, surrounded by beautiful objects, some of which were all that remained of beautiful people who had died horribly, and she let herself drop into the abyss wordlessly and without any outward changes to the cool veneer she presented the world.

One of the other donors shook her hand and thanked her for her contributions. She couldn't remember his name, only that his wife had seemed bored and lonely when they met for the first time two days before. For a fraction of a second, she thought of Laura. Alas, the thought didn't serve as the cautionary tale it should have, and she found herself lingering over the wife's features longer than was strictly necessary. She could hardly remember her now, except for vague impressions. Another donor stepped into their conversation. *Patrick?* She thought she might remember him from an event years ago. He was a collector of photographs taken by artists who weren't primarily photographers. It was unusual, and she found he was less tiresome to talk to than the others who all had their obligatory prized Manet or Whistler or whatever it was.

"Will we see you at the dinner tonight?"

"Hmm?"

"Forgive me for interjecting. But I do hope you'll be at the dinner," Patrick said.

"Oh yes, I—"

"Indeed. It would be so lovely to have you," not-Patrick with the pretty wife said.

Bel nodded and offered some noncommittal reply, but she sensed she would be there. Where else would she go? The void was open and there would be no painting today. Why not spend too much money to drink too much alcohol with people whose company she did not enjoy?

Another dead Dave. Wolf hated herself for thinking it, but he was the third Dave she'd watched die from this shit. He was the second Dave she'd carried. Her brain simply couldn't do anything else but start making a file of names, like the endless files of claims she tucked away in the big metal cabinets at Cait's office. Here he was, another dead Dave tucked into some small miserable part of her consciousness. *Or was it subcon-*

scious? No, she was thinking it now, really thinking it. For the moment at least. The funeral had been hours ago, but she could hear the awful wailing of his lover still, and she wanted to do anything at all to make it stop. That was why she said yes to going to the rally. It was a small one. Someone she didn't know all that well was encouraging her to join. She said yes. *Sure, why not?*

Wolf forced herself to focus.

Look at what's in front of you. Watch where you're going.

She thought about the streetlights. Waited for the walk sign. There was the wail again in her memory. A flash, but perfectly clear and utterly absorbing. Then it was gone and she was walking, and the people next to her were talking about Christmas shopping, and the street was just ordinary traffic.

The dinner Patrick had been so keen for her to attend was the usual affair. She wished Marek were in town so she wouldn't have to endure it alone. Everyone was eager to mingle and drink and make it seem like they were ending the AIDS crisis with one bold stroke of the pen across their checkbook. The famous people had turned out at other events in other parts of the city, but this was for their less recognizable but infinitely richer peers. Bel didn't bother thinking what the cost of a seat at the table was. Price was irrelevant. All she cared to think about was the way the gin didn't quite seem to blunt the idiotic ramblings of the man seated beside her. His attempted repartee was so profoundly boring she was almost excited to see Patrick and the other man from that morning approaching her, faces aglow with triumph.

"I hope we're not interrupting, but I thought you might like to see this new acquisition. Meyers just outbid everyone," Patrick boasted on his friend's behalf.

"I'll share it with the public of course, eventually, but I'd be honored to have you give it a look. You did say you enjoy abstracts?"

"I did." Bel felt momentarily annoyed because she couldn't remember his name. For all she didn't care for him, he had saved her from being bored to death. In a mood of gratitude, she let herself be led away to a suite of rooms down the hall. There, another party was underway, almost indistinguishable from the last except here paintings arranged on easels around the outer perimeter of the room gave the effect of a gallery. People milled about. At first glance most of the works were of a sort she found tiresome, but even a personally uninspiring work of art was better than talking to strangers. Alas, it seemed conversation would not be completely off the table as their entrance prompted a small cluster of partygoers to turn and walk in their direction. Soon enough they were surrounded, and a round of introductions and handshaking began. She listened to their names without hearing them; only Petra stood out. She looked no happier than the last time they'd met, but she smiled prettily enough when introduced to Bel.

"We've met before, haven't we?" she asked, still holding Bel's hand.

"You were at the planning committee."

"Yes, that's where it was. So much official business and so little time to meet new people. But I see John lured you over for a bit of socializing."

At the mention of his name, her husband—John apparently—turned toward them both and smiled without breaking away from whatever Patrick and the men were discussing.

"I suppose he wanted to show you the Krasner."

"Ah, Krasner, he didn't say." Bel felt genuinely charmed. Maybe she had been wrong about old John. She'd taken him for a traditional man's man, the kind who would balk at her wanting access to the club pool. A fan of British Marine Art or Catlin's images of the West. The idea he had purchased something abstract was surprising enough, but a Krasner? Well, perhaps she had gotten him all wrong.

"We are being awful hosts, I'm afraid. You have nothing left in your glass. Vodka was it?" John interjected.

"Gin," she replied.

He walked her toward a small but well-stocked bar. Petra joined them. With their drinks refreshed, John led the way to his newest purchase. "There it is." He motioned with his glass of scotch toward an easel.

Bel stepped closer and examined the work. It was a drawing, not tiny, but not overly large. Charcoal on paper, probably from the 1930s or '40s. Before Krasner married. Bel could feel her gaze being pulled deeper and deeper into the image as if the two dimensions were actually endless.

"Christ, all that money for this? You should have held out for a Pollock at least," someone grumbled to John.

Bel closed her eyes for a second and then opened them again, still facing the drawing. The movement in the line was exquisite. She'd seen Krasner once at one of Whit's gatherings. She was old by then, and Bel had been too young and insecure to walk up to her.

"Ah, it'll mature nicely. Don't you worry. Lady artists are all the rage these days," John replied easily and everyone laughed.

Bel tilted her head ever so slightly and saw Petra wasn't laughing. She stood close to Bel, gazing at the floor.

"You think it's good, don't you?" Patrick asked.

"I think it's beautiful. I didn't know it was for sale or I might have bought it," Belinda replied calmly. Petra looked up and watched their exchange with interest.

"I told him he ought to get the opinion of someone in the know. I remember hearing one of the curators say you know a great deal about this modern stuff."

Bel smiled politely. Patrick seemed too good of a person to be in this group. Maybe he was sleeping with Petra.

"Ah, you see. We have further confirmation of a good investment," John said smugly.

"Are you Whitney's Belinda?" one of their companions asked tentatively.

She couldn't place him but answered without thinking. "Yes, that's right."

"Oh, we were so sorry to hear about Whit. We were all shocked."

It had been ages since she'd been to an event like this. She had in fact done everything in her power to avoid being around anyone who might know Whit. Still, when the museum reached out about doing something for World AIDS Day, she had felt compelled to contribute. She should have known Whit might come up, but even so, mention of his death felt like a slap in the mouth. She just stared.

"Lung cancer. And at his age. A damned shame."

Well, that rumor certainly traveled.

Bel averted her eyes from this stranger who seemed determined to talk about Whitney's death. She looked at Petra and noticed that it was the set of her mouth more than anything that made her seem sad. Bel thought for a moment how she might smile if truly moved to do so.

"That's what we ought to be putting all our money into—a fight against cancer. Yet here we are prattling on about the addicts and the fags. Well, what can you do? Politics, I guess," John muttered.

"Indeed," another of them concurred.

Petra flinched. Her petite angular body seemed to contract. A momentary glare formed in wide gray eyes. Looking at her, a jolt of perverse amusement passed through Bel as she thought, *Oh John, I should seduce your wife, you stupid boy.* She threw back the rest of her drink as if it might burn the thought from her head.

"Whitney would be very pleased with the work we did today. If you'll excuse me. Petra, it was a pleasure meeting you," she kissed her cheek and God help her, the woman blushed. Bel turned and walked away.

Bel didn't know where she was going. In truth, she was a little drunk and more than a little angry. She'd already walked farther than was wise in the shoes she wore, but she didn't want to stop. Overhead the clouds held in a miasma of lights and sounds. It was a warm night for December, and she felt like wandering. She longed for the beach like one of Pavlov's dogs. A night of contending with condescension and bald-faced hypocrisy called for the sea. She thought perhaps if she closed her eyes, the traffic might sound like waves. She could ignore the honking. Think of it as gulls. But no, there was no replacement for the ocean, no trick she could sufficiently play on herself. Manhattan was an island, but she might as well be in the middle of the country for all the solace it offered.

She tried to think of Petra, to imagine her outrageous head of golden blonde hair, but when she went to grasp for the image what she found instead was a memory of Wolf awkwardly coming aboard her father's sailboat. The unaccustomed vulnerability in her dark eyes, the feeling of her hand clutching Bel's as if it were her lifeline. Then, as if by some cruel trick of fate, she turned the corner and found she was skirting the edge of a demonstration. It was dark out, and she didn't quite understand who they were or what they were yelling about, but soon enough she got the point. There was a tragically familiar set of slogans emblazoned on the signs. Chants that had rung out all over the city and in other cities, too, reverberated yet again. It was a small rally, a hundred people at most, and some were there just to gawk and heckle. It made her queasy.

What's the point? She supposed sometimes there was a point, at least in a theatrical way, but she was not convinced by any stretch that these protests served the people who were sick.

A wave of nausea crested in her gut with the thought that those bastards back at the ballroom were accomplishing more than all of these people in the streets.

Money.

Money moved the world, even if those doling it out despised the people they were supplying. It struck her as brutally ironic to think John was stopping AIDS, and Wolf was only grinding herself down. There was a third option, and she wanted to take it. Ridgeway was going to make a difference. She would make it make a difference.

Again, a chant of "Fight AIDS" was raised. Someone not far from her shouted "Shut up, fags!" She didn't bother to look at him. The police set up blue sawhorses, trying to get people under control. It wouldn't be long before things would either break up and resolve or intensify into chaos and arrests. It was about this time when Cait would have ushered her away and Wolf would have vanished into the thick of things.

Maybe she's already there. Bel scanned the crowd, inched closer to the barricade, and looked. There were plenty of women in the mix, and many wore the same uniform of blue jeans, leather, and cropped hair, but no Wolf.

I hope she's not here. Her gaze moved over the crowd again, pausing on faces which seemed vaguely familiar.

Then, like a switch had been flipped, the scene contracted. A few sharp whistles. A flurry of shouts. Some people walked away still holding their banners. The police harassed a smaller group of men who were locked together arm-in-arm. Then, running up the street like someone was chasing her, Wolf.

With an uncharacteristic burst of clarity, the kind that usually came only from work, Bel turned and followed. She couldn't catch up; she knew Wolf was too fast. Besides, Bel's shoes were already giving her fits, but she could keep the girl in her sights if she hurried. Finally, Wolf stopped a few blocks away and dipped into a phone booth. Bel watched her dialing, and as she got closer she could hear one side of the conversation.

"Miller and Bill Mac. I don't know who else but those two for certain."

Wolf thrust a hand in her pocket and dropped another coin in the slot.

"They're arrested for sure. Saw the cuffs go on. Yeah, I'm going back over."

She shook her head.

"I'm going back."

A longer pause.

"Fine. No, you're right. I'll see you in the morning."

Bel stood at the booth like she was waiting to use it. Wolf had hung up the phone but was standing there, hand still on the receiver, perhaps deciding who else to ring. Bel saw a glint of sweat on the back of Wolf's neck despite the cold. Then Wolf turned around. At the sight of Bel, her expression changed. Not happy exactly, but not disappointed either. She slid open the door.

"Where've you been?" Wolf looked her up and down.

It was only then that Bel remembered what she was wearing. The deep blue silk party dress, nonsensical shoes. "A benefit."

"For lost poodles? Bankrupt debutantes?"

"You're bleeding," Bel observed. She hadn't stepped out of the doorway, and Wolf still stood in the phone booth looking a little stunned.

"And you're panting."

"Well, you're fast."

Wolf's expression shifted again. More of a smile this time.

"You should clean that cut. Don't want to ruin your pretty face," Bel taunted, but her eyes were having difficulty seeing anything besides the perfect curve of Wolf's mouth.

"Fast and pretty. Well, with all these compliments someone might think your opinions have changed. But I don't really respond to flattery." The smile turned sneer but with none of the malice it could sometimes convey.

Bel leaned in and kissed her.

The moment their mouths touched she knew she had made a serious miscalculation. She had thought fucking Wolf would feel like fucking the system. It would be the horrifying pulse in her ears as the police tried to corral them. It would be the sting of tear gas filling an alley as they ran, or the raw thrill of screaming "Shut it down!" But Wolf tasted like the color of fresh honey in glass jars. Bel closed her eyes and saw the raw white of a fresh canvas expanding there behind her eyelids. Wolf's tongue in her mouth was the piercing brightness of noon daylight through an ocean wave.

She gasped. It was too late.

They were in the phone booth, Bel's body pressed to Wolf's.

Wolf's hand slid up her thigh, not at all like storming Wall Street, but sailing smooth and sure. Bel's breathing seemed to stop for a moment and resumed only when she felt the subtle pressure of Wolf's stare.

"Is this okay?" Wolf's dark eyes were searching hers, wanting only the truth.

She's offering an escape. But there was no escape. Not when this was what she wanted.

"Yes," she breathed as she leaned in closer, pressing her lips to Wolf's, and again she knew she had been wrong about everything. She ran her fingers over Wolf's face, along the curve of her ear and down her throat, letting sensation guide her, like painting in the darkness.

A police car, siren blaring, passed by, the red-and-blue light slashing through the dim shadows that sheltered them.

"We probably shouldn't stay out here," Wolf whispered into Bel's mouth.

Bel kissed her again, wanting her to shut up, but Wolf was right. It wasn't safe or sane or even sanitary the things she was thinking she might do. "I know."

"I can drive you home." Wolf's voice was hoarse, more of a whisper.

"It's all right, I can hail a cab," Bel answered. Her voice too was not yet returned to normal. There was an electric trembling all through her that made it difficult to stand and speak.

"No, don't do that. Really, I'll take you anywhere; it's no problem."

Wolf seemed to be speaking earnestly, not at all noticing the double entendre, and it made Bel wonder if she, too, was shaken by what had just transpired. Was she also realizing she'd been mistaken? Or did she think it was a mistake?

"Where's your van?"

"Not far from here."

"You know, never mind. I'm headed to the train station anyway. I can walk."

"You are?"

"Yes." *I am now.*

Wolf looked at her skeptically. Her eyes seemed to be taking in every detail, calculating every inconsistency. Bel had no bag save for a slender clutch purse. She was dressed for a party, her jacket too thin for anything colder than the current conditions.

"I'll walk with you."

"All right. But you don't need to. I'm a grown-up you know."

"I know. But I need to wash my face, right?"

Bel nodded and did her best not to look at Wolf too intently. She needed to get out of the city. She needed to see Marek and put a little space between herself and this girl. They walked up Forty-Second shoulder to shoulder, occasionally brushing against each other as pedestrians streamed around them in both directions. She was conscious of a lingering need to feel Wolf close to her and she tried to lean away, but the crowds of travelers, tourists, and holiday shoppers made it impossible.

"I didn't know you were in town," Wolf said as they waited to cross Lexington.

"I haven't been. I had some business to attend to this evening."

"Right. The benefit."

Bel shrugged. "We raised almost a million dollars."

"But it wasn't very fun, was it?" Wolf laughed.

"Not at all."

"Well, I'm glad we ran into each other then. Here you are." She gestured toward the train station.

Bel surveyed the damage on Wolf's cheek, carefully committing the shape to her memory. "Let's go wash your face."

Are there secret places for rich people everywhere? Wolf wondered as Bel led her to a part of the station she'd never seen before or even imagined.

Bel opened the door to a restroom that was clean and empty. The fixtures looked as old as the building itself but in good repair as if they'd only just been installed.

Wolf leaned forward and brushed her finger across the abrasion brightening her cheek. "It's not too bad."

Bel ran the hot water and, to Wolf's surprise, it was hot; a faint cloud of steam rose from the tap. Bel took a small white cloth from her clutch and ran it under the water, the spill of liquid over her fingers a visual igniting a memory of how their mouths had felt.

"Are you carrying a first aid kit in there?"

"No, only this handkerchief, I'm afraid." Bel squeezed the fabric and put one finger to Wolf's chin.

"I can—"

"I know." She applied the faintest pressure, and Wolf let the angle of her head be directed by the warm point of contact. Bel pressed the cloth lightly to the wound and then a bit more firmly.

The heat felt good, and she fought to keep her eyes from closing. The terrible temptation of comfort surged through her. It was never wise to lean into a sensation like this one. Especially now. They hadn't seen each other in a month. Their only contact had been an anonymous envelope of cash delivered to Wolf via courier. Now? Now she remembered the taste of Bel's mouth.

Bel took the cloth away, rinsed it, and patted Wolf's face again. "Does it hurt?"

"Not as much as you'll hurt me," Wolf mused. She hadn't intended to say it aloud, but what little filter she had was ruined by adrenaline.

Wolf forced a smile, and when Bel gave no reply, she stood away from the sink and headed for the door. "You had better go catch your train. I'll find my way out."

Her heart hammered as she walked. It hadn't beat this hard at the protest. Not when her face scuffed the brick wall. Not when she ran to call Cait. But it hammered now, an unremitting throb in her throat that felt like it was choking her. She walked outside and wished with all her might that the heavy clouds would open up and rain.

Marek's car was parked at the curb. Bel saw him leaning against the front fender. He looked like he had come straight from a business meeting. His black shoes caught the reflection of the city lights. He wore the better part of a three-piece suit—only the jacket had been discarded—and his shirt sleeves were rolled to the elbow. She knew he'd been out with members of the Harrington and Cardwell board earlier in the evening, and by the looks of it they had kept him busy for some time. He was smoking in leisurely puffs, his face tilting toward the sky as he exhaled. It was a bit colder in Boston, but still unseasonably warm. She walked over, letting the sound of her shoes on the pavement announce her arrival.

"To what do I owe the pleasure? It was all so dramatic, an after-hours call. Meet me at the station," he said in a fairly accurate imitation of her more sultry tones.

When he teased her, she could see a trace of how he'd been with Whit. The two of them always so polished on the surface, but often barely suppressing a laugh. Bel grinned. She had been feeling dramatic, but a few hours in the mostly empty business class car had helped to settle her nerves. She felt she could almost close her eyes now and not see Wolf there in front of her. "I was eager to hear what you learned from your tête-à-tête with your friends at H&C."

"Bel. Please. We're above this sort of thing. Or perhaps we're beneath it, but either way, you don't rush off to Boston in a cocktail dress just to hear how my meeting went. I don't need the whole truth if it's too sordid, but some of it surely."

"Hmm. Give me a puff." She reached out and took the filter between her fingers. She hadn't smoked since her little jaunt around Central America with Michel, but now Marek's cigarette looked irresistible.

"Something bad then? Your mother?" he guessed, reaching in his vest pocket for his cigarette case.

"No. Miraculously, I managed to avoid her despite being just down the road from the city house. Maybe we could go somewhere off the street for this conversation? Or are you busy?"

Marek shook his head. "I'm at your disposal. Where do you suggest?"

"Anywhere," she replied and tried not to acknowledge the tone of desperation she heard in her own voice.

Marek didn't mock her, just finished his smoke and held open the passenger door. He drove her through the city, not filling the silence with chatter the way some might. Bel hoped it was a sign that he was simply comfortable, and not worried about her. She was, at that moment, a little worried about herself, but determined to shake it off.

He pulled up to an all-night diner and led the way inside. As far as Belinda could tell from the look of things, the Sunrise Cafe was where vampires waited for their shift to end. A cluster of black-clad teenagers filled the corner booth. Another slightly less theatrical, but equally pale, collection of youths debated the merits of studying Latin as their waitress poured steaming coffee into their cups. Beyond the smoking section, a tantalizing mix of strong brewed espresso and greasy breakfast foods laced the air.

"I hope this will do." Marek nodded at their surroundings.

"It's perfect." Bel glanced at her watch. "God, it's late, Marek. I'm sorry I called you."

She didn't want to talk about Wolf, but their kiss was all Bel could think about, and this student cafe made it worse.

"No trouble at all, Bel. I was still with Verne, watching him drink twenty-year single malt like water."

"Hmm, a companion for my mother, should the alliance with Old Sheridan dissolve."

"Verne's too sweet for your mother even if he has her liver of steel."

They ordered coffee and omelets. When the food arrived, Bel realized she was famished.

"All right, you've managed to put it off long enough," Marek said after they'd eaten.

Bel made a face of friendly defiance. "Do we still own the building in Back Bay?"

"You own it, yes."

"And it's not been rented out?"

"Not yet, no. It goes on the market at the end of the month. The renovations are mostly complete, though."

"I need a unit."

Marek seemed on the verge of saying something, but Bel pressed on before she lost her nerve.

"Two actually."

"Two apartments? In Back Bay?"

"Right."

"All right. Consider it done. When will you need them by?"

"By the beginning of the year?"

"No problem. I'll have someone confirm when everything is ready for you," he replied, unable to keep the suspicion out of his voice.

"So, Verne. What did he have to say?"

"Bel. Really? Okay. Verne said nothing to suggest there was anything unusual about the situation. The grant is through the NIH, as Pamela said. A team of H&C researchers wrote a proposal and it was selected. Very standard procedure. He didn't know the specifics of the research, but it is certainly AIDS-related, and he said everyone seemed excited about it. You know most of these board members are there purely on their financial backgrounds and social connections, so I'm not shocked he isn't exactly brimming with scientific data. From a financial side, though, everything sounds good. There was nearly unanimous support from the board when the proposal was first mentioned, and now with the money secured even those who were dragging their heels have fallen in line."

"So what's the Ridgeway connection?"

"Hmm, he said Nat wasn't the one to suggest it. Which surprised me. The suggestion came from a man named Dell who is the head of one of the primary H&C labs. He's apparently used Ridgeway for some sort of specialized sensor before and he thought they would be up to the task on whatever this is."

"So, serendipity?"

"That was the impression I got."

"Did he know how large the grant was?"

"Yes, just over a million dollars."

"Well. Nothing to sniff at."

"Not at all, and there are other funding streams. At least five million is projected for this project, but Verne seemed to think there would be more once they start their initial tests."

"Provided they get a result," Bel clarified.

"Of course. You know, I've asked all of the treatment research guys if they've heard of this." He leaned forward as he spoke, his voice softer as if someone might be listening, though Bel was sure no one in the cafe gave a damn about them.

"And?"

His mouth compressed in a disappointed line. "Nothing. I'm sure things will get out into public hands at some point, but it's all sealed up for now."

"Marek, what would you advise me do?"

He leaned back and sighed. "Well, there are no openings on the board at the moment. I asked. We could try to create one of course, but anything even remotely hostile will cause a stir. And you'd have to mingle with Nat. Not ideal."

"Stocks? Some sort of activist investing?"

"It's a possibility, but I don't recommend it, not now anyway. I think Verne is more than happy to talk to me about this. He's an old queen, you know."

"Oh?"

"Don't be shocked. There are countless married old men who are very much part of the extended family. At any rate, Verne and I understand each other. I think he's privately quite pleased to be working on this project, and it bolsters his ego to have me taking him out and asking him questions. And, since you've asked for an apartment in Back Bay, well two apartments in Back Bay, I assume you have your own plan brewing. Perhaps something involving our kidnapper friend?"

"She's not a kidnapper."

Marek laughed. "Well, she is quite dedicated to the work."

"Exactly, I never doubt her sincerity," Bel explained, not realizing until she said it how truthful the assessment was, nor how much she valued the fact.

"Indeed."

"Besides, can't I take an interest in the family business?" she feigned innocence.

"Of course you can. I'm sure Natty will find it amusing to learn you've suddenly decided to specialize in laboratory equipment. But you're right; this is where the action will be. H&C and Ridgeway are both based in the vicinity. Even if Natty insists on acting like DC is home, all of the on-the-ground action will be here. He might even appreciate having you around if you can make him think it was his idea."

"How do you propose I do that?"

"Leave it to me. You know Nat has always wanted me to visit his Washington office? Maybe I'll drop in."

"Nefarious."

"Indeed. And, speaking of dirty deeds, what sent you fleeing from Manhattan if not mommy dearest?"

Bel laughed, but it sounded like a sigh. She could tell him something and it would be enough. "Oh, I went to the museum this morning to watch them cover the art. It was harrowing, I suppose. Then some donor talked me into joining him at a benefit this evening, well last night."

Marek nodded, his eyes full of patient waiting.

"The bastard had the audacity to mention Whit in one breath and call people faggots in another. It was all too much."

"I see."

She could tell he wasn't completely buying it, but was too polite to press for more.

The Plan
December 1992

HE'S MARK NOW, Bel reminded herself as they walked together into the meeting. His gold, round-rimmed glasses made it easier to remember the ruse. They made him look younger somehow, or maybe it was the way his white-blonde hair flopped over his forehead when he didn't glue it up in its usual private banker position. Either way, men adored him and she wondered to herself how many of them he'd slept with. It wasn't the kind of thought she was proud of, but it would have been impossible to ignore the way his charm and good looks brought others to his side.

She supposed she might have the same kind of appeal if only she could be more open, easier to approach, quicker to laugh. But she had never been any of those things. Prickly, her grandmother had called her, and she supposed that's what it was like trying to get close to her. A thousand tiny pricks. For all of her time in these meetings, she knew only a handful of people by name, and none of them appeared to be present.

She tried not to feel let down. It was smart to stay connected with the movement, but she knew full well she'd only agreed to come because she thought Wolf would be here. Where else would she be? It felt like there was no meeting too small nor rally too rowdy for her to be a part of. Bel looked around, but there was no sign of her.

"She'll show up," Marek whispered.

"What?"

"Cait. Oh, or is it Wolf you're looking for?"

Bel felt the unpleasant heat of her response to his question and only hoped it didn't show. There wasn't much time to worry, however, as the marshals had already begun to assemble, giving directions to the masses and handing out leaflets with all of the pertinent information. She fell in line with Marek and followed him into the street.

Compared to the last time she'd witnessed a rally outside of the cathedral, this gathering seemed subdued. There were chants and cops and plenty of gawkers looking for an argument, but over all it was a smaller and less vibrant crowd. She couldn't help but wonder if it was the work of the disease itself or if people were losing steam. Above all, she couldn't help but wonder, where the hell was Wolf?

The disappointment of failing to find Wolf at the protest was still fresh on her mind days later when Bel and Marek arrived at Cait's office. On the face of it, the director of Violet Mission had stayed the course with the same affinity groups she'd been a part of for almost a decade, but she was also one of the people everyone recognized as a powerful resource for those with questions about new drugs and treatment research. Whatever she didn't know off the top of her head, she usually managed to find. Her background in medicine helped, and Bel thought Cait probably had sympathetic friends or former co-workers in one or more of the big research hospitals. It was therefore quite a surprise when Marek asked her for information on SEAFOAM and she drew a complete blank.

"I'm sorry. So far I'm just not turning up anything. Mark, are you sure you have the right trial name and funding stream?"

Marek looked at Bel who shrugged. She had a sinking feeling.

"Well, this is what I have on the companies you mentioned and on any HIV-related research they've done up until now. It's not much." Cait pushed a folder of material in their direction. It looked like a lot to Bel.

"We appreciate it. We'll read this over." Marek put the folder in his bag.

"Is it rare? Not being able to find information on a grant?" Bel inquired.

Cait shook her head. "It takes time for things to process and to get everything into the system. If it's a newer project, it might not have been through the mill yet. I'll keep checking back in. After the new year, there's always a batch of reports released. I'm sure we'll find it."

"Thanks, Cait. We missed you at the cathedral," Marek said casually. Bel could have kicked him. Since last week he'd hardly let up trying in subtle and not so subtle ways to figure out who Bel had been looking for and why.

"Right. Some of our people were there doing the usual street team stuff, you know handing out kits and fliers, but I had to talk with someone over at immigration."

"Problems with a worker?"

"No, trying to get homeless people with AIDS into shelters, but there are so many barriers. Especially for immigrants. The paperwork is making it harder than it needs to be. You know how they love to murder us with red tape and then pin a little red ribbon on it. Frustrating, but I think we're making some progress. Wolf wrote a whole thing about it."

Practically on cue, Wolf opened the door, pushing off her hood, and thumping a black bag onto the desk to the left of Cait's.

"Hi, Wolf. We were just talking about your write-up on the immigration thing."

Wolf looked at them. As her gaze passed from Cait to Marek to Belinda in turn, her expression shifted from total preoccupation to something less clearly defined. Bel could only think of the last time they'd seen each other. The memory of Wolf walking out of the train station bathroom had gnawed at her ever since.

"I got all of the fliers posted." She deflected the conversation.

"Oh great. Donovan called about the photos; he's going to use them for the trifold."

"Sounds good." She looked down at the desk, rummaging in her bag, looking anywhere but at Belinda, and the feeling of being purposely ignored stung all the more because Bel knew she deserved it.

"Wolf, are you headed toward Audrey's by any chance?" Cait asked.

"I wasn't going to but if you need me to drop something off, I will." Her voice weary but willing.

Cait held out a stack of pink photocopies. "You're the best."

"Yeah, yeah."

"Mind if I walk with you?" Bel asked. Wolf shook her head but made no reply. Bel couldn't help but notice the flash of self-satisfaction playing over Marek's features. Ordinarily she would have tried to be more subtle, but *fuck it.* She had been waiting too long, and after not finding Wolf at the protest she'd started to wonder when she might run into her again.

They descended the stairs and headed south toward the bar, neither of them saying anything. As they neared Audrey's, the signature blend of tobacco smoke, partly metabolized liquor, and a mélange of colognes enveloped them. *I could use a drink,* one part of her groaned but another cautioned against cowardice. She needed to face this.

"Are you coming in?" Wolf held the door.

Bel followed. The bar was dim and mostly empty, but the music blared as loud as ever. A group of women who must have been regulars passed a dog-eared copy of *On Our Backs* between them and shouted enthusiastically about whoever they were looking at.

Wolf leaned against the bar and waved at the young woman behind the counter. The girl beamed at Wolf and hurried over, tucking a rag into her belt loop as she approached, which seemed to accentuate her swagger.

"Wolf, it's been a while." The girl's voice was crisp and shockingly unaccented.

"Yeah. Busy, busy. Cait wanted me to bring these over," Wolf replied. She smiled, but her usual easy magnetism seemed dampened.

"Cool. You want a drink? On the house," the girl offered as she took the papers. She wasn't quite leering, but there was something in the way she eyed Wolf that was unmistakable. Bel sized her up as a college girl. A junior maybe. Probably at NYU although Columbia wasn't out of the question. Her teeth were remarkably straight and white, her haircut roguish but professionally done, and the ring she wore on a chain around her neck was most definitely an antique Harvard signet.

"I'm okay, thanks. Bel, you want something?" Wolf turned her back on the girl, who looked stunned by Wolf's refusal. Bel knew she shouldn't feel smug about it. It wasn't as if the girl were her competition. It wasn't as if Wolf belonged to either of them. Still, it did give her a jolt of pleasure.

"No, I'm fine."

"We're good, thanks. Tell Maggie I say hey," Wolf instructed over her shoulder as she walked toward the exit.

"You disappointed her," Bel chided once they stepped outside.

"Nah. Anyway, where are you headed?"

"Home, I suppose."

"Want me to walk with you?"

"If you're free."

They walked on. Wolf relaxed enough to talk about Cait's meeting with the people at immigration. She spent a few minutes bemoaning the plight of those detained at Guantanamo. As was often the case, Bel had no clue what she was talking about, but she got the sense it was an outrage, at least as far as Wolf was concerned.

"So what have you been up to?" Wolf asked as they walked down Broome.

"Not too much, visiting with friends. I went to the protest at St. Patrick's."

"Did you? Did you hold a sign and everything?"

"I did."

"Well, well, well. We are radicalizing you after all." Wolf smirked.

Bel stopped walking. She had gotten in the habit of never letting anyone walk her all the way to her door. It was better this way. It kept the studio as a world apart. "I've been thinking about what you said. When we were at the train station. You said I'd hurt you."

Wolf looked at her directly, and Bel felt herself falling into her gaze as if it were a painting of tremendous power.

"Hmm. I've been thinking about it too. The thing is, I'm not afraid of pain," Wolf said.

"I know." Bel's voice was a whisper. She had planned a few things to say, but those words were nowhere to be found. She had wanted to be reassuring, but it was clear now that Wolf didn't want to be reassured. Bel let her hand brush against Wolf's skin, which was cold from being out all day. She lifted Wolf's hand and held it between her palms, half hoping that the warmth spreading through her could communicate something of the truth, whatever the truth was.

Wolf bent a finger and softly stroked the inside of Bel's palm. "So, do you live here?"

"No, it's a few blocks away. Do you want to see it?"

"Yeah, I'd love to."

Slowly, Bel let go of Wolf's hand and led the way to her studio. Somewhere, a small voice inside protested *don't give up this space. Don't fill it with memories.* But the voice wasn't loud enough to warrant her attention, not when Wolf was beside her walking down her street, coming into her building, stepping into her elevator.

Bel pulled the gate closed and pressed the button.

"Bel?"

"Yes?"

"Can I kiss you?"

Wordlessly Bel leaned forward and slid her hands up the sides of Wolf's neck. She pulled her close, reveling in the sensation of Wolf's muscles taut beneath her cool gold skin. She pressed her lips to Wolf's and felt any thought of resisting this impulse evaporate in a rush of desire.

The elevator stopped.

"We should probably not linger on this thing," Bel said, though she didn't want to.

Wolf nodded and straightened up.

"Would you like a drink?" Bel turned the key in her lock and pushed open the door.

"If you're having one, I'll join you. But let's not get drunk, okay?"

"No?" she asked as they stepped into the apartment.

"I don't want to be drunk, Bel."

Belinda closed the door and leaned back against it with a sigh. *Don't complicate this.* "What do you want?"

"To be with you. But I thought that was obvious."

"Show me."

Wolf stepped closer and slid her hands under the hem of Bel's shirt, the contact of her palms cool, light, and steady along her sides. Bel took a deep breath and pressed forward. She wanted Wolf to ruin her, but she couldn't shake the feeling that this tenderness was what would ultimately destroy her.

"When's the last time you tested?" Wolf whispered, her lips brushing the pulse point just below Bel's earlobe.

Of course you would ask. "A while ago."

"Hmm. I'm waiting on results, so we probably should be creative."

"I can be creative."

"I see that." Wolf nodded over her shoulder at the shelves of paint and piles of canvas.

"I told you I'm an artist."

"Sure, but everyone says that in the Village."

Bel laughed. "This is SoHo. Take off your boots."

Wolf did and Bel kicked off her shoes. Without her heels, their height difference was slightly more pronounced. It amused her to look up at a woman; it was so rarely the case. She hooked a finger in the belt loop of Wolf's jeans and tugged. "Come here."

They walked deeper into the studio. Bel took a folded piece of canvas from a shelf and spread it on the floor. "So you believe in safety first?"

"Absolutely."

"All right then. Sit right there."

Wolf sat cross-legged on the canvas and looked up hungrily at Bel. With a little shake of her head, like she almost couldn't believe what she was doing, Bel walked across the room. Under a stack of newspapers and sketch pads dusty with neglect was a beautifully crafted drawing bench made of red oak. She cleared the rubble off and wiped down the surface with a soft cloth.

"I can feel you watching me," Bel said without turning around.

"Really? How does it feel?"

"Like you're rethinking your commitment to safety."

"Never," Wolf replied.

Bel placed the bench directly in front of Wolf. "Are you nervous?"

"No. Just excited. Curious."

"Is it your first time?"

A laugh exploded from Wolf. "I'm not sure what you mean by 'first time.' But we've gone over how old I am so I hope you don't mean sex."

Bel smiled, relieved.

"Is it yours?" Wolf asked sarcastically.

"I'm going to get us a drink."

Bel walked to the kitchen keenly aware of the way her clothes brushed against her and of how much she wanted Wolf to change her mind about this whole safety-first policy. She came back with two glasses of wine, each only half full.

"In honor of your admirable restraint." She handed a glass to Wolf and sat on the end of the drawing bench.

"Will I be on the floor all night?" Wolf sipped the wine and smiled.

"It depends how well you manage to keep up your commitment."

"Ah, well in that case I might as well make myself comfortable." Wolf pulled off her hooded sweatshirt.

The heater kicked on and hummed. Bel wished for once she had a cozy room with a raging fire or at least a functional radiator, but she wasn't about to let the chill stop her from getting what she wanted. Besides, she probably had the cold to thank for the most exquisite image of Wolf's nipples hard under her paper-thin *Dykes Do It Better* T-shirt.

"Now you're the one staring," Wolf observed as she took another drink.

"Hmm, well, I think looking is one thing we can do safely."

"Looking is approved."

"Good. You can be our safety monitor. I'll ask and you answer."

"Okay." Wolf scooted closer. She could have laid her head in Bel's lap, but instead she sat at attention, ready to respond to Bel's inquiries.

"I suppose you need something to see." Bel stood up and slowly unzipped her pants. Wolf watched with obvious enjoyment as the fabric slid to the floor and Bel stepped out of them. She wished she'd planned for this, picked something more alluring to wear, but Wolf didn't seem like the kind of person to be especially captivated by lingerie.

Wolf leaned back and let her eyes drift over Bel's legs then back to her face. Her lips were parted ever so slightly, and Bel wanted to feel her mouth hot and insistent against her. She considered asking but knew that wouldn't be approved.

"Of course, kissing is allowed." Bel stepped forward and bent at the waist. She put her finger under Wolf's chin and tilted her head back ever so slightly until their lips touched. Wolf leaned up into the kiss and steadied herself by clutching Bel's thighs. As much as the feeling of her fingers delighted, Bel couldn't resist the little game they'd fallen into.

"Is all of this touching safe?"

"Quite safe, so far." Wolf trailed her hands from Bel's thighs to her ankles and then back up, finally cupping her ass and pulling her closer. From that vantage point Bel knew Wolf couldn't possibly not notice how wet she was. Her breath caught for a moment as Wolf pressed her face to the damp cotton of Bel's underwear and placed a kiss.

"Dangerous maneuver," Bel cautioned.

"Yes. Unpleasant?"

"No. Not at all. I'll tell you. You don't need to worry." She ran her hands over Wolf's head. She'd let her buzz cut go a bit shaggy for winter, and Bel stroked her hair with an almost reverent adoration she hadn't known she felt. The cuts on Wolf's cheek had healed, and only a faded pink blotch remained. She passed her thumb over it. *I won't hurt you.* But she knew not to say it. She knew it might not even be true, but she felt it in every nerve.

"Perhaps we had better put a little space between us. Just to make sure you aren't tempted." Bel backed away from Wolf by a few inches and pulled her underwear to the ground.

"Fuck." Wolf sighed and slid her hands under her own thighs as if to restrain herself.

"I'm really quite surprised you aren't more prepared," Bel taunted.

"Me too. I gave my last kit to a kid on the subway; can you fucking believe it?"

"You're a community hero." Bel ran her hand lazily over her thighs; she was aching for Wolf, but her own hands would have to do.

"It was a bigger sacrifice than I intended." Wolf gave a sad little laugh.

"Don't worry, safety monitor. You'll get your results soon. And tomorrow you can take me to the testing center and make sure I'm safe to play with." Bel sat down on the edge of the drawing bench and spread her legs so Wolf could see how shockingly wet she was.

"Ye-Yeah, sounds like a plan."

"Is it a good plan?" she asked.

"It's very good."

"Mmm. I'm going to fuck myself, Wolf, and I'm going to imagine it's you, all right?"

"O-okay."

"Are you okay, Wolf?"

She nodded and swallowed hard. "I'm great."

Belinda let her hips rock forward and was delighted by the way Wolf sucked in sharply and bit her lip in delectable concentration. Never in her life had Bel considered doing something like this, but in the moment, spread out in front of Wolf who watched her every movement as if it were the most riveting thing she'd ever seen, Bel felt as though this were something she'd always longed for.

"How about spit? Is spit safe?"

Wolf made eye contact. Bel could see she was having trouble focusing on the question. She couldn't blame her. It was only the ecstasy of taunting Wolf that kept her from losing all self-control.

"It's, um, well. It's mostly safe. Safer, yes."

"Open your mouth, Wolf."

She did as she was told, and Bel leaned forward and slipped two fingers in. The sensation was more luscious than she'd expected, and she shuddered as she slid her fingers under Wolf's tongue. Wolf closed her eyes.

"Watch me, Wolf. Looking is safe, remember?" She took her fingers from Wolf's mouth and pressed them into herself with a groan.

"Oh fuck."

"Do you wish it were you?"

"Yes."

"Me too. Would that be all right? You using your hands right now like this?"

"No, probably not. I mean, maybe, but, uhh no, not really. Oh fuck," Wolf moaned as she watched Bel rock against her own hand, her breathing growing more and more ragged.

As much as she wanted Wolf to give in, Bel had to admit that her resistance was alluring. She was sitting there on the canvas writhing with desire, her eyes virtually tearing up as she watched Bel, and the sight of her response was a more powerful aphrodisiac than Bel had anticipated. "Lie down, Wolf. Lie on your back."

"Okay."

"Put your arms out. Yes, just like that." Bel walked to Wolf and stood over her so that her toes just brushed the edge of Wolf's armpits. Standing there she pulled off her shirt.

"I, oh, damn," Wolf mumbled. She took a deep breath and watched with fascination as Bel knelt down and straddled her chest.

"Am I too heavy for you?" She rubbed herself against the place where Wolf's breastbone made contact with her body.

"No, fuck no."

"And is this approved, safety monitor?"

"Yes. It's, yeah, safe."

"I'm going to cum on you," Bel whispered sliding her fingers back into herself and grinding down on Wolf. She felt Wolf tremble at the sight.

"Can I touch you?"

"Of course you can. I want you to." Bel pressed deeper into herself and leaned against Wolf so she could feel just how much Bel wanted her.

Despite the coolness of the air around them, their bodies were slicked with sweat. Wolf's fingers coasted over Bel's back, traced down her spine, and rested on her hips, pulling her closer. Bel closed her eyes and thought she could feel the space between them collapsing into darkness; there was no space, only pressure, and the occasional sense of rising out of her own skin.

As Bel edged ever nearer to the inevitable, she bent back and pressed her hand over the zipper of Wolf's jeans. "Safe?"

"Oh fuck, yes," Wolf whimpered and lifted her hips to Bel's hand.

She wanted badly to work her way under the fabric, to feel for herself the soft slick heat of Wolf's body, but that was out of the question.

For the duration of their time together she had been thinking of her hand as Wolf's working inside of her, driving her on, but suddenly she thought of her hand as her own, and of her body as Wolf's body. She imagined what it would feel like to fuck her, and was capsized by a new more potent wave of longing.

"I'm so close," Bel rasped.

Wolf nodded and made an incoherent sound of agreement, her breathing unsteady. Bel matched the rhythm of her hands and watched Wolf's face transform in ecstasy. Her eyes fixed on Bel's looked to her like wet obsidian, the jet black of new paint glimmering in the fractured light of the city. Not a void, but an opening into a new world.

Wolf grabbed the collar of her own T-shirt and shoved it in her mouth to stifle a scream.

Bel made no effort to silence herself. She came with a cry unlike any she'd ever heard. It emerged from a place inside her so obscure she had not known it existed, had not known it made sound, yet there it was echoing through her. Wolf's palm was flat on Bel's chest, fingers tracing the column of her throat and she wondered what the sound had felt like in her lover's hand.

"Creative enough for you?" Bel asked after a moment. She looked at Wolf and smiled.

"Very creative. I can verify you are indeed an artist."

"I told you." Bel tried to stand up, but Wolf held her and rolled her down to the ground beside her.

It was a reflex to hop out of bed after sex, to put some space between herself and whoever it was she'd slept with. Especially when it had been Laura, who hated to linger and would always rush toward the shower as soon as she'd gotten off. As Wolf wrapped her long lean body around Bel and pulled her close, Bel half wanted to worm away from the embrace.

Wolf kissed her face, her cheek, her lips, her forehead.

"Are you cuddling me?"

"Yes. Obviously."

"Hmm." Bel groaned.

"What? You don't like cuddles? Too passé?"

Bel shook her head and let herself relax for just a moment. It was cold on the floor, and Wolf was warm, she told herself.

Bel woke up an hour later from a half-formed dream of floating in the sea. Her face was flush with the side of Wolf's left breast, Wolf's arm under her head cradling her.

Jesus.

She got to her feet and Wolf yawned awake.

"You can sleep here." Bel gestured toward a plush couch against the wall farthest from the studio. It was tucked under the overhang where her own bedroom loft jutted out.

"You can join me," Wolf offered playfully.

"No, I think I've had my year's worth of cuddling." Bel snatched her shirt from the floor and shook it out. She felt as though her body vibrated at some strange new frequency. Well, it had been a long time since she'd been with anyone, she supposed.

"You don't need to get dressed on my account."

Bel chuckled and walked to the kitchen for a glass of water, pulling her shirt on as she went. She needed a little distance, but Wolf was on her feet and following close behind. Bel wanted to turn, stop short, and let them collide. To feel the way Wolf would inevitably reach out and catch her, but she didn't. "Are you busy tomorrow?"

"Yeah, taking you to the clinic remember?"

"Oh right." Bel took a long drink of water, and handed a glass to Wolf.

For a moment they stood in the kitchen, inches apart.

Finally, Bel gestured to the right. "Well, the bathroom is over that way. I'm going to go shower in a bit."

"Want me to join you?"

"Ha, no, I don't think that will pass the safety test."

"We could resist."

Bel felt herself leaning imperceptibly closer. "Maybe you could, you're very good, but I'm not so sure about myself. Go on. You shower first, and I'll get you some sheets."

When Wolf returned, the couch was made up in a worn set of linens, a comforter tossed over the arm.

"Want to tuck me in?"

"Go to bed, Wolf. I'll see you in the morning."

Wolf sprawled out on the couch and sighed.

Bel woke up early. She had fallen asleep easily, her mind unable to fix on any anxiety or even form a coherent thought. Now, in the smoky gray blue of a morning not yet broken she lay alone in her bed thinking about Wolf on the couch below. If sleeping together had been a mistake, which she strongly suspected, why didn't she regret it? She supposed she would wait and see how the next few hours went before deciding if it had been a disaster. Well, perhaps disaster was too strong of a word. Disasters required feelings. She would wait to see if it had been a blunder. *Yes, a blunder.* She sighed and stretched, dimly aware of how the dawn was painting a pattern of bright white waves on the wall below. She wanted the water, the sun of autumn mornings, the sensation of Wolf's fingers on her throat.

Coffee.

She sat up to stop herself before her mind ran too far afield.

As she descended, the wooden stairs let out a soft groan of complaint. The floor was cold on her feet, but she welcomed the sensation as one of those rituals bringing her more fully into consciousness. In the shadowy cubby under the loft, Bel saw Wolf still sleeping curled tight under the covers. She pushed away the urge to be near her and went to the kitchen instead. If things went according to plan, this might be one of her last mornings here for a while, and she wanted to enjoy the pleasures of the shack, the blue flame of her stove, the way the Moka pot ticked as it heated.

"Mmm, do I smell coffee?" Wolf's voice was soft and sleepy.

"Yes."

"Do you have enough for two?"

"Of course."

"Nice."

Bel stood on her toes and reached around the top shelf for a second cup. She had never needed a second cup before. The thought was like the brush of an errant hair ghosting along her cheek, not unpleasant but distracting. The coffee brewed. Outside, a bank of clouds rolled in and obscured the sun, but the glow of morning still streamed down through the skylight. There, at the edge of illumination, lay the square of canvas where they had been together the night before, and Bel's body twitched with a pleasant stab of memory. She prepared two servings of her usual breakfast, espresso with three shortbread cookies, and walked toward the low table where she had taken to eating when it was too cold for the patio.

"Wolf, clear this off, would you?" She gestured at a pile of magazines tossed on one of the chairs.

Wolf stopped folding her blankets and did as she was asked. "You eat cookies for breakfast?"

"I do. You can too if you like, or I have some fruit in the refrigerator."

Bel put down the plates and took a seat.

Wolf joined her and eagerly munched a cookie. A few buttery crumbs fell, which she brushed off. "Ah, your latest print." She examined her shirt, which bore a stark reminder of the night before.

"I have something you can wear instead."

Wolf laughed. "Why? I like it."

"I'm sure you do, but I'll get you something else after breakfast," Bel reiterated. She put her lips to her coffee cup to hide her own amusement.

"So, how was your night?"

Bel rolled her eyes. "So-so. Yours?"

Wolf sat up straight and affected the tones she used when pretending to be someone who could mingle with the Sheridans. "Oh, I saw the most exquisite show. It was quite moving."

Bel snorted softly. "Is that so?"

"It is. So, will you be accompanying me to the clinic today? I'm sure I can get us an excellent table—I am quite familiar with the maître d'."

"Hmm. Yes, I imagine so."

"So it's a date?" Wolf asked.

"I suppose."

The clinic was always busy. Wolf figured it was a good thing—the more people tested, the better. Cait insisted everyone who worked for her get regularly screened. For the past few years, Wolf had a standing second Monday of the month appointment with Peg, the phlebotomist. Being a regular, Wolf had never had to wait this long before. Sitting in the dingy room, Bel stood out in the crowd. People with money like hers had private doctors, freshly painted waiting areas with tasteful decor and soft music. Wolf wondered why she'd agreed to this. Bel was probably wondering the same thing. As she looked around at the people anxiously waiting their turns, Wolf was glad this clinic only took samples for testing. Results were given elsewhere. She didn't think Bel would do well weathering the sights and sounds associated with waiting in a place where people regularly learned their lives were about to end or at least be radically altered.

Wolf took a deep breath remembering her first few months on the street team. Every visit to the clinic had felt like standing at the very edge of a subway platform. Death, imminent death. The refrain beat in her head every time, even though she didn't shoot up, and the risks from what she did to get by were lower than the risks some of her friends took. Even when she was given the all clear, she would remember the wails of the newly diagnosed or, worse yet, the sight of those people who walked in cheerful and left in a veritable fugue. Those sights and sounds would rattle around inside of her for days after.

"Belinda," a nurse finally called.

Bel stood up and glanced at Wolf. "You coming?"

"If you want me to."

"It's up to you. "Wolf stood and followed her down the familiar hall. The fluorescents' glare on the glossy, pea-green cinderblocks had never much fazed her, but when she considered how it must look from Bel's point of view, the place seemed daunting. The nurse ushered them into a tiny exam room papered with public health posters. The sleek mass-produced images advertised everything from condoms to flossing.

"Someone will be back in a minute."

Bel stood by the exam table. She looked tense.

"You good?"

"I don't like needles."

"Oh. It's fast. They know what they're doing here." Wolf fought the urge to touch her. The instinct to give a comforting gesture warred with her sense of Bel as someone who would hate to be seen in a place like this being touched by someone like Wolf. Again, she wondered why they'd come to this particular clinic. Maybe it made sense somehow. A fancy clinic meant the possibility of Wolf being seen in Bel's world. That might raise eyebrows. But here, nobody looked at anyone too closely.

When the door opened, Wolf was glad to see it wasn't Peggy. She didn't know if she could handle the kind of familiar banter they tended to fall into.

"Hello. Who's getting tested? Both of you?"

"Hello. No, just me." Bel replied.

Wolf had never heard her sound anything less than brutally confident. Even when they'd first met and Bel was new to the meetings, she had managed to seem like the world was hers and everyone else was a visitor. Now, the subtle fear in her voice was remarkable.

"HIV test? All right then." The tech marked the little paper on her clipboard. "And when was the last time you were tested?"

"Um, years ago."

"Ah, okay. How have you been feeling? Any fevers, night sweats? Unusual skin irritations?"

"No, nothing like that."

"Okay, just precautionary testing then?"

"Right."

"Okay. You'll need to take off your coat and roll up your sleeve." The technician turned away and rummaged around in the drawers behind her, gathering the necessary supplies.

Bel sat down and draped her coat across her lap. She pushed the sleeve of her black silk shirt up over her elbow. Wolf's eyes traced the bright blue vein in her arm.

"It'll be quick," she whispered again.

Bel grabbed her hand and squeezed.

As the tech placed the needle and the vial, Bel looked away, but Wolf watched intently. She had never thought of herself as particularly kinky before, but it was undeniable—the sight of Bel's blood struck something in her. As it filled the vial, Wolf was potently aware that Bel's blood was bright and dangerous. And it was hers, part of her that had been hidden but was now brought to light. She felt a pang of longing. It wasn't even the blood itself that was so striking. Wolf had seen people getting tested more times than she could count, but Bel was doing this thing she was afraid of only because Wolf had asked her to. Because they were sleeping together and Bel wanted more. It was an offering. Something precious, and it made Wolf feel such a peculiar sensation, much more than a thrill.

They had agreed to meet at the cafe around six. Bel arrived first and sat outside sipping wine, wishing it were something stronger. The hands on her watch read five minutes past. A creeping sensation slid through her. *A blunder.* The holiday crowds hadn't thinned. Anticipation of the New Year brought people in droves to the city, and even this far from Times Square it was obvious. Young city couples with parents who had flown in from some rural place or another thronged around the neighborhood sipping hot chocolates and enjoying the sights. Bel didn't envy them, though she could see clearly how they were comfortable everywhere, elevated in the most mundane ways. She looked at her watch again. Another minute had passed. More crowds of tourists meandered by. She observed a clump of tall-haired teenage girls attired in matching jackets. *Rockville High Cheerleading.* One was blowing a massive pink bubble while another snapped a photo with a disposable camera. Nearby, she heard another shutter click, too loud to have come from the one she was looking at. Bel turned and Wolf fired off another frame.

"I thought you were using that thing for the revolution," Bel said.

She grinned. "This is the revolution."

The waiter looked at Wolf like he was about to shoo her away, but Bel waved him over.

"Ma'am?" He asked, all deference.

"What are you drinking, Wolf?"

"I'll have whatever you're having." Wolf put the camera back in her bag.

The man nodded and returned a moment later with another glass of chardonnay.

"It's crazy out today. The warm weather I guess." Wolf shrugged out of her leather jacket. She was still wearing the shirt Bel had given her after breakfast.

"Indeed. It's pleasant though."

Wolf nodded and took a drink. "So, did you paint today?"

Bel's eyebrow raised. "I didn't. I had meetings."

"Rich people stuff?"

"Precisely," Bel replied.

"Don't you have people to do those things for you? I mean, isn't it one of the perks?"

"Hmm. Indeed. But you still have to meet with your people at some point."

"I guess that makes sense. Are you coming to the meeting tonight? Cait's bringing some lawyer. I didn't catch the name, but she's going to talk to us about the legal challenges we've been coming up against with immigration."

"Perhaps—Wolf, do you like the city?"

"This city? Sure. I mean, it's home I guess."

"Do you think you'd ever leave?"

"I don't know. Maybe. I mean if I had a reason to, sure. I'm not one of those New York crazed people. It's a great place but—" She shrugged.

"Yes."

Wolf looked at Bel inquiringly. "What about you? Do you like it here?"

"I have connections here. I have my studio. It's an important place for the art world."

"Right, of course. But do you like it?"

"I have mixed feelings."

"Yeah, it's bittersweet, right?"

Bel exhaled softly. "Exactly right."

—⁂— —⁂— —⁂—

Wolf took another slow sip of wine. Like everything about Bel, it was exceptional, and she didn't know how she'd managed to find herself in this position. The other shoe would drop, of course it would, but in the meantime, she wanted to absorb every delicious bit of what was happening between them. Maybe someday she would ask her why she kept all of her paintings turned backward, or why she had put her on a sheet of canvas, or why she hated to cuddle, but for now Wolf just watched as Bel ran a finger pensively around the rim of her glass.

"I wonder if you would do something with me?" Bel tipped back her drink as if summoning the courage to ask.

"I'd do anything f-with you."

Bel's lips twitched in amusement. "F-with me, hey?"

Wolf wished she could smack herself, but there was nothing to do but carry on. "Cut it out. What do you want me to do?"

"I want to hire you."

"Huh?" She must have made a face that gave away her first and horribly unflattering thought.

Bel's expression shifted, suddenly serious. "No. Not like that. Don't be dense."

"I just—" Wolf shrugged and shook her head. It was no time to admit that she more or less had whored herself for years. Bel probably knew all she needed to know on that score from Cait or Brenda or from watching the way people treated her at the bar.

"I have an idea, but I need help."

"You need a spy?" Wolf asked.

"Yes. Sort of. I'm going back to Boston to keep an eye on this deal with H&C."

"The research thing?"

"Right. I want to know what's going on. I want to be there to push things along if I can."

"That sounds smart. What would I be doing?"

"I want you there with me to get to know the community. I want to have some connection with the pool of trial applicants."

"People with AIDS?"

"Yes. Cait knows people in the activist world out there, and she can put us in connection with them. You'd be doing pretty much what you do here, but you'd also be helping me out. I want to know what's going on with SEAFOAM, not only from inside the company, but on the outside as well."

"How the trials are running from the patients' point of view?"

"Exactly. You'd be paid of course."

"Of course," Wolf smirked. There was no point arguing about money with Bel; she knew better by now.

"It would require a commitment of several months."

"A commitment? Already? Wow. Classic lesbian."

"Now you're the one who should cut it out. This is a real offer, Wolf, and I had hoped you would give it serious consideration."

"I'm sorry. I'll be serious for a minute. Go on. You said several months?"

Bel inclined her head. "Yes. I wish I could be clearer about the timeline, but the truth is I don't know how long it will take to figure things out. The most critical thing is, you'll need to move."

"Move in with you?"

Bel's eyebrow raised, and she looked as if she were about to call the whole thing off.

"Move to Boston?" Wolf made her tone as serious as she possibly could before Bel rethought the whole offer.

"Yes. I can provide a place for you."

"Provide a place? A room?"

"An apartment."

"Seriously, Bel? Are you sure you're not in the mob? This is pretty fucking weird."

"It's not weird. I own property, and I'm asking you to move. Providing a place for you to live would be part of the compensation for your time and relocation. It's fairly standard."

Wolf shook her head, unable to put into words the gulf dividing them on this matter. Even if she could explain, she couldn't see how it would do her any good. Besides, Bel was there across from her at the table looking not vulnerable so much as hopeful. It wasn't an expression Wolf had seen before, and she was willing to admit, if only to herself, it was beautiful and she didn't want it to end.

"Will I have to wear a suit?"

"Occasionally, yes, but you won't have to lie about what you do. When you accompany me, we'll say you're my assistant. Which will be true enough."

"What if someone sees me and remembers I'm a photographer. Won't it seem suspicious?"

Bel shook her head. "No, I will simply tell them what they already know, that art doesn't pay the bills so I hired you."

"I've never been to Boston."

"It's not New York, but it can be charming."

"Would I still be able to fuck you?"

"Jesus. You are direct, Wolf."

"I am."

Bel blinked slowly. "Are you asking to fuck me?"

"I'm asking if fucking you would be off the table if I take this job."

"No. I'm not saying it will happen. I haven't thought about it, but it wouldn't be off the table."

"All right then, I'm in."

The Connection
October 2002

WOLF ROLLED OVER IN bed and squeezed her eyes tightly closed. From outside came the plaintive sound of birds, autumn migrants chirping in their last frantic search for seeds before leaving. Warm gold light seeped through the curtain's edge and crept up the wall in a slice of brilliance. It was pretty, but Wolf missed the city. Not New York so much, not even Boston, but any proper city where she might be completely anonymous. She wished she could walk through the masses unnoticed and unfamiliar. She had tried to replicate the sensation downtown the night before, but had only run into Vic. The model put her hand on Wolf's arm so casually and squeezed her bicep as if she were testing her. "Let's get a drink," she offered. With smiles and a little flirtation she'd done her best to maneuver Wolf toward a night of drinking and probably sex.

It was hard to decline without being rude, but Vic raised the hairs on the back of Wolf's neck. She couldn't be trusted. And after their last outing, turning her down was easy.

Never sleep with a source.

She retreated home and spent a few hours trying to make sense of her life until finally sleep claimed her. Now, watching the sun creep up the wall she found herself mentally running through the same thoughts she'd had the night before. She had left a good job to write a book, she had come to Iowa, she had found Bel.

Each thought was a little more troubling than the last. Her cell phone trilled mutely. Wolf fished around under the pillows until her finger found the plastic brick.

"Y'ello," she mumbled, her voice still drowsy.

"Deb, is that you? Sorry, the connection isn't great on my end." The voice came bright and cheerful through the static.

"Yes, this is Deb."

"It's Sandy! How's it going?"

"Oh Sandy! Hi." Wolf couldn't imagine why Sandy would be calling. They'd always been on friendly enough terms, but Wolf's sudden exit from *The Globe* had left her former editor in a lurch. Maybe this was an overture to come back to work? Or, more likely, a freelance offer? Wolf hadn't burned all of her bridges, but this one felt shaky at best.

"Hey, how's that book coming?"

Wolf held back a groan. For no particular reason she had the sense Sandy didn't think much of Wolf's shift to long form. "Sorry Sand, I can't hear you very well."

"I know, sorry about that. I'm on the road right now outside of Bridgeport. Not driving, don't worry. Though my husband's at the wheel so I don't know if we're any safer."

Wolf summoned a polite laugh through her mounting anxiety.

"Listen, I was just visiting my brother-in-law. You know he works with one of the big presses in Manhattan, and I was telling him about your book."

"What?"

"Yeah, I mean you're still writing it, aren't you?"

"I uh, yeah, yes, I'm still writing it."

"Great. Because I'd look like an ass otherwise. I gave him some of your shorter stuff, those profiles you did when you were in DC, and I told him about what you're up to. He's very interested."

"Really?"

"Yeah, look, I know it's short notice, but he wants to meet you. He's leaving for LA soon, so it's a tight squeeze, but he wants to take you for dinner and talk about the project."

"Really?"

"Yes, stop asking that. You're a rock star, Deb Wolf, and I can't wait for you to publish this book."

The shock of Sandy's praise embarrassed her.

"Oh, um, well. I'm in Iowa right now."

"Iowa? Oh right, the thing for Gemma."

"How did you—"

"Come on, Deb, we all know each other in this business. New England is tiny. So can you get to New York in a few days?"

"Yeah, sure."

"Great. Get a pen, I'm gonna give you the number for Tom's secretary. Call her. Seriously, call her today."

"I will, I promise."

Wolf sat on a paint-spattered folding chair in the hall outside of the studio. Although there was no sound, save for the low hum of music forced through a cheap set of speakers, she knew Professor Coltswood was on the other side of the door. A small pink paper placard read *Coltswood: Advanced Painting Studio 2-5 p.m.* Wolf looked at her watch. The publisher wanted her on a plane out of Cedar Rapids later that night. The ticket was waiting for her. It had been a long time since Wolf had felt so utterly trapped. She didn't deal well with these kinds of situations. As a general rule, she went with her gut, and it rarely failed her. Her gut right then was telling her stay.

But she had transformed her life in order to pursue this book. It was one of the reasons she quit what seemed to many like a dream job. Journalism had taken her places and put her in the same room as some very powerful people, but it had worn her down physically and mentally. The things she saw never went away; they merely piled up with all of the other corpses she'd collected in her consciousness over the years. Still, the idea of making some lasting monument to the women she'd known and been directly or indirectly mentored by was something that gave her a reason to get up and go on no matter how difficult. This publisher was the ticket to the book. They believed in it. They wanted to back it. They wanted her in New York.

But she didn't want to go.

At five minutes after five the door opened. Two women emerged, each lugging a crate of supplies. A short time later, another trickle of students departed. Clusters absorbed in their own conversations—plans for dinner, the offer of a ride across town, a joke. Their laughter followed them down the empty hall. Wolf stole a glance inside. Bel was taking a final turn around the room, looking at each of the canvases with a tilt of her head and a critical gaze. She was alone, and Wolf wanted to watch her for a moment longer, to pretend they were somewhere else and that time had never passed.

"I can feel you looking," Bel said.

"Can you?"

Bel turned around. "Oh, it is you. We didn't have an appointment."

"No. I came because I have to go back to New York. I've got a meeting with a publisher and I—"

"That sounds promising."

"I suppose. I don't know, it's tentative."

"Well, it sounds like good news. See, you don't need me for this project of yours."

"I—"

"I'm very pleased for you." She ushered Wolf into the hall and locked the studio behind her.

"Bel, I—"

Belinda glanced at her watch. "I'm afraid I have a faculty meeting I need to get to. Have a safe journey. And thank you for your work on the Hirsch bio; it really was very well done. I'm sure your book will be even better."

Bel didn't wait for a reply but turned and walked away.

The Move
January 1993

EVERY TIME SHE FLED New York Bel left by train. The rails were a comfort. Somehow, they made the transition real. The hours in the station and seated in the familiar plush blue seats gave her time to put away Manhattan, which so often loomed like a dangerous specter behind her as she went. This time felt different. She looked out of the windows at the world rushing by and wondered if riding in the van with Wolf might have been a better option. She could have talked to her about the plan, explained what little she knew about the H&C project and Ridgeway's role. Wolf was a fine driver, Bel knew from experience, but the thought of rolling through the darkness in a work van full of boxes had seemed entirely unappealing. She'd tried to convince Wolf to hire a mover with company money. *They'll have all of your things packed up in a day at most*, she had told her, but Wolf had insisted on driving herself.

Bel pulled a novel from her bag and tried to settle into the story. It was difficult to concentrate with so many thoughts churning. She hadn't seen the apartments in Back Bay, which gave her pause. Of course, Marek could be trusted, but who had he hired? It was idiotic, she knew, to fret over linens, but all she could think about was the sheets. Had they gotten something suitable? Had they made both units up sufficiently? Wolf wouldn't care about the thread count, but Bel cared. And she tried desperately to keep her mind on those little things so she would not notice how much she wished Wolf were there beside her. Wishing for Wolf was something she was absolutely not prepared to do.

Cait's apartment, so often packed with people, felt eerily quiet with just the two of them. The affinity group had long since cleared out. Even Brenda had gone, though she sulked about being sent away. Wolf sat at the kitchen table sipping a mug of ginger tea that had gone cold. She swirled the liquid, watching the tea bag tip back and forth in the current. She felt like that, wobbly.

"So she talked to you about this plan?" Wolf wasn't sure if the fact made her feel better about things or worse.

"She did. She asked if I could spare you. Of course, you are irreplaceable in some ways, but I can spare you if you want to be spared." The creases at the corners of Cait's eyes deepened.

"I feel like I'm running away." A new city, an adventure, a cause, and Bel. Of course she wanted to go.

Cait shook her head. "Don't. That's not what's happening here. You know Belinda has connections none of us have. She can get access to spaces we can't. Not to mention, she's helped us and I think we ought to lend her our support. Besides, if she can influence how those drug trials are performed, it might make a real difference."

"I know."

"And for whatever reason, she trusts you." Cait rolled her eyes.

"Well, we have spied together before."

"Uh huh. Well, I think you'd be an idiot to say no. She likes you."

"You think so?"

"Obviously. Apart from all that, she's offering better pay than I ever could, and she's giving you one hell of a chance to get something done in this fight."

Wolf fidgeted. "I don't want to leave you in a jam, though."

"Please. I can find someone to file papers and hand out kits. You've outgrown this job, Wolf."

She sighed and slouched over the table. "I guess."

"You guess? Get off it. You ought to be planning for the future. Bel will help you, Wolf; she will."

"I don't want to plan for the future, Cait. There is no future, there's only now."

Cait relented. They'd had this fight too many times already. "Okay, okay. No big plans, but there's tomorrow. She told me she needed you in town by mid-month. You're dragging your heels."

"I'm not. I plan to leave in the morning. I just didn't want to go without talking to you first."

Cait nodded. "All right. Don't back out because you're worried about me. Or because you think this isn't real activism. It's as real as it gets. These people are the ones calling the shots, and you could be in the room with them."

"What if I fuck up?"

"Don't. Wolf, you don't fuck up. You take risks, you act on instinct, but you don't fuck up. Deep down, do you want to go to Boston and help with this project or not?"

"Of course I do." *Of course.*

"Good. Then go."

Wolf sighed. Cait never made things complicated. Wolf loved that about her.

"Here, take this." She pushed a spiral-bound memo pad across the table.

Wolf flipped open the soft cardboard cover. Names, numbers, addresses, some crossed out.

"They're all the people I know of who are based in Boston or have some roots there. I haven't talked to some of them in a while, but if they're still alive, they'll be happy to meet with you and tell you what they can."

If they're still alive.

It occurred to Wolf how many people she knew who might not be alive when she got back to New York. The thought gnawed at her. But then again, maybe what she was about to do would be the difference between life and death.

Sleep was impossible. Wolf mashed her face into the pillow with a grunt. No matter how she twisted and turned, each new configuration of blankets and limbs was as unpleasant as the last. Outside, the city—or at least the particular side street where she'd parked for the night—was finally quieting down. But rather than soothe her, the lessening din made her thoughts seem louder. She blinked her eyes open and stared at the ceiling. With a resigned sigh she reached into her hoodie pocket and took out the bit of cardstock, which had bent under her body weight. The slip bore directions to an unfamiliar address. She had planned to start driving as soon as she woke up, but as she lay in the dark watching her breath crystalize in the air, she began to think now was as good a time as any.

At least with the engine running there'll be heat.

She rubbed her cold-numbed fingers over her eyes until the sleep cleared. Her boots were beside one of the banana boxes she'd pillaged from a bodega and used to pack her clothes in. They added a smell of fruit-damp cardboard to the usual scents of dryer sheets and leather that permeated her living space. She laced her boots, dug her keys from her pocket, climbed into the driver's seat, and started the engine.

"I'm not abandoning you," she said aloud to the darkness where Dave and Danny, and all of the others whose names ran on in her mind, seemed to be watching her and wondering what the hell she was up to.

She wondered the same thing.

She'd rarely driven east out of the city, and she was thankful for the feeling of a fresh start even as her gut tightened with anxiety. Not far past Hartford, the traffic thinned. Wolf sped on, her mind casting around for some sort of anchor as everything she'd known for years slipped away in the rearview.

She tried to imagine the future. Cait said she ought to. But everything came up blank. She tried something a little more specific. Bel had written the address where they would meet on a small cream-colored card. Wolf conjured images of what the address might look like. Would it be somewhere discreet? A place suitable for spies? A clapboard house on a nondescript road? A loft in an unassuming warehouse? Who knew. And where would she put Wolf up? A bedsit in the gay part of town? Was there a gay part of town?

I don't know anything.

Maybe it was best not to think too deeply because when she thought about what she was doing it almost felt like someone was playing a joke on her. An apartment for free? No such thing. Getting paid to watch a drug company who might, for all they knew, be developing a vaccine or a cure? Sleeping with Belinda once and maybe again, even if that were only a remote possibility? It had to be a hoax. At least she had the van. If things went sour, she'd have a roof over her head and a way back to New York.

Outside of Boston, the traffic suddenly multiplied and slowed. Cars and trucks squeezed into the city through the narrow chutes of tollbooths. She dropped her coins into the waiting hand of the operator. Exiting the interstate, she found herself quickly deposited into a warren of unfamiliar streets. She was thankful for every red light that gave her an opportunity to consult her notes.

Finally, she passed the address Bel had given her.

"No way."

The sensation of being pranked grew stronger. Wolf drove around the block one more time. She laughed and checked the card again. The numbers written in Bel's distinctive scrawl were the same as the ones posted in brass on the door of a high-end brownstone.

Wolf parked the van.

Looks like I need to suit up.

She glanced at the passenger's seat where the suit from Fielding was draped carefully, sealed in its protective bag. The street still hovered in the space between yesterday and today, but soon it would be full of people who would see her and know instantly she didn't belong. With the careful movements of a person used to dressing in cramped spaces, she slid out of her leather, hoodie, jeans, and T-shirt and into the tailored gray wool.

Satisfied with her attire, she sat back in the driver's seat for a moment gathering her nerve. Wolf let her gaze trace the shape of the building. It was almost ominous in its beauty. A column of round bay windows jutted out in a curve like a castle turret. The top of the facade was lined with wrought iron. The topmost floor consisted of a line of small square windows trimmed with pale green copper. All were dark save for one, which glowed a soft gold from within. It looked warm and welcoming and she knew, or thought she knew, Bel must be inside. The sensation of a secret current vibrating between them surged, and she laughed at herself for being a fool.

There was, as far as Belinda could tell, no reason to be anxious yet she felt a cold prick of fear when the telephone rang. Perhaps an early morning call always had this effect, for what good news could come before the sun was even up? She grabbed the receiver and mumbled a greeting.

"I'm sorry for ringing at this hour." Marek sounded contrite, but not frantic.

She remembered he was in London, and his calls tended to come at odd hours.

"It's all right. I'm just a little disoriented. New place and all." She sat up and flipped on the lamp beside her.

"Of course. How is the apartment?"

She gazed around the room. "It's very well done. I'm impressed."

"Good. The other units aren't quite finished, but I've told Lucas and Vincent to hold off on any construction until you're ready for them to proceed."

"Thank you. I don't think I could live in a work zone."

"Ah, it's mostly finishing touches at this stage, but still. I imagine the less you have to deal with the better, at least while you're getting used to life as an active member of the Ridgeway Unit."

"Indeed."

"Has Nat reached out?"

She huffed softly and twisted the phone cord around her finger. "He has. Yesterday in fact. It seems he'd been hoping to get a little more family oversight on the project, and had been thinking of sending someone in to work as a liaison with H&C."

"Oh splendid. And who did he think might make a good liaison?" Marek teased.

"Wouldn't you know it. He asked me if I'd be willing to serve as an ambassador on the project since I have a home base in Boston. I don't know how you do it, Marek."

"Well, your brother is painfully easy to read and always eager to look smart in front of others."

"Hmm. True. He's very pleased to have my support."

"I should think so. Speaking of support, has your kidnapper arrived yet?"

"She's not a kidnapper."

"No? I certainly remember you saying she kidnapped you," Marek joked.

"She was trying to look out for—No. She hasn't."

"Ah. When do you expect her?" His voice was serious now, and she sensed she had given too much away with her response.

"I don't know. I told her we'd start on the eleventh, so before then."

"I see."

She swore she could hear him smiling through the phone. She didn't want to sound defensive, but still she said, "I think she'll work well."

"I do too."

"Hmm. Then why do I feel like you're, I don't know, having some sort of disparaging thought about it."

"Not at all, Belinda. I'm actually quite fond of the idea of you two running the show. I suppose you don't want a paper trail linking our little friend to Ridgeway, so I'm routing her pay through alternative channels. Nothing for you to do or worry about. It's all very much under control. If Wolf has questions, you can direct her to me. As Mark of course."

"Of course. Shall I give her your number here in Cambridge, or the London number?"

"Give her both. I should be back soon, though. Things are almost finalized here."

"Thank you, Marek."

"Any time, Bel. Ring me if you need anything at all."

"I will."

She placed the phone gently back in its cradle and sat in bed wondering what Marek was thinking. Marek's thoughts were more pleasant to speculate about than trying to manage her own unruly imagination. Her first few days in Back Bay had been acceptably quiet. She walked around the neighborhood and reacquainted herself with the shops and cafes. She carefully avoided the North End and anywhere she might find especially packed with memories of Whitney or Laura. The problem, however, wasn't so much thinking about either of them, but rather a persistent and irritating longing for Wolf.

Wolf stood on the step, tugged at the crisp white cuff of her shirt, and smoothed a hand over her tie. A few cars passed through the street, but other than the light in the window and a lone man walking a Pekingese there were no signs of life. She glanced over her shoulder and tried to shake the nervous feeling creeping up her spine. In the shadow of the doorway, she examined a brass plate affixed to a wall of massive reddish stone. It contained an empty list of what should have been last names next to pearl-white doorbell buttons. She tapped her finger lightly over the surface of No. 4. If she pressed the button and anyone other than Belinda came down, she wanted to have a plan in place. Who was she? Who was she looking for? Belinda Sheridan. Or was it Meredith? The house in the Hamptons said White-Meredith, but Nat was called Sheridan. She couldn't remember.

You're an idiot. She swallowed back her self-recriminations. She'd driven through the predawn darkness toward a woman whose full name she didn't even know.

Fuck it. She'd done stupider things. She pressed the button. There was no sound on her end, but she chose to believe the bell had worked. She waited, running over a number of possible responses to probable questions. Who are you? What do you want?

Despite her overactive imagination and her earnest attempt to think of every possible contingency, never had she imagined having the wind knocked out of her as a good thing, but as her breath rushed from her body in an exquisite release at the sight of Bel, she revised her previous opinion.

"Reporting for duty," she said with an effort to seem calm.

Bel smiled and leaned against the door frame. She wore a matching set of pale gray pajamas, quite open at the throat.

Wolf tried not to stare. "Did I wake you?"

"No, I've been awake for a while, just lounging. You're in a suit." Bel's eyes scanned the length of Wolf's body.

"I didn't want to look suspicious."

"Of course. Come in. I'll show you around."

Bel's first feeling was relief. Somewhere deep inside she had never truly doubted Wolf. The girl wasn't the kind of person to make a plan and then break it. Of course she would show up. Troublingly, Bel realized her relief was merely a product of being together again. She wanted to grab her hand, her face. Instead, she turned and calmly led the way up the stairs, conscious of Wolf's presence, the sound of her boots on the tiles, the warmth of Wolf's gaze on her back.

"You're on top."

"Beg pardon?" Bel looked over her shoulder.

"Your apartment. It's the top floor, right? I saw a light on."

"Yes. You're on 3. We'll have to go to mine for your key." She pushed open a heavy wooden door and stepped onto a landing. The floor was an antique mosaic of pale green-and-toffee gold tiles, edged with white marble.

"Are you serious? Look at this place," Wolf whispered in awe as Bel swung open the door to her apartment.

Whit had bought the building not long before his diagnosis, and the restoration had been on hold for ages. It still wasn't fully completed, but the work so far had been top-notch. Bel took a key from a hook on the wall.

"Bel, I can't live here."

"What? You don't. You live downstairs. You haven't even seen it yet. Let's go take a look." She gave Wolf no chance to argue, and the fact that she didn't try to put up a fight suggested she was open to being persuaded.

They went down one flight and stood on a landing not unlike the one above. Bel turned the key and opened the door. The entryway led into a double parlor with a bay window in one corner and a fireplace against the back wall.

"It's unbelievable, Bel. I can't possibly earn enough to afford this."

"It's part of your pay."

"But—"

"Wolf, I own the building. It's under renovation. I can't rent it out yet, so it costs me nothing to put you up here. Now, here's your key. I don't have a spare, so look after it."

"I will." She put it in the pocket of her suit coat, and Bel tried to keep her eyes from lingering too long on the way Wolf smoothed the fabric protectively.

"I have my first meeting at Ridgeway next week. We'll need to go over a few details before then, but I expect you'll want to get settled in first. Working lunch?"

"All right."

"Good. I'll be back at noon. We can go somewhere that won't require a suit, handsome as it is."

Wolf smiled and Bel showed herself out, feeling proud for having avoided any kind of overt display she might later come to regret.

The cafe was in a part of town dominated by university students. A discordant punk song played from a mounted speaker, and the walls were plastered with Polaroid photos and dollar bills. Wolf wouldn't have imagined Bel spending time in this kind of place, but she seemed familiar with the man behind the counter who took their order.

"Is this one of your hangouts?"

"Artists are a lively bunch," Bel replied.

They took their meal to a table on the mezzanine. To one side a pair of young tie-dye clad women shared a slice of cake and discussed a concert only one of them had attended. One table over, a professor counseled an anxious redhead who seemed insistent on the possibility her literature review was too clunky and incomplete. Aside from that, they had the place to themselves. After a few bites of salad, Bel slid her bowl aside and splayed a black leather portfolio on the table.

"Looks professional."

Bel arched an eyebrow as if she thought Wolf might be teasing her. "Hmm. It's new."

Wolf nodded and kept eating. Bel was uneasy about something, and Wolf sensed it was better not to press.

"The truth is, I know so much less about this kind of thing than I ought to. As you so eloquently pointed out the other day, I have people who deal with these things. Personally, I've avoided it all as much as possible, but now it seems I need to learn quickly."

"How can I help?"

"I don't suppose you understand the ways of corporate intrigue any better than I do," Bel answered with a sigh.

Wolf responded with a soft laugh. She wanted to be useful, but she couldn't deny her own incompetence. She had no idea what they were getting themselves into.

"Are you having second thoughts?" Bel looked more at her glass of wine than at Wolf.

"Not at all."

Some of the tension drained from Bel's expression. "Good. Having you here is helpful. My friends can teach me what I need to know for the boardroom, but there are things you can do that I can't. There are people who will want to talk to you because you're you. And not just in the activist circles, but at the business meetings as well. You're young, you're bright, and you're new. You can ask questions and get to know people in a way that would be almost impossible for me. Do you understand what I mean?"

"I think so." Wolf made a mental note. *Young and bright and new.* She would lean into those traits as needed.

"I want you to build rapport with the local activists. Let them know you're interested in treatment development. Join any medical or treatment groups you can. I'll funnel information to you when possible. I want you to tell me what people are hearing about the new H&C project. Anything about the company or the name SEAFOAM."

"Cait gave me a list of contacts. I'll start reaching out today."

"Perfect. Additionally, I hope you'll accompany me to certain events."

"Are we dating?" Wolf asked with a playful smirk.

Bel scowled. "Hmm. No. Board meetings, any kind of godawful social events the H&C people might invite me to, things of that nature."

"Of course. Happy to spy."

"Good."

"Will you come to the activist meetings?" Wolf asked.

"Probably not. I need to keep a low profile. The H&C people put me through a background check."

Wolf leaned back, a nervous flutter in her throat. "Am I going to uh—need that?"

"No. I don't plan to take you on site. Board meetings aren't held at the labs, and as far as I can tell no one on the business side has been vetted the way those of us with lab access have. Even so, I'll ask around about how assistants are treated vis-à-vis security."

"Thing is, I won't pass a screening. I've got form. Juvie stuff, and a few protest things, nothing major."

"Juvenile crime? Oh dear, Wolf, what did you do?" she teased.

"Slept on a bench."

"What?"

"Nothing." It was better not to talk about the past.

"I'm sure we could get it expunged. I'll ask some of my people about how that works."

"Really?" Wolf's voice raised with the tiniest note of hope.

"Perks of the job," Bel replied as she jotted something in her notepad.

Wolf tried to steer them back toward the matter at hand. "Have you been to the lab?"

"I have; they gave me a tour. It all looks very scientific. I couldn't tell you a thing about it. Lots of white coats and charts. They didn't really explain anything to me, only a tour of the facilities. I think they wanted me to be impressed with the look of it."

"And were you?" Wolf asked, though she could tell by Bel's tone she hadn't been.

"Eh, in a way. But I suppose a lab, is a lab, is a lab. It probably looks about the same whether they're developing skin cream or vaccines. I don't know. I'll be impressed by results. Also, I don't like it when people try to butter me up. It felt—"

"Buttery?"

"Yes. Slick. I'm sure they sent their best PR person to show me around. They know who I am. They know my family. They know I'm the liaison between their facility and Ridgeway. I suspect they also know something of my brother's political connections and ambitions."

"Natty?"

"Right. So they want me on their good side. They want me to send back glowing reports, and I'm sure they've done enough research to know I'm not a scientist or even a business person, so they're probably trying to fleece me."

"Yeah, that seems possible. How will you deal with it?"

"Ah well, as you know, Wolf, I have people. I have friends who understand the business, and friends who understand the science, and friends on the ground who know what's happening with treatments. And soon I'll have a friend with the activists and the patients." She touched Wolf's hand for just a moment. Her skin was cool and dry, but Wolf felt warmer all the same. "Between all of us, we'll sort out what's going on and apply pressure as needed."

"Sounds ominous." Wolf felt a distinct thrill as she listened to Bel plotting.

"I'm hoping it won't need to be, but—" Bel leaned back and held up her hands as if to say *that's not up to me.*

"What kind of pressure?"

"Financial mostly, but I wouldn't hesitate to make a spectacle if need be."

"Protest?"

"Absolutely. But, like I said, I hope it won't come to that. The whole point of being on the inside is to get things done before people have to get desperate. If we do our jobs, there should be no reason for a protest."

"You're optimistic?"

"Atypical, but yes, I am."

Bel walked alone down Massachusetts Avenue, the hem of her long black coat fluttering against her legs in the wind. It was cold and gray, threatening to snow, but she needed to do something to dissipate the anxious impatience coursing through her. After lunch, Wolf had gone looking for a friend of Cait's, eager to make connections and to establish herself with the local activists. She told Bel it would take time to build trust even with the backing of a friend. Bel had thought she might spend the rest of the afternoon reading in bed, but that plan was foiled by an innocuous-looking piece of mail with *Community Health* stamped in blue on the return address.

Bel stood for a time on the landing staring at the envelope in her hand. She had insisted on getting her test results by mail. The nurse had been adamant that an in-person consultation was the standard, but Bel wanted to see it in black and white. *I'll be in Boston*, she said and left an address. That seemed to settle it. Now here was the day of reckoning. That night with Wolf she had been so sure she was negative. Wolf's insistence on safety seemed to verge on paranoia. Even the next day in the clinic her only real concern had been the needle. But as days went on she had begun to wonder. She and Whit hadn't done anything risky in years, but Laura? She certainly seemed cozy with Peter, and God only knew what he got up to. Worry seeped in. Anything was possible.

Standing at the mailbox with the letter in her hand, her legs felt boneless and weak. She wasn't given to fainting, but she leaned against the wall anyway, desperate for support. Somewhere in her mind she thought *I won't let myself waste away*. And the brutal clarity of that knowledge steadied her somehow. She opened the letter and ran her eyes over the text, searching for her results. *Negative.*

A nearly manic laugh burst from her chest, and she sagged back against the wall again and stayed there for a moment just reminding herself to breathe.

"Thank fuck," she muttered softly as she read the letter again. She wished Wolf was with her; there wasn't even time to push the thought away. No, she wanted Wolf there beside her to share this. *I should have waited.* But she knew even as she thought it that she could not have coped with Wolf seeing the word positive, could not have borne being the object of pity and disgust. *Wolf wouldn't.* She knew Wolf wouldn't think those things, but she would and it would have been awful.

Too awful.

Slowly she stood up and brushed off her coat. She needed a walk and so she found herself sometime later briskly moving through a part of the city she didn't ordinarily travel on foot. Around her the walls of factories somewhat fallen into disrepair loomed tall and white. At least one was still in operation, and whatever they were making smelled of warm sugar. Bel took a deep breath and tried to savor the facts. She was moving through an invisible swirling sweetness, she was negative, and no matter what the challenges at Ridgeway might be, Wolf had come to Boston. Bel wished she could paint, but she had left everything back at the shack in an effort to focus on her new profession.

The scent of candy faded away, and the buildings seemed to shrink—still brick and battered, but less ominous to walk between. It occurred to her that Harvard Square must still be a long way off, but a good cup of coffee and a copy of *Le Monde* were now her primary objectives. She kept walking, determined to meet her goal. At the next corner a splash of pink neon light in a dark window caught her attention, and when it dawned on her what sort of place she'd stumbled upon, all thoughts of French news evaporated.

She would never have ventured into a shop like this of her own accord, but today it felt as if she were destined for it. Belinda opened the door and stepped inside. A woman behind the counter gazed up from her work and smiled. She was young and pretty with badly bleached hair and a silver chain swaying from a ring in her nose to another in her earlobe.

"Welcome. Let me know if I can help you find anything," she said as if she were shelving books at the local library and not slapping price tags on a stack of neon vibrators.

Bel simply nodded and walked around the room. The assortment of implements astounded, yet she was looking for something particular. Probably the girl would know where to find it, but what would be the fun in that? Bel didn't believe in the afterlife, not really, but it amused her to imagine how Whit might enjoy watching over this particular moment as she thumbed through a rack of vinyl thongs, each pair a bit more outrageous than the last. He would have loved them. In an instant her throat grew tight, her eyes burned, and she thought she might finally cry. *How ironic.* But no, the moment passed, and she felt certain that Whit would be happy for her.

"We have a sale on the leather ones." The girl tipped her chin in the direction of another rack.

Bel smiled. "Thank you, but I was looking for latex actually. Not clothes per se. I have a friend who is very keen on safety."

It was a little after ten by the time Wolf got back to the house. The guys from the Action Center would have kept her longer, but she told them she needed to be ready for work in the morning. In truth she was exhausted.

A string of sleepless nights, coupled with all of the anxiety of the move, had left her feeling ready to keel over. The brownstone that had seemed so surreal and ominous in the early morning light now looked like a welcome oasis. Wolf's eyes flicked to the windows at the top floor. A gold glow emitted from one, and a shadow passed behind sheer curtains. Bel. She wished she could go up and tell her all about the day she'd had, but that would be weird. She'd have to settle for slumber instead.

Wolf went inside and locked the main door. As she climbed to the third floor, she let herself drink in all the little details of the building. The warm wood of the banister, the citrus smell of polish, the patterns that the tiles made under her boots. Just outside her apartment door, there was a small brown paper parcel. *The planner?* She and Bel had discussed getting a date book for Wolf so they could coordinate meetings and contacts, and so Wolf could look the part of an assistant when the time came. She grabbed the package and opened the door. Inside, the room assailed her once more with its beauty. There was furniture and bedding, and a few books propped on the shelves with plenty of room for more. Her things were still in two boxes neatly stacked just inside the entryway where she'd left them.

Wolf put the planner on the table and poured herself a glass of water. She considered unpacking. If she took those things out of their boxes, what did it mean? That she was staying? She drank and listened to the soft sound of footfalls overhead. She intended to stay, wanted to. Wolf carried the boxes into the bedroom and pulled the lid off the first. It was stuffed with clothes. Blue jeans and T-shirts. All threadbare. A few thermals and mismatched socks. The other was a haphazard collection of notebooks, dog-eared novels, a pile of photos and ephemera she didn't need but couldn't bear to toss away. She put her clothes in a drawer and paused to look out the window at her van. A few flakes of snow drifted through the orange-yellow street light. She was halfway through sorting the second box when the phone rang.

The instinct to say *Violet Mission, Wolf here* was strong, but she caught herself.

"Hello?" It came out like a question.

"Hello. Did you have a productive day?"

Bel's voice in her ear—why had she never considered how it might feel? She sat on the bed, a little stunned.

"Wolf? Everything all right?"

"Yeah, yes. It was good, sorry, just not used to—anything I guess."

Bel laughed. "I know the feeling. I hope it's okay that I called. I heard you come in."

"No, of course. Call anytime."

"So how did your day go?"

"Good. I found the first guy on Cait's list. It wasn't too hard."

"And he's still active?"

"Very. He's running a youth education program and also heading up one of the affinity groups in town. I think he'll be helpful."

It was true. Andrew Cyrus would be helpful, but he hadn't been exactly happy to see Wolf, at least not at first. He'd slammed the door on her and then cracked it open just enough to take a long inventory of her features before calling Cait.

"Excellent."

"He's a bit paranoid."

"Paranoid? Is he—not well?"

"No, he's fine, at least as far as I could tell, but I guess he and his group have had some problems with the police and with people making threats. Apparently, no one wants fags talking to their kids about condoms," Wolf explained, unable to scrub the irritation from her voice.

"Hmm," Bel replied. Wolf noticed she seemed to make that sound in a variety of tones and flavors. This one sounded like sympathetic annoyance.

"Once he was sure I was okay, he warmed up. He took me out to meet some people, and I think one of them has ties with the local clinic. That should help us. I also got a list of meetings that should be exactly what we're looking for." Wolf got up and went to the kitchen, thinking she ought to write those dates and times in the planner. She cradled the phone against her shoulder.

"Very productive."

Wolf slipped the twine off the package and peeled back the paper, revealing a pack of black latex gloves. She didn't say anything, but she was aware of how her breathing changed. *Fuck.*

"Everything okay?"

"Oh, yeah. Yeah, I uh—just opened the—"

"Oh. Did you? I wasn't sure if I got the right size. You should try them on."

"I—I don't want to waste them."

"Why would it be a waste?"

"I—uh—" she swallowed with some difficulty.

"Should I come down and see how they fit?"

"I—yeah, yes. Sure," Wolf replied, unable to think of anything except the deep and intensifying throb, which seemed to be scrambling her capacity to speak. She didn't fully realize Bel had hung up the phone until she heard a knock.

Opening the door did nothing to ease her back to normalcy. Belinda stood in the hall wearing a black silk robe that fell to her mid-thigh, and nothing else as far as Wolf could tell. It hardly seemed fair that one person could be smart, rich, and beautiful all at the same time, but there she was, further proof of the world's cruel inequalities. Bel let herself in and shut the door as her eyes flicked to the box of gloves and then to Wolf's hands.

"Are you tired?" she asked, as if suddenly realizing the time.

"Not anymore." Wolf looked down at Bel's bare feet and tried not to trail her eyes over every exposed inch of skin, but it was hard as hell to look away. *Definitely not anymore.*

"Good. So, try them on."

Wolf opened the box. The smell of latex had never been arousing. It reminded her of sickness, and fear, and sex under duress, but those usual fragments of memory vanished when she slid her hand into one of the gloves Bel had bought for her. This was different. She wanted Bel, and Bel wanted her, and these black gloves looked so fucking sexy stretched over her hands.

"They fit?" Bel inched closer.

Wolf watched the sinuous line of light and shadow along Bel's chest shift and could tell she was breathing a little heavy at the sight. It was wildly satisfying.

"They do."

Bel moved closer still, just inches away. Wolf could smell the clean woody perfume she wore. "Good. I have something else to show you."

"Show me anything."

Bel slipped her hand into the pocket of her robe and pulled out a sheet of paper. She unfolded it and held it up for Wolf to read.

Community Health. HIV Test: Negative.

"So, are we safe?" Bel asked.

"We can be."

"You'll make sure of it, will you?"

"Of course I will."

Bel smiled. A bright almost reluctant gesture, which never failed to make Wolf feel like she'd accomplished something.

"Thanks for the gloves," Wolf said softly.

Bel smirked. "I thought they were the sort of thing a kidnapper might like."

"Yeah?"

"Yes."

"Should I kidnap you?" Wolf meant it as a joke, but her voice was muddled with lust.

"You could try."

Wolf slipped behind Bel and lifted her easily off the ground, delighting in the sensation of Bel's writhing mock resistance. Wolf pulled her closer, one arm crossed over Bel's chest and the other around her waist. Her lips brushed the curve of Bel's ear. "Say the word and I'll let go."

Bel said nothing, but tried to bite Wolf in reply.

"Careful of the gloves unless you want me to use only one hand," Wolf cautioned.

Bel made a low groan then turned her head and sunk her teeth slowly into the bare flesh of Wolf's wrist.

"Good." Wolf tightened her grip. She thought about dragging Bel to the bedroom, but temptation overrode her senses. The couch was so much closer. Wolf detoured to the entryway and hit the lights so they were left in the half-glow of the city.

"Protecting my virtue?" Bel asked in a breathless rasp.

"Hardly." Wolf brought one hand up under Bel's chin and tipped her head back. She ran one gloved finger over Bel's lower lip before kissing her lightly on the neck. Bel whined and squirmed in Wolf's arms. The memory of the train station burst into Wolf's consciousness; the adrenaline of the protest could not compare to the rush she felt now. She knew, too, that they were no longer those people. The woman she'd grabbed in Grand Central had been precious to the movement. Important to Cait. That was all. Now she was Bel.

Bel.

Wolf wanted to stop thinking because every thought floating in her mind seemed dangerous and unspeakable. Thankfully, Bel bit her again, and she focused on the sharp jolt of sensation.

"Are you going to tell me what you want, or should I guess?" She had no shortage of things she'd like to try on Bel, but the memory of Belinda narrating their last encounter charged Wolf with an ache to hear her say exactly what she wanted.

"You're a clever girl. I trust you'll think of something." There was a break in the ordinary rhythm of her breathing as she spoke, perhaps because she felt her legs go flush against the arm of the sofa, or perhaps because she could sense the way Wolf's own breath caught in her chest.

"I can think of a lot of things," Wolf whispered, though in fact at the moment all she could think of was what it would feel like to have Bel wrapped around her, of how warm her body felt through the thin fabric of their clothes.

Bel tried to look back over her shoulder. "Pick one," she breathlessly demanded.

With controlled force, Wolf pushed Bel forward and leaned down over her. "Tell me if you want something else."

Bel nodded. She looked like it was taking a great deal of concentration to remain quiet.

"Say you understand." Wolf ran a hand up Bel's thigh and nipped her ear softly to see how she responded to the pain.

"Ah," she hissed—a breathy note she probably would rather not have made. Wolf felt it echo in her own throat. "I will. I'll tell you. Now are you going to fuck me or not?"

Wolf smiled. There she was—the princess, the commander of spies. "Of course." Wolf trailed soft kisses over Bel's neck and shoulder as she peeled the silk robe away, revealing nothing but the perfection of Bel's body.

Fuck.

The confirmation of Belinda's nakedness beneath the robe was thrilling. She had come to Wolf wanting this to happen. Hoping it would.

Wolf followed the retreating line of silk with her mouth. Tasting the dip and rise of Bel's spine, the curve of her hip, the lonely dark birthmark at the top of her thigh, the hot hollow behind her knee, the long taut muscle of her calf.

"Goddamn," Wolf muttered softly to herself. The floor was cold and hard under her knees, but as she watched her black gloved hands slide up Bel's legs all she could think was *I could worship you.* Bel was shaking but silent. Wolf stood. From this vantage point the faint city light illuminated Bel's face. Her eyes were closed, teeth sunk into her bottom lip.

Wolf let one hand trail over the curving lines of Bel's body as she undid her own leather belt and let her jeans fall to the floor. The sound of metal meeting hardwood broke the silence, eliciting a single trembling gasp from Bel.

Bel had been thinking of Wolf's hands for hours, and now she was about to find out exactly how they felt inside of her. She was shaking and wondered if Wolf could tell. But there was no time to dwell on the question as Wolf's hand slid between her thighs. The gentleness remained, Wolf's mouth a soft sensation against the smooth slope of Bel's shoulder blade, the teasing sway of Wolf's T-shirt-clad breasts against her back, but there was a power and insistence in her fingers that sent an instant knot of light and pressure to the base of Bel's spine. She wouldn't last. She knew she wouldn't, but what did it matter?

"Oh fuck." The cushion muffled her cry. She felt exquisitely captured, bandied between the thrust of Wolf's hips and her hands. Wolf leaned in and bit the tight cord of muscle between Bel's neck and shoulder. That was it. The pain surged and with it the unbearable pleasure of Wolf inside her, against her, over her. She buried her face further into the couch and unleashed a wild note of guttural release. Wolf kept her pace, slowing only when Bel was gasping; then she ran her hands tenderly over Bel's back for a moment before wrapping an arm around her and lifting Bel to her feet.

"You good?" Wolf held her in a softer version of the way she had in Grand Central. Bel gazed down at the vein in Wolf's forearm as it crossed over her chest. A band of olive gold against the bright white of Bel's body.

"Yeah, yes. I'm good." She felt hazy and unsteady. Thankful for Wolf's grasp.

Wolf kissed her cheek and laughed. "Sit down."

The leather of the couch was cool under her and now probably ruined, she mused. Wolf stood in front of her, looking at her, eyes still dark with lust.

"Why do you have so many clothes on?" Bel asked.

"I was busy."

"Hmm. Take off your shirt."

Wolf smirked and pulled off the threadbare T-shirt. "Still like a goddess?"

Yes. "I suppose it's too much to ask you to take those off too?" Bel gestured at the pair of boxer shorts.

"Are you asking to fuck me?"

"Sadly, we aren't the same size glove." Bel held up her slender hand. *Why the fuck didn't I buy gloves in both sizes?*

"There's always tomorrow," Wolf teased. She got on her knees in front of Bel and traced her hand over Bel's calves. The sensation, which might have been soothing in some other context, was also unusually erotic.

"I suppose there is." She shifted her hips slightly, aware of how much she wanted Wolf not just now but, yes, tomorrow.

Wolf kissed Bel's knee before gently moving closer between her thighs and whispering "Could you go again?"

The Darkroom
July 1993

A LOW BANK OF clouds had parked over the city, neither moving nor breaking open but sitting heavily on the tops of buildings, pressing down to the horizon. Wolf drove north at midday wondering when the rain would start. She flicked on her headlights as the road dipped into the Sumner Tunnel. The traffic crept along. Above them the bay lapped and shifted with the tides, but here there was only one way to go. Wolf kept her foot poised over the brake. The blocky lights protruding from the tiled walls blinked in and out of service, casting and then retracting a yellow haze that colored more than illuminated the space around them. The crawl toward Logan was monotonous and the air thick with fumes. Wolf drummed her fingers on the steering wheel. The song on the radio was one she knew by heart without particularly enjoying, but it helped to pass the time.

She wondered if Bel would find it irksome, being met at the gate, but she also didn't especially care. She had gotten used to having Bel around, and a week without her had felt more disorienting than she'd anticipated. Maybe Bel felt it too? It wasn't like her to catch a flight—Wolf knew she preferred the train—but her answering machine message had said she would be in Logan by six.

The short-term parking lot was surrounded by concrete blocks with two points of entry, each manned by a drowsy security guard. Wolf parked the van and slung her camera around her neck. She'd gotten in the habit of taking it everywhere, and the habit had paid off. While her stories didn't get much further than the weeklies, some of her photos had made good money with the *Herald* and the *Globe*. Bel had let her set up a darkroom in the apartment upstairs. They no longer even pretended it was Bel's place—what was the point? Since March they'd rarely spent a night apart. They weren't a couple—neither of them would have called it a relationship—but they were something.

Wolf waited at the base of the escalator. All around her, drivers with little white placards had lined up looking for their traveler. She wished for a moment she'd done the same; they could have made a game of it. As it was, the best she could pull off was paparazzi. She checked her camera against the light. It would be too dark to do much, but she'd manage a shot just for the fun of it. Even something blurry would amuse her because it would be Bel in the blur moving toward her.

A few well-dressed men hurried down the steps, unwilling to wait. Behind them, another small cluster of passengers came into view. Bel stood out among them, the only woman, her short dark hair smooth against her scalp, her eyes hidden behind a pair of dark glasses. She looked the part of a star hoping to remain incognito. Wolf lifted her camera and took aim. The shutter issued its clear report. Wolf advanced the film and slowed the speed a bit more. Bel was closer, halfway down the stairs but still not looking in Wolf's direction. She wanted to wait, to see if she could capture some subtle shift of features. Bel often looked stern, a cool authority in the set of her jaw, the way she turned her head slightly to take stock of the others in a room if indeed she regarded them at all. But when she looked at Wolf, something changed. Wolf wasn't sure exactly what.

The escalator filled behind Bel. A man in a black suit edged his way down at her left side, and she scowled at him for a fraction of a second before returning to her usual unruffled state. The top button of her over-sized white silk shirt was open, and her skin was faintly gold beneath. The color of summer. Wolf focused. In an instant there it was, a curl at the corner of her mouth, a twitch in the cheek. Not a smile, but a shift which changed everything. Wolf's finger pressed the release and the shutter sounded a distinct opening and closing as it gathered the light.

"Really, Wolf?" Bel tried to sound incredulous. She spoke in a low whisper and stood nearer to Wolf than was her habit with other people.

"Of course," Wolf replied. She whispered too, trying to get Bel to lean in even closer. She took a deep breath, wanting to immerse herself in Bel's scent.

"You couldn't wait?"

"I didn't want to."

"Hmm. Very well." She took off her sunglasses and let her gaze pass gently over Wolf's face.

Wolf's apartment on the third floor was larger than the one upstairs. That's what Bel told herself when she occasionally wondered why she spent so much time there. The fourth floor had become a shared workspace, the bathroom almost entirely devoted to photography and the master bedroom transformed into a painting studio, the bed pushed into the living room and unused except for moments, like this one, when she felt compelled to prove to herself she wasn't particularly attached to the reckless anarchist she had dragged east from New York.

Belinda lay on her side looking out at the dusky skyline. There was a trace of electric pink in the clouds, which seemed thicker than they had been even while flying into the city. Murmurs of impending lightning had made travel tense. While in the airport Bel had positioned herself close to the desk, listening intently for any sign the crew might not fly. The thought of a storm delaying her flight made her restless. Flying had never particularly pleased her, but she wanted to come home. And now she wanted to pretend this bed on the fourth floor was what she had meant by home.

For a moment, she quieted her mind and tried to listen as if she might hear through the mattress and the floor the sounds of Wolf doing whatever it was Wolf did when she was alone. There was only the muffled hum of her own blood whirling through her body. Then a knock.

"Coming," she muttered like it was a chore, but she leapt from the bed and was pleased to see Wolf standing in the hall. She forced her face to stay neutral.

"Is it all right if I do a little work? I'll keep it down."

Bel stepped back from the entryway. "Of course."

"Sorry. Don't let me bother you. I can let myself out," Wolf offered. She was playing along, Bel thought, or maybe she was convinced when

Bel said she wanted to decompress by herself tonight. At any rate, Wolf did not linger, but walked purposefully to the darkroom. The sounds from behind the door were familiar and comforting: Wolf prying the canisters apart, the plastic click of the spools as she placed the undeveloped film on them, the snap of the rubber lid onto the developing tank.

"Can I come in?"

"Yeah, it's all in the tank now."

Bel opened the door and stepped inside. She didn't bother turning on a light.

"You missed the darkroom?"

"Have you been busy?"

"Very." Wolf agitated the tank. For a few minutes the soft swish of chemicals over film was the only sound between them.

Bel found she liked being in the dark with Wolf as she worked. The quiet blackness allowed her space to imagine. She closed her eyes and let form and color drift into her consciousness. Wolf poured the chemistry out and turned on the tap. More swishing. Bel sensed Wolf was close to her, close enough to touch if only she would will her fingers to reach out, but she stayed still. Every nerve pulled her toward the warm shadow beside her but her mind remained master over all of them.

Wolf poured out the last of the chemistry and turned the tap on again. The rinse. They could have flicked the lights on at any moment, Bel knew, but Wolf must have loved the darkness too. Bel let her mind drift deeper, listening to the water run from the faucet to the canister, through the spools and over the images waiting to see daylight. Then she felt Wolf behind her, pressed to her, their bodies fitting together seamlessly. Wolf's arm around Bel's torso pulled her closer. She nuzzled her face against Bel's shoulder and kissed her softly.

Bel sighed and leaned into Wolf. The solid strength of her body made Bel want to fall back further, to let go completely, to let Wolf catch her. She kept the impulse at bay.

"Is this all right?" Wolf whispered, her lips moving against the sensitive skin of Bel's neck.

"Yes."

"Can I fuck you tonight?"

"Here?"

"No. Downstairs?"

"No, I'm sleeping in my own bed tonight, remember?"

"Of course." She let her teeth close over the skin of Bel's neck. A light pressure, then a bit more.

"Oh fuck. Now?" Bel asked.

"No. I have to finish this."

Bel groaned and leaned back a bit harder as if grinding herself against Wolf might change the balance of power. Wolf kissed her cheek and flicked on the lights.

"You're always better at restraint than I am."

"You want to be restrained?" Wolf's voice was casual, but the look she gave Bel offered a clear challenge.

Bel could hardly summon a response. If she said no, she was lying, and if she said yes, well, what did that say about her? Wolf opened the developing tank and worked the negatives from the reel. Bel watched her long fingers move through the water.

"Gorgeous," Wolf whispered at the image in her hand.

"What are they?"

"Fire-eating lesbians."

"What? You're just developing those now? Didn't you want to sell those?"

"No, not these. This roll is for us."

"Us?" The word felt wrong.

"The community, you know. Just for us to have, not for sale. I did sell some photos from that day. Why, are you raising my rent?" Wolf teased.

"No. Of course not. What else have you got there?"

"There was a rally this morning over in Cambridge. A bunch of students are organizing to protect student rights in the public schools. I got shots there. Most of the roll is just everyday stuff. Meetings. Hanging out. There was a speaker, some big-shot novelist, I don't know. I tried this new film stock so I can shoot inside without a flash. It looks pretty good." Wolf held the negatives up to the light and turned toward Bel so she could see.

"She's cute." Bel pointed toward a few frames.

"Uh huh. Kelly Westland, no, Westmore. It's in my notes. She's one of the organizers. I wrote an article on the rally. The weekly wants photos.

I wouldn't have interrupted you otherwise." Wolf hung the negatives to dry and unspooled another roll.

A nagging feeling flitted in Bel's gut. Was it jealousy? Wolf owed her nothing, but still it was difficult to face the fact, especially when she was still aching for her touch.

"This one's even cuter." Wolf held up another strip of images. She slid her finger over the dark edge of sprockets just above four frames of Belinda in the airport.

"You're ridiculous."

Wolf hung the negatives and turned toward Bel. "Is that your unrestrained opinion?"

Ridiculous. Belinda rolled her eyes, but Wolf grabbed her by the wrists and pressed her to the wall with a sudden kiss that stole her ability to think of anything except the luscious wave of heat rolling through her body.

"How about now? Am I still ridiculous?"

Bel tried to laugh, but the sound from her lips was more of a gasp.

Wolf tightened her grip. "Besides, what's so funny about admiring a beautiful woman?"

"Nothing," she whispered.

Wolf kissed her, softly this time, though the strength of her fingers still bit against Bel's wrists. The juxtaposition of sensations was so uniquely Wolf and Bel.

"Are you done decompressing? Can we go downstairs now?"

Bel nodded, unsure if her voice would crack.

Wolf kissed her lightly one more time and released her. "Good. I'm hungry. I'll make us something to eat."

The kitchen light was the only one on, and it illuminated the spot by the sink where Wolf ran a dry white towel over the last of the supper dishes. She knew Belinda was getting tired of waiting, but there was something so pleasant about making her wait. Bel's upbringing had clearly trained her to endure irritating situations with grace, but Wolf knew her too well. She could see the strain in the way Bel kept subtly shifting her posture.

"So, what did you want to do tonight?" Wolf watched Bel's features darken just a bit as she struggled to maintain her composure. "I was supposed to teach you something, wasn't I?"

"I don't know, were you? It's been so long now I've forgotten," Bel replied.

"Ah well, maybe it was nothing. I suppose I'd better go make some prints," Wolf said. It was a daring move. Bel might retract her offer at any moment, but Wolf didn't think she would. The look Bel had given her when pressed to the wall had been too raw, too hungry.

"Don't tease me, Wolf."

Bel sat on the leather couch in the center of the room with her legs crossed. The men's button-down shirt she wore hung invitingly open. Wolf didn't want to tease her anymore; she wanted her. "No?"

"Not like that."

"How should I tease you?" Wolf walked closer and stood in front of Bel so she had to look up to meet Wolf's eyes.

"I'm sure you'll figure it out."

"I'm sure I will." She ran a finger under Bel's chin and tilted her head back further. "Serious question, Bel, and I want an honest answer, okay? Any answer is fine, but just the truth."

She nodded.

"Do I need to get a kit or are we good?"

"We're good."

Wolf could feel Bel's breath tremble as she spoke. It was a dangerous game, trusting a lover. Wolf had seen how badly it could go, but Wolf did trust her. And she wanted to taste her, to feel her with nothing between them. "Good. Pass me your belt."

Without a word, Bel reached for her buckle and worked it open. The sound of the leather sliding through the metal made the hair on Wolf's arms tingle. Bel handed it over and began undoing the buttons on her shirt, her eyes fixed on Wolf's. The apartment was warm, perhaps a bit too warm. The weather, which had been threatening rain, had only made the air heavy and damp. Wolf thought about taking off her own tank top, but she knew from experience it would be better to wait. She loved the feeling of Bel frantically pulling at her clothes as if Wolf's nudity was what she needed for her sanity.

"I'm probably going to cum the second you touch me," Bel admitted as she laid her shirt on the floor.

"That's okay. I'll have you more than once."

"I thought this was an exercise in restraint." Bel slid off her pants and placed them beside her shirt.

"Yours, not mine."

The truth was, neither of them was very good at refusing the other, and the belt lashed around Bel's wrists did nothing to change the fact. Hours later they collapsed together on the disheveled bed. Belinda made no motion to leave, though she had insisted over dinner she wouldn't be spending the night.

"I should have taken you with me." She looked toward the window, and Wolf admired her profile in the dim haze of the city glow.

"Is that a subtle way of saying you missed me?"

"No. IV was insufferable asking after you. Wanting to know how the photography was going, asking about your work."

"Really? Natty missed me?" Wolf chuckled. She trailed her fingers lazily over the curve of Belinda's back.

"He always wants what he can't have."

"Your brother wants me?"

"Not like that, pup."

Wolf smiled. "That's good to know."

"He always wants whoever wants me."

"Does he know?"

"Know what?"

"Nothing."

"That I fancy women or that we're sleeping together? I don't know, but I am sure he suspects both. We were not raised to ask those sorts of questions. It's indecorous."

"Clearly."

Bel rolled over and faced Wolf. "There's an exhibition next weekend. Will you come?"

"For work? Like a fundraiser?"

"No, not for work."

"Oh, a date?"

"If you wish." Bel sighed.

Wolf wrestled her into an embrace, which she only half-attempted to wriggle out of. Outside the rain started to fall, and a cool breeze blew across their sweat-dampened skin.

"I'm glad you're home," Wolf whispered.

Bel did not reply, but her body relaxed as she shifted slightly closer.

The museum was as busy as Belinda had feared, but thankfully she recognized no one save for a familiar curator who merely smiled at her from across the room. She could have pulled some strings and requested a private showing, but Wolf was already teasing her about the night being a date. Any plausible deniability would have been shot with a solo viewing. Bel resolved to endure the masses and to keep Wolf at a respectable distance, if only to torment her.

"Are you sure I shouldn't have worn the suit?" Wolf asked as they passed from the entryway into the rotunda.

"You're fine. Didn't you ever go to the Met?"

"No, I mean, I've been by it. Looks pricey."

"Jesus, Wolf, I'll take you when we're back in the city. They have a nice collection of photos."

"Thanks, sugar daddy," Wolf said with an enthusiastic smile.

Bel shook her head, giving every impression of an annoyance she didn't feel. "Come on, the exhibit is this way."

They climbed the stairs. Bel could tell by the cluster of people on the landing above that the show had drawn a crowd. It was no less than the artists deserved. For too long they hadn't gotten their due. Most of the people milling around looked like students. *Just as well.* She remembered with no decrease in bitterness the evening she'd gazed at one of Krasner's drawings while a team of idiots discussed the dubious merit of investing in women's art.

Crowded or not, when Bel entered the hall, it was as if everyone else vanished. Only Wolf remained in the edge of her consciousness, but she secured Bel's full attention with a genuine gasp.

"Holy shit," Wolf muttered.

"A sound of approval?"

"Yeah, I mean look at it!" Wolf smiled at one of the large paintings like she was gazing at the face of a long-lost friend.

Such honest delight colored Wolf's features Bel could have kissed her right there in the midst of the dozen aspiring painters filling the space around them. "I like that one too. Very much."

"It's beautiful. I like your pink and gold one better, though."

Bel leaned over and poked Wolf subtly in the side. "Don't flatter me; we're already sleeping together. There's no point."

Wolf made a face.

The exhibit hall was loud, but Bel refused to be moved. She took her time at each image. The tours thinned out, and soon only a handful of admirers were left still staring at the artwork.

Wolf lifted her camera.

"No flash photography," a stern voice warned.

"No flash," Wolf confirmed for him, and the guard went back to his station by the doorway.

She took a shot and advanced the film.

"Is there enough light in here?"

"Just about."

"Let me see." Bel held out her hand and took the camera. She hadn't taken a photograph in years. Whit's illness had stripped away the pleasure of documenting their lives, and lately Wolf had taken more than enough for the both of them. "Is it all set?"

"Sure, I mean, you can adjust it if you want."

Bel pointed the camera at Wolf; behind her was DeFeo's "Loop System No. 1."

"Should I do something?" Wolf asked, evidently uncomfortable with being on the receiving end of the lens.

"Go on, smile. Show me that little twisted tooth."

"Rude." Wolf laughed.

"No, bless it. I couldn't love you if you were perfect."

"Oh, you love me, do you?"

"Shut up, Wolf."

She smiled, and Belinda snapped a photo.

The Storm
(August 1993)

OUTSIDE, THE SKY FLICKERED with heat lightning. Wolf dozed, only vaguely aware of the cool linen against her palm. The spot where Bel ought to be was empty. The sound of water running in the bathroom permeated Wolf's groggy haze and she tried to remember if she'd rinsed her last batch of prints for long enough. The battery on the timer needed to be replaced. She would do it tomorrow.

"Are you asleep?"

"No. Just resting." She rubbed her eyes. Bel stood naked, toweling her hair in the doorway between the bathroom and the bedroom, a perfect shadow backlit by the pale light over the sink.

"How was the meeting?"

"About the same as usual. Jimmy's man died."

"Tim?"

"Ted."

"I'm sorry."

"It's all right. I think he was probably glad to go. Last time I saw him it was pretty rough." Wolf didn't want to talk about it. Didn't want to explain how the sound of sobbing still pulsed in her head at odd intervals.

"Understood. Any news from the guys on the wait list?"

"Nothing."

"Fuck. I think it might be time to push a little harder. My friend on the board is telling me that they've got over a thousand people on trials, but that can't be so. How could they have a thousand people and we can't find a single one?" The frustration in Bel's voice made Wolf wish she were nearer.

Come to bed. "I know. Something doesn't add up."

They had been patiently trying to sort the situation out for months. At first things seemed to be going well: the drug that H&C claimed would slow the progression of viral replication was in animal trials. A few more grants had been secured to support expanded testing, and in late spring they were ready to move on to human trials. There was no shortage of willing participants. Even with all of the risks attached to participating in a drug trial at this stage, men and some women were lining up to volunteer. At every treatment meeting Wolf had to field scores of questions about how to get on the list or who might be able to bump them up in line. Jimmy had actually begged on his knees for Wolf to get them in. *We'll try anything,* he cried.

Wolf asked Bel, Bel asked the people she worked with, but there was never a straight answer. Two weeks ago, Bel had told her she would give them until the end of the month to prove they were actually conducting trials with local participation. The deadline loomed, and nothing seemed to have changed.

Wolf watched Bel hang her towel. The flashes of light at the edge of the clouds seemed to come less frequently. Bel had spent the night out with a few people who were insiders at H&C, and still she apparently did not have any answers that satisfied her. She turned off the bathroom light.

"I think we're going to have to go public soon. Something isn't right. I can feel it."

Wolf knew she meant a takeover, storming the offices and locking down. Media coverage of a kind that would be hard to spin or avoid. She'd been thinking about it for days. There were plenty of people she could trust with the task. She'd take the lead, and Bel would be there to negotiate on the company's behalf. "What do you think's going on?"

"I don't know," she whispered. She slid into bed and let her leg rest against Wolf's.

"Just tell me what you want done, and I'll make it happen." Wolf turned her face toward Belinda. It was too dark to make out her features, but she could sense Bel looking back at her.

"I know you will."

"You don't have to be there, Bel. It could get rough." Wolf had been wrestling with her conscience over this for days. A protest could shift into a brawl, and she knew firsthand what it was like to be caught in the melee, to be arrested. Of course, Bel had every advantage—lawyers, money, friends in high places—but it wouldn't stop a club in midair.

"I want to be there. If you're there, then I'm there."

In the darkness, Wolf reached for her and pulled her close. She smelled like her fancy shampoo—beeswax and cypress and something else like a hint of leather. Sometimes Wolf caught that smell on her own skin while she was out photographing or trying to pitch stories to the local rags. It pierced and soothed all at the same time.

"Do you have everything you need?" Bel asked, her fingertips tracing lazy circles over Wolf's torso. Bel's breathing in the dark, soft and steady. Wolf felt they might both drift off at any moment.

"Not quite, but we can get it. When are you thinking we'd do it?"

"I want to go to this party first."

Wolf laughed sleepily.

"Barry will be there."

"Barry?" Wolf yawned.

"Barry Elliston. He's a congressman, and now it seems he might be aiming his sights a bit higher. At any rate, he's a friend of Nat's."

"Natty," Wolf mumbled and laughed again. She was far too tired for this kind of conversation.

"Yeah, Natty. I'll tell you tomorrow over lunch, okay?"

"Yeah, lunch is good." Bel's hand ran down the length of Wolf's arm, and she allowed herself to close her eyes.

The train was approaching South Station. Bel watched a group of women dressed in off-the-rack business suits and nearly neon sneakers fidget with their belongings, each readying for their dash to the commuter rails back to suburbia. A real shiver of revulsion passed over her. Whatever her life had become or might become, at least it wasn't that. She sighed and looked away. If she were being honest, she was rather enjoying life lately. It was unusual but true. Bel watched the walls of the tunnel rush by, a great smudge of sooty warm black punctuated with occasional flares of yellow paint and tiny red lights. Another round of passengers filled the car. The train moved on.

Her mid-morning call with Marek had been pitifully brief. She missed him, wished he were closer, or more often in Boston. But he was so busy these days with some London project that he didn't expect to be back stateside until autumn. She suspected he had a lover, but Marek gave nothing away on that matter, though he prodded at every chance for any scrap of information about how she and Wolf were getting on. *We work well together* was all Bel had conceded.

Being so occupied abroad, he didn't have much information to offer on Ridgeway or H&C, but he had heard from Verne that Barry Elliston was indeed planning a bid for senator, and most of the H&C board actively supported his ambitions, not least because his brother Thomas had been their treasurer for years. Marek cautioned her, "Don't get too excited Bel; lots of politicians get support from these kind of businesses." He was right, of course. That was the way of the world. It was all normal, fundamentally normal. Still, where were the patients in all of it? Where were the drugs? She told him about the trials, about the activists and the sick people desperate to get involved. As they were wrapping up their call, Marek said in a soft voice, "You know I support any decision you make. If it needs to be grand, so be it." Grand. Their code for radical action at Ridgeway, a grand affair. Marek approved.

"Watch out for Wolf, though; don't let her get arrested." He still hadn't managed to get Wolf's record cleared and that rankled them both, though Wolf remained untroubled. She seemed to think the notion of a clean record was unlikely at best. Besides, Wolf didn't need access to the lab. Everything Wolf needed was in the streets, activists' apartments, and meeting centers. Still, Bel worried what a record might mean for her in the long run, especially if things at Ridgeway got out of hand.

The train stopped at Harvard, and Bel made her way to the door. The station air—train fumes and close-pressed bodies—dissipated as Bel hurried up the steps and onto the plaza of sun-warmed bricks above. As on any summer day, the place hummed, startlingly alive. Masses of youth, mostly black-clad, but some in every available hue, thronged in the semicircle. Punks, hippies, activists, would-be artists and wannabe vampires—it might have taken her a moment to pick Wolf out of the assembled crowd, but the girl was impossible to miss. She stood on the top of a set of stairs, leveling her camera at a cluster of impossibly young-looking activists trading pamphlets.

Catching sight of Bel, her expression changed. Wolf's dark eyes locked on her. The serious line of her mouth transformed. The moment, instantaneous and then gone, lit a bright ache in Bel's chest. She did her best not to give it heed and simply shook her head affectionately as the young people parted to make way for Wolf who leapt down the steps in Bel's direction. They stood close. Wolf made no move to touch her, but her smile felt like a caress.

"Good afternoon, pup," Bel said softly as they walked together in the direction of the cafe.

"Good afternoon, princess. How was the T? Not too many dreary peasants I hope."

Bel laughed and leaned against Wolf for just a moment. She didn't want to hold her hand, not really, but she couldn't stop thinking of the night before, how Wolf had drifted off mid-sentence, the warm press of her thigh against Bel's. Somehow the memory made her want to be closer.

The cafe around the corner hummed with music and banter. They found a place on the second floor with a good view over the street. The light along Wolf's brow and jaw made Bel think of a painting she'd loved as a freshman. She took out her planner and skimmed the page, hoping it might hone her attention or at least give her something else to look at.

"So, big party tonight," Wolf said over the rim of her coffee cup. Mischief. That was the look in her eyes. Bel adored it, but now wasn't the time for making trouble.

"Very big. You'll go to the tailor?" Bel asked, not rising to the challenge in Wolf's tone.

"Of course. Are you coming?"

"I wish I could, but no. Besides, it's just final touches. Shouldn't take you more than twenty minutes."

Wolf nodded. The dark linen suit had been a month in the making, and Belinda had enjoyed every moment of the process, but today there was a meeting at Ridgeway she couldn't afford to miss. Natty had even phoned ahead to remind her.

"Anything else I should get?"

"Not that I can think of."

Wolf had been marshaling supplies for the action. Duct tape, hand-cuffs, and a few two-foot lengths of PVC they would need to lock down. Wolf said Andrew knew how to make the right kind of blockade link. The kind of thing where the cops would have a hard time breaking them apart. Paint and sheets and cardboard for signs. Cameras and film. Bel tapped her pencil against the planner and wrote *Maps* invisibly over the page. She couldn't be idiot enough to write any of this down, but the motion would remind her. She felt Wolf watching.

"Party planning?"

"No." She took a drink to ease the tension from her voice.

"So, you were telling me about something when I fell asleep. Barry?"

"Elliston. He's been a congressman for a while now, but he's trying for Senate."

"And he's a big AIDS research guy?"

"His brother is on the board at H&C, a friend of Nat's so he's interested."

"Right."

Bel saw tension at the corners of Wolf's mouth. She sensed how it must sound. How it was. Elliston was interested in AIDS for the political clout, for the firepower it gave him in debates, not because he feared it would obliterate his every hope and leave him gagging in the dark. "He wants to meet with the SEAFOAM team privately for a few moments. He's looking for an adviser to take on the campaign trail."

"Natty?"

"God, he would love that, but I don't know. I do know he wants us to bring him up to speed on what's happening with SEAFOAM."

"Will it all be bullshit? I'm sorry, umm, political spin?" Wolf adjusted her diction with a smirk.

Bel shrugged. "Behind closed doors with a political ally? I don't know. I've never been in on something like this. It certainly might be nothing but lies, or perhaps they'll tell him everything as bluntly as they can and leave the PR to his people."

"We'll see."

"Exactly."

"So he's a friend, this Elliston guy?" Wolf asked.

"To whom? Me?"

"No, uh, to the cause I guess?"

"Oh, well. He's a compassionate conservative, as they say."

Wolf made a face.

"We'll have to play nice. Just for tonight," Bel replied.

The waiter passed by and refilled their cups.

"Am I your assistant tonight? I mean, will I be allowed in the meeting?"

"I don't know. There hasn't been any clarification on who exactly is invited. I only know myself and Greg from H&C for certain. It's a different level than what we're used to," Bel mused. She didn't want to discuss the problems with Wolf's record. There was no point. Everything that could be done was already underway. Results would come, she'd make sure of it, but for now—Bel sighed internally and tried not to let her concerns show.

Wolf tapped her fingers on the side of her mug for a moment, clearly considering what to say. Finally, she looked up and met Bel's gaze. "Don't worry. I'll play along. I won't do anything to embarrass you."

Without thinking, Bel shot her hand across the table. Wolf started, unused to being touched in public, but Bel caught her hand and held it. "You couldn't embarrass me."

"Oh, couldn't I?" she asked archly.

"No. I'd have to care about them and I don't."

Wolf smirked, but something in her face still looked as if she didn't quite take Bel's meaning. Bel wanted it to pour out of her skin and into Wolf's blood—*you couldn't possibly embarrass me.*

"I don't care what they think." *Do you see?* Bel wanted to believe she could.

Wolf scoffed. "Me either."

"Good, now let's go over these notes." Bel slowly let their hands move apart.

Again, Wolf's face was radiant with the knowledge of what was to come.

The car moved through the darkness swiftly liquid, sliding around every obstacle seen or unseen. Wolf wanted to move like that. She wanted to be somewhere else. A memory of Bel's moan, the blueprints of the Ridgeway office building, the soft rustle of her new shirt flickered through her mind in a series of waves. Beside her, Bel gazed out the rain-spattered window. They hadn't spoken since the ride began, both too anxious about what might be overheard. The driver was a company man. Natty had insisted. Wolf had left her camera at home, but now her eyes traced the contours and angles of the world bathed in night, spotting over and over again something beautiful she wished she could capture on film. The sensation was strongest when she turned toward Belinda.

"What?" Bel whispered.

"Nothing." *You're beautiful.* There was no point in stating the obvious. Wolf let her gaze run from the curve of Bel's ear, down the sweep of her neck, shoulder, arm.

"Hmm," Bel replied, looking back into the darkness.

"I meant what I said, you know."

Bel turned, her eyes more intense than Wolf had expected, but she kept her voice low. "So did I."

There was no time to say more. The car rolled to a stop.

It was going to be a long night. Wolf sensed it the moment they were ushered inside. The band played elevator music. No one danced. The waiters passed through the room, and Bel grabbed two glasses of wine, handing one to Wolf with a wink.

Over the lip of her wine glass, Wolf scanned the crowd for familiar people. Her capacity for observation served her well. She had become fairly good at approximating the way people behaved in these situations, and she had also discovered an uncanny memory for faces although names sometimes eluded her.

"Your tour guide is here." Wolf tipped her chin in the direction of a voluptuous blonde who worked her way through the crowd in a pinstriped pencil skirt.

"Allison Talcott," Bel whispered, voice laced with dislike.

Allison had been the one H&C foisted on Bel her first day at work. Talcott turned up at nearly every H&C event. She was important, even if she tried to play the giggling hostess.

"She'll be there, I'm sure."

"In the meeting? I wouldn't be surprised," Bel replied, her lips scarcely moving.

A man in a navy-blue suit made a beeline toward them. Wolf didn't recognize him, but the man seemed to know Bel.

"It's been too long," he said. For a moment he seemed inclined to hug her but apparently thought the better of it and shook her hand instead.

Not a friend, Wolf decided by the way Bel's brow tightened. The man shook Wolf's hand, but after that obligatory courtesy his eyes never strayed from Belinda. They spoke about nothing in particular the way acquaintances often do, and Bel broke off the conversation at the first available opportunity to guide Wolf in the direction of Greg Dell.

"I'll tell you later," she muttered as they left. Wolf tried imagining what it would be, a former suitor maybe? He certainly had looked disappointed enough by Bel's obvious lack of interest.

Greg Dell was a familiar face, his position at H&C comparable to Bel's at Ridgeway. He was the one who theoretically ought to know exactly what was going on with the drug trials, but if he did, he gave nothing away. The night dragged on.

Wolf spotted the man who must be Elliston the moment he appeared. A tight and mobile mass of young well-dressed assistants circled around him like flies over shit. *Play nice,* she reminded herself, but it was difficult to imagine how this man could possibly be an ally. She supposed he might have cleared the way for funding of some kind or at the very least not been obstructive, but he radiated a sort of love-the-sinner-hate-the-sin false friendliness.

Bel must have caught her looking his way. She brushed the back of her hand against Wolf's. The momentary contact brought Wolf to attention.

"We had better go put ourselves in Elliston's line of sight." Greg glanced in the man's direction.

"Hmm. Yes. I'll be along in a moment," Belinda replied.

"Of course."

Bel turned, and Wolf followed her down the hall in the direction of the restrooms, feeling this might be their last chance to speak openly before the doors closed between insiders and outsiders.

Elliston had kept her and Greg behind late into the night wanting to look at files and talk profitability and probability. In all of that talk, nothing answered the pressing question of why there were no local men or women with AIDS in the trials. She'd seen numbers. More numbers than she'd been privy to before, but nothing in the binders of data told the story of what was happening with SEAFOAM. Was the project likely to boost shareholder earnings? Yes. Were they seeing results in the trial? Yes, though some were unexpected. Here Greg inserted a monologue of biochemical jargon neither Bel nor Elliston was likely to understand.

The moment Natty's driver deposited them in Back Bay, Bel turned to Wolf. "This Thursday?"

"We're ready when you are."

"Good."

They went inside, and Wolf grabbed her hand and kissed her in the hall. Bel leaned in. The night had been exhausting, and relief washed over her as she locked the door behind them.

"Are you nervous?" Wolf pulled away from their embrace just enough to look in Bel's eyes, searching.

She was. Excited too. "It needs to be done."

"Yeah. But still. It's okay if you're nervous."

Belinda leaned in and kissed Wolf hungrily. "I won't embarrass you," she whispered at last.

Wolf laughed and moaned in equal measure as Bel pressed her body close. They were bound for the bedroom when the telephone rang.

"Shit," Bel muttered.

"It's okay. Take it. I'll go shower."

Marek was on the line, eager to hear about Elliston. She knew it would be him even before she heard his voice. As they debriefed, Bel was distracted and vaguely aware she was thinking of Wolf, imagining herself in the shower. Imagining the way Wolf would close her eyes as

Bel ran her mouth over the divot where Wolf's throat and collarbones collided. Marek could tell she wasn't quite paying attention and finally, with a bit of teasing, let her go.

Wolf stood in the kitchen drinking water, dressed in nothing but a T-shirt, her skin faintly pink from the shower's heat. Bel went to her and slipped her hands under Wolf's shirt.

"We should get you out of that dress." Wolf pressed a finger under the edge of the fabric and slid it further down Bel's arm.

"Zipper."

Slowly, Wolf undid the zipper and the dress fell to the floor.

"I ought to shower."

"I don't mind."

"Oh, I know, but I'd rather wash off this evening first."

"Understood. I'll wait out here." Wolf selected a book from the shelf and flopped back onto the couch.

Something in Bel wanted to change direction: turn back and lie atop Wolf, fuck her until she couldn't speak in sentences, only broken syllables and half-formed groans. There was something so pure in it—a hue. Absolute. Unmuddled. She would paint it someday, maybe when this was all over, and it would be over soon enough. After the lockdown they could go back to New York, or maybe—she stopped herself.

Don't.

Bel walked to the bathroom and turned on the shower. Her muscles eased in the heat, yet her mind wandered down unpleasant paths. Police and prisons and Wolf. What would happen to her in a place like that? What already had? Bel blinked the thought away and scrubbed at her skin. Safety first wasn't a motto Wolf followed in the streets, and Bel had seen enough to know she would hurl herself into confrontation if it came to it.

I'll have to make sure it doesn't.

They'd talked it over. Wolf understood Bel wanted them to generate attention, but nothing more. No damage, no fights. Wolf agreed. Wolf always agreed beforehand, but in the moment when things flared, she rushed in. A low pull deep in her gut reminded Bel of what she would rather not acknowledge: she cared. She pushed that thought away as well and replaced it with a vivid memory of Wolf naked beneath her.

As she dried off in the bedroom and pondered whether she should bother getting dressed, the phone rang again. *Damn.* She threw on a shirt and answered the call.

Belinda found Wolf on the couch, her eyes closed, one hand tucked under her head and the other resting on her chest, which rose and fell with the gentle ease of sleep. *We're going to change the world.* She knew Wolf had a plan. She didn't need the details. She trusted her. In two days they were going to force SEAFOAM into the light. Transparency, if nothing else, would finally prevail. She let her fingers skim over the soft contour of Wolf's shaved head.

"Let's go to bed," Bel whispered.

Wolf mumbled something semi-coherent and slowly opened her eyes.

"Come on, we've got a big day tomorrow."

"And an even bigger one after that," Wolf agreed as they made their way back to the bedroom.

"Come here." She drew Wolf close and lifted the hem of her T-shirt.

"I don't think I'm awake enough for this."

"It's okay." She pulled off the shirt and kissed Wolf's chest once. "Me neither. It's just hot in here," she explained as if it mattered.

They climbed into bed. Bel pulled a thin sheet over them.

"Who was it on the phone? Things okay?" Wolf asked, her voice heavy, her eyes closed.

"My uncle Anders, do you remember him?"

"Mmmhmm."

"He's in town for some reason and asked me out for dinner."

"Mmmhm"

"Go to sleep, Wolf. We can talk about it in the morning."

"Mmkay."

Bel lay in the dark listening as Wolf's breathing evened out into the slow soft rhythm of sleep. There was no chance she'd join her anytime soon. Her mind raced. Anders? Natty must have told him how to reach her. Well, whatever the old man had to say she was sure it wouldn't be of any real interest. Bel had known flirting with the family business was bound to send the wrong message. They had always hoped she might give up what they called her "bohemian life" as if she'd been living in a squat along the Seine. Now that she'd worked for Ridgeway, they'd be trying to pull her in deeper. Anders was the type to try maneuvering her.

Well, one more way I'll disappoint.

She rolled on her side and watched Wolf sleep. There were faint dark smudges under her eyes. Bel knew the last few weeks had been difficult. Wolf didn't talk about the funerals, the dying, not in any detail. Belinda found it a kindness, even as she considered the toll it must take. Wolf talked logistics, and music, and funny things that happened on the T. She talked photography and newspapers, and sometimes politics, though less now than she had when they first met. Part of Bel wanted to rouse her, to hear her voice even in mumbles, but a better part knew Wolf needed the rest. She needed to be at her best for what they had ahead of them. Clear minds and quick thinking were a necessity.

All night, in the ballroom, and then again in the backroom, she had been waiting for them to be alone together. The realization troubled her less than it ought to have. Now here they were. Wolf shifted in her sleep and sighed, the sheet sliding from her. Bel reached out her hand and brushed her fingers tentatively over the curve of Wolf's ribs, down along her obliques. This part of her that rarely saw the sun was so much paler than the rest. Belinda thought of the cliffs along Mallorca, the cool sea caves where the high sun never penetrated. In that secret shelter you could hear the echo of rock and water endlessly tolling. *When this is over—* She didn't complete the thought, but her mind rushed wordlessly through a catalog of warm and beautiful places where Wolf might rest beside her. No cops, no death.

God, Wolf. I hope this works. Slowly she inched closer and let her hand trace the thick knot of scar tissue on Wolf's side. They didn't talk about that either, but Bel knew. *You're so solid but so breakable.* She hadn't even seen the worst of it firsthand, but she knew. She saw the little reminders everywhere etched on Wolf's body. With a sudden jolt she thought of DC, of the moments before Brenda and Cait rushed her out of the crowd. *I've seen clubs coming down on you, and I've wanted to throw myself in front of them, but I can't. I'm not like you.* A sensation like choking forced her to slow her breathing. The ghost of that old feeling, the absolute terror and helplessness of watching Wolf run into the fight she had so desperately wanted to flee from assailed her. They hadn't been anything to each other then, not even quite friends, but she had seen that shining black wall of violence closing around them, had seen Wolf's body vanish in the fray, and she had felt—*something*. She blinked. Forced it back.

Bel looked at Wolf's face, still, soft. She remembered watching her pick dried blood from her hair in a truck stop bathroom. Then again, bleeding as they kissed for the first time. She thought about Ridgeway, about the blueprints she'd brought home. She thought about the way Wolf had studied them, and the way she talked about her plans to shut the facility down. *For the revolution.*

Bel's fingers circled the scar again. *I'm not like you, but I'll protect you.*

"I won't let anything happen to you," she whispered, her lips brushing Wolf's shoulder.

"I love you too," Wolf mumbled in her sleep.

Bel pressed her face to Wolf's body and closed her eyes.

The Second Ask
October 2002

THE AIRPORT WAS SMALL, more like a slowly fading shopping mall than a terminal. Wolf slumped into one of the uncomfortable tweedy benches and pushed at her bag with the toe of her boot. She had flown to Iowa feeling so much. It wasn't hope, not really, but a kind of humming thrill of anticipation. Now she felt heavy and disappointed. Around her the gate crew readied the plane for boarding. A pair of flight attendants in their smart blue uniforms hurried from one gate to another, apparently looking for a wayward pilot who was meant to be at A6. Wolf chewed absentmindedly at a piece of dry skin on her lip, and fought back an overwhelming rush of sadness.

"Well, look who it is."

A voice not entirely unfamiliar drew her gaze. Vic leaned back against one of the benches by the window at A7. She raised her hand in a half wave before hopping up and walking toward Wolf.

"Headed to New York?" she asked, though it was obvious from the sign posted at the desk.

"Yeah."

"I'm off to Chicago myself. A conference on techniques for the measurement of mental distress."

Wolf tried not to make a face, but she felt her muscles betraying her.

"Not everyone's cup of tea, I know. So are you all done with the professor? Did she spill the goods on that whole torrid affair business?" Vic sat on one of the benches opposite Wolf.

"It never came up."

"Oh, disappointing. I thought you were an investigator."

"Hmm," Wolf replied. It was a response she'd deployed over the years as a defense against her impulse to argue when annoyed by someone she was interviewing. Diplomacy had never been her strength, but a well-timed *hmm* helped her get by.

Vic smiled. She clearly understood she was being deflected, but she didn't let it disrupt her come-hither looks. "I wondered if we'd cross paths again. I hoped we would—here take this."

Wolf took the proffered business card and glanced at it briefly. It had all of the standard information arranged beside a very official-looking University of Iowa seal; Vic's number was written by hand on the back.

"If you're ever in Iowa again, give me a ring. I think we could have a nice time together."

The announcement for the Chicago flight cut in.

"Oh, that's me. Well, call me. Safe travels." She hoisted a backpack over her shoulder. As she walked off, she shook out her long blonde hair like a parting shot of flirtation.

Vic's come-ons felt oddly familiar and distinctly unpleasant. While Wolf had always preferred directness, this felt braided with some ulterior motive, something illicit Wolf couldn't quite name.

"The 10:46 flight to New York will be boarding soon. Please have your tickets ready."

Wolf couldn't pin down what was wrong with Vic, but she could name what was troubling her the most. She didn't want to go. She had an interview lined up. She had questions she wanted answers to. And Bel had those answers.

Wolf picked up her bag and slung it across her body. Sandy's publisher brother would have to wait. She wasn't about to pass up her chance. Wolf had been betrayed a number of times in her life, both professionally and personally, but she had never betrayed herself.

The Art Department office occupied the south side of the second floor and smelled strongly of copy machine toner mingled with overcooked coffee.

A low wooden counter separated the staff from visitors, and behind it a woman who wore her hair in a tight helmet of pale brown curls watched over the shoulder of a young man as he frantically typed. Neither of them turned to look at Wolf as she entered, allowing her the opportunity to browse the mailboxes. Coltswood, B. was empty.

"How can I help you?" the woman asked in a warm voice that invited conversation. The plaque on her desk read Sally Feeny.

Wolf turned toward her and smiled. "Hello, yes, I'm trying to find Professor Coltswood."

"I see."

"I thought she would be in class." Wolf looked at her watch as if to emphasize she was aware of the date, time, and ordinary schedule of Belinda's work routine.

Sally plucked a pencil from the can of writing implements and ran the eraser side across the massive calendar on her desk. "Ah, yes. I'm sorry, the professor canceled class today."

"Is that, is she well?" Wolf asked, surprised by the genuine concern she felt.

"I can't say—"

"I'm sorry, I should introduce myself. I'm Deborah Wolf. I'm with the Hirsch Prize. I'm sure you know Professor Coltswood recently won a very prestigious award."

"Oh, yes. We are so proud of her accomplishment. The dean made quite an announcement."

"Yes, I would expect so. Well, as I say, I'm with the Hirsch Prize and I need to speak with the professor as soon as possible."

The woman's naturally thin lips compressed even more tightly and she nodded in understanding. "I'd like to help, but it's not in my power to pass on any personal information about a faculty member."

"No, of course not. Perhaps you could call her on my behalf? We were supposed to have an interview, but it seems I must have got the date wrong." Wolf smiled in a self-deprecating way that often inclined people to help her.

"Well, I suppose I could do that. Let me find the number." She flipped through a massive Rolodex and stopped on a card toward the front of the wheel.

With the smooth practiced motion of a professional, Sally lifted the phone and nestled the curved black plastic handset against her shoulder. She dialed and waited while tapping her fingers lightly on the Rolodex knob. Wolf heard the line ringing and for a moment feared Belinda wouldn't answer.

"Hello, Professor Coltswood. It's Sally from the second floor. Yes, everything is fine. There's a person here looking for you, and they asked if I'd give you a call."

She paused.

"Uh huh, yes. That's right. They said they have an interview with you? I'm sorry, is this something I should have booked on my end?"

Another pause.

"I see. All right then. Yes."

Sally looked up at Wolf and held out the phone. The cord didn't stretch far, and Wolf had to lean against the counter to hold it to her ear.

"Hello, Professor," she tried to keep her tone professional.

"Ah, it is you. Why are you lurking around the secretaries? I thought you were supposed to be hobnobbing with the publisher."

Wolf had to admit it wasn't the most cordial greeting, but Bel's note of playful harassment amused her. "I didn't want to miss our interview."

"Is that right? But we never arranged a time, so how could you miss it?"

"No, I know. But I thought perhaps we could finalize a time. I have quite a bit of availability just now."

"Since you blew off your publisher?"

"Right."

"Well, the problem is, I'm not in Iowa at the moment, so I suppose that may put a kink in your works."

"You're not?"

"No."

Wolf dug her notebook and pencil from her bag. "Where are you? I could come out and meet you."

"Hmm, could you? Well. What a gracious offer. The funny thing is, I'm in my studio."

"Your studio? Where's that?"

"Oh, I'm sure you remember the place."

The realization made Wolf want to both laugh and groan. "In New

York? Are you in Manhattan?"

"Indeed."

"Were you following me?" Wolf whispered into the phone, hoping Sally was as distracted by her data entry as she was pretending to be.

"Clearly not, since you're in Iowa."

Wolf couldn't argue with that. "So, when should we meet?"

Belinda sighed. "I have things to do this Saturday. I could meet on Sunday night."

"Sunday night. Okay. Eight o'clock?"

"Make it seven, I have to get back to teach eventually."

"All right." Wolf jotted down the date and time.

"Do you remember the way to the scene of the crime?" Bel deadpanned.

Wolf held in a laugh. "Sure."

"Okay. See you then."

The line cut off and she shook her head.

Classic.

The First Question
November 2002

REARRANGING THE FLIGHT PROVED simple enough. Tom's secretary took Wolf's excuse of a faulty rental car in stride and arranged a dinner with Tom, who was apparently a big shot if his choice of restaurant was any indication. He met her at a swanky bistro in The Village, perhaps trying to bolster his credibility as an ally. But by the way the staff greeted him, it seemed possible he was a regular.

They went through the usual round of small talk. The unseasonably warm weather, the challenges of flying, the nice things Sandy had said about Wolf. As soon as drinks arrived, Tom launched into business. "It is a remarkable project. There's a market for it these days, much more than people realize, I think, but we've always been a bit ahead of the trends."

Wolf didn't respond, but a small muscle twitched under her jaw.

Ahead of the trends.

She took a long drink of water and raised her brow just enough to let the man know she'd heard him.

"I appreciate the chapters you sent. Captivating stuff. And from the looks of it, you've collected so many interesting stories in this piece." Tom paused, perhaps testing how Wolf would receive the compliment.

Bel had once advised her to be suspicious of flattery in settings like these, and she found the advice easy to follow. Wolf was naturally skeptical. Tom waited, clearly wanting a reply.

"They did amazing things under duress."

"Yes. I'm almost too young to remember it, you know."

He wasn't. He looked at least her age, probably five years her senior. "Hmm." It was all well and good to be interested now that things seemed better, safer, profitable.

"I'm very excited to see the final draft. Sandy tells me you're still conducting interviews, but if you could get us the draft before the holidays it would be great."

Wolf thought it was interesting how much he presumed she would want to work with him. She supposed it was an unusual position for an author to be in, getting wooed by a publisher instead of clamoring for a scrap of attention.

"Not to worry."

"Did Mary mention our timeline?"

"She did."

"Wonderful. I'm so excited for this one. I think it's terrific."

Wolf forced a smile, her focus almost entirely on her impending meeting. From their table at the window she could see the corner of Broome Street.

The waiter inquired about their interest in dessert. Wolf would have gladly passed on the opportunity, but before she could summon some diplomatic refusal, Tom put in an order.

The waiter looked at Wolf.

"Just coffee for me." She fought the urge to leave and ignored the phantom sensation of moving through the city darkness, pulled in the direction of Belinda Coltswood.

Her mind was so fixed upon the moment that when it finally came, it felt surreal. She had been to this building exactly twice in her life, but she found her way with ease, every step reminding her of that first time when she and Bel had walked from Audrey's talking about protests, politics, anything but the kiss they'd shared. It was certainly ironic. Here she was again planning to repeat the process. Wolf paused in the doorway and mentally ran over a list of interview questions. She had been refining them over the past eight months, and always ran through them right before her interviews. Doing so now, she pretended there could be something ordinary about what lay ahead.

Wolf ignored the tremor in her hand as she raised it and pressed the button for Bel's loft. The buzzer sounded, followed by a click from deep in the metal door jamb. Wolf went inside. The building had hardly changed, though the old freight elevator had been redone and seemed more welcoming, less likely to hold her captive.

Deep breath.

Her heart raced. *Don't freak out,* she scolded herself. She was too seasoned, too experienced to be unnerved by Bel. She wanted this interview; she'd been willing to blow off a publisher for it. The only thing to do was carry on. The elevator stopped. She opened the door and saw Bel waiting for her on the landing.

"So you did remember the way." Bel ran a hand along the nape of her neck and dropped it casually to her side, three slender silver bracelets chiming together.

"Of course, how could I forget?"

Bel blinked slowly, and Wolf wondered if it was a gesture of surrender or recoil. Either way, it was impossible that Bel had forgotten either. She'd called it the scene of the crime after all.

She opened the apartment door and stepped aside. "Come in. Wine?"

"Why not."

Belinda poured her a glass of something red and motioned to the couch, which hadn't been there before.

"I can get you a chair if you prefer."

"No, this is fine." Wolf sat down and took out a small tape recorder.

"We need to have some ground rules, don't we?" Belinda asked. She sat at the other end of the couch and turned her body toward Wolf. She seemed remarkably more like her old self in this setting, or perhaps in this room Wolf was unable to separate the woman in front of her from the woman she had been years before.

"Yes. Of course. May I?" Wolf nodded toward the recorder, and when Bel agreed she pressed the button. "It's November third, and I'm speaking with Professor Belinda Coltswood. You were saying you'd like some ground rules."

"I would. I can pass on any question. If I decide I don't want to do this anymore, we stop and you give me any notes or recordings you made during our interview process."

"I agree." It was no different than what they'd established beforehand, and Wolf felt at ease with the arrangement.

"I also wondered something."

"Hmm?"

"Are you in the book?"

"Am I? Well, I'm the author. I mean, I'm everywhere in the book," Wolf replied with a measure of uncertainty.

"Right, but how is the thing arranged? Is it word-for-word interviews?"

"No, it's a narrative based on interviews. I had it arranged by interviewee originally, but I might change that, I have some other ideas."

"Ah. Right. Well, what I'm curious about is whether or not there'll be some of your story in the book. I mean, if I'm worth interviewing, surely you are too."

Wolf made a face.

"That's my ground rule. You interview me, and I'll interview you. If you have a specific set of questions, I promise to follow it to the letter, but if it's more free-form, well, I'll come up with something."

"Bel, I'm not—" There was no point resisting her. Not now. "Oh, fine. Sure, okay."

"And it goes in the book." She glared at Wolf over the rim of her wine glass.

"Fine. Yeah, why not."

"Wonderful," Bel smiled. "Go ahead and ask me a question."

Wolf sipped her wine. Before it hit her palate, she knew it was strong. Bel always could outdrink her. She'd need to watch herself if she wanted to stay in charge of the process. "All right. So, I'm sure I don't know the full extent of your work during the '80s and '90s, but I know you were in the city in the early '90s and supporting a variety of activist endeavors around HIV/AIDS. How did you initially get involved?"

Bel looked at her in a flat way. Not as though she wanted a fight, but she simply wasn't amused. "You know how. Why waste time?"

People often bristled at this question, but she had decided to keep it first in her rotation nonetheless. Not because she wanted a contentious relationship with her interviewees, but rather because she preferred to get what was often the most difficult part over with first. She leaned back against the arm of the couch and kept her voice level. "No. I never asked you and you never said."

Bel's face contracted slightly as if she were scanning a part of her memory she had let lie dormant for years. "Hard to believe."

"I know, but it was the kind of question we didn't ask each other. It felt like too much. If someone wanted you to know, they would say. You know how it was. People were always giving testimony so you often did know how folks got involved, but for those who didn't offer the information, we never asked. I certainly never asked."

There was a long pause, and Bel nodded. "Hmm. Yes, I suppose you didn't."

"Never."

"I assumed you would have heard from someone. People certainly knew. Cait knows."

The fact wasn't shocking. Cait and Bel had been friendly for a while before Bel decided Wolf was worth her time. She wondered and found it difficult to tell whether Belinda was trying to wound her with this. It hardly mattered. "Cait wouldn't tell a story that wasn't hers."

"No, I suppose not. And all our time together it never came up? I just—"

Wolf understood her disbelief. They had shared a great deal, and they had taken risks together. "It felt sacrilegious to talk about what came before. I don't think we talked much at all about our lives before. We talked about the work and the research, and bail, and treatment, and what to eat, but never much about our lives from before we worked together."

"Worked together," Bel quietly scoffed.

"You know what I mean."

Her shoulders stiffened, her impeccable posture restored. She drank before replying. "Of course. Does it matter?"

"I don't know. I think it does. I think it's an interesting thing how many women were involved, particularly lesbians."

"Is your book all lesbians?"

"No. Would that bother you if it were?"

"Not at all." She held Wolf's gaze for a tick longer than was customary.

Wolf made no reply, but was glad for the insight.

"I suppose most people got involved for the same reasons. Either they were sick or they knew someone who was sick," Bel mused and took a long drink.

"That's fairly common, yes. Is that what got you involved?"

Bel nodded.

"A friend? A family member?"

She shook her head and sighed. "My husband, Whit. Don't look shocked; it was one of those things. Two wealthy queers who needed cover and the legitimacy of marriage to ensure their fortunes. A story old as time."

Perhaps it was a story old as time, but Wolf had never heard it. "You were both in the closet?"

"No, not really. I met Whit when I was eighteen. I think I knew what I was, but it hadn't occurred to me to do anything about it."

"No?"

Bel shrugged. "Whit was a professor of art history. A medievalist, fascinated by walled cities. Anyway, he asked me on a date and I accepted. We went to a gallery opening. Basquiat—can you imagine it? A medievalist at The Fun. You probably don't remember the place, but I would never have imagined it myself. Still, that's where he took me. And he was so charming and generous. It was impossible to not like Whit."

"So you married a professor?"

"I did. It's funny, I feel like I'm living some strange shadow of the life he left. He didn't need to teach. He did it for his own amusement. I think he enjoyed being around idealists, and no one is more idealistic than a university student."

"Is that what you enjoy?"

"Pfft. Hardly. I find their optimism tiring at best and often galling, but as I said, my life is a shadow of his. He was the golden child, and I'm, well, not. Not by a long shot. Still, they are rather compelled to keep me with all of the money I funnel into them." A wry smile contorted her lips.

"The university?" Wolf clarified.

"Of course."

Wolf shook her head and made a note. Somehow, she was never worldly enough to understand Bel's life or the kind of wealth that upheld it. "When did you marry?"

"We waited a year. Like I said, he was a perfect gentleman. Never pressing me to do anything I didn't want to do. Probably because he didn't want to do it either. I appreciated that, and, more importantly, he took me seriously. He offered me opportunities to be in the room with other artists. Do you remember the painting I showed you in Boston?"

"*The Huntress*"?

Bel laughed, a real laugh this time, not her usual scoff. "No, not that one. The one I photographed you with."

"Oh, of course, yes, I remember." Wolf thought it had been one of the better nights of her life, though she had often tried to forget it.

"He took me to Oakland to meet the artist. I was so enamored. Like a lovesick child, and Whit knew it. I think he saw it for what it was. Much more than professional admiration, but a crush in every sense of the word."

"Did you sleep with her?"

"Is this for your book? Or simply a prurient curiosity?"

Wolf smiled, caught out. "The latter."

"No, not a chance. I could hardly speak with her, but it was a wonderful experience all the same. It was the kind of thing that can sustain you through a difficult time: the idea that you've been close to greatness, even if you can never compare."

Wolf wanted to remind Bel that she had accomplished what many others had failed to, but she knew better than to say anything of the sort. Bel would brush her off or, worse, think Wolf was an idiot for suggesting a prize was the same as greatness.

She looked down at her notebook. "You said 'he saw it for what it was.' Did he know you were gay?"

"Ah, well. I think so. I think he figured it out long before I did. It was probably part of the attraction. But I remember the night he told me he knew."

Wolf waited. It seemed Bel might not say more, but then she went on.

"We were at an opening. Some colleague of his. Dreary paintings, but people turned out in droves regardless. All night I was milling around trying to make the best of it. Whit was surrounded by admirers, and at some point I saw him talking to one of the servers. I couldn't hear him as he was across the room, but something in his posture told me what was happening. Later that night he was helping me out of my gown and I asked him."

"If he was gay?"

"I asked if he fancied the boy serving wine. He smiled, so indulgently.

I think he was happy I'd caught on. He said, 'Of course I did. He was beautiful. Didn't you?' Well, I didn't reply right away. I was processing it, I suppose, and Whit touched my shoulder and said, 'But you don't really feel that way for men, do you?' Just as plain as could be. After that night, we were closer than ever. All of our pretending we wanted an heir and fumbling around once or twice a month went away and we were friends. Great friends. We did whatever we wanted. We enjoyed ourselves."

"What year was that?" Wolf tried to imagine Belinda as so young and naive. It seemed unthinkable.

"Oh, umm, '83 I suppose. We hadn't been married long."

"Were you worried?"

"About what? Being outed?" She looked incredulous, but Wolf thought even that would have been a fair question given the time.

"No, AIDS," she clarified.

Bel breathed in deeply and shook her head. "No. I should have been. Looking back, I can see how I should have been, but I wasn't. I never even thought about it. It wasn't until Whit got sick that I really—No."

Wolf made a note.

"I should have been," Bel repeated softly as she lifted her wine glass. She was thinking about something far away.

Wolf said nothing. She agreed of course from this vantage point, but had she been any wiser before sickness made its way into her own life? No, she'd never given it a second thought.

"I didn't start worrying until after I saw what it did to Whit. Then I was looking for signs everywhere."

"Signs?"

Bel nodded. "In the faces of our friends, people I knew who had the same tastes, maybe even the same lovers. I was terrified for them."

Wolf knew the feeling. This part of the interview always brought it back—the simmering panic residing in her bones. It lived in her silently, and when she listened to another person acknowledge their terror she felt her own flare. Somehow, she hadn't fully considered what it would be like to hear Bel talk about her losses. If she had, she might not have gone through with this. But here they were.

"You must have gotten numb to it," Bel hazarded without accusation or bitterness.

"No, never. I just live with it. It helps to know nothing lasts. Good or bad."

Bel huffed softly as if she couldn't quite agree, but wouldn't push it.

"You mentioned friends. Did you have a lot of gay friends?"

"Hmm, it's an interesting question. There were men around, men I'm sure were gay, are gay, but there was a code of silence, too. And Whit honored it, more or less. So we did and we didn't. I didn't know any openly lesbian women until after Whit died."

Wolf couldn't control her expression. She looked and felt incredulous.

Belinda shrugged. "I know. It seems insane. Of course, we had connections in the art world, and that crowd was more open, but they weren't really our inner circle. And they were almost all men. I did know women who were gay but not openly so. I dated a number of women, but all in secret. Always very discreet."

The way she hissed that final word was full of bitterness. Wolf clicked her mechanical pencil.

"I—"

Whatever Bel had thought to say, she stopped herself. Ordinarily Wolf knew how to move things along, what buttons to press, how to crack someone open, but in this context it was difficult. She wanted to know and was afraid to ask, afraid Bel would withdraw, and refuse to go on. She steered them back to safer waters.

"You said he took you seriously. About art you mean?"

"Yes. My parents thought it was a joke. Painting. They never approved. Whitney thought I had potential."

"He was right," Wolf replied without thinking. Bel's face registered her pleasure and her immediate dismissal of Wolf's comment.

"Maybe. It doesn't really matter, I suppose. If I'm good, or only a dilettante, it makes no difference."

Wolf wanted to pursue the question. While she mentally ran over the best possible approach, she let her eyes linger on a painting across the room.

"What?" Bel asked, a hint of confrontation in her voice. They knew each other well enough for Wolf to recognize the tone. Bel had sensed Wolf's disagreement, and she wanted to have it out. Not a fight so much, but a debate.

"Nothing. I don't remember that one." Wolf gestured toward the far end of the room where a canvas hung against a bare brick wall. It was mostly black with hints of blue-green and slashes of gray that seemed to flow outward and draw back in at the same time.

"It's newer."

"Yours, though."

"It is."

"What's it called?"

"*The Urchin.*" Her voice was cool and matter of fact.

"Hmm." Wolf tilted her head from side to side, admiring it.

"Oh, that's the good hmm," Bel observed.

"Yes."

"Do you still do the other one? The um, oh, what did you call it?"

"The diplomatic hmm."

"Yes."

"Of course. It's very useful," Wolf replied.

"I'm glad."

Wolf set down her wine glass and walked across the room to look more closely. There were fine threads of gold she hadn't noticed before in the overwhelming darkness. "It's sad."

"It was a difficult time."

"Do you want to talk about it?"

"No. Not really," Bel replied, the fight having gone from her voice.

The Urchin
February 1995

THE HALLS WERE EMPTY; not even the graduate students lingered. Bel locked the office door behind herself with a sigh, amazed by how she could become accustomed to some things—the dark, the quiet, the loneliness. It seemed to almost suit her. Outside a heavy snow had barely been cleared away from the walks and roads. No pedestrians, no bikes. Only an occasional vehicle hazarding to pass by. Her house would be empty too, and if it hadn't been for the want of wine and a soft bed, she would not have bothered leaving the office at all. But she had a certain set of requirements, and those could only be met in the understated bungalow she now pretended to call home.

She straightened a pile of papers and shoved them into her bag, wondering why she had bothered assigning her Introduction to Painting students an essay. But she had, and now she faced the consequences. The next few days would be filled with nothing but pretension and awkward prose.

And wine.

Outside, the city had a haunted quality. The sky dropped even more precipitation, a sleety mix. She moved with a tight careful stride, painfully aware she should have called for a cab. By the time she arrived she was more than ready to end the day, but Marek would ring soon enough. It was time for his weekly update on her fortunes, which, despite all appearances, were doing well. She hung her damp wool overcoat in the entry hall and pulled off her boots. Everything ached. She paused to massage a bit of warmth back into her feet before putting on a pair of slippers and heading to the kitchen and the wine rack, the only testament to the life she had abandoned.

No, not abandoned.

This resembled exile more than abandonment. Though maybe it wasn't even exile. After all, no one could force her to stay in Iowa, but staying did not feel like a choice either. She worked the cork from a bottle and pushed away all philosophical questions regarding her geographic location.

She would spend tonight the way she had spent hundreds of nights before. Her sense of indignation had lessened over time, but there was always a moment, often preceding her first drink, when she had to ask herself if she'd done the right thing, was doing the right thing, and did any of it really matter anymore? Marek would call and run some numbers; then he would tell her to go back to New York or to start over in London. He said it as an offering, an attempt at inspiration. She supposed it was the talk of a man who did not understand how she needed desperately the punishment and refuge of Iowa. A memory-less place, at least for her—a place where she could live without being alive.

Even after these eighteen months, she remained an outsider with no connections beyond those forged by the ruts of lives running parallel—the familiar barista, the usual checkout clerk. There were also the tenuous professional links maintained by force of habit—the people in her department whom she was compelled to meet with every month, the glad-handing dean who tried to invite her to every donors' event. Then there were the students, some of whom verged on acquaintanceship. However idiotic she sometimes found them, there were a few committed to their craft, and an even more select group who actually possessed talent, for all the good it would do them without money and friends in high places. She supposed someday she might become one of their patrons, but thus far she had refrained.

Having waited barely long enough to start feeling bitter and maudlin, Belinda sipped from her glass of Château Cheval Blanc. The drink eased her mind and helped her to endure Marek's call. She even managed to laugh at his story of a chance encounter with Michel in Paris. It was funny, but the tale affirmed her decision to stay, knowing how easily paths might cross even in a city of millions.

Again, she assured him she was fine, and he assured her there was money enough to do anything she wanted. The conversation went nowhere. She advised him on donations, approving almost anything he suggested, but always resisted the urge to ask questions about New York and their ongoing philanthropy there. With the usual reserved expressions of fondness they would end the call. "Take care, Marek." In those words were every hope for his happiness, his safety, his joy. Things she could and would never say, and which he returned in the same constrained manner. "You too, Bel."

Weeks later, with the sky a bit paler and the weather a tad warmer, they repeated the call with uncanny similarity. It was Chicago on Marek's mind then.

"Come to Chicago for a week. We could catch a show."

They had not seen each other in so long. Not since London. She would not go.

"Sorry, but the term is in full swing."

And she told him to take care and he said, "You too, Bel."

She intended to.

But through no fault of her own, the connections she sought to escape had closed in around her in a most unnerving way. Two days after their call, she'd sat on the back patio of her little Iowa house and watched the clouds turn from gold to violet to darkness, knowing the distance she'd surrendered to could not help her, because in what felt like a Grecian twist of fate, Laura Worthing was in Iowa.

"Oh my God, Belinda, is that you?"

She had known that voice without turning. She'd felt the snare cinch around her.

"I can't believe it; look at you!" Laura wrapped her arms around Bel and pulled her close with a carnal familiarity that would have been more than welcomed years before but in the moment turned Belinda's stomach.

"Laura. What are you doing here?" She had stepped back just enough to maintain politeness while also making space between them. It was the sort of discreet posture Laura herself had always insisted upon in public.

"I'm the writer-in-residence."

Of course.

The school was known for its commitment to creative writing. There were always authors hosting workshops, readings, courses. She should have known this might happen one day.

"I'm so glad to see you, Belinda. It's been entirely too long. Never mind me; what are you doing here?"

It was too much of a question. The real answer was not something she would ever share, least of all with the likes of Laura-fucking-Worthing. "Working in the Art Department."

"Oh wonderful. I'm so pleased to have a friend in town."

The irony astounded. No mention of Whit, no acknowledgment of the last almost seven years. Belinda knew how to play this game, but she wasn't sure she could. After that first chance encounter she avoided anywhere Laura might be, but the sense of inevitable collision loomed. For better or worse, some things could not be avoided.

When their paths crossed again, they were both drunk. Bel hated herself for being there. She hadn't even wanted to go, but some sick curiosity had driven her to the party. The moment Laura smiled at her from across the room, Bel knew she would pay dearly. Perhaps she deserved it. Laura was in her element, surrounded by people who were fawning over her latest book and clamoring to know about her next project. She held a glass of white wine in one hand and gestured with the other. Her admirers nodded and smiled. Bel wanted to slip out, but she was cornered by one of the museum curators who had helped dress the room for the event.

"Do you think the paintings are too much in this space?" he asked with a real desire for Bel's opinion. It occurred to her he might be flirting. His eyes strayed from the two bright abstracts to the exposed skin of her collarbones. She stifled a laugh at the utter ridiculousness of the moment. A reception in a beautifully appointed university building. Her former lover, the one she had believed would be her everything, leaning against the hearth a mere yards away, and a man she'd never give a second glance staring at her chest.

Oh rich irony!

"I'm sorry, is it funny that I asked?" He pushed his glasses up his nose. They were wire-rims, round like Marek had worn to the activist meetings.

She had laughed without realizing it. *So much for self-control.* But before she could answer him, Laura put a hand on Bel's arm, effectively dismissing the man in her very particular way of sending lesser people off without a word.

"I thought he might be pestering you," Laura whispered as she leaned in so close Bel could veritably taste the floral notes of her skin.

"He's harmless, just a professional chat."

"Oh, Belinda, you always were oblivious to how men want you. It's as if your lack of interest in them has blinded you entirely."

She smiled and Bel felt the familiar pull between them. She was sure if she had been sober she would have found a way to tactfully extract herself, but under the influence of one too many glasses of middling chardonnay, she found she didn't back away.

"These things always bored you to death," Laura mused. The warmth of her hand around Bel's wrist seemed to feel suddenly all-consuming.

"I've learned to manage."

"Beautifully," Laura replied. She raked her eyes over Bel's body. However well Belinda managed to tune out the attention of men, she was painfully aware of Laura's gaze.

A waiter passed by with a tray of drinks, and Bel took another. "How's Peter doing these days?" She wasn't sure what she wanted from the question, but Laura's sharp laugh surprised her.

"Oh, hang him. We've been split for ages. Belinda, it has been too long." She sighed the last sentence and inched closer.

It was easy to give in, especially knowing how badly it would end. As a rule, Bel hated reminders, but she let Laura into her bedroom with an almost deviant craving for the night to scrawl itself all over the walls. What better than to remember how foolish she could be? Perhaps it would help her down the road. Sleeping with Laura now was no different than it had ever been, save for the fact that Bel no longer loved her. She knew the moves she was expected to make, and she made them. If she was out of practice or too intoxicated, it hardly mattered. Bel's body remembered what to do. Years of hopelessly pursuing Laura had seen to it. When she'd had enough, Laura hopped up and went to shower the same way she always had. Bel sighed and sprawled out on the soiled sheets, feeling hollow.

You get what you deserve.

A few moments later Laura emerged, wrapped in a towel. Smiling. Sated. Water dripped from the ends of her hair. She nodded toward the bathroom, which still emitted a haze of steam. "All yours."

The water was too hot, but Bel made no adjustment, hoping the discomfort might fend off a memory that welled up from the depths of her subconscious and threatened to swallow her.

Laura. Laura.

She forced herself to think of the woman she'd just serviced. But Laura was not a candle driving out darkness. She no longer had the capacity to override Bel's senses. The memory was unstoppable, and the face behind her eyelids was not Laura's. Bel slid a hand between her thighs and tried again to fix her mind on any detail she could, anything at all that might edge out what was flooding in. The water streamed scalding down her body as she came and remembered.

A gasp. A sob. And there was no escaping the regret and revulsion tearing through her. Still, even in the moment, she knew she would do it again.

Bel stepped out of the shower and looked at her reflection. Did it show? Would anyone looking at her know how awful she felt? How sick with herself? And how perversely justified? There was a sad shadow under her eyes, but all in all she looked fine. She passed a towel over her hair and put on a robe.

Exiting the bathroom, Bel paused. Laura stood at the dresser. She had a wooden cigar box open in front of her, riffling through the contents with a light whisper of amusement curving her mouth.

"Belinda, who are these people? My goodness, look at them." She waved a black-and-white photo.

Bel stepped closer. Generations of good breeding and years of careful training prevented her from screaming *leave those alone*. "Just reference material. I think we should probably call it a night. I have class tomorrow."

"Of course," Laura agreed, but continued to flip through the photos. "My God, look at this little urchin! What a face!"

Laura held up a photo of Wolf and laughed.

The Follow-up
November 2002

BELINDA WATCHED WOLF EXAMINE the painting as if she were she reading fine print. Her dark eyes narrowed, focused. Could she see it? Was it plain how much the picture contained everything Bel could not say?

I missed you. I miss you still.

But you can't say something like that to a person you left behind. You have no right. Belinda took a slow breath, and drank.

Maybe Wolf could read it in the places where the palette knife had bit through every layer of pigment, or maybe she saw nothing at all, only an interesting arrangement of colors. Bel supposed she'd never know. Though Wolf had given her the chance to explain, how could she?

"Whit bought me this place." She hoped at least she could give Wolf what she came for, an interview. Something interesting for the book, though she couldn't see how she mattered enough to be included. There had been so many others who had done so much. Bel had just tagged along.

"This place? The loft?"

"It was an engagement gift."

"Hell of a gift," Wolf replied. Her eyes moved across the room.

"It was. I was quite won over. I thought even if I couldn't love him the way I was supposed to, I'd be well cared for, and I'd always have this."

"But you did."

"Love him? Yes, absolutely. Especially once we could be ourselves."

Wolf looked at her notes. "You said you enjoyed yourselves. What was life like once you both knew?"

"Oh, it was lovely. Whit was always traveling for business and I went along. We sailed, visited those walled cities he found so captivating. He had friends in the best museums and galleries, and I saw some of the finest art in all the world." She shrugged, self-conscious. "Rich people stuff."

"It sounds nice," Wolf replied, her tone more neutral than Bel expected.

"It was. It didn't change a thing, though. Ultimately, he got to die somewhere beautiful, but it didn't stop his suffering. We went to France. We tried everything, and I think right up until the end Whit believed he'd get his way; he always did. But not this time. A friend got us access to some experimental drugs, but nothing helped."

"I'm sorry," Wolf said, not as a reflex the way so many people did, but with a depth of understanding Bel knew came from years of her own close experience with illness.

"When Whit got sick, our social life contracted to such a profound degree. It was almost unimaginable. He had always been outgoing. He threw lavish parties and people clamored for invitations, but when it came down to it, most of them were nowhere to be found." The sting of those facts still pained her.

How could they have left him?

Wolf sat at the opposite end of the couch and leaned forward, her attention fixed on Bel. She would have been one of the people who stayed. She hadn't abandoned her friends in need. Wolf had stayed even for strangers. It had been hard for Bel to fathom at the time, but now she appreciated it more deeply than she ever had.

"The only people who stood by us were Michel and Marek."

"Your friends in France?"

"Michel, yes. He's a curator in Paris."

"Gay?"

"Oh absolutely." Bel laughed thinking of the times she had traveled with him under the pretense of being his beloved. "I suspect he and Whit were lovers at one point, but he's still managed to stay negative. He always was more cautious than Whitney. But when he heard what was happening, he opened his home to us. He put us in contact with some doctors who were working in France and Switzerland. He stayed by our side. Literally."

"And is Marek his partner?"

"No. Whit's cousin, and yes, also gay." She remembered how the two men had teased each other with their conquests. Challenging each other to secure the interests of the most handsome men in any room.

"A cousin?" She made a note.

"He and Whit were very close, like brothers, only a few years apart. They grew up together, attended the same boarding school, then the same university. I think when Whit died it shook him, perhaps even more than it did me. I don't mean it the way it sounds. I loved Whit dearly. His death was a profound loss, but I don't know. I wasn't shattered by it the way Marek was. I wasn't transformed on a political level. I might have carried on without ever getting involved in the fight if not for Marek. It was like my consciousness of AIDS stopped at Whit, but Marek saw further. He saw how we were needed, how something could be done for those who were still alive." She had never admitted to Wolf before how easily she might have left the fight to everyone else. How effortlessly she might have insulated herself from any future mention of HIV, but she suspected Wolf knew, and had known all along.

"We owe him a debt."

"I'll never stop owing Marek. I couldn't cry for Whit, but Marek gave me a way to honor him." *And he gave me you.* She wished they were drinking something stronger, something that might give her an excuse to let out these awful truths, but some things were better left unsaid. She stuck with wine, even if it meant having to rake through the past unarmored.

"So when you say he got you involved, what did your involvement look like? Did he take you to meetings? Send you literature?"

"No. He was never one for half-measures when he set his mind to something. He took me to Wall Street the day protestors shut it down."

Wolf perked up, and in her face Belinda saw so clearly the old Wolf, always exhilarated by a fight, ready to rush into the fray. "Really? I was there. What a day!"

"Yes, it was. He took me into an office and had me watch things unfold. Then he told me we should be doing something to help. I agreed to a few donations, but he wanted me to stay in the city and become an activist." She laughed. It sounded as ridiculous now as it had then.

"What's so funny?"

"Me, an activist."

"You were, though."

"After a fashion, I suppose. I never made the grade, though, did I? I went to some meetings but . . ." She shook her head and laughed again. Marek had made a wonderful activist, Wolf was the very definition, but her—no, she was a satellite to their movement, though perhaps a useful one.

Wolf didn't press the point, though Bel could tell she had plenty to say on the matter by the way she furiously scribbled in her notebook. Bel considered asking to see what she was writing, but decided it was perhaps better to not know.

"What made you decide to work with Violet Mission?"

"'Work with' hardly describes my involvement. I signed off on donations. Marek manages a philanthropic foundation that had been under Whit's control. When Whit passed, it became my responsibility, and Marek wanted to put the money toward fighting AIDS. He identified a number of groups he believed would benefit from our support. Then he turned the final decisions over to me. He arranged for a meeting with Cait. We had drinks, she told me what she was doing, and I approved the funding. I could see she was very serious about her work, and she was doing something meaningful."

Wolf nodded. Cait's diligence was hardly information to her, but Bel supposed readers might want to know. A dark tendril of hair fell over Wolf's brow, and she pushed it back before making another notation. Bel tried to remember if she'd ever seen Wolf's hair so long, short as it still was.

"It was a substantial amount, wasn't it? I only ask because I feel like things really amped up around the time we met."

Bel smirked. What did Wolf consider their first meeting? "When was that?"

"Not long after Wall Street. We met at an office, not sure whose. You gave me champagne—no, not champagne but it was wine. Fancy wine."

"Good memory."

"It has its uses." Her face went blank for a fraction of a second, and Bel knew how a good memory could also be a curse. Wolf recovered her composure and returned to her original question. "So it was substantial?"

"I suppose. I don't have the figures, but they'd be easy enough to track down."

Wolf tapped her pencil on the edge of her notebook. "When you have that kind of money, it must be tempting to control how it's spent."

"Maybe for some people. Or on some occasions." Bel knew she had insisted Marek earmark a line of funds for medical and legal support to be used in the event of anyone at Violet Mission being injured or arrested in the course of their work. An entirely inadequate response to the news of Wolf being stabbed after a rally, but it had covered the bills and ensured adequate care.

"Were you and Marek interested in directing the Mission?"

Bel pursed her lips in a brief flash of annoyance. Ever since Wolf had walked into her office she had been expecting some kind of fight, but this was the last thing she expected to be accused of. "No. Not at all. Cait knew what she was doing. She had years of experience as a medical provider and as an organizer. I had nothing but money. It wouldn't have served anyone's best interests to have me calling the shots."

"I think you're right. It's too bad not everyone feels that way."

Bel seemed unsure of what to say and Wolf knew she'd been an idiot to even ask the question. It had poured out before she'd been able to fully consider what it might cost her.

"I'm sorry . . . I didn't mean to suggest," Wolf fumbled uncharacteristically. "It's just, not many women are in charge of such large donations and I was curious. I wanted to have something of that perspective in the book. I never thought you seriously—"

"Wanted to control the Mission?" Bel shook her head.

"Right. I know you didn't. But you have to admit, it's not unheard of."

Bel raised her brows in acquiescence. "No, it's not."

There was a defeated note in Bel's voice, and again Wolf wished she hadn't mentioned it. Money had always been a sore spot between them.

"Wait, is Cait all right?" Bel asked suddenly.

"What?"

"Is there someone pressuring her, a funder?" Bel asked, her voice low. Wolf had almost forgotten that tone. There was a fierce familiar brightness in Bel's eyes although for the most part her posture and expression remained neutral.

Wolf smiled. If nothing else, Bel still cared about Cait. "No, no. She's okay. She's doing really well, actually."

"Oh good. I'm glad to hear it." Bel leaned back and sipped her drink. "So how did you get involved?"

"Me?"

"Yes, I'm asking you questions too, remember?"

Wolf nodded. There was no backing out of it. "Of course, yeah, go ahead."

"I know when we met, you were already working for Cait, at least in some capacity, and apparently you were at Wall Street. So when did you get started, and how?"

Wolf's body tensed a little. This was the question so many people struggled through, and apparently she was no more at ease than any of her interview subjects had been. "I guess it must have been the winter of '88."

"Should I take notes?" Bel asked, eyeing the notebook on Wolf's lap.

Oh no you don't.

"You can if you want to, but I've got the recorder on."

Bel didn't look satisfied so Wolf dug another slender blank book from her bag and handed it over.

"No lines," Bel observed as she ran her hand over a page to smooth the book open.

"No."

"Do you sketch?"

"Hardly, but you're welcome to." Wolf passed Bel one of her preferred drafting pencils and watched Bel twirl the diamond-cut metal grip between her fingers.

"So, what happened in the winter of '88?"

"I met Cait in a bar."

"Like a date?" Bel sat up a bit straighter.

"No. I was, uh, hanging out, dancing." Wolf wasn't prone to blushing, but she felt warm just thinking about where this conversation would lead.

"I don't think I ever saw you dance."

"Probably not. You never liked to party with us. I think you thought we were a little too rowdy. I suppose you may have been right."

"It wasn't that. I just—" Bel shrugged.

"No, go on. You just what?"

"I felt out of place," she admitted.

"Aw come on. I would've danced with you. Cait would've too. And Brenda, shit, Brenda would've loved to dance with you."

"Brenda!"

They both laughed. The long-forgotten sound echoed through her body, from within and without resonating together in the cool air of the studio.

"She ended up with Cait, you know? They're still a thing." Wolf's expression projected her bewilderment.

"Really?" Bel shook her head. "Well, go on. Tell me how you met Cait."

Wolf lifted her glass. Remembering the bar required a drink.

"Do you need a refill?"

"No, not yet. Thanks. Um, so I met Cait at Audrey's. They were having a party."

"How old were you?"

Wolf scowled.

"I'm serious. You couldn't have been legal to drink."

"Is this for the book or for your personal curiosity?" Wolf echoed the question Bel used on her.

"What gets in the book will be out of my hands."

Wolf shook her head. "No, it won't. I'll show you the chapter. You can veto anything or ask me to add anything. I'll do it."

"The publisher will love that."

"Fuck 'em. If they want to publish it, great. If not, someone else will. But I'm not going to publish anything unless you say okay."

"All right then. Still, how old were you?"

Wolf rolled her eyes. "Um, early December '88, I was almost eighteen." The memory of the day despite all of the intervening years still lingered, visceral, near to the surface. She remembered how her extremities ached from the cold. She felt the gnawing uncertainty that hounded her well into the night.

"Almost 18? Are you trying to rile me up?"

"Not at all."

"So you were 17 at Audrey's," Bel restated. She looked as if she were trying not to let on how much the notion shocked her.

You don't want to know what I was doing there.

"So you met Cait at a holiday party. Were you already working for the Mission then?" Bel asked.

"Not yet. I had seen them around the city. In those days it seemed like the street team was everywhere."

"Did someone introduce the two of you?"

"Sort of." Wolf swirled the wine in her glass. She remembered looking for a hookup desperately all night. It was too cold to survive outside and she had missed last check-in at most of the shelters. Not that she wanted to be in one of those places ever again. What she needed was for someone to take her home. A college girl had seemed interested, bought her drinks, even kissed her, but nothing came of it.

Bel's eyes narrowed, but she said nothing.

"Maggie introduced us. You remember her? The bartender? She introduced me to Cait. I think she wanted me to start working with the street team, probably sick of me mooching free drinks." Wolf forced some levity into her voice.

Probably worried I was going to catch something.

"I still can't believe you were seventeen in the bar. Didn't your parents notice you were gone?"

Wolf nearly choked on her drink. "No. They uh—no. I was on my own by then, had been for a while. Anyway, Maggie introduced us and I asked Cait for a dance."

That night after a few dances she'd asked Cait directly, "Could I come home with you tonight?" And Cait, handsome Cait, had said, "Wolf, I'm not going to fuck you." Too drunk to think, Wolf had countered, "Well, that's okay, I'm usually the one who does the fucking." Wolf laughed to herself as she remembered it. It was funny now; some people would find it funny, but probably not Bel.

"She took you up on it?"

"Ha, sort of," Wolf replied.

Bel tilted her head, waiting for clarification.

Wolf thought about the interview process. What did she want when she asked a question? What did she always want from this experience when she was on the other end? *The truth.* A good story, sure, but more than anything, the truth was what interested her. "She danced with me, but I tried to hustle her."

There, that's that. But she didn't feel relieved.

"What do you mean 'hustle'?"

"You know what I mean."

"I'm not sure I do. Do you want more wine?" Bel held out her hand for Wolf's glass.

As she had so often, Wolf wished Bel were more readable, but her upbringing seemed to make her capable of turning her emotions off completely, or at least shielding them from view. "Thanks, but I'm still working on this one."

"Very well."

Bel walked away and Wolf noted with some self-recrimination how watching the easy movements of Bel's lithe body still generated a ripple of pleasure.

"Are you watching me?"

"Force of habit," Wolf replied.

Bel shook her head. When she returned, she held her glass in one hand and the bottle in her other. Settling at the far end of the couch with her legs crossed on the cushion, she rested her glass in the hollow between. It was such a relaxed pose, startlingly familiar, unlike anything Wolf had seen from her in years.

The wine works wonders.

"So, tell me more about your hustle. Were you trying to scam her?"

"No. I was trying to get a place for the night."

"Oh." A small sound, a whisper. "Oh, I see."

"Do you?"

"Yes, I think so." She drank, letting her eyes close briefly as she swallowed.

"She offered me a job instead and gave me a long serious talk about safer sex. She took me to get tested the next day."

"That sounds like Cait. Did you actually sleep together?"

"Ah, who's being prurient now? No, we didn't. I was drunk and under-age and she's not a creep. I know there were always rumors about the two of us because she let me live with her sometimes when the weather was bad, and she looked after me, but no. We were never a thing."

"You never told me about this." Something in Bel's eyes looked almost hurt.

"Hustling?"

"Right."

Wolf ran her fingers over the spot above her ear. It was a place she'd been hit so many times before, and she touched it almost automatically when she was afraid. She pulled her hand away. "Why would I have? I was already below your pay grade. I didn't need to make it any more obvious."

"I never thought that," Bel protested.

Wolf rolled her eyes. "Oh, come on, Princess. You let me know what you thought at those meetings." She worried once the words were out, but Bel just feigned ignorance.

"I did? I don't recall."

Wolf suppressed a scoff. They had fought with each other furiously in one of the first breakout sessions Bel attended, Belinda calling Wolf a "sanctimonious delinquent." It was all some people talked about for days, especially Brenda. If Bel wanted to feign ignorance, though, that was fine by Wolf. She seized the opportunity to shift focus away from herself. "Okay. Let's talk about what you do remember. So Marek put you in touch with Cait. When was that exactly?"

"Not long after Wall Street. Maybe a few days later. It was all straightforward."

"And just like that you decided to start coming to the meetings?"

"No. Just like that I signed some paperwork. And then I met you."

"And it was less straightforward?"

Bel smirked but quickly reined it in.

"No, simply the order of affairs. You were the messenger who brought the paperwork," Bel explained in a mock snobbish tone she knew Wolf would find amusing, or would have all those years ago.

"Indeed. So, what made you decide to get more actively involved?"

"I think it was the kidnapping. I don't know if you know, but some ruffian grabbed me out of Grand Central station one afternoon."

"Oh yeah, I think I heard something about it. A daring rescue as I recall. A lonely heiress snatched from a tumultuous mob."

Bel made a face, but not unkindly. How could they slip so easily back into this ritual of joking? The familiarity pained her. "It's hard to say what changed my mind. I'd certainly never planned to deviate from the original course of action. I put money into the Mission, I received regular updates from Marek and Cait, and that was the extent of it for a while. I was satisfied. They were satisfied. I went abroad with Michel, our friend from France. He needed a woman to make him look, well, acceptable while touring for business. We had a lovely time, but it reminded me vividly of how much I had lost. How friendless I had become. When I came back, I decided to see Cait in person."

"Socially?"

"I suppose. I don't know. I had hoped so. She was in New York, we were already communicating regularly about the Mission, and I thought we might become friends, at least go for drinks." Bel couldn't explain how horrible returning to Boston had been, nor could she admit the need she felt for connection, however tenuous.

"And Cait convinced you to get more involved?"

Bel nodded. It wasn't the full story, but close enough.

"She is good at recruiting."

"Exceptional," Bel agreed.

"Was the needle exchange session your first meeting then?"

"I think so."

"March '91," Wolf said without consulting a calendar or notes.

Bel wondered at the elaborate timeline Wolf seem to have stored in her head. So much of Bel's own life was a hazy mishmash of events. "That sounds about right."

"What do you remember of it?"

Bel ran one hand plaintively over her soft denim-covered knee. "I remember it was at Cait's place and the room was packed. Absolutely jammed. She told me it would be a smaller meeting. That's how she got me there."

"It was small."

"I gathered as much later, but in the moment I was stunned. There must have been thirty or more people in that little one-bedroom flat. And everyone was so loud. I can say without reservation I'd never been to a gathering like it. Not even the pre-break meals at boarding school were as raucous. It was disorienting."

"I can imagine. Not boarding school, but that Cait's place was a lot to take in."

"I might have turned around and walked out, but I wanted Cait to see that I keep my word. It would've been rude to go, so I stayed."

"And argued with us."

"Well, arguing seemed de rigueur." Bel waved her hand in the air.

Wolf smiled. "You said what you thought. I respected that."

"Really? You didn't seem to care for my opinions as I recall."

"I didn't. No, you were wrong, but you said what you thought. That's all we can really ask for—honesty."

A tight pang gripped Bel's chest, and she soothed it with wine. The feeling passed.

You wouldn't like my honesty now, Wolf.

Wolf's expression softened. "I remember being so pissed off, but also impressed at how you kept debating. Most people fold."

"When you yell at them," Bel asked.

"When anyone challenges them at all. But yes, especially when I would yell at them." Wolf teased. "How often would you say you ended up attending meetings after the first one?"

"Infrequently. Cait or Marek would sometimes talk me into them, but it was never my scene. I didn't feel alive when we argued, I felt—"Bel struggled to find the words to express what it had been like going home after a night among the affinity groups. She looked around her loft and thought how strange it was to be sitting in the same room she'd come back to after that first meeting. What was the sensation? Tired, yes, but something much more.

"You look like you're deciding if you should say something," Wolf prompted.

"Not so much if I should say it. I'm trying to figure it out, how it felt. I remember coming back here exhausted, but it was more than simply tired. No, it was—you know when you stand outside for too long when it's bone cold and damp?"

Wolf nodded.

"At the time, perhaps you don't notice how cold it is. I suppose you get used to it. Your brain tunes it out or focuses on something else, but later when you come inside—"

"It hurts."

"Yes," Bel practically whispered.

"The meetings hurt?"

She straightened up. "In a way. I felt raw, wrung out. I thought you must all be mad for going back as often as you did. Week after week."

"Multiple times a week."

"Unthinkable," she muttered and took a drink. "Every time Cait or Marek would talk me into going I would say to myself, Bel, it'll be different this time. It's a different topic, or a different group. I'd give myself a little pep talk about keeping my mouth shut, but you know I wasn't always good at keeping quiet."

"Oh, I know the feeling."

"But you loved the fight, didn't you? You always seemed so ready to charge in."

"At the time, I think I did love it. I felt like I was doing something right. And there was so little we could do. There was so much hopeless watching. Watching people wither, watching the government turn its back. It was nice to believe I was doing something at all. But it takes a toll. Do you think you got anything useful out of the experience? Do you feel you learned anything?"

"Of course. I learned so many things in those meetings about how people were feeling about their loss and their chances. I learned their logic for taking such awful risks, their motivations, what they thought they might gain. I saw how some people could put aside personal fights and press on with other things. And how even when reconciliation wasn't possible, people would bond with others and go off to start something new. It was never stagnant. People were always pressing forward. I'm not like that. I'm constantly pulled back. I creep ahead an inch or two and then I'm drawn back, back, back. You know?" Bel wondered if Wolf felt the same. She must, taking on a project like this one, choosing to sit here with Bel and rehash it all. Only someone who felt the unrelenting grip of the past would bother.

Wolf didn't reply. She made a note in her book.

"It was also in one of those meetings where I learned you didn't thoroughly despise me, so that was instructive."

Wolf looked up from her writing with a curious glance.

"The dress."

"Oh yeah, the dress." Wolf smiled slowly, remembering.

"You stood up for me."

"It was an argument on principle. Nothing to do with you." Wolf repositioned herself against the arm of Bel's couch. "And it was a great dress. Brenda was so pissed off with me. She said I was breaking ranks and siding with straight women."

"Moi?" Bel fought the urge to laugh.

"She and I were always scuffling over something."

"Well, that day it was me. I tried to follow you."

"Did you?" Wolf's eyes brightened, but her mouth looked sad.

Bel shrugged. She shouldn't have said anything. It didn't matter, then or now. "Anyway. What did you get out of those meetings, aside from a feeling of doing the right thing?"

"Oh, I don't know. Friends, family. It was nice to not feel alone. When I started spending time with the Mission, I felt like I was a part of something bigger. People cared about me. They wanted me to go to meetings, and they were happy to see me. It was nice."

"There were always girls swooning over you, too, so I suppose that helped."

"Pfft. Not my deal. I mean, you're right, there were those people who used meetings like an occasion for cruising, but I wasn't one of them. I've never been much for that kind of thing."

"Sleeping with other activists?" Bel clarified.

"Right. I mean once I had the van, I wasn't sleeping with anyone. I needed a break."

"That wasn't the impression I had of you."

"No? What was your impression?"

"You seemed, I don't know. Like you were getting what you wanted when you wanted it. At least as far as women were concerned," Bel surmised.

Wolf made a face, partly stunned and partly amused. "Fuck no. I was freaked out. I had some friends get sick. Women. It made me extremely cautious."

"Safety monitor."

"Exactly. As soon as I had the option to be selective, I was very, very selective. People flirted with me, sure, but I hadn't slept with anyone freely in ages."

"Shit." Bel sighed. The thought had never occurred to her.

"Yeah. Shit."

For a fraction of a second a twitch at the corner of Wolf's mouth told Bel how completely wrong she'd been.

Of course, she had been wrong so many times before.

The Novel
May 1996

BELINDA LET HER EYES LINGER on the cafe bulletin board while a gangly youth prepared her morning coffee. Posters layered upon posters announced every manner of social, political, and academic event of interest to the university clientele. None of them mentioned Laura. The book she had been writing while in residence was published sometime in April, and the expected fanfare accompanying it had served as an advanced warning, each poster and email a reminder of Laura's impending return to campus as part of her book tour. Belinda made use of the ample notice to avoid any unplanned interactions. Even now, the habit of being on alert had remained.

"Double shot cappuccino." The boy's voice cut through the din.

Bel took her paper cup and began the final stretch of her commute. The weather was warm, the sky clear. Along the lane evenly spaced trees with tiny pink and purple flowers unfurled their buds in a vibrant display. Bel considered taking her color theory students outdoors. She sipped her drink and realized with some measure of surprise that for the first time in a long time, she was not actively unhappy.

The hazy wine-addled weeks she'd spent with Laura last spring had been a kind of misery sharp enough to dull a deeper pain. Each of their sexual exchanges left Belinda feeling she had wronged herself. Still, she always went back for more. The compulsion to give in was unstoppable. Each cry of pleasure extracted from Laura was a lash of self-reproach Bel could not resist enduring. Then there was Wolf; the inescapable memories of Wolf, which would flood her in the bitter afterglow, part balm, part brand. Ending the affair was probably the only kind thing Laura had ever done. It had been months now since Laura had stopped calling. In the past, her withdrawal might have felt like torture. Now, the feeling of relief Bel experienced in Laura's absence alarmed her.

Belinda opened her office door and set down her things.

"Psst. Belinda." A hissed whisper from the end of the hall drew her attention. "Come here for a sec."

The conspiratorial tone felt misplaced. There was no one in the entire state whom she considered a friend, yet Professor Neal hailed her in such a way that anyone passing might have thought they were close.

Neal's office was standard issue: a metal desk and filing cabinets topped with an overload of textile scraps and partly finished projects. Bel had to practically push aside the welter of detritus to make room for herself.

"Did you go to the book talk?" Neal asked in hushed tones.

"No, why?"

"Are you and she—you know?" Neal waved her hand in a tight nervous circle as if the motion were a universally understood sign for something.

"Who and I?"

"The author, the one who wrote *The Hidden Portrait*. I thought I saw you two at one of her talks last year, but maybe I'm misremembering."

"We know each other from Boston. But I didn't go to the book talk, no."

"Ohh, it was steamy."

"Was it?" She didn't care and she couldn't imagine why Neal thought she might.

"I hope nothing comes of it."

The words rendered Bel thoroughly confused and more than a little annoyed. She fidgeted with the thin silver bangles on her wrist and let her gaze rest on one of the embroidered panels of her co-worker's coat. What had Laura written? Ultimately, what did it matter?

Bel excused herself and went to class. She spent most of the seminar wondering how on earth Laura had managed to stir up discord from such a distance. It made no difference to Bel if people knew they had been lovers. It wasn't as if she were ashamed. And, more to the point, it wasn't as if she valued the opinions of anyone around her. The only people she cared about were far away or long dead.

Having wasted a few hours running these thoughts over in her mind, she wasn't much surprised when Dean Kenneth Jay Hoffstetter intercepted her. A naturally slender man, he looked like a caricature of a bookish academic at the best of times, pale and pinched, but this morning the effect was pronounced.

"Professor Coltswood, I need to speak with you immediately."

She didn't bother asking why. On any other day, she would have suspected his urgency was the product of a missing signature on a grade form or a last-minute request for her to dine with some notable guest or donor. Today, she suspected it would be about Laura. She followed him to his office, neither making any effort to engage in small talk.

He motioned for Bel to sit and she did. To her right, on a shelf dedicated to Socrates, was a fine bronze figure of Artemis and her hounds. Her eyes traced the curves of Artemis, and she thought of all the other things she would rather be doing than sitting in this room, and of the only reason she was here at all.

"I assume you know this book has caused quite a stir." He lifted a copy of *The Hidden Portrait* from his desk.

"I wasn't aware."

"Belinda, surely you've read this book?"

His incredulity angered her. The way he said her name made her sit straighter, her body preparing for an argument, but she maintained her composure. "I certainly have not read the book, nor do I intend to. What is this about?"

"Read this passage." Two spots of color brightened his face as he held the book out to her. A tab of paper marked the page, and a line of highlighter yellow illuminated the words.

Melinda Yearling-Forrest had not known how deeply she longed for the touch of her teenage protégée until their bodies melded together in a sinuous knot of unbridled lust.

Bel looked up at Hoffstetter. "It's not her best work. Bit of a mixed metaphor really."

"Belinda, you must recognize the rumors this has instigated."

"About my relationship with Laura?"

"No. Oh, if only it were so simple. Belinda, a student of yours has suggested this book is a very thinly disguised version of actual events.

Her parents are naturally quite distressed."

"A student of mine?" She almost laughed. The idea that she would have any kind of sexual relationship with one of those half-formed, bright-eyed fools was eminently laughable.

"That's right. Missy Barnes. She was one of your Introduction to Painting students." There was an edge of whining in his voice.

"Intro? Hardly a protégée then." Bel huffed.

"It's not funny, Belinda. Her parents have withdrawn her from the university and are threatening to contact a lawyer."

"A lawyer. What's the charge?"

"Assault, damage to reputation, sexual harassment. Who knows?" He threw up his hands.

"This is absurd."

"I assure you it is very serious. You've broken the trust that parents place in us when they send their children here for an education."

Belinda stood up and leaned over his desk. "The fact is, Kenneth, I didn't sleep with her or any other student, but what if I had? What of it? I remember Miss Barnes. The girl is in her third year; she's at least eighteen. So, no, this isn't about children and broken trust. This is about the scandal of lesbianism. Some homophobe complains because their daughter claims to have had a tryst with me."

"Belinda, that's not fair."

"No? When I was nineteen, I married my art history professor. He taught the Medieval to Renaissance course. No one batted an eye. He was wealthy and well regarded, and a man. If I were a man, we wouldn't be having this conversation, Kenneth. You and some of your best donors would be lining up for wedding invitations. But I'm not, so it's an outrage. Christ, in your way of putting it, it sounds like a crime. But the fact is it never happened. Never. Frankly, she's not my taste at all."

"Belinda! Jesus! Don't say things like that."

"I'll say what I damn well please."

"If they go forward with this lawsuit, we'll need to talk about the possibility of termination."

Belinda scoffed. "All right, let's talk termination. Take it up with the people who handle the endowments. In the meantime, I'll be taking my sabbatical effective immediately."

"Belinda. Professor Coltswood!"

She walked out of his office and headed directly for the airport, fully intending to never return.

The Third Question
November 2002

WOLF ADJUSTED THE NOTEBOOK on her lap. She knew her face gave too much away, and she didn't want to think about how much Bel had meant to her. "Look, let's talk about something else, okay?"

"What do you suggest?"

"I don't know. Do you mind if I get a glass of water?"

Belinda nodded toward the fridge. "Help yourself."

The sensation of Bel's gaze at her back made Wolf's joints ache.

"Do you want some?" she asked without looking over her shoulder.

"No, thank you."

Filling her glass, Wolf imagined they were in the Back Bay apartment. In their eight months together, how many times had she gone for a glass of water? A sense of déjà vu overwhelmed her. Had she been alone, she might have wept from the feeling.

"Are you getting tired?" Bel asked from the living room.

"No. I'm all right. Besides, you're headed back to Iowa tomorrow, aren't you? We should make the most of tonight."

"Indeed."

"Well, I suppose one question we haven't covered is legacy." Most people enjoyed talking about this. Wolf figured they could both take a breath.

"Legacy?"

"Right, how would you imagine your work lives on and how has your participation affected your life since?"

Astonishingly, Bel's eyes narrowed and for a moment Wolf thought she might say something cutting, but she merely sipped her drink and held back whatever thought had moved her features. "Everything in my life now is a direct result of what happened in those days."

"How so?"

"I think I might want to pass on this one."

Nobody passed on this one, but Wolf had promised to grant Bel leeway. "Sure. Okay. Well, would you say anything good has come out of the work you did?"

A pause. Shadows moved across Bel's throat as she swallowed, then spoke. "I suppose some of my students, a few of the talented ones. I wouldn't have known them otherwise, and I wouldn't have been in a position to support their careers without—you know."

Wolf wasn't sure she did know; she hoped Bel would explain if given the chance. Still, she was nervous now, worried Bel might cut the process short. "Are you close with them? Your students? I mean, I know you said their idealism is tiring, but the talented ones?"

"I'm not close with anyone. I'm not in the habit of developing friendships. I haven't the knack. But there are a few students I've remained in contact with over the years. I mentor them professionally when I can."

Wolf made a note. "Can I ask you something?"

"You've been asking questions all night." Bel laughed.

"Right, but not for the book and obviously you can tell me it's none of my business, but Vic mentioned—"

"Oh Vic. Hmm. Did you sleep with her?"

"What? No."

Bel held up her hand as if to forestall Wolf's objections. "Obviously it's none of my business, but she does have a bit of a reputation for, well, you'd be just her type. Forget I asked."

"No. I didn't sleep with her although I got the impression she was interested. No, it's something she said."

"About Shawn?"

"No. Who's Shawn?"

"A student of mine, well, former student, a talented one. She and Vic were an item. Vic suspects I had a hand in their breakup. Absurd, but you know people aren't always logical."

"No, she didn't mention anything about a breakup. She said there'd been some sort of scandal and I just wondered." Wolf feigned nonchalance.

"Oh, did she?" Bel sucked a breath between her teeth, and Wolf thought it wouldn't be great to be Vic in the coming weeks.

"You don't have to tell me," Wolf reiterated.

"I know I don't. But I will. Did you read *The Hidden Portrait* by any chance?"

"No. I never read it." Wolf jotted the name of the book in her notes and drew a line under it. When she looked up, something in Belinda's eyes seemed troubled. There was anger, clearly, but something more. Bel stood and paced into the studio then back to the couch. She perched on the arm as if she might hop off again at any moment.

"Well, don't bother reading it. Here's the summary: Melinda Yearling-Forrest takes a young lover from among her undergraduate students. Their relations are unconventional, and it drives the girl to attempt suicide, which is blessedly unsuccessful. Melinda, apparently unruffled by these events, begins cultivating another lover from among her pupils."

"You're kidding."

"I wish I were."

"Sounds like a hit piece." Wolf clicked her mechanical pencil, trying to master her own outrage.

Belinda raised her brows for a moment and then shook her head. "The dean wanted to fire me, but it's difficult to fire someone who essentially pays their own salary."

Again, Wolf felt the gulf of distance between her own life and Bel's.

"I would have left and not gone back at all, but—" She shrugged. Under different circumstances, Wolf might have pounced on that gesture, insisted on knowing what lay beneath, but she was too preoccupied with other more pressing curiosities.

"The author, what reason could she have had for writing something like that?"

"Lack of creative vision, a fixation with old pulp novels, a perverse desire to wound, I don't know."

"But why?"

"We'd been lovers."

Jealousy squeezed Wolf's insides, immediately followed by an instinct to laugh at herself. She suppressed the urge. It had been eight long years.

Of course, there had been other women. Wolf had enjoyed a few encounters, but no one she would have called a lover. The word suggested a kind of intimacy she'd been determined to avoid. "You don't have to tell me."

"I know, but I will, if you're curious." There was an unexpected softness in Bel's offer.

Of course Wolf was curious. "Okay. Who was she?"

Belinda drew a breath and steeled her nerves. The story had festered for so long. She had kept it to herself even when pressed to reveal it. She had never imagined Wolf would be her confessor. "Laura Worthing and I had been together for years before Whit died. I met her at some ridiculous gala, and we hit it off instantly. She was married, but of course so was I. Like a fool, I thought we were in the same situation. I believed everything was above board. Whitney knew about Laura, and I assumed, probably incorrectly, that Peter, her husband, knew about me.

"I was delusional about Laura. Whit always laughed about my being so besotted. He had a better grasp on love than I did. He knew how to separate lust from feelings, but I never quite got the hang of it." Certain all of her feelings were on florid display, Bel hoped Wolf wouldn't look at her just then. Thankfully, Wolf seemed preoccupied with something else across the room, the painting perhaps.

Oh my urchin, do you see yourself there?

"I thought if Laura was with me, she must love me, and eventually we would have a life together. I was misled or, more truthfully, I misled myself. Our relationship was always one-sided. She would get her fill and I would wait for her, wanting more. It went on like that until Whit got sick; then so many of our friends disappeared. Laura and Peter were among the vanished. It was, I don't know, demoralizing, but at the same time it revealed a truth I had been very carefully avoiding. She didn't love me; she loved the things I did for her."

"Oh Bel." Wolf sighed softly. Belinda looked at her with amazement. She sounded genuinely sorry.

How can you pity me? Regardless of her disbelief, a warm sensation spread across her collarbones and throat. It felt for a moment like standing in the sunshine. She cherished it and loathed herself all at the same time.

"I thought so much of her, but I saw who my true friends were when Whit was dying and she wasn't among them. I didn't see or speak to her again for years. Who needs false friends? Who needs to feel themselves being worked upon by lies and their own treacherous impulses? I was much better off without her. But, at any rate, she turned up in Iowa."

"What are the odds?"

Bel managed a chagrined chuckle. "You would think not very high, but the school has a strong writing program, and she managed to attach herself to it. I don't know why she wanted to write this particular book, or why she said what she said. More troubling, though, a student got it in her head to claim the story was about us. I think you can well imagine how unlikely my sleeping with an undergrad would be."

"Did you break her heart?"

"The girl?"

"No, God no. Laura?" Wolf laughed mirthlessly.

"How could I? I was an object to her, and she got her use from me."

"I'm sorry."

Bel waved her away. "I cause my own misery."

"We all do to some extent, but I can't see how you caused this."

Belinda shrugged; she could not let herself off the hook quite so easily. She had gotten what she deserved. She didn't deserve the soft care in Wolf's voice no matter how much it soothed her. "Let's talk about something else. Are you quite sure you don't want a little more of this?" Bel lifted the wine bottle from the floor.

Wolf held out her glass. "Sure, thanks."

"My pleasure. If you don't mind me asking, what made you want to do this?"

"Interview you?"

"No, well, yes. But the whole thing, the book. It seems like such awful memories to dredge up. Not only for the people you talk to, but for you."

Wolf scoffed as Bel knew she would. "Like I said when we first spoke about it, I think there ought to be a book focused on women's experiences and contributions. The men's stories are getting out there and when people think of those days that's who they think of, but there's a missing element that I believe deserves some attention."

"Of course you're right, but, it—Who have you interviewed?"

"A few lawyers, particularly the lesbian civil rights collective who helped keep us out of jail. Some musicians. A few people who ran the puppet-building workshop over in the garment district. Some of the women in Harlem who led the push for better prevention education in schools." Wolf stopped listing.

"Is it difficult getting people to agree to talk to you?"

"Not really. Some people don't want to talk about it, and I can understand why, but loads of people are still doing things that came out of those movements, those experiences. They still have the work on their mind, so it's natural for them to reflect on what they learned during those years. And I think for some of the people who remember me or Cait, it's nice to be interviewed by someone who knows what it was like."

"I'm sure. But it *is* difficult, surely?"

"Of course, it can be."

"So why do it? Masochism?"

Wolf made a face.

"Seriously, though, what made you decide to start writing this book? Was there some particular event?"

"I suppose," she looked pensive.

"Tell me, for the record."

The Puff Piece
April 2001

RIDING THE TRAIN CAUSED a twinge of nostalgia, though she wasn't sure what for. This late at night, the observation car was mostly empty. A few people huddled dozing under blankets. Wolf took an empty seat and watched the retreating lights of Washington. She had been stationed in DC for the past two years, covering anything to do with public health and policy. It had been a natural progression from where she'd started as a freelancer. AIDS was less and less in the news, but Wolf knew better than to think her transfer had been all about numbers. The plan to move her to the Boston office felt like a kick in the face, but she would suck it up.

When they'd delivered the news, they hadn't mentioned who she was being sent to replace and she didn't bother to find out. Wolf evacuated the office in less than twenty minutes and had her apartment all but scrubbed in a weekend. Having no roots helped when things like this happened. A lover, a family—those would have made life harder. It was better to be agile. There were contacts who would need to be informed and a few friendly acquaintances to bid farewell, but aside from the feeling of being robbed by an idiot boss, the move was quick and uncomplicated.

Living in Boston would be less simple. It was true she had broken a major story there. The enormity of the scoop made her a real reporter. There had been offers of work and a steady market for what she wrote, but it had not been enough to keep her in the city. She had looked for ways out at every opportunity and took the first out-of-state post she'd been offered. Now it would be Boston again and, with it, all of the memories she had worked hard to shake free from. Wolf slumped back in the seat and rested her feet on the gray plastic window frame, hoping sleep would claim her.

The train stopped in South Station just after nine in the morning. Stepping out onto the platform, she knew she'd been right to worry about going back. A strange, almost weightless sensation started in her hands and tingled its way up her limbs.

The air smelled of winter.

She couldn't move. She looked down at a long cold season's worth of salt stains crystalized on the concrete. Commuters flowed around her, a stream breaking around a rock. Wolf took a breath, and then another. What did winter smell like? She wanted to make it into words, to make it make sense. It was the smell of fearfully waiting in a tailored suit outside of a gorgeous house. It was the smell of walking through Back Bay for the first time. The smell of coming home late and answering the phone and Bel—

Don't do it.

She took one more breath and then headed inside.

You can do this.

She had been back in Kenmore Square for less than a week when she ran into Sandy McIntyre while trying to decide between Peruvian Perk and Bali Blend at the co-op. Her hand was poised on the little plastic lever ready to finally commit to a pound of coffee when an unmistakable squeal caught her attention.

"It can't be! Deborah Wolf, is that you?"

A half-second later, a soft caramel-colored cashmere embrace enveloped Wolf as Sandy pulled her close and shook her gently with enthusiasm.

"Sandy!" Wolf tried to sound upbeat, but there was no matching Sandy's energy.

"Are you visiting? Are you back? Oh my god, do you need a job? I have the perfect thing! Well, maybe not what you'd consider perfect, being all front-page splash as you are, but it's a good one if you're looking."

Sandy had a habit of speaking in a rapid succession of thoughts. She'd been in charge of obituaries and personal ads at one of the small daily papers when Wolf first got to the city, but anyone could see she was destined to climb. She had an unbeatable memory for names, dates, and tiny details. People found her charming and easy to talk to. Underneath all of that, she was bright and singularly ambitious.

"What are you doing these days?" Wolf asked.

"I'm at the *Globe* now."

"Well, good for you!"

"You're looking at the managing editor for Arts and Lifestyle."

"No kidding?" It made perfect sense.

"Well, as I said, if you need a job, I mean it seems like fate. We've got a slot opening. Look, I know you've got your areas of focus and you're thinking *Sandy, I don't want to do puff pieces.* And hey, maybe reporting on the recent revival of bocce in south Boston isn't as exciting as what's happening at the CDC, but it sure would be fun to work together, wouldn't it?"

Wolf wanted to say *I have a job.* Or maybe even *What makes you think we'd have fun?* Instead, she gave Sandy her number and they agreed to meet the next day to discuss the position. A few weeks later, Wolf walked into Sandy's office ready to receive her first assignment as a lifestyle reporter. The gig was an amusing change of pace. She interviewed a ferry boat captain, and she learned more about the history of campus coffee shops than she'd ever imagined possible. For the first time in her life, she wasn't constantly confronting the horrors of the human condition. It pricked her with guilt, but it soothed her too. Sandy, for her part, tried to see the political possibilities in every story as if Wolf, even after taking the job, still needed to be beguiled into staying.

"Hey, Wolf, look here, we've got a new bakery. It just opened up on Beacon."

"Exciting?"

"Oh, come now, you can't resist a good croissant," Sandy observed.

"Guilty as charged, but does it warrant an article?"

"It was the best croissant I've ever had and the owners are gay."

"Okay, I'm listening."

"One is from upstate New York; the other is French. Both very cute, not that you'll notice."

Wolf shook her head. "I'm gay, not blind."

"Perfect. Why don't you swing by and see if you like what they have to offer. We could use something upbeat and adorable with a dash of political angst."

"Ah, my specialty," Wolf conceded. She grabbed her reusable coffee mug and headed in search of a story. She predicted this would be the pun-perfect epitome of a puff piece.

The man behind the counter was about what Wolf had expected, given Sandra's description—meticulously groomed and tall with dark hair and eyes. His voice had a slight French accent as he welcomed her and told her the day's specials. He was handsome and Wolf would have noticed on her own, but she was more drawn to the artfully arranged cakes and pastries. Wolf sensed she would be back again no matter what came of the interview.

"A croissant and dark roast coffee, please."

At the back of the shop, another man, presumably the boyfriend, slid a tray of proofed breads into the oven.

Wolf sat by the window enjoying her breakfast. *New Common's-side cafe serves croissants with class…* it would write itself. The morning rush was over. A selection of jazz standards at a moderate volume designed to allow conversation or concentration emanated from above. Outside, a woman in a thin gray coat dashed toward the subway station. The drizzle had taken a turn toward outright rain. The traffic pushed on, weakly spraying water from the road onto the sidewalk. Wolf wrapped her hands around her cup and let the warmth seep through her skin. There was an edge of melancholy about everything, and the familiarity of the scene outside only intensified the sensation. She felt a memory creeping in, and she forced it down with another deep swallow of scalding brew.

Wolf took out her laptop and started a draft. Describing the shop gave her something to focus on. As often as she felt bad leaving her old beat behind, she had to admit there were perks to being the one who wrote about coffee shops and vacation cabins. Her nerves needed a break.

"Hello, would you like a sample of our newest—oh, I'm sorry but you look—"

"Daniel?" If she hadn't been seated, she surely would have fallen. Standing by her table holding a tray of tiny confections was Daniel Bauman in the flesh.

"Deb Wolf!" He put down the tray and half-hauled her out of the seat and into a crushing embrace. He smelled of sweets and aftershave. "I can't believe it." He kissed her cheek.

"Oh my god, Daniel! I thought you were dead," she squeaked, too stunned to notice her voice was still capable of making such a sound. Tears rushed to the surface, and she sobbed against him, suddenly aware of every ghost she had been carrying.

"Not yet, and hopefully not for a long time."

The Penultimate Question
November 2002

THE SACRILEGIOUS FEELING WOLF got from talking about the time before AIDS had helped her conveniently avoid discussing a number of unsavory aspects of her life. Hustling, homelessness. She had never mentioned Danny to Bel. "I guess what really got me thinking about all of this was running into an old friend."

"An activist friend?"

"No, a friend from before I got involved."

"Interesting."

"It—I thought he was dead."

Bel leaned forward at full attention. "Well, go on. For the book."

"Right. Um, well, I was working in Boston, and my editor sent me to interview some people. One of them turned out to be my friend Danny, which was quite a shock."

"I imagine so. Only, why did you think he was dead? Had someone told you that?"

"No, but he was diagnosed in '88 and he'd gone upstate with his sister. We lost contact but after all those years, I mean who survived? Hardly anyone, so I thought he must be gone. Every time I saw the quilt I'd look for his name. But I never found it. Then, last year I was in a coffee shop in Boston and—"

"And there he was."

"There he was. I couldn't believe my eyes. Not only alive, but happy and strong, better than he'd been when he left. It was amazing. I'm honestly still amazed."

"How did it happen?"

"He got into some trial up in Canada and it worked for him. He's been on a variety of cocktails over the years, but he's stable, healthy."

"Incredible," Belinda whispered.

Wolf swore there was something affectionate in her gaze. *How bittersweet.* How long had Wolf hungered for Bel's affection, which had never been quite freely given? It didn't shock her to realize she hungered for it still, but even if there was real tenderness in this look, Wolf knew she shouldn't read too much into it. Bel had left her. Whatever they'd had ended long ago.

Lifting her pencil, she shifted back to journalist mode. "It really was. We started talking, and the more I told him about what I'd been up to over the years, the more I realized that the world I experienced is something not many people know about. It's something interesting and important. So why not write a book?"

Bel nodded. "Perhaps I'll ask you the question you asked me. How did you phrase it? Legacy, how has participation shaped your life?"

"Well, just as you said, I think AIDS shaped everything in my life. Danny's diagnosis raised my awareness in an undeniable way. Then, meeting Cait set everything in motion." Wolf swallowed back the next part. The part where she and Bel had planned to change the world. The part where Wolf finally started believing in a future.

Bel waited for her to say more.

"My career in journalism started with Grand Central Station, and until recently I've stayed focused on health policy and research. That's what I'm known for."

"Until recently?" Bel pressed.

"I switched jobs a little over a year ago, decided to take something lighter."

"And promptly supplemented it with this." Bel gestured toward the recorder and smiled.

"True." Wolf picked up the recorder and paused it, eager for something to do with her hands. She didn't want to mention how seeing Danny had seemed to punch a hole in her. Happy as the reunion had made her, she found she could suddenly think of nothing but the past. Departed friends. The smell of death. The weight of coffins. The thin but precious hope she had felt in those months by Bel's side. It ruined her sleep and left her constantly on the edge of weeping. Finally, she told Sandy she needed time off. She took the first bus to Manhattan and spent a few weeks immobilized on Cait's sofa. The book had been her way back to life.

She drew a new tape from a pocket in her bag and clicked it into place, leaving the other beside the machine. "Tape two of the November third interview with Professor Belinda Coltswood."

Bel leaned across the couch and held out the wine bottle. Wolf refreshed her own glass.

"So, what's the new position?"

"Lifestyle at *The Globe*," Wolf replied with a laugh. It was laughable.

"Ah, is that how you ended up with the Hirsch assignment?"

"No. I had taken a few months off, long story, but Gemma needed someone to take over for her when her dad got sick. I needed some paid work so I took it. I didn't know you were the winner until I heard the tapes."

"Would you have taken the job if you had?" Bel asked with an aloof expression Wolf could tell wasn't quite genuine.

"Of course."

"Of course?"

"I wasn't the one who vanished." Wolf gripped her pencil, willing the tension in her hand to ease the tension in her throat. She hadn't meant to say that out loud.

Bel raised her brow, but seemed unruffled. "Touché. When did you realize what you'd gotten yourself into?"

"On the plane. Can we come back to this later maybe?" Wolf didn't want the interview to end, and an unpleasant ending seemed the only way this line of questioning could go.

"Of course. So you've done well for yourself."

Was that a question? She suspected Bel knew more than she let on, but Wolf played along. "I've done all right. My first big story took down a company so I can't complain. Even if it had ended there, my career's been worth something."

"Sounds like quite a scoop." Nothing in Bel's face showed any sign of recognition.

"They were defrauding their investors and the federal government out of tens of millions of dollars."

Again no reaction. Part of Wolf wanted to weep and another to laugh. For years she had lived under an illusion. In her mind, Bel knew what they had done together, or at the very least she knew what Wolf had accomplished without her, but now it seemed disturbingly apparent: Bel knew nothing of the sort.

The Dossier
September 1993

TWO WEEKS HAD PASSED since she woke up alone. Every day, Wolf expected someone might show up to evict her, but no one came. Wolf knew she should leave. She knew lingering in the apartment wouldn't change anything, but her body wouldn't comply. She made it as far as the kitchen, looked at the bottles of wine neatly arranged on the rack and wondered if she should smash them all. It might make her feel better. It might make her feel something.

For about nine days she had been totally numb. So numb that she wondered if she'd had some kind of psychotic break. She should be upset. She was upset, but somehow everything seemed quiet now. Empty. She went back to bed and lay face down. The pillow still smelled faintly like Bel.

Wolf didn't hear the knock at first, and when she did, a mortifying burst of hope propelled her toward the sound. It was a mortification made only worse when she opened the door to find a bike messenger standing breathless on the other side.

"I'm looking for—" he glanced down at a small notebook then up at her. "Wolf."

She could only imagine how ragged and out of place she must look standing in this luxury apartment, her hair shaggy and unwashed. She wore one of Bel's oversized button-downs and nothing else. Not that she could make herself care. She stared at him, realizing once more Bel wasn't coming back. Maybe this was the eviction notice she'd been waiting for.

She cleared her throat. It had been days since she'd said anything out loud. Finally, she forced out the words. "I'm Wolf."

"Great!" He put a package in her hands.

The heft surprised her. "Did the sender request a response?"

"Nope."

Wolf grabbed two of the fancy wine bottles and thrust them toward him. "Bring them one and keep the other."

"Really? Thanks." He tucked the bottles in his bag before bounding downstairs.

Wolf looked at the package—plain brown paper, no writing. The image sparked a chain reaction. Brown paper, black latex, Bel. A sound, small and angry, forced itself out with her next breath. She shook her head and opened the wrapper, not knowing what to expect. The accordion folder she found inside confused her, but when she pulled out the contents a clearer picture formed.

Wolf emptied the documents onto the counter. Spreadsheets and memos. A few shipping invoices. Photographs of people she didn't quite recognize, but who seemed familiar. She stared at them until names percolated into her mind.

It took a few hours of reading to comprehend the gravity of what she'd been given, but when that took hold, Wolf finally understood. Bel hadn't wanted her, but at least she had wanted to complete their task.

Revived, Wolf picked up the phone.

"Violet Mission, Cait Hanson here; how can I help you?"

"Cait." Wolf's voice rasped from disuse and emotion.

"Wolf? Everything good?"

"Eh. It's okay. I have some paperwork I need your help deciphering."

"Sure thing."

"I'll fax it over."

Belinda's home office had seemed over the top, like everything else, but Wolf felt grateful for it now. She sent a small batch of documents to the Violet Mission fax number and waited.

"So, how are things in the City?" Wolf asked, desperate to forestall any inquiries about Bel or their project.

Predictably, Cait launched into a robust update, and Wolf listened attentively, asking for clarification whenever she could just to keep the focus off of herself. If Cait noticed, she didn't let on. "Oh, the fax is coming through now."

Wolf heard Cait shuffling stacks of paper. Then a pause.

"Huh. What is this?"

"I was hoping you could tell me."

"Well, it looks like the kind of records you'd keep in a drug trial but, hmm, do you have more of these?"

"Yeah, there's a stack of them."

"Send a few more. Just grab some at random from the pile, but pay attention to how they're filed just in case."

"Um, yeah, hold on." A buzz of excitement punctuated her movements as she grabbed a few paperclips to mark the places she sampled from. It was the best she'd felt since that brutal morning fifteen days before. This was what they had come for. Answers, one way or another. She sent the fax.

"I'll call you back in a half hour, Wolf. Hang tight, okay?"

"Call collect. I'll be here."

Wolf hung up and went back to reading the documents, making notes in the journal she'd been keeping on all of their Boston activities. When Cait called back, Wolf could tell by the sound of her voice that she had found something.

"What've you got, Cait?"

"This is fishy. I mean, really fishy on a few levels."

"Tell me."

"You see the numbers on these lab reports?"

"Sure."

"They're too similar. I mean some are exactly the same."

"Um, yeah, but that could happen, right? Like we could have the same T-cell count. There's nothing saying that couldn't happen."

"No, but it shouldn't happen like this. This is too regular. I think some of this is falsified, maybe all of it. And that's another thing. Do you see anything on here that looks like a typical HIV/AIDS lab?"

Wolf looked though the documents again. No T4, no T8, no viral load numbers. "No."

"Right. If this is supposed to be some kind of HIV treatment, those numbers would be front and center. But they're not here."

"Could this be a control group or something?"

"No. Even if it were we'd have that information. Furthermore, the numbers in the right-hand corner look like group numbers, and across all of the data I don't see anything that would make me think they were working with HIV."

"Maybe it's a vaccine trial?" No matter how much she wanted a vaccine, Wolf felt stupid even asking.

"No. No way. I don't think we're close to that yet, but if that's what this was, we'd see regular HIV tests. These subjects, if they're real people, aren't positive. Or maybe they are and no one knows because no one is bothering to check." Cait sounded furious.

"What do you think they're working on?"

"Getting rich is my best guess," Cait grumbled. "What does Belinda think of all this?"

"I don't know."

"What do you mean? Ask her."

"I can't; she's gotten clear of the blowback." Wolf surprised herself with how easily the words came. Thinking of things tactically made anything possible to bear.

"Where is she?"

"No clue; it's probably safer that way, right?"

"Wolf?" Cait's voice went soft.

"I mean it's best that she not be around when shit hits the fan, right? She's a donor, and we can't afford to have her getting in trouble."

"Wolf, are you all right, buddy?"

In an instant, she felt as though she couldn't breathe. She swallowed and swallowed despite the fact that every effort worsened the sensation. "Ah—" A traitorous squeak of a sound slipped out before she ground her teeth together so hard her molars ached.

"Wolf?"

Five deep shaking breaths—then she spoke, her voice almost normal. "This project is almost over, Cait. Bel is safe and I've got a ton of evidence to work through. It might take me a little while, but this is almost over."

"Wolf, are you okay?" she asked again.

"Sure. Talk to you soon." She hung up. The concern in Cait's voice was unmistakable, and it threatened to open the wound in her chest. She didn't have time for that shit. She was here for a reason. For the revolution.

The Unavoidable Question
November 2002

WOLF FELT BEL ANTICIPATING an answer, but she needed a moment to reorder her thoughts. How could she have gotten something so important so wrong?

Belinda took another sip of wine and waited a few moments longer. "So, how did it happen? Who were you working for? Not *The Globe*?"

"No, I was freelance still."

"I see."

"A dossier landed in my lap. It was a gold mine. Proof of fabricated data, fraudulent grant applications, maleficence all through the company. Even a helpful senator."

"That is something," Bel mused, making a note. "You weren't going to leave this out of the book, were you?"

"I don't know. Maybe I was. It's had its fifteen minutes of fame already. It launched my career and it tanked Ridgeway Labs."

Bel leaned forward, eyes bright. Her lips curled. She looked for a moment like she might kiss Wolf, and the thought sent a spasm of fear and longing racing through her.

Well, that got a response.

"Ridgeway?" Bel asked, almost breathless.

"You must have known." Wolf leaned back, desperate for a little space.

"No. You know I'm awful with these things." Bel regained her mask of indifference.

"But you knew they folded?"

"My family and I are not on speaking terms."

"Oh." Wolf knew they had never been close, but still, the revelation was alarming. Belinda owned part of the family business. How could she have failed to notice Ridgeway closing? Was she that rich? "It was a big story."

"I'm sure it was."

"You really didn't know?"

"I cut ties." She forced a smile, the clearest tell of all. Something in this had wounded her, badly. She wanted it to mean nothing, but it still hurt. Bel reached for the bottle of wine. Wolf wanted to stop her, but it wasn't her place. Even so, her body betrayed her, and she ached in a sympathetic echo of the pain she saw so clearly in Bel's expression.

Instantly she recalled how they'd planned to confront Ridgeway, to force them to open their trials to local people with AIDS or to at least go public with their test results. Wolf had rallied a team of people willing to chain themselves to the doors. She planned to lock down in the front offices. Bel would be on site; she would make sure the protestors were listened to and not mistreated.

Memory gripped her. She didn't want to think about that last night, which was etched indelibly in her mind. Belinda in a cocktail dress, Wolf in a suit. Expensive cocktails and soft jazz. The two of them had slipped into an unused room and kissed like teenagers, afraid yet giddy.

"Trust me," Belinda had said.

And Wolf had leaned in and pressed their mouths together before whispering *I do* with all the solemnity of a vow.

Upstairs, the music played and people danced, and rich men got richer.

Do you trust me? Wolf asked, knowing the risk Bel took was so much weightier than her own.

She grabbed Wolf's wrist, pushing her throat against Wolf's hand.

Do you feel that? Bel's pulse throbbed under Wolf's fingers. Then Bel put her own hand over Wolf's and squeezed until they both gasped. *I trust you with my whole life, Wolf.*

How many times had she replayed that memory, trying to understand what had happened?

Wolf watched Bel drink, watched the movement of her swallowing, and remembered intimately how much they had trusted each other.

"You weren't the one who sent the files?"

"No. But I'm glad you wrote that story. I hope you destroyed every last one of them." She filled her glass again and drank.

"What happened, Bel?"

Bel closed her eyes and shook her head. "Next question, please."

"No, I'm sorry, I can't just leave this. I wasn't going to ask, I really wasn't. I swear it was never my intention to ask about this, but—"

"But what?" she snapped, though Wolf heard fear lacing her tone, not anger.

"Something happened. I've thought about it a lot, and it never occurred to me it had to do with the company, but now—the look on your face. I don't know. I can't drop it. You left me without saying anything. I never thought you were a cruel person, Bel, never, but it—I let myself think I was wrong about you, about us, but now." Wolf shrugged, wishing she could shake some of the resurfacing heartache from her bones. "Something happened and I want to know what."

Bel looked at Wolf wordlessly and Wolf didn't look away. She realized she'd been avoiding too much eye contact, but now Wolf let herself stare back. Pain and something like terror flickered there inside a woman who otherwise seemed calm to the point of disinterested.

"What happened?" Wolf asked again more softly.

I don't want to hurt you, but I need to know.

"Just forget it."

"I can't, Bel. Don't you think I've tried to? But how do you forget something like that? Have you forgotten it?"

Bel closed her eyes. "What do you want from me? Do you want me to say I loved you? That I would've done anything to protect you? That I did do anything to protect you? You don't need a confession. You know it already deep down. Look at your life. Look at your career. And look at mine."

Wolf started to speak, but Bel raised her hand. "I know this all looks impressive from the outside, but I am clawing my way out of a fucking hole. And I am no happier for it, believe me."

A hole. How apt.

Wolf raised a hand instinctively to her chest but let it drop. The darkness in her that filled every space had been that way for as long as she could remember.

"I thought it would be okay, that doing the right thing would feel good. It always did with you, but I suppose that was the difference," Bel said at last.

"Tell me what happened, Bel. Because as fucked up as it is, I do believe you, but I deserve to know."

Belinda emptied her glass and filled it once more. It seemed for a moment she wouldn't speak, but then she sighed. "Do you remember my uncle Anders?"

The Ultimatum
August 1993

THE CLUB OFF BEACON Street was not the place she would have chosen, but it suited her uncle. As a young man dressed in the club's livery guided her, she took a moment to observe Anders staring into his glass of amber spirits, his fleshy body tucked into a deep blue suit. He was a gentleman, most would have supposed, but when she imagined men of refinement and taste, Anders was the furthest thing from her mind. He could make himself look the part in this room of mahogany wainscoting and polished silver, but Anders was a man about money and power. Everything else he deemed inconsequential. Whit had despised him.

"Mr. Meredith, your guest has arrived." The young man deposited Bel at the side of her uncle.

"Belinda, I appreciate you taking this meeting with me." He motioned for her to sit.

"Of course, Uncle Anders. I was surprised to hear you're in Boston."

"Indeed, it must be a surprise. Well, I thought I owed you a visit. I heard you were acting liaison between the family interest at Ridgeway and H&C. I suppose the task is quite a change of pace for you."

"It is," she confirmed. Under his comment she heard his absolute disdain for the life she had chosen. *If you only knew.* Oh, how she might have enjoyed telling him if only to see his jowly shock and disapprobation. For a moment she wished she'd invited Wolf along.

"It can be quite trying to take on a task like this. Good help is so hard to find."

A waiter appeared with a bottle of wine, and Anders bade him fill their glasses despite the fact he was already drinking something stronger. Bel didn't argue. She would need a drink or two to make it through this evening. It was tiresome already, trying to make nice with her uncle while Wolf waited for her at home.

"I've been fortunate where help is concerned," Bel replied.

"Oh, have you been? You mean Marek?"

"Of course, Marek and Wolf. I believe you met Wolf at Natty's party?"

"Ah yes, your assistant. I heard you've had a devil of a time getting Wolf's record cleaned up."

Something inside Belinda grew tight. A sudden contraction of the muscles holding her up. A stab of pain through the deepest part of her. All around her things went blurry, only to shift into sharper relief than they had been before. *I'm in danger,* she realized, but there was no escape.

"Artists, what can be expected?" he guffawed.

She said nothing.

"Listen, Belinda, I know you've had some rather important realizations about life, the world. It's all well and good to play the philanthropist. I admire that. Philanthropy builds a name, a memory. But you're stepping a bit too far in the deep end, my girl."

"Beg pardon?"

"I know what's been planned, and as your uncle I want to caution you strongly against carrying this plan out. It won't serve the purpose you think it will. Quite the contrary."

"I'm sure I don't understand you."

He leaned forward. Even old and fleshy, there was something predatory about Anders. "You do understand, Belinda, but in case I've been unclear, let me spell it out further. I know you are colluding with some ne'er-do-wells who think they can strong-arm companies and governments into doing their bidding. They've made quite a show of their contempt for our industry. I know you plan to aid those people in their efforts to disrupt our project. I don't make threats, Belinda. It's beneath me, but as you are family and my family means a great deal to me, I am warning you."

"Are you mad, Anders?"

"No, Belinda. I'm telling you, you have been compromised. Surely you must have noticed something feels off. You're in trouble and I want to help you."

"I don't know what you mean."

"Where's Marek? It's been a while since we've seen him," Anders coolly lifted his glass of scotch to his lips and smiled.

She felt a shiver trace up the nape of her neck. "He's in London."

"I'm quite sure he is. Probably trying to figure out how to tell you about your change in fortunes. You see, I have it on good authority that the Hall empire is crumbling. A shame really. I always thought Marek was a smart one, but the market is ever a gamble."

She took a deep breath trying to steady a faint tremble building in her gut. If Marek had gambled and lost, he would have told her. Anders was lying. He had to be, but he was unreadable.

"You haven't a head for business, Belinda; you never did."

"I'm sure Marek and the businesses are fine."

"Are you? Well, I hope for your sake that's right because the Sheridans have shut you out. Your stock is gone. Your inheritance gone. I have no doubt Marek is fretting over how to break the news. Belinda, I know what you are planning to do. The details are not perfectly clear, but I am aware of the generalities, and I have someone on the inside who will make sure arrests are made."

"Anders, please, you're being ridiculous. I didn't come here for an argument."

He went on as calmly as before. "As I say, arrests will be made, and when they are, I will continue to use my connections in the courts to see to it those pesky juvenile issues will be the least of your assistant's problems. Activism is such a dangerous business. Tempers flare, don't they? People lose their head."

She was thankful for all the years of family dinners and boarding school and parties with people she detested, for they had prepared her well to make no outward sign of the absolute rage and revulsion coursing through her. "And what are you asking?"

"Ah, I see you are interested in your old uncle's requests. Very good of you. You are a woman with some feeling for family after all. I have a dear friend in Iowa—"

"Iowa?" She said the name of the place like it was a far-off planet. It might as well have been, for Anders had never mentioned anywhere in the center of the US save for Chicago and Houston.

"Indeed. At the local university, and he has mentioned to me they're looking to expand one of their programs. I, of course, enjoy philanthropy, as I said, and I mentioned your name to him. He'll be in contact shortly. I want you to help him out."

"You want me to give money to a friend in Iowa? But I thought I was a pauper now?"

"Oh, hardly a pauper. But a woman in need of a profession, I should think. No. I want you to listen to what my friend has to say, and then help him. You should do this, Belinda, because if you do, everything will be fine, I'm sure. You'll have a very respectable career doing what you like, and your friend Wolf will have a life."

"So you are threatening me."

"Not at all." He snipped the tip of a stubby cigar and smiled. That smile held more of a threat than anything he'd yet spoken. Bel knew Anders sorted out all of her family's troubles. No problem was too great for him, and now she and Wolf were one of those problems. Something to be eliminated.

The waiter brought their food without asking for Bel's order. She knew better than to leave the table, and ate what she was offered as if it had been poisoned. The whole time Anders said nothing more about the matter. He spoke of Natty's new appointment as an adviser to the Elliston campaign, his son's new real estate venture, his favorite new television show. All in a tone that suggested nothing was amiss. Just an old man visiting his niece in the city.

"It has been such a pleasure catching up, Belinda. Give my regards to Wolf," he said at last before rising from the table.

Bel said nothing.

The waiter cleared the table and poured her another drink. She sat motionless for a long time staring at the chair where her uncle had been. Sometime later, a man in a deep blue suit approached her and bent solicitously in her direction.

"Miss, your uncle has a car waiting for you whenever you're ready."

"No, I'll call my own car."

"Miss, your uncle rather—"

"I would prefer if you would call me a cab," she said and summoned a smile she knew would make him yield.

Her mind raced with memories. Bel had seen Wolf run toward danger too many times. She didn't know what to do, but she knew she could not go back to Wolf.

The Answer
November 2002

BEL'S EYES FLICKED DOWN to her own hands for a moment before returning to Wolf's face. "Anders knew about the plan at Ridgeway. Apparently, we weren't the only spies and I was stupid to think we were."

A surge of something like horror coursed through Wolf. She put her notebook down and shivered, but shook it off. Of course they hadn't been the only ones keeping an eye on the project. She had known this for years, but she'd never thought about the possibility of spies for the company. They had been fools not to consider it.

Everything made perfect sense; still, the memory of waking up alone, fearing for Bel's safety, waiting anxiously in the apartment only to be told by some corporate office a few days later that Bel had "departed of her own volition and did not wish to be contacted." Those were things Wolf couldn't forget.

"You could have talked to me. You could have told me what was going on."

"He threatened you. You don't understand. Remember when you used to ask me if I was in the mob?"

Wolf sat at attention. *Fuck.*

"I'm not, but sometimes the difference is so fine. Do you understand?"

She didn't, but she could imagine.

"Families like mine, we have ways of resolving problems. Anders is our solution, always has been. I don't know what his limits are or if he even has any, but he has police and lawyers and judges on his side. I don't have those connections. I'm not that kind of person, sadly."

"I'm glad you aren't. But I wasn't a child. I didn't need you to make decisions on my behalf."

"He destroys people. And you were an obstacle. He wanted to ruin you. He said as much. I couldn't let him."

"We could have run," Wolf whispered, feeling all through her the urge to run even now.

"Oh, come on. The fight was everything to you. You lived and breathed it. I couldn't take you from it. What was I supposed to do? Take you to Iowa? I could never." Bel held her head up, chin pointed defiantly a bit higher than usual as if daring Wolf to argue the point.

"You could've asked me."

"No, I couldn't."

Wolf grunted in frustration. She hadn't wanted to argue with Bel, but it was hard to hold back. Even as she argued, she could not ignore the anguish in Bel's eyes. *This hurt you too? Why?* "You could have, but you didn't."

"I couldn't face you saying no. I knew you would say no, and I didn't want to hear it. I'd have understood. Of course I would have understood. Iowa? A life without the city, without the protests, without being a part of something bigger? I didn't want to take all that from you, and I didn't want to watch you choose it over me."

"I would have gone anywhere with you. I was in love with you, for fuck's sake."

A moment of stunned recognition registered on Bel's face before she managed to regain her cool composure. "It's easy to remember it that way now, but all we had was the fight, and you would have resented me in the end if we'd run. Think about it. How much of what we've said today was first-time information? Did we even know each other?"

"Don't. Don't pretend we didn't know each other. You always wanted to convince me that I was disgusted by you, by your money, your family, that hot little vintage car, but I never was. I saw you, Bel. You were trying. Most people never gave us a second thought. They would have let us suffer and die and never tried at all. You were one of us. And now you want me to say I didn't know you. Maybe not entirely, sure, but I wanted to know you. I've always wanted to know you—isn't it obvious? Look at me. Even now, after all that happened—I'm here because I want to know you. Ugh,

I can't do this." The words had tumbled out so fast. Probably she'd made no sense at all to Bel who stared, eyes wide and sad. Wolf had no more words. She held up the recorder and tape as if to say *do you want this?*

Belinda shook her head and Wolf dropped them in her bag. She headed to the door, but Bel rushed forward and put her body between Wolf and the exit. She didn't touch her—the look on her face said she didn't dare—but the way her hand moved gave away the urge.

"Wolf."

Her name in Bel's voice, spoken like a plea, ricocheted through every inch of Wolf's body.

Why are you making this harder?

"Please. Please don't go. I'll go. I'll give you some space, but please, don't leave."

"Why?" Wolf held back her tears but just barely. The last thing she wanted was to break down. She'd been doing an admirable job of holding it together, all things considered, but this conversation was proving to be too much. The look in Bel's eyes was too familiar, too open.

"I don't want you to go, please. I need a cigarette anyway. I'll leave. Will you stay?"

"Will you be back?" she scoffed, the bitterness in the question unavoidable. Bel visibly flinched.

"Of course. It's my studio."

"You've left me in your place before."

"I know, but—Why would I ask you to stay and then not come back? Wolf, I know I shouldn't ask anything of you, but I am asking. Believe me. I don't want you to go. I'll be back, and I hope you're here when I am."

Wolf stood in the entryway and watched Bel leave. She heard the elevator crank on. *What am I doing?* She put her coat on and touched the doorknob.

She could leave.

What was the point in staying? She had her interview. She had enough to write a few interesting pages at the very least. She even had her answer for the question that had loomed in the back of her mind for years. Bel had left her due to some pathetic mix of cowardice and altruism. It didn't make her feel better. If anything, Bel's explanation only pressed on a half-healed wound.

Wolf had talked herself into so many more likely scenarios. Ultimately, she'd picked one that made sense. Bel had enjoyed their romp but had never taken it seriously. When push came to shove, she couldn't hack the idea of a confrontation, with either Wolf or her family. The documents had been her parting gift—mission accomplished without getting her hands dirty. No fuss, no muss. It didn't comfort her, but it made sense and she had lived with it.

She walked away from the door and sighed.

I loved you. I would have done anything to protect you. Fuck, Bel. Why say it now?

Wolf closed her eyes and passed her finger over the edge of her hairline just above her ear. Was this the first time Bel had said those words out loud?

Why now?

Wolf took another deep breath and paced across the studio toward the painting. She stared at it. Bel's signature seemed scraped into the surface with a fine edge. A partial smoke-gray fingerprint lingered at the limit of the canvas. A few unstoppable tears leaked from the corners of her eyes. She didn't bother trying to stanch them. Dull pain radiated through her like the aftermath of a punch, a familiar feeling, not entirely welcome, but comforting. Outside, the city sounds were the same as ever. It could have been yesterday when she lay on this floor with Bel standing over her. It could have been only this morning when she woke up on the couch feeling happy and uncertain of how long it would last.

But it wasn't.

"It wasn't," she said aloud to herself in the empty expanse of the room. *Why am I always looking back?* What was it Bel had said about going back? Wolf pulled out the recorder and rewound the tape. Play. Stop. Rewind. Play. Stop. Rewind.

"People were always pressing forward. I'm not like that. I'm constantly pulled back."

Through the tiny speaker, Bel's voice was not quite as smooth as the real thing, but this way Wolf could hold her close, lift the sound to her ear, and listen again and again.

I'm constantly pulled back.

Her tears fell faster.

The Clapper and the Bell
November 2002

IT WASN'T A REAL rain shower, only a mist heavy enough to collect on her coat and her hair. Bel walked down the empty street. Her pace suggested a woman with purpose, but she was going nowhere. Wolf would leave. Of course she would go. There was no reason to stay, but Bel couldn't watch it happen. She told herself it would be fine. She would go home like it was any other night, and the studio would be empty and it would be all right. It wouldn't stamp itself into her mind the way the sight of Wolf walking out would.

As she wandered without any sense of destination, she swore she could hear Marek's voice from all those years ago. *She loves you. Go home!* Marek had been her port in the storm. She had taken a cab from the club directly to Logan, and from there she'd gone to London. When he had opened the door to find her, his expression was one Bel had never seen. A mix of outrage and pity had darkened his eyes. "God, what have you done, Bel?"

London had been waking up, and Marek's face bore the marks of sleep interrupted. Of all the things he might have expected from a knock on the door, surely Belinda in tears was not one of them. He took her in and made her tea. The fine rain had soaked through all of her clothes. She sat damp and exhausted in his sitting room. Her heart kept making a strange sensation. It was the feeling of falling from a great height, but the landing never came.

We can salvage this. He had seemed desperate for her to listen. Her friend, not her adviser, not her co-conspirator.

Belinda had forced herself to straighten up and accept her fate. *No. God, Bel, let me help you. We can set you up in London. Bring Wolf.*

She had dried her eyes and refused. *That won't satisfy him. I've upset the order of things and he wants me to suffer. He wants to know I've been humiliated, isolated. Set up the endowment. I'll leave this afternoon. You know what Anders is capable of. Believe me, it's safer this way.* She had to turn off her feelings. She summoned a memory of her mother's cool half-drunk eyes. She could do this; she was born to it. Then the phone rang.

The sound of Wolf's voice cut through the distance, a rising panic hitting its crescendo. Marek had held the phone in Bel's direction, pleading with his eyes, but she shook her head. He spoke then. *No, I haven't heard from her. Don't worry, I'll make sure she's okay. Stay put, Wolf. Someone will be in touch. No, don't worry—*Then a sob, a sob across the ocean, a sound she had never imagined could come out of Wolf's mouth. Only it had, she had heard it, and she had been the cause.

She gagged as bile and a wounded helpless cry from somewhere deep in her own body knotted her throat. Her skin felt tight, her pulse stuttered. She hurried down the hall and locked herself in Marek's bathroom. If she could not control herself, she could at least hide. He finished the call, waited outside of the door, and when she emerged, he could only say, *She loves you. Go home.*

Years passed yet she remembered it vividly. Often unexpected, that day rose up and plagued her. A cold fire shooting through her nerves, the feeling of her body revolting against the choices she had made. She remembered, too, the awful certainty that it was the right thing to do, with Marek's assurance that Ridgeway would be handled, and his promise to discreetly make sure Wolf was okay.

It seemed she finally knew what he had meant. Wolf was fine. Better than fine. And Ridgeway was ruined, not that she cared about any of them. Bel couldn't regret the outcome even if it had broken her heart. Still, that sound, that memory of a sound revived itself and tore through her. Bel shivered and walked on. The moment Wolf had stepped into her office, she'd known she was in trouble, known she would be forced to feel everything all over and to finally feel the weight of Wolf's anguish turned to disdain or maybe not even that. She wended her way back toward the studio and did her best to focus on the world as it was. The here and now.

Bel shook the heavy mist from her hair. The landing outside of her studio door was illuminated only by a street lamp, which shone through a small window to her right. Under the door itself a thin strip of pale light offered no clue to what lay beyond. The glow could mean anything. Wolf was there. Or she had gone without flipping the switch. Bel studied the bright edge, calculating which hues would adequately replicate the colors there. Which pallet knife might best produce this quality of line. If she stayed on the landing, she could suspend time. There would always be the possibility of something more.

Preserving potential. More like dwelling in delusion. She opened the door. The single light that illuminated the sitting area glowed over an empty couch. A half-empty glass of wine sat on the table. The bottle lay on the floor. Tears pricked the corners of her eyes. Wolf had gone. An awful sinking feeling passed through Bel. Like a fool, she had dared to hope.

"I knew you'd hurt me. Remember?"

Bel turned and saw Wolf seated on the floor amid half-finished paintings, in the shadows of the studio, knees pulled tight to her chest. Without thinking, Bel walked to her.

"I didn't want to hurt you, Wolf. I never wanted to hurt you." She let her fingertips brush the back of Wolf's head. Bel expected her to pull away or turn on her, but Wolf didn't move.

"I believe you. I wouldn't be here if I didn't." Wolf sighed and leaned her head back into Belinda's hands.

Bel let her fingers sink deeper into the soft black waves of Wolf's hair.

"I told you from the start I wasn't afraid of pain."

"I recall." She recalled too how she had sworn to herself it wouldn't happen that way, though in the end it had been exactly as Wolf predicted.

"It's still true, but the thing is, even if I'm not afraid, I think I've had enough. It feels like I've lived too long and seen too much," she scoffed with a half-choked sob.

The sound of Wolf crying right beside her was too much to bear. "Don't say that."

Wolf shrugged but seemed to inch closer. Her back touched Bel's legs, though she still didn't turn to face her. Wolf took a steadying breath and swiped at her tears. "Earlier you called me a masochist."

"Did I?"

"You did. And maybe it's true. I told myself you didn't want to be with me, but you cared about our mission. It hurt, but I lived with it. Now? God, the truth is worse, and I can't look away. I loved you so much, Bel. Right from the start I told you I'd do anything for you. Why didn't you know that I meant it?"

"I was afraid. I'm not like you, Wolf. I wanted to be with you. That's never stopped." Bel surprised herself with the taste of a truth she'd never spoken. Wolf's hair slipping between her fingers was a strange comfort, and she clung to that feeling. "I didn't know what to do. And I don't only mean in that moment with Anders. I didn't know what to do with any of it. With you, with how I felt about you. I was learning."

"Were you happy?"

"With you? Yes, so strangely happy. It was the happiest I've ever been."

"Me too." Wolf shook her head like she couldn't reconcile the stupidity of it all, but she didn't move away from Bel's caress.

Bel wanted to wrap herself around Wolf's body, to vanish into the warmth between them, but words and these tentative touches were all she dared. "Everything with you was so different. I had no frame of reference for how I felt or for how to behave. I had a habit of dating women who made me chase them, but who never let me catch up."

"Laura?"

"A fine example. I thought they were my people. Same schools, same tailors. I thought they were the women I belonged with. If there was such a thing. But if they were like me at all, it was only in the most shallow ways. And by the time I figured that out, well … It doesn't matter. It was too late. When I met you, I tried to run."

"I noticed." Bel stroked Wolf's brow. *Of course you did.*

"I thought maybe I ought to be chased for once. But you never chased, and still you caught me. I would leave and be drawn back to you. You're like a tide. The more I fought, the more I drowned."

Wolf closed her eyes.

"It troubled me at first, that pull between us, but lately it has kept me sane. In the worst moments I've told myself we're linked somehow. I made myself believe we'd meet again. I thought it would be here. That you'd turn up, in the Village or at some rally, so for years when I thought Anders might still be watching, I stayed away to keep that from happening. To keep you safe. But when I was at my lowest, I told myself the day would come. I never let myself imagine what it would actually be like. Then, when you turned up in my office, I was—" Her hands trembled. She didn't know when that had started, but she was powerless to stop it.

"What, Bel?" Wolf leaned her head slightly to the left. Bel's hand cradled her face, her skin still damp with tears.

"Terrified." Defeat colored the word. "I saw you on the other side of my desk with your notebook and your professional demeanor, and I didn't for one second believe you could feel anything for me but contempt." Her voice broke on the word. Hot tears slipped from the corners of her eyes.

"No," Wolf replied with quiet finality.

Bel still found it hard to believe.

"You showing up, it was exactly what I wanted and I froze."

Bel didn't know what she expected. A chastisement? A lecture on the importance of courage? How could Wolf not want to say something? Bel waited. The loft was silent save for the sound of their breathing and the steady patter of rain.

Bel's fingers traced the soft shaved sides of Wolf's head and over the curve of her ear. She looked at the spot where Wolf had been bleeding the first night they kissed and drew a spiral over it with her finger. She had thought of that spot so many times in the intervening years. She had painted and wept and hated herself to the memory of it.

"Sometimes the temptation to look for you was so strong, but I couldn't bring myself to look because what if I was wrong? What if we weren't connected? What if I forced it, only to be shown my own stupidity? What if I chased you and in the act of chasing I lost even the hope of you? I had to believe we'd come back together as if by gravity."

Wolf leaned her head fully back in Bel's hands. Her eyes held a challenge and a promise. "Here I am."

Bel pressed a tentative kiss to Wolf's temple and heard her sigh in soft relief. In that sound, a feeling so bright, like light piercing a wave, reverberated through her. "Yes. Here you are."

Acknowledgements

When I started writing *Coltswood*, I lived in a world my characters could only dream of, a world my younger self scarcely dared to imagine. Now, on the eve of the book's completion, I find we are staring down the barrel of profound political cruelty which feels tragically familiar. Although the need for activism has never gone away, it seems more pressing now than it has in a long while. I hope remembering the work of those who fought so hard in the 1980s and 1990s can inspire us to battle through this new wave of violent indifference and ferocious intolerance.

I am deeply grateful to every person who has participated in the long and ongoing struggle to end AIDS. When it comes to this book, I am especially thankful for those who have kept alive the memories of those earliest moments and people through their writing, music, art, and archival work. *Coltswood* could not have come to life without the chronology and archive maintained by ACTUP New York, the work of Sarah Schulman, Deborah Gould, Ron Goldberg, and Peter Staley, and the video and film productions of David France, Jim Hubbard, and DIVA TV. While many details have been invented or changed for the sake of fiction, I hope the energy and passion of those who fought remain recognizable in these pages.

I was a teenager in the years central to this story. I could not have survived those days without the support of the older LGBTQ people in my life who treated me with kindness and respect. Special thanks to Sage, Jessica, Bud, and Auntie Judy for connecting me with a world of protest, zines, safe sex education, public radio stations, lesbian dances, and late-night poetry. Wherever you may be now, I wouldn't be here without you.

Thank you to all the people at Bywater Books for taking a chance on this manuscript. Salem, Ann, and Christel, your support and guidance have been amazing. It's an honor to be part of the team. To my editors, Rey Spangler and Anna Burke, your enthusiasm for this story and these characters means a great deal to me. Thank you for everything you did to help me make *Coltswood* as good as I could in this moment and not letting me fixate on the illusion of perfection, which can so quickly become a destroyer of worlds.

Thank you to the GCLS Writing Academy folks who had the pleasure/pain of experiencing a few very unedited scenes, to Jennifer Steil who so generously provided feedback and encouragement on my first one hundred pages, to my journalism and investment savvy friends who answered my endless questions, to Ren for listening to me talk my way through this idea, to Kirsten who endured my divided attention on our many academic projects while I was writing, and to Neebinaukzhik, Marissa, Riley, and Jan, whose diverse insights and opinions helped me think more deeply about how readers might receive these words. (Sorry, Jan, still no epilogue.)

Finally, *go raibh mile maith agat* to L, my ultimate alpha reader, who has filled my days and nights with joy for the past thirteen years. Reading this book with you has been a delight, each and every time.

About the Author

The product of a semi-feral childhood, Jules Revel writes stories that explore courage, chance, and the role of magic in our mundane lives. Her debut short story, "Make Me a Sword," was published in *By Her Sword: A Sapphic Fantasy Anthology* in 2025. When not writing, Jules can be found researching environmental activism, taking analog photos, or rescuing animals with her girlfriend.

Bywater Books believes that all people have the right to read or not read what they want—and that we are all entitled to make those choices ourselves. But to ensure these freedoms, books and information must remain accessible. Any effort to eliminate or restrict these rights stands in opposition to freedom of choice.

Please join us by opposing book bans and censorship of the LGBTQ+ and BIPOC communities.

At Bywater Books, we are all stories.

For more information about Bywater Books, our publishing mission, authors, and our titles, please visit our website.

https://bywaterbooks.com

The 2024 Foreword INDIES Publisher of the Year award was presented to Bywater Books for its twenty years of ushering in the coming of age of queer literature.

"In a year when LGBTQ+ communities faced renewed attacks and the names of DEI efforts were sullied by those in power, Bywater Books remained firm in its commitment to publishing titles that celebrate queer existence and that embrace diversity. Their world-widening books make us laugh, make us cry, and stand as enduring testaments to the breadth of love and the human experience."

—*Foreword Reviews*